NO MORE SEA

NO MORE SEA

Keith Jacobsen

to   Sam

with all best

wishes

Keith

May 2010

Book Guild Publishing
Sussex, England

First published in Great Britain in 2010 by
The Book Guild Ltd
Pavilion View
19 New Road
Brighton, BN1 1UF

Typeset in Baskerville by
Ellipsis Books Limited, Glasgow

Printed in Great Britain by
CPI Antony Rowe

A catalogue record for this book is available from
The British Library.

ISBN 978 1 84624 421 6

*To Sam Llewellyn, with deepest thanks
for all your help and encouragement.*

'And I saw a new heaven and a new earth:
for the first heaven and the first earth were passed away;
and there was no more sea.'
Revelation, 21.1

Prologue

A tall, gaunt figure stumbled along the rough path between the two granite headlands, his plimsolled feet sliding on the streaming stones, the rain driving through his thin sweater and sodden jeans. He held a torch loosely in his slippery left hand, the tiny puddle of faint light zigzagging drunkenly from one side of the path to the other.

For some minutes the crashing sound of the waves had increased with every step. The cliff must be very close now. He stepped off the path, leaving his torch beside it. He groped his way through the solid darkness across the saturated grass and gorse. For a moment a distant flicker from the lighthouse was just enough to outline the edge. He sank to his knees, pushing his hands in front of him until he was lying flat on the ground. He crawled forward, the tufts of slippery grass becoming ever smaller and sparser until there was only sloping mud, crisscrossed by rivulets of rainwater. There was a taste of slime and grit in his mouth.

At last he felt his fingers grip the edge. He eased his body forward until his face overhung the drop. He could hear the waves slap and boom against the rocks hundreds of feet below, sending up a salt spray like inverted rain. Centuries ago, the sea had cut away the base of the cliff, leaving the rock above to hang over and at last to fall in a huddle of huge stones, now sculpted smooth and round by the endlessly swelling and retreating tide. At the

1

top, right at the edge, a layer of earth only a few inches thick was left unsupported, the layer on which he was now stretched out.

High tide. Perfect. He eased himself back into a kneeling position. Very slowly, he started to push his hands into the soft mud. As he felt it yield, he pushed harder, pulling his hands back and beating them against the ground with the weight of his upper body. Barely perceptibly at first, then with increasing momentum the beaten earth began to give way. He sensed the tremor running through his body as the long fissure spread out on either side of him. There was a rumbling sound, distant at first, then ever closer to his ears. He stood up and held out his arms towards the black void above him and the abyss below. He cried out, the wind and rain bearing away the sound. The dislodged earth groaned and hurtled down.

A small Moroccan cafe by the old harbour. Not a suitable place for a woman on her own. The treacly evening air. Smells of oil, tar, brine, bougainvillaea. Strong, sweet coffee, thick as mud. Waves slapping sluggishly against the harbour wall, boats creaking at their moorings. Passing chatter in a French as strange to her as a foreign language, used as she was to Paris. The lilt of the Midi, intermingled here and there with the sing-song of North Africa.

A man sat down opposite her. His face was deeply tanned. Wind and sea had furrowed his skin. He had a large white moustache, drooping at the corners. He wore blue serge overalls, the clothes of a deckhand. He waved to the *patron*, who was inside, wiping a row of small glasses. The *patron* nodded and came outside, bearing a tray upon which were two glasses of brown liquid. He put them down on the table between them. The man smiled and pushed one of the glasses over to her. She sipped it and coughed noisily. It was a local brandy, burning the back of her throat like hot cinders. The man laughed. He spoke, a medley of harsh, rasping sounds in a language she could not identify. Not Greek or Turkish. Somewhere from the Balkans, she guessed. In French, then again in English, she told him she did not understand. He shook his head.

She looked over to where they were standing. The grey shadows did not move. The one with the black hood and cloak seemed to be nodding at her.

She looked up at the stranger. Her eyes held his, trying to tell him she understood. So, who was she? I bet you never asked her name. Where was it? A bar or a brothel in some tiny port where you had taken shore leave. A port like this one. Perhaps it was this one. You were lonely, desperate, careless. For the price of a few drinks you sought comfort in her body. Now you see her face in every woman you meet. You are a messenger of death, as she was. Soon, you will meet your own.

She rose and walked slowly away, in the direction of the tiny, squalid hotel where she was staying. She heard his footsteps padding softly behind her.

1

May 1995

The tramp emerged from the path through the woodland and began to follow the trunk road which after a further 10 miles would take him to Land's End. He was hot and thirsty. At the top of a rise he could see a strip of sea on each side of the land which stretched ahead. It was late afternoon and the strip seemed to surround him with silvery light. The large cultivated fields had given way to small fallow ones with untidy drystone walls. Houses were few and scattered. It was as if a skin of modernity had been peeled back to reveal the ancient landscapes beneath. In deference to their venerable age the modern road wound around rather than through these old fields, forcing cars to a moderate, respectful pace. Not that any of the drivers slowed enough to respond to the lethargic movement of his hitchhiker's thumb. They passed close enough to see the drab and torn condition of his loose brown jacket and baggy grey trousers, imagined the smell and the dirt in the smart interiors of their cars and drove hastily on.

The miles slid away beneath his feet. His beard and stooped gait belied the briskness of his pace. A few miles before Land's End he took the left turn he knew would lead him to the coastal village of Porthhella. A wide sweep of sand lay to his right, to the left the outline of the village crouching beneath a steep hill.

The water was a placid lake of ruby and gold beneath the setting sun.

Of the day trippers to the beach, only a few stragglers were left, irritable parents, fractious children, making their way to the car park. Nobody gave him as much as a glance. He stopped by the tap near the beach and drank clumsily, most of the water streaming onto his shirt and trousers. He walked on along the sea front, through the old fishing quarter of the village and on to the deserted coastal path. He struggled up the steep slope to the first headland, crowned by a tiny, castellated circular building, long since fallen into disrepair. Only part of the roof remained. But there was sufficient shelter from the sea breezes and no rain was forecast. It would serve him well enough for that night. And maybe a few more after that. He took off his jacket, spread it on the litter-strewn floor, and unpacked a stale sandwich he had crammed into one of the side-pockets. From the other he took out a crumpled sheet from a newspaper. Carefully he smoothed it out and read through the article until the fading light began to hurt his eyes. He was not able to finish it but it did not matter. He knew it off by heart.

The next morning he walked on along the path, in the direction away from the village. The ground was level now, easy on lungs and legs which were still weary from the long walk of the preceding day. He reached the massive granite cliffs, pink from the surface of the water up to the point where they began to slope land-wards. There the lichen gave them a green tinge. At a junction where the main path turned inland, a narrow side-path led on to a Bronze Age fort whose stone outlines were still visible, clinging precariously to the cliff-top. Beyond it, towards the horizon, a lighthouse marked the end of a string of tooth-like rocks projecting from the water like the scales of a partly submerged dragon.

Between two headlands the path turned back towards the sea and the cliffs. He came to a rope slung across the path between two metal posts, barring his way. Beyond the rope the path was still visible, though an overgrowth of grass and gorse bush was beginning to claim it. His eyes followed the line of the old path for a few hundred yards to a point where it almost brushed the cliff edge. Far too dangerous now. Once it had been a safe distance away. That was before the earth had fallen. By the rope was a warning sign, diverting him to a new path which led back inland. He followed it between dense, bright yellow gorse bushes. Stonechats, a haze of brown and orange, flashed and darted among the bushes, sometimes taking noisy and assertive possession of the sharp top of a branch.

After half a mile the new path rejoined the one which had been roped off. He passed a number of small inlets with narrow pebble beaches. He gave them barely a glance. At last he came to an inlet just about large enough to be called a bay. It had a narrow strip of sand, of a darker yellow than the sand near Porthhella. The path led downhill towards this mini-beach and rose again on the other side. The land behind the beach was a gentle rise, in contrast to the surrounding cliffs. The lake-calm water in the bay was turquoise at the mouth and dark green closer in to shore.

As he rounded a sharp corner the house was there. It stood on a plateau about halfway up the hillside. It was a solid-looking structure, faced in grey stone, with two large downstairs French windows and four upstairs bay windows. Sunlight flashed into his eyes, reflected from three skylights set into the sloping slate roof. All the windows on the first floor were shuttered, giving the impression that the whole building was wearing a severe frown. What was it the newspaper had called it? A house of sickness, madness and death.

He turned back along the path.

2

The lady who was locking the door of the art gallery on the sea front was silver-haired now. She stooped a little. But Madeleine had changed much more than Brenda had. Would she even recognise her?

'Hello, Brenda.'

The silver-haired lady stared at Madeleine. 'Good God, it is you. I heard they let you out. I never thought you'd come back here.'

'And it's good to see you again, Brenda.'

'How long has it been? Six years? Now look at us. I've become an old lady, and you look like a ghost. No point in our scratching each other's eyes out, I suppose. I'm not going to pretend I'm pleased to see you. But I've had time to get over the way I used to feel about you. Even my hate can't survive six years of not seeing you, of trying not to think about you. I'm too old and tired. Have you gone back to live at the house?'

Madeleine shook her head. 'I'm not going to live there again. I only came back to these parts to see Megan. But I can't face going up to the house yet. I don't know if I could handle the memories. Me being arrested, Megan screaming at the police to leave me alone. I need to prepare myself.'

'Where are you staying?'

'At the inn.'

'Come and have a cup of tea. I've closed up early today. Hardly any customers. Still a few more weeks to high season.'

Brenda's home was only a few yards away, a pink-washed picture postcard conversion of an old fisherman's cottage. The door opened straight into a spotlessly clean and tidy lounge. A large, beige three-piece suite with neatly embroidered antimacassars over the backs of the armchairs took up most of the floor space. Madeleine wondered why she needed so much furniture. She was sure she was the first person Brenda had ever invited over the doorstep.

Brenda served tea in tiny china cups, with shortbread biscuits. Madeleine stared at her cup as if unsure what to do with it. When she picked it up she held it tightly in both hands as if afraid she would drop it. She wondered if Brenda had noticed the slight tremor in her fingers and wrists.

'So, when was it we last spoke to each other?' asked Brenda.

'Let me see. It must have been that time you came round to see me about Michael's will, a few weeks after the funeral. I refused to let you in and I told you to get lost.'

'I think you used stronger language than that. In a very loud voice so the entire village could hear. You said I was a scheming bitch – I'm editing now – who had wormed her way into Michael's affections just to get my hands on his money, and you wouldn't take any leftovers from me to save your life. That wasn't fair, Brenda. I had only come round to see if you were all right. To check that you and Michael hadn't come to any understandings which were not reflected in his will and which I didn't know about.'

Brenda nodded. 'I know. I knew it wasn't fair when I said it. If you had been a gold digger, Michael would have realised. He would never have let you stay. I wasn't in the mood to be patronised by you of all people, that's all. Michael and I had come to a mutual arrangement years before. He had made the gallery over to me. I never wanted or expected anything more. How long have you been out?'

'I was discharged a year ago. I had to live in a hostel for a year, under supervision. Relearn my daily living skills.'

'I'm surprised. I thought . . . after what you did . . .'

'Come on, Brenda. Out with it. You're surprised they let me out so soon. You expected me to do at least twenty years. You expected and hoped it, didn't you? It's all right, I understand.'

'All right. I admit it. I am a little surprised.'

'They decided I was crazy. I had no motive for what I did. So I was detained at Her Majesty's pleasure for as long as I was thought a danger to myself or to others. I was in a secure hospital, not a prison.'

Madeleine thought of the crumpled sheet of paper she carried in her handbag, the passport to her early discharge. She wondered how Brenda would react if she knew. She would certainly destroy the cup from which Madeleine had been drinking, probably the armchair as well.

'And how are you now?'

'Well, I'm out. So that must mean I'm no longer a danger, you'll be relieved to know. I was going to go straight up to the house. Then I lost my nerve. Came down here instead. When I was discharged I had no idea what to do. I asked them at the hospital whether there was anybody connected to the old lady, anybody I could apologise to. Make it up to them in some way. But there isn't. Her sister-in-law died. There were no other relatives. She was about to die anyway. It was the most pointless killing in history. I sometimes wonder if it was my way of killing myself. I was too cowardly to do what David did. Jump off the cliff. Make a nice clean job of it. So I killed someone in a way that caused minimal damage. Somebody who had no husband or children, who was dying anyway. To make sure I would be put away.'

'Who was she, Madeleine? Who was Laura? The papers only said she was a friend of Michael's. One of them was convinced she was the main beneficiary of Michael's will, but you had looked after him all that time so you thought you should get everything. You killed her, hoping nobody would notice.'

'But she was dying anyway. And killing her wouldn't have made me the beneficiary. No, there was no doubt about his will. Everything came to Megan and myself. You really don't know who she was?'

'No idea.'

'She was David's mother . . .' Her voice trailed away. She shuddered.

Brenda leaned forward and shook her arm. 'Madeleine, are you all right? You shivered as if a goose just walked over your grave. Do you know what you just said?'

Madeleine shook herself. She stared at Brenda. 'Yes, yes, I remember. I'm sorry. I get like that sometimes. Don't mind me. All those drugs. Sometimes I lose concentration. I said she was David's mother.'

'But David's mother was that French woman who was killed in a car crash. The one who married Michael's brother, George.'

'That was what Michael wanted the world to believe. He passed David off as his orphaned nephew. He never had a nephew, as far as I know.'

'So Michael really was his father?'

'You don't sound too surprised.'

'I'm not. I did wonder from time to time. How did you find out?'

'Find out what?'

'That Laura was David's mother and Michael was his father? Did Michael tell you?'

'Good Lord, no. It was his great secret. I can't remember how I knew. It just came to me one day in the hospital. I knew it had to be true. I'd been there for months, all the time trying to remember who she was. Hoping that would help me remember why I killed her. Only it didn't. That's all still a blank. I may have seen some papers Michael had left in the house somewhere. He could be forgetful at times towards the end.'

'But assuming you're right, why should you want to kill David's mother?'

'Exactly. There's no possible motive. I gained nothing by it. It proves I was crazy. I'm a paranoid schizophrenic, apparently. We can't always distinguish between dreams and reality. Perhaps I thought I was dreaming. Have you ever killed anybody in a dream?'

'Maybe. Haven't we all? Look, I have read about schizophrenics killing total strangers, imagining they're CIA agents or God knows what. But Laura wasn't a total stranger to you, was she?'

'I didn't know her. I have a vague memory of her coming to the house to see Michael, a few weeks before his final stroke. He let her in. He thought I was asleep upstairs. I didn't meet her then. I saw her from the landing. She never saw me.'

'But you knew who she was and where to find her. You went all the way to Portsmouth to see her.'

'Maybe Michael had left an errand for me. Something he wanted me to give her or tell her. But if so I can't remember anything about it. I certainly didn't leave anything with her, or with her sister-in-law. I remember her name was Naomi, the sister-in-law, that is. What Naomi said to the police was that I told her Michael was a mutual friend and I wanted to give Laura the news of his death in person. Perhaps that was it. Michael just wanted me to visit her, check out how she was, see if she needed anything. Feeling guilty, perhaps.'

'Guilty about what?'

'I never knew about her. Neither did you, obviously, though you had known Michael for much longer than I had. So where was she all that time? After their affair he must have sent her away somewhere, until he was ready to take David from her. Gave her money, I suppose. On condition she kept out of his life, out of both their lives.'

'If you're right, he would have had his reasons. He would have wanted to protect Celia.'

'Yes. But after Celia died he didn't take Laura back. Only her child.'

'I suppose he might have felt guilty about that. Again, assuming you're right. Neither of us knows for sure.'

'It might explain why I went, and it fits in with what I told

Naomi. I remember going to see Naomi first. She took me to the hospice. Laura was in a private room. There was a nurse outside at a nursing station. Not directly outside, about twenty yards up the corridor. Naomi told her I was a friend who wanted to see Laura. Then Naomi looked into the room to see if Laura was awake and ask her if she minded another visitor. She came out and nodded to me. Naomi left me there because she had already been in to see Laura earlier that day. I went in on my own. Laura was there in bed, very sick, only a few days to live, so Naomi had told me.

'I left the room an hour later. I knew that because while I was waiting for Naomi to come out I had noticed the clock on the wall in the corridor and I looked at it again when I left. I found my way home, in a daze. The strange thing was that I couldn't remember why I had gone or what we had talked about. I couldn't remember anything that had happened in that room during that hour.

'The police came the next day. They had traced me through Naomi. She told them I had mentioned Michael. Maybe she had heard of him. Or maybe I had said he was a famous artist and I had lived with him. They got the address from the Royal Academy. They showed me photographs of Laura, dead, with purple bruising around her lips and cheeks. Apparently I had pulled the pillow from underneath her head and pressed it down on her face. She was too weak to resist. It didn't take long. There was no doubt I did it. Nobody else could have. It was just the two of us in that room. Only I just can't remember.'

Brenda said nothing. Madeleine's cup rattled slightly as she placed it slowly on the table.

'Thanks for the tea, Brenda. I've said what I came here to say, about me not being after Michael's money. There are plenty of reasons why you should think badly about me, but I didn't want that to be one of them. Oh, there was something else I wanted to ask you. About the cottage. I haven't been back there yet. I just wanted to have a look. Is anybody living there now?'

13

'Not the owners. They live in Truro. They rent it out in the high season. It's empty at the moment. But you can go inside if you want. I have the key. I do some cleaning jobs around the village. It keeps me occupied when the gallery's closed. And I find the extra money useful.'

Useful for what, Madeleine wondered.

'Here you are. You can drop it back here through the letter box when you've finished.'

She took a tarnished Yale key off a hook near the door and handed it to her. There was a cardboard label attached to it, bearing the words 'Cove Cottage'.

Madeleine's hands grasped clumsily at the key, nearly dropping it as she stood up. She shuffled towards the door. Brenda closed it firmly behind her.

God, you've aged, poor girl, Brenda said to herself, looking out of the window to make sure Madeleine had gone. How old are you? Forty-five? Forty-six? About the same age as your mother when she died. You look more my age. You shake like a leaf and you've got a terrible cough. I'll have to spray some disinfectant around the place. Why in God's name did I invite you in? I must be getting soft in my old age.

She walked over to the sideboard and took out a slender gold bracelet from the back of one the cupboards. She opened it out and looked at the words engraved on the inner rim: 'To Ceridwen with love'.

I suppose I should give this to Madeleine, now she's back. But as she knows nothing about it I'll keep it. I earned it. It should have been mine from the start. She returned the bracelet to its place and closed the cupboard door.

So, Michael, David really was your son, was he? And now this crazy girl has cleared up the mystery of who his mother was. Or she thinks she has. God knows what's going on in her head. But she could be right. Poor Laura! What did you do to her, Michael, to keep her out of the way? Did she give David up to you willingly or did you have to force her?

And Madeleine can't remember why she would want to kill her. Perhaps I could have helped her out there. Jealousy is always good for a motive, in my book. I know all about jealousy. Why shouldn't Madeleine have been jealous of any woman Michael had known in his prime, any woman he had made pregnant? After all, by the time Madeleine finally decided she wanted to be with Michael he was old and sick. I saw them together sometimes, watched them from the coastal path, going out for walks together. He leaning on her arm, stopping every few yards to catch his breath. What sort of relationship was that for a woman who was still young and attractive? A very frustrating one, I would have thought. Yes, she could well have been jealous of Laura's past. But jealous enough to kill her? Not in cold blood, perhaps. But in the heat of a quarrel, if she had rejected Madeleine's offer of help and sympathy, taunted her with her passionate past with Michael? Who knows?

I can tell she's not pretending. She really doesn't remember. I wish to God she had had a motive and confessed it to the police. She would still be in prison. Instead of coming back here to haunt me again.

She poured herself another cup of tea and sat down. Then she got up again and went to look out of the window. She had seen the tramp again that morning, watching her as she unlocked the gallery. She was sure he had been there again as she locked up. She had been about to go up to him and speak to him, tell him to stay away because he would put her customers off. But the sudden sight of Madeleine had distracted her. There was no sign of him now. She would catch him the next time. She would give him a piece of her mind.

3

'And I'm telling you, it's her! I recognised her as soon as she walked past me to get her key, when I were going through the other bar to take a leak. Her picture were in the papers again only a couple of weeks ago. She looks much older now but it's her.'

The three weather-beaten faces glowed in the reflection from the log fire in the main bar of the inn. A sharp-edged breeze had blown off the sea all day, so the landlord had lit the fire, knowing they would complain bitterly if he didn't.

'Well, I suppose she signed the register, so let's ask John. John, over here!'

The landlord did not bother to look up from his copy of the local paper. He knew where the voice had come from. The rest of the bar was deserted. But that corner near the fire was never empty from seven o'clock onwards. The three former fishermen, their boats long since decommissioned, were part of the fabric of the building. If it ever had to be demolished in his time they would have to carry them out first, and he was prepared to swear that each would still have a pint mug of beer in his hand.

'Finished those beers already, gentlemen? I only pulled them ten seconds ago.'

'No, we don't need filling up. We wants private information. Not shouted across the room. So do us a favour and get over here. Your legs are younger than ours.'

John Foster sighed and walked over. He was not a local and they never let him forget it, any more than they let him forget that he was 30 years younger than they were. Until two years ago he and his wife had been advertising executives in London. They had bought the inn in pursuit of a dream of a quieter, more fulfilled life, close to nature, attuned to the cycle of the seasons instead of the 6.40 a.m. train to Paddington. They had made their decision in one drunken moment in a West End pub. They had had two years to regret it. Instead of a dream come true, John's life was now a nightmare of ever-rising debts as he fought to maintain the building and keep it warm and occupied in the teeth of the daily onslaught of wind and salt water from the Atlantic. Six months earlier his wife had given up the struggle and returned to London, moving in with a former lover in Clapham.

The company in the bar were no consolation to him. He had dreamed of spending his time with real country people, people of the sort he had never met in his entire life. He had dreamed of people who were wise in the ways of the land and the sea, stoic in the face of storms and natural disasters, fixed in the traditions handed down by their ancestors, real people, the salt of the earth. He had dreamed of being a million miles away from the empty, shallow, back-stabbing chatter of his Paddington office and the neurotic snobbery of the Berkshire executive housing estate where they had lived.

And here they were, his dream. George, Samuel and Charley. They were now the centre of his universe. His heart sank every time they came through the front door. It lifted only slightly when they stumbled out again several hours later because he knew they would be back the next evening. He was never busy enough to have an excuse to avoid joining them for at least half an hour each evening. The Porthhella Mutual Moaning Society, he called them, when they were out of earshot. They were enough to make him long for the London cocktail party circuit from which he had fled.

And the worst thing was that these men fulfilled all the criteria of his dream. Each of them had faced death on the high seas, night after night, year after year, for a pitiful living. They had survived the flooding of their homes, the sinking of their boats, the loss of sons and nephews swept from the decks in storms which had risen without warning. From their early teens to the threshold of old age they had lived a way of life which would have killed him within hours. But somewhere along the way they had forgotten to read the script. They had not emerged with the nobility of soul which might have revived John's withered spiritual faculties. He did not mind the fact that they taunted him and teased him. What he resented intensely was that their hardships had not nourished their spirits in a way which would allow him vicariously to nourish his own. They did not sing local ballads in obscure dialects, or send chills down his spine with ghost stories about haunted tin mines and shipwrecked sailors told so convincingly that they had to be true. They did not dispense folk wisdom and remedies which had been tried and tested down the centuries. He could not forgive them one simple thing. They bored him.

'That young woman as is staying here,' said Charley.

'What about her?'

'Samuel here reckons as she were the one used to live up in the big house on the bay, a couple of miles along the coast. The one as went out of her head and killed some poor old lady in Portsmouth. She had a cottage here before she moved up there.'

'What was her name?'

Charley turned to his colleagues for help. 'Reed, weren't it? Madeleine, that were it. Madeleine Reed.'

John shook his head. 'Can't be her. That's not the name she's signed in the register.'

'So what name were that then?'

'Russell. Mary Russell.'

All three of them, with uncannily synchronised movements, clapped their hands and took long draughts from their mugs.

'There's the proof then,' said George.

'Proof of what?' asked John, utterly bewildered.

'That it's her. Mary Russell. Madeleine Reed. Same initials. Must be her. Going under a nom dee ploom.'

'Don't be daft,' said Charley. 'You mean a pseudo-name. Didn't they learn you anything at school?'

'Well, what if it is her?' asked John.

'You can't let her stay, that's what. She's killed somebody. We're not safe. Might be murdered in our beds. She's crazy. That's what the judge said. She were sent to a looney bin.'

'Well, if she's here, that means she must have recovered. They wouldn't have let her out otherwise.'

'That's as may be,' said Samuel. 'But her sort only ever brought us trouble here. It weren't just her. He started it all. The rot. That Michael Wallace. Artist chap.' If he had said 'serial killer' he could not have pronounced the words with more venom. 'The last thing we needed around here. This were a proper working community before he came. Farmers, tradesmen, fishermen like us. Over at St Ives they'd been going all poncey and arty for years. But not us. Then he came. Did up the old capstan house as an art gallery. That were a working building for the boats in my young days. He brought that Brenda Rogers woman in to run it. So all the arty types would come and look at the pictures and then look around and see how quaint all the little cottages were. And then they bought them all up and drove up the prices so none of us as had given our hearts and souls and the sweat of our brows to this place could afford to buy them. She never fitted in either. Came from up north. Funny accent.'

'But he never lived here, did he, that Wallace chap?' said Charley.

'No, that were the trouble. He were too high and mighty for the likes of us. So he lived in that big old mansion up the coast. But the damage was done. He planted that gallery here. In a few years time it'll be like St Ives here.'

There was a collective shudder from the three of them, followed by a collective consolatory swig from the mugs.

'After him came Madeleine Reed's mum,' continued Samuel.

'Bought Cove Cottage. Real stuck-up city type, she were. Never fitted in, either.'

'But she were worse than that Brenda Rogers, though,' said George, with a wink.

'Her mum – she had a fancy Welsh name I could never pronounce – she were what you call a fatal femme. In her late thirties, on her own, quite a beauty. When she were walking about the village my Susan wouldn't let me out of doors. Not that she would have honoured any of us with so much as a glance.'

'Well, she did the decent thing in the end,' said Charley.

There was a long pause.

'What was that?' asked John. For the first time since he had bought the pub, the trio had caught his interest. The moment had been so long coming and been paid for so dearly in accumulated tedium that he was determined to hear the full story, or at least their version of it.

'Walked off the cliffs. Killed instantly. Mind you, I've never been sure as it were an accident.' They shook their heads, solemnly.

'What, then?' asked John.

Further shaking of heads, accompanied by mutterings. He was clearly not yet worthy to share all their secrets.

'Then that Madeleine Reed came along,' said Samuel.

'I don't suppose she fitted in, either,' sighed John.

'Too right she didn't. She were like her mum to look at. On her own as well. Next thing she were at it hammer and tongs with old Michael's young nephew. Disgusting it were. So I heard. I never saw them together.'

Another long pause.

'So what happened?' ventured John, timidly.

'Oh, nothing much,' responded George. 'The young nephew went mad and fell off the cliffs as well, old Michael died of grief, Madeleine Reed went mad in her turn and killed that woman so they took her away.'

John gaped at them. He felt doubly betrayed. All along they had kept this to themselves. Night after night they had moaned endlessly about the decommissioning of boats, the state of the harbour wall, the price of local cottages, the absence of their owners during the winter months, the presence of their owners during the summer months, the overflow of parking from the beach car park onto the sea front, the installation of ugly double yellow lines to prevent it, the lack of any buses when needed, the presence of buses when peace and quiet were wanted. And all the time they had been concealing this epic local drama from him. It was exactly the sort of thing he had craved. And now, when they had at last chosen to reveal it, they had crammed the whole of the last three acts into a single, throwaway sentence.

'Anyway,' continued George. 'We wants to know what you intends to do about it.'

'About what?' replied John, testily.

'About that woman, of course. She can't stay here. I mean, as you know, we are as open and welcoming as anybody.' John wondered how the four people in their story who had never fitted in would have reacted to that. 'But my Susan would never allow it. And as the man in the house she'd expect me to do something about it.' This last comment caused the others to choke on their beer.

'Well, gentlemen, it's a free country.' The three faces stared back at him, deeply unimpressed by that argument. John's spirits sank. He had enough problems filling his rooms before high season as it was. Miss Russell had given every indication of wanting to stay for some time and the last thing he wanted was to put a perfectly good customer out onto the street. On the other hand he could not afford to alienate his regulars. 'She's entitled to stay here if she wants.'

'We're only asking you to speak to her,' said Samuel. 'Make it clear she's not exactly welcome here. Find out when she intends to move on. For her sake. We wouldn't want any harm to come to her. Not from us, of course. From those with less understanding and toleration.'

There was a general nod.

'And if she still wants to stay?'

'Well, I hate to say this but you may find as your most loyal customers takes their custom elsewhere.'

John smiled. He would do his best to remain on good terms with them but he knew they were bluffing. The inn was the only place in the village they could get a pint and a warm fire. The nearest pub otherwise was three miles away and they would first have to climb the steep hill up to the main road. And none of them wanted that.

'I'll have a word with her. I promise.'

Cove Cottage stood on the steep hillside behind and overlooking the village. The only access to it was via a narrow lane, too small for cars, too steep for bicycles, lined with giant fuchsia bushes. The cottage itself was rather too large to deserve the designation and it was neither pretty nor quaint. It was not thatched. The garden on the landward side was so steep that the gate, almost hidden by fuchsia shrubs, was on a level with the roof.

Madeleine clambered down the path, now barely visible beneath the encroaching weeds. The new owners are economising on gardening services, she thought. There was the familiar brass doorknocker in the shape of a smiling man's head. She stepped into the hall. It had been painted chocolate brown in her day. Now it was hung with garish wallpaper of yellow flowers against a pink background. The kitchen and the bathroom, on either side of the hallway near the front door, had all been refurbished in stainless steel and pink and yellow ceramics. Bright, modern and functional. Perfect for a holiday let. She walked through into the main living room. Through the two wide bay windows the panorama of sea and sky spread across the bay to the right, down on to the village below and over to the rocky headland to the left. At least they couldn't modernise the view, thank God.

She looked at the wall above the huge iron stove, a feature which the new owners had obviously thought quaint enough to retain. To her intense surprise the picture was still there. An ink drawing of a nude woman. Her face was not visible. A broad sweep of back, hips and buttocks. The tiny pencil signature in the left-hand corner.

She descended the steep staircase which had been set into a corner of the room near the window. The owners had installed a safety-gate at the top of the stairs. For children or drunken adults or both. The main bedroom was downstairs. This had been the original cottage, a single low-roofed storey built into the side of the hill so the only windows, ill-fitting sashes, faced out to sea. The room clung on to the damp from the rain and sea, and never caught enough of the afternoon sun to dispel it. She touched part of the wall on the land side. Some flakes from the thin layer of whitewash came away in her hands. Nothing here had changed. The iron bedstead, the solid oak cupboards and chairs, were the same. The moveable full-length mirror was still in its place in the corner, silent, heavy with the secrets of everything it had witnessed.

She shivered and climbed hastily back up the stairs. She stepped through the living room and out through the front door without a backward glance.

On her way back to the village she lingered only to drop the key through Brenda's letter box. A few minutes later she found herself outside the main door of the inn. She was about to enter, then stopped herself. Why should she go back up to her room now? The narrow, bare walls would crowd in on her, stifle her, like those of her hospital room. But then she had had no choice. Now she was free. She could go where she liked, return when she liked. She was still not used to the idea. She walked slowly along to the bend in the road and on to the empty beach.

She remembered what it was like in high season. By mid-morning the beach would be noisy and crowded, though the village was barely affected by the daily invasion. The cars and motorbikes would crawl in a patient queue down the steep approach road descending from the main route between Land's End and Penzance. The beach and its large car park would beckon to them, siphoning off the flow of humanity before it had a chance to notice the village, tucked out of sight around the corner. The few who drove on would find themselves passing the sea on the right-hand side and, on the left, a row of spacious houses built in Edwardian times for visitors taking the fashionable sea air. The road finished abruptly. Just before the end, opposite a lifeboat station, was a turning-space for the local bus which visited twice a day. The space, and the double yellow lines which ran along the entire sea front, were a stern invitation to the unwanted cars to turn around and go back. Few casual visitors would ever find the old fishing quarter, with its jumble of thatched cottages, looking as if they had been cast up there at random by a particularly high wave. Hardly anybody would ever find the way to the narrow lane behind Cove Cottage.

Today was not a day for visitors. The breeze was strengthening by the minute. An inlander would not hesitate to call it a wind, though the locals would scoff at the idea. For them, a wind was what caused the waves to rise over the sea wall and strew spray and foam across the road. Madeleine had lived for months in Cove Cottage, and then, for a much longer period of time, in the far more exposed house on the bay. But she had never become acclimatised. She was still an inlander at heart. What she was feeling now was definitely a wind. Not to mention the sand which penetrated her thin loose shoes and irritated her toes and the soles of her feet.

She turned round, walked past the inn again and on towards the fishing quarter. The gallery over which Brenda Rogers presided was one of the oldest buildings in the quarter, perfectly round in shape and sited just by the harbour. It had once contained a large wheel used for drawing boats up the harbour beach when the water was low. Now the ebbing tide would leave the flotilla of tiny boats which comprised what was left of the inshore fishing fleet forlornly on the sand until the sea returned to refloat them. At night they would slip out unobtrusively into the bay, slinking back at dawn before most inhabitants were awake. Nets and lobster pots in various states of disrepair lay strewn around the edge of the harbour. The harbour wall, the only protection against the Atlantic breakers, was just a few yards long. As she threaded her way through the cottages to the end of the village she found herself on the coastal path. With her eyes she followed it up to the first granite headland, on the far side of which were the cliffs where her mother, and then David, had perished. She went only a few yards along the path before she retraced her steps.

Along the sea front, she turned to face the sea, gripping the rail on top of the harbour wall, letting the moisture-laden air beat into her face. She glanced around. The sea front, the entire village, seemed deserted.

So why had she come back to this bleak, lonely spot that she had always hated? She had lied to Brenda, partially at least. It was of course true that she had come to see Megan. She was desperate for the kindness of Megan's eyes and voice. Megan was the one person who would not judge her, who would not ask her why she had done what she had done. But there was another reason. She wanted to recover her memories of the killing. She wanted to know the worst before it was too late. She had forgotten because she had remembered. That was what the therapist at the special hospital had told her, a few weeks after she had been detained. On the advice of the lawyer appointed to handle her case she had pleaded guilty to manslaughter on grounds of diminished responsibility. The psychiatrist who had prepared reports for the court had diagnosed paranoid schizophrenia with severe long-term and short-term amnesia. He had recommended therapy to help her recover her memories. So for a few weeks she had therapy sessions, twice a week. They were a complete waste of time of course. She had remembered nothing as a result of them.

He had asked her about her childhood. She had expected that. So she told him she had had a very happy childhood, had been very close to both her parents, had been saddened by their early deaths. So, he asked her, why had she been compulsorily admitted to hospital at the age of 14 with cuts on her arms, cuts she had inflicted on herself? That had been a misunderstanding, she had told him. She had been clumsy, she had cut herself accidentally. Perhaps she was still upset about her father's death a few months before. But she had never deliberately harmed herself. Her mother had overreacted. So if there had been nothing wrong why had she had herself admitted four years later to a rehab clinic for drug addicts? Okay, she had experimented with drugs. Didn't everybody at that age? Hadn't he? She had only been there for a few weeks. The treatment had been completely successful. She had never relapsed. Well, not onto the hard stuff anyway. By then she and her mother had gone their separate ways but there was surely nothing unusual about that. As for her father, they had always been very close. She had helped him with his research for his books, sat in with him when he gave tutorials. She had been grief-stricken when he died of cancer.

The therapist accused her of idealising her childhood. He told her she had serious gaps in her early memories, which she had filled with images of the childhood she would have liked to have. He even had a word for it. Reconstruction, that was what he called it. It was quite common, he advised her. We all do it to some extent. He suggested that some of her early memories had come back to her at the time she had been with Laura. He questioned her closely about Laura. Had she known her before she had come to the house to see Michael? If not, was it possible that Laura reminded her of someone she might have known in her childhood, someone who had frightened her? If her early memories had momentarily returned when she had been with Laura, then the shock of what she did to her had caused them to be suppressed once again, along with the memory of the killing itself.

Amnesia is a learned reaction, he had explained. We use it to protect ourselves, and when another threatening situation occurs we use it again. But it is dangerous because the emotions of terror and loss associated with the memories are not suppressed. They stay with us until we recover and confront the memories, until we know them for what they are. Then we need no longer fear them.

She had not believed him then and she did not believe him now. She accepted that the moment of the killing had been erased from her mind. But the rest seemed nothing more than an elaborate fantasy designed to fit in with his own jargon-ridden theories. She had forgotten because she had remembered. What nonsense! Thank goodness they had stopped the sessions, or she would have been driven even crazier than she was already. But she did want to remember about the killing. She wanted to know what had been going through her mind. She was curious. Nobody but a psychopath could see into the mind of a psychopath. And if that was what she was, she had a unique chance to see what the workings of such a mind looked like. She was sure she was now harmless. She need not fear she would repeat her crime. Looking into her past thoughts, however evil or misshapen, would be like looking into the mind of another, someone as remote from her as it was possible to be. She had no fear of knowing the worst of what she had been, not now she was just a shadow, waiting to join all the other shadows who had already passed beyond the grave.

Like her mother. Like David and Michael. She had plenty of memories about those. And if thinking about them helped her towards the secret door in her mind behind which the lost memories might be hidden, then she would think about them. And to do that the best place to be was here, where they had lived and died.

She would start with her mother. At the age of 37 her mother, for reasons she had never explained and about which Madeleine had never asked, had come to a run-down cottage right at the edge of the country. She had followed the road to the point where the narrow, tapering land finally tumbled over the cliffs and into the sea, leaving only a scattering of black, shiny rocks at the surface still clawing at the air, until the waves at last closed over them. Had she then simply waited until it was time to follow the road to the end, to complete her journey? Seven years later she had done so, quickly, dramatically, decisively. Had she come at last to the point where she had realised that there was only one thing left for her? There was no way back to the life she had left. And the only way forward was into the sea.

Her first thoughts had indeed been that her mother had killed herself. But she was wrong. The truth was much simpler. She had been walking on her own along the cliff-tops. She had lost her way in torrential rain and pitch blackness. She had stumbled to the edge and fallen over. That was what the police had told her, when she went to identify the body.

4

'If it's any consolation to you we believe she died instantly,' said the inspector. 'Her head hit a sharp rock.'

'Who found her?'

'A couple of climbers. They use that cliff for training quite a lot. It's very dangerous. The rescue helicopter gets called out regularly.'

'Can I see her things?'

'We've got the clothes she was wearing when we found her. I can show you them if you like. I can't release them until after the inquest.'

Madeleine glanced inside the carrier bag the inspector handed to her. 'Is that it?'

'That's it, Miss Reed. Everything she was wearing when we found her.'

She took the items out of the bag and examined them, one by one. A voluminous brown tweed skirt, a thick woollen jumper unravelling in several places, oversized off-white underwear from a cheap High Street chain, tights with several holes in them. All had brown stained patches.

'There wasn't much blood,' said the inspector, following her thoughts. 'Except from the head. So that wouldn't show in her clothes. Her body was badly bruised. A lot of broken bones.'

29

Madeleine stared at him. She wondered if he was testing her, trying to find her breaking point. She turned her attention to the bag once again. It was not yet empty. She took out a pair of flat, thin-soled water-stained shoes with worn heels and a thin, badly crumpled raincoat, torn and spattered with dried mud.

'Nothing else? No watch? No jewellery?'

'Nothing at all.'

Suddenly she started to giggle. Then she put her hand to her mouth.

'What is it, Miss Reed? You find something amusing about the clothes your mother was found dead in?'

The inspector stared at her in his turn. He was in his fifties, she guessed, balding, unshaven, grown careless in appearance and manner as he whiled away the time in his last job before retirement. His voice was flat, with traces of Cockney. Cynicism had grown into his features from beneath the surface of his skin and hardened them into the face which would now stare at him unchanging from the bathroom mirror every morning for the rest of his life. She wondered what he had done to deserve a posting to this backwater as the climax to his career. Her mother's death was probably the most exciting thing to have happened round there for years. And he was too hardened, too lazy or too bored to get any enjoyment out of it.

'I'm sorry,' she said, shaking her head. 'I was just thinking that I wouldn't be seen dead in these things. Then I realised it wasn't an appropriate thing to think. In the circumstances.'

'If I may say so, Miss Reed, you don't seem too upset by what has happened.'

'I can't say that I am, really. I haven't seen my mother for some time. We had grown apart. She came down here to live and I left Oxford to work in London. Christ, was she really wearing this stuff? She used to have such a good dress sense. We were the same size. We could borrow each other's things. But this underwear is hideous. And this skirt, it's like a tent. She must have put on weight. Was this really everything? You said she was out walking on the top of the cliffs. It was very wet and windy. She had nothing else? Not even a headscarf?'

'That's it, Miss Reed. No headscarf, no handbag. Nothing we could identify her from. Everything else is still at the cottage. What there is. A few clothes in the wardrobe. A suitcase. A few books. Romantic novels. Not my sort of stuff. My wife likes it. I'm not a reading man myself.'

'It shouldn't have been her sort of stuff. She used to have a brain. Gave it up when she married.'

'You can claim it all after the inquest.'

'How did you find out who she was?'

'We sent the uniforms down to Porthhella to make house-to-house enquiries.'

'Porthhella?'

'Yes, that's where she lived. You didn't know that? You never went there to visit her? Never wrote to her there? It's the nearest village to where it happened. In one of the first houses they came to, the wife of an ex-fisherman told our chaps about a lady who lived in a cottage nearby who answered the description. Said she had gone to live there a few years ago. She didn't know the lady's name. Said she kept herself to herself. They went round to the address. There was no reply. They knocked at the cottage next door. Retired accountant from Bristol. He didn't know your mother's name, either. Had seen her around and said good morning sometimes. He confirmed the description as well. He said the same thing, that she kept herself to herself. They went back to her cottage and found a key under a pot plant near the front door. That's how she would have got back in. It explains why she had no key on her when we found her. They found her handbag inside. That's here as well.'

He pushed the bag over to her. Madeleine thought she recognised it. It had to be at least ten years old. It was in black leather, coming apart at the seams, the silver buckle tarnished and loose. It was empty.

31

'We took everything out. You can have it all, including the key . . .'

'I know. After the inquest.'

'Not that there was much. No letters, no receipts, no credit cards, no passport. No photographs. Only a few pounds in cash. Nothing with her name on it.'

'Make-up?'

'No mention of it on this list. Tissues. Cough sweets. That sort of rubbish. Not what I would have expected. Now take my wife's handbag, for instance. That has her whole life history in it, such as it is. A whole forensic team would need a week to go through it. I'm sure yours is the same. All they found was a card with the address of a Mr Wilson. An office in Oxford.'

'Yes, that's our solicitor.'

'I rang him. He told me who she was. Said she had one surviving relative. He promised to pass the message on to you. He didn't think it was strange that we found nothing on her or in her cottage which mentioned you. But, speaking personally, I find it just a little bit strange.'

'Do you?'

The inspector shuffled in his seat and leaned forward. She was uncomfortably aware that he had suddenly become interested in the case, if for no other reason than the scope it gave him to embarrass her. She braced herself.

'Miss Reed, can I ask you a personal question?'

'I know you're going to, with or without my permission.'

'How old are you?'

'Is that it? That's the personal question? I'm twenty-five.'

'And when did you last see your mother?'

'I suppose it was about seven years ago. Yes, that was it. When I went to London to work and she came down here.'

'And she never told you where she was living?'

'Yes she did. Through our solicitor.'

'And you never told her where you were.'

'Yes. Through . . .'

'I know. Through your solicitor. Miss Reed, I've heard of divorced people only communicating through their solicitors, but a mother and daughter? Doesn't that strike you as a bit odd?'

Madeleine shrugged her shoulders.

'So what did you fall out over?'

'We never fell out. We were good friends. We just drifted apart, that's all.'

'So you had a good relationship until you were eighteen, then you went to London, she came down here and you never had sight nor sound of each other from that day since. That's more than drifting apart if you ask me. That's one bloody great falling out if you ask me.'

'But I'm not asking you. You asked me. And I told you. I'm sorry if you don't believe me.'

'Before you and your mother separated, was she ever depressed?'

'Depressed? No, of course not. She was always full of life.'

'Were you like her? I mean, I can see you look like her. But you said you and she were good friends. So were you full of life as well? Did you enjoy the same things? Shopping, conversation, you know the sort of thing I mean.'

'I'm not sure I do know. But yes, we enjoyed the same sort of things.'

'But she came down here to live. In a tiny little village in the remotest part of the remotest county in England. You would never have wanted to come here, would you? What do you do for a living?'

'I work in a merchant bank. What exactly are you getting at?'

'I'm getting at this, Miss Reed. She was full of life and the two of you shared the same interests. But she came and buried herself here. Then one night she went wandering up on the cliffs in the wind and rain with the sort of clothes that wouldn't get you through a damp afternoon in Hyde Park. In the meantime you're living the high life in London. She dies, aged only, what . . .?'

'Forty-four.'

'Thank you. She dies in a tragic accident, only forty-four. Just half an hour ago, you saw her for the first time in seven years, all laid out cold on the slab. Then you see her clothes and giggle about not being seen dead in them. What I'm getting at is that your mother was depressed, and one reason she may have been depressed is that her daughter had turned into the cold-hearted bitch I'm talking to now. That, Miss Reed, is what I'm getting at.'

'So you think she killed herself? And you think I may have had something to do with it? Even though I hadn't seen her for years. For reasons which are none of your business.'

'Actually, no. I don't think she killed herself. But after meeting you I can imagine she might have had reason to. Where are you staying?'

'Hotel in Penzance High Street.'

'Did you bring anybody with you? Husband, lover, girlfriend? Anybody to help you through this difficult time? No, I bet you didn't. You're very independent, aren't you, Miss Reed? Very self-sufficient. No, as I was saying, I don't think it was suicide. Not that you would give a damn anyway. There was no sign of a suicide note, either at the spot or in the cottage. Have you seen her will?'

'Not yet. Mr Wilson told me she left everything to me. She was a widow. I'm an only child. You're not going to suggest I murdered her for her money, are you? Laid in wait for her at the top of the cliffs?'

To her surprise, he laughed. 'No. I'm afraid not. Though God knows it would be interesting to have a murder round here, just one before I go. I'd think more of you if you had done that, you know. It would show you cared passionately about something. And that you had a sense of the dramatic. But sadly, neither is true, is it? No, it's all very clear, unfortunately. Those cliffs are dangerous even for experienced walkers in daylight in good weather. Anybody who did what she did needs their head examining. She was crazy, in my view. But suicidal? No. She would have found an easier and more comfortable way, don't you think?

34

'Of course, it's not for me to decide. That's for the coroner. The inquest will be in a few days. You'll need to be there. He may want to ask you some questions. Probably he won't. It'll just be a formality. You don't mind if we release her name to the local press, do you? They've been on at us ever since it happened and we like to keep them sweet.'

'Is that all you intend to release?'

He leaned back in his chair. 'You're worried in case they come knocking at your hotel room door, asking about the rift between mother and daughter which drove the mother to throw herself off the cliffs. It makes a good story, you have to admit. And round here the press are desperate enough for those. No, I won't say anything about you. I'll just tell them she was a widow, came to the area a few years ago, tragic accident, well-known danger spot, all that sort of stuff. They might spot you at the inquest. Just ignore them. I will.'

The inquest took place in a cramped, stuffy office near the town hall in Penzance. A very thin, bearded young man in an open-necked check shirt sat at the back, scribbling into a notebook. She assumed he was from the local paper. To her relief he ignored her. Apart from the inspector and the police doctor there was only one other person present, a tall, distinguished, fair-haired man, probably in his late forties. The coroner, an elderly, bald man with a distracted air, listened to the witnesses, nodded and pronounced a verdict of accidental death. The witnesses, the journalist and the other man hurried out without a glance at her.

She stood outside the street entrance, wondering what would happen next. She would need to arrange to claim the body. Then there would have to be a funeral. Christ, how would she go about organising that? She knew nobody there. She did not know if her mother had made any friends who would want to attend. She would need to go to the village where she had lived and contact the local priest. But her mother had never gone to church in her life, as far as she could remember. The priest would probably have never met her. And how was she to find the place? She could not even remember the name the inspector had given her. She would need to get the full address from him. She shuddered at the prospect of another interview with him. Perhaps the desk sergeant could get her all the information she needed, without referring her upwards.

Through her rising sense of panic she was aware that the man who had been at the inquest was still in the street, standing a few yards away and staring at her. Now he stepped up and spoke to her.

'You must be her daughter.'

She realised too late that she had taken his proffered hand. She pulled it back sharply.

'I'm sorry, you're not a journalist, are you? I saw you in there but I assumed the young chap was the only one from the press. I don't really want to talk about it. The police said they wouldn't tell you she had a daughter.'

He laughed, heartily. She felt a surge of embarrassed relief.

'Good lord, no. I've been taken for a few things in my time but never a journalist. Michael Wallace. I knew your mother a little. Please accept my deepest sympathies. Dreadful thing to happen. But those cliffs have claimed quite a few lives in their time. I was wondering if there would be any family here. She never mentioned anybody to me. She said she was a widow. That's all I knew about her. If there had been nobody else I would have volunteered to arrange the funeral. As a mark of respect. Spare her the indignity of a local authority funeral.'

'I'm sorry, Mr Wallace. What an insult, to be taken for a journalist. No offence meant.'

'None taken.'

'My name's Madeleine. Madeleine Reed.'

They shook hands again.

'Reed, you said? I knew your mother as Ceridwen Williams.'

'Williams was her maiden name.'

'Were she and your father divorced? Before he died, I mean.'

'No. He died of cancer when I was fourteen. But, Mr Wallace, how did you know . . .?'

'Michael, please. You're very like her indeed. You must have been told that many times.'

'I have heard it said. I suppose you read about it in the press.'

'Yes, but I didn't know who it was, of course. All it said was that an unidentified woman had fallen from the cliffs. Could have been a tourist or a day tripper. They tend to be the ones who don't treat the cliffs with the respect they deserve. Then I saw her name yesterday in the same paper. It was quite a shock, I can tell you. The police had released the name, so that meant somebody had identified her. If possible the police prefer family to do the identification. So I thought I would come down and see if there was anybody here. I'm sorry if I scared you. It must be something of a shock to be approached in the street by a strange man, right after the inquest into your mother's death. I came on my own because my wife is ill. Is it just you? Are you the only surviving relative?'

'Yes, I'm afraid so. You said you knew her a little. Were you a neighbour?'

'Yes, I suppose you could say that. I don't live in the same village. I have a house a couple of miles along the coast. But that counts as neighbour around here. Come and have a coffee and we can discuss arrangements. You're a stranger to these parts, are you?'

She walked beside him as he moved briskly along the pavement.

'Yes. And I'm afraid I was rather a stranger to my mother as well in recent years. We got on very well before I went to London. When it's just mother and daughter you get very close. Like sisters. But since she came down here we seemed to grow apart.'

To her relief he did not press her further about the separation. She had had enough of that from the inspector.

'Please let me help you in any way I can, Madeleine. You'll be able to claim the body when they've done the paperwork. I'll get my housekeeper to ring them about that, and keep ringing them until it's sorted. After we've had coffee I'll take you along to see an excellent funeral director I know, here in Penzance. Very discreet and sympathetic. He arranged my aunt's funeral. Then we'll collect my car and I'll drive you round to see the minister at St Olave's. I'm sure he'll be happy to conduct the service and have her buried there. It's within the parish where she lived. I have a family burial plot in the churchyard. Plan to be buried in it myself when my time comes. Lovely little church, in a very peaceful spot. It's by the sea but sheltered. I can't imagine a better place to be laid to rest. I'm sure the minister will agree. Unless, of course, you have other plans. Or you know anything else about her wishes.'

'No, I talked to our solicitor before I came down. There was nothing in her will about wanting to be buried anywhere special or have her ashes strewn over the Welsh mountains or anything like that. What you propose is fine by me.'

She returned to London the next day, already anxious about the time she had missed away from the office and the effects it would have on her next bonus, leaving the arrangements for the funeral in Michael's hands. The next day he rang her home number while she was at work, leaving a message to the effect that the funeral would be two weeks hence. He had arranged for the body to be reclaimed and deposited with the funeral director. She rang back to thank him and agreed she would meet him outside the church.

The day before her journey, she took a couple of hours off and caught a taxi to Bond Street. She was painfully aware that she had nothing suitable to wear. She had never dressed herself for a funeral before. She could not remember her father's, but she presumed her outfit then had been arranged for her. If she had gone at all. She had only been 14, after all.

After searching through numerous boutiques, she at last found something which she thought would be suitable. It was a plain, black, knee-length woollen dress with a wide collar edged with grey fur. She also bought a matching overcoat, a few inches longer than the dress. She could wear it open so that the dress would not be completely hidden. She would need something to cover her head but she detested hats. After long deliberation, and numerous suggestions from the endlessly patient member of staff, she chose a black silk scarf. The overall effect was in her view dignified but not overdone.

The tiny old church was just outside the village of St Olave's, though the single row of miniature terraced cottages barely deserved to be called a hamlet.

Michael was waiting for her outside, as arranged. He looked as dignified as when she had first seen him at the inquest, but with an added measure of solemnity in his demeanour. A plain black suit, white shirt and black tie. How much easier it is for men to dress for this sort of thing, she thought. Next to Michael was a stout, middle-aged woman. Her loose overcoat, scarf and feathered hat presented a haphazard mixture of dark browns and faded greens. Madeleine was surprised to see that Michael and the woman seemed to be together. They made a bizarre couple. Surely this was not his wife? She seemed much older than he was. She looked in good health, though he had mentioned at the inquest that she was ill.

She clambered out of her red sports car with as much dignity as she could, suddenly aware that the car was the one thing which clashed with both her outfit and the occasion. She should have left it somewhere and taken a black taxi. But it was too late now. Michael and the woman came up to her. He shook hands warmly.

'Hello, Madeleine. Good to see you again. What a beautifully coordinated outfit. I'm sure your mother would have been proud to see you today. She must have been proud of you, full stop. I wonder when she was going to tell me about you. What a pity she didn't have a chance to see what you have become. Oh, this is Megan, my housekeeper. Been with me for years. A real treasure.

I couldn't do without her. She never met your mother, but I didn't want to come on my own. And I thought you would appreciate an extra person. My wife is still not well, I'm afraid.'

Megan smiled and stepped up to shake hands. 'Very sorry about your poor mother's sudden death, my dear. Must have been such a shock, and you being so far away.'

Megan spoke in an unfamiliar accent and Madeleine had some difficulty in understanding her. But she sensed a warmth in her manner which she did not find in Michael's carefully worded compliments. She decided Michael had made the right decision in bringing her.

Apart from the four pallbearers only the three of them followed the coffin into the church. She was here for seven years, thought Madeleine. Did she make no friends at all, apart from this Michael? And even he had been at pains to stress that he had not known her well. Did she not invite people from her village round for coffee, go to their cottages for afternoon tea and exchanges of gossip? Where were they all? Then she remembered what the inspector had told her. Apparently nobody in Porthhella had known her name.

The minister, the Reverend Colm O'Brien, was young with a musical Dublin accent. He seemed unsure what tone to set for his address. Only three people there, and nobody crying. He had some notes in front of him, which he had compiled when Michael had taken Madeleine round to see him. Now they seemed to be little use to him. Madeleine felt a twinge of guilt for his predicament, remembering that she had been able to tell him very little about her mother, and nothing at all about her life within their community. He struggled with some opening platitudes, then with visible relief seemed to find in the manner of her death a theme he could develop. He warmed slowly to his subject.

'Ceridwen Williams was still a young woman in the prime of her life. She had a sense of adventure. Sometimes that brings danger with it. She fell to her death, falling into the arms of the sea that she loved. But we who are left behind must not hate the sea because of this tragic accident. The sea brings forth life and sometimes by the will of God it brings forth death. I love the sea. I lived near Dublin Bay as a boy in constant sight and sound of it. There is a passage in the Book of Revelation with which I have to confess that I have always had some difficulty. It seems to say that one day there will be no more sea. Well I for one do not want to see that day, if it literally means the sea will disappear. But I do not think the author of Revelation, in his divine inspiration, really meant that at all. He was referring to the sea which divides people.

'We may all have friends and relatives over the sea. I meet many people round here who do. But to them we may be close in our hearts. Others may be only a few miles away, or in the next street, or next door, or even in our own homes with us. But between us and them there may be a whole raging ocean. An ocean of suspicion. An ocean of lovingly nursed grievances for past wrongs. And how lovingly we nurture our grievances, watering them, giving them a place in the sun, watching them grow from seeds and tender shoots to tall, sturdy plants and trees, which then take pride of place in the inner landscapes of our hearts. Those mighty oak-like grievances might, when they were still only seeds or saplings, have been consigned to oblivion for ever through a word of regret or the offer of a hand of friendship. But we never spoke that word or offered that hand. So there they stand like the sea between us and those we love. No more sea. Well in that sense I for one will welcome the day when the events foretold in the Book of Revelation come to pass, and there is indeed no more sea.'

As the sermon unfolded, Madeleine felt her face redden. She bit her lip. She was furious with the minister, her sympathy for him long since dissipated. She was sure his words were aimed at her, condemning her in a public place for her estrangement from her mother. At least the inspector had attacked her in private and been discreet with the press. What business was it of the minister's anyway? She was convinced he was staring at her as he spoke.

41

In her embarrassment she looked round. There were two more people in the church. They were sitting at the back, in shadow. One was a woman. She wore a black veil across her face. By her side sat a very young, dark-haired boy. He could only have been five or six. Madeleine looked back towards the front of the church. She noticed Michael. He was also looking behind him towards the place where the woman and the boy sat. She had the impression that he was nodding in their direction. After a few more minutes she looked round again. The woman and the boy had left.

She began to feel sick. She rose and made her way outside as quickly as possible. She felt the eyes of the others upon her back as the final cadences of the sermon rolled away into the beams and rafters of the low wooden ceiling. She stood just outside the door, gulping in the sharp air. Then she noticed that the woman and the boy were standing a few yards away behind a tombstone, staring at her. The boy smiled and started to move forwards towards her. She was too surprised to smile back. The woman, her features still concealed behind the veil, restrained him. Then without a word the woman turned away, pushing the boy gently but firmly in front of her. As they moved up the path towards the gate the boy looked back at her over his shoulders. The woman quickened her pace and tightened her grip on his arm. Madeleine stared after them, then started to walk slowly up the path.

Had they just been passing by and dropped in to watch the service? No, St Olave's was not a place you just passed by. And they had been dressed for a funeral. And she was sure Michael had known them and made some sort of communication with them. So who were they? His wife was ill. Was the woman his girlfriend, with their love child? That had to be the explanation. His girlfriend had known her mother and had wanted to attend the funeral. But Michael had not wanted her to meet Madeleine or Megan. Perhaps Megan did not know about her and Michael did not want her to find out and say something out of order to his wife. Anyway, it was their business. Nothing to do with her.

She turned back towards the church and waited for the coffin and the others to emerge. When they did so, Michael came up to her and put his arm round her shoulder. Instinctively she pulled away.

'Sorry about that dramatic exit,' she said. 'Very stuffy in there. I felt a bit sick. I'm better now. I needed the sea air.'

'I understand. And all that business about sea and trees. Like one big mixed metaphor. I couldn't follow it at all. Colm's a nice chap but he does get carried away sometimes. Imagines he's preaching in St Paul's to a congregation of thousands.'

After the coffin had been lowered and the final words of the service spoken, she thanked the minister, concealing her anger with him behind a taut smile, and turned back to Michael. Megan had withdrawn to leave them on their own, no doubt in accordance with prior instructions. She walked round the churchyard with him.

'Michael, I wanted to speak to you about her cottage.'

'Well, of course it's all yours now. You're the only surviving relative. Unless she left it to an animal charity or something.'

'Oh, no. Everything comes to me. I'm sure it's very nice.'

'Not really. It's very run down.'

'But I thought you said you didn't live in her village.'

'I don't. But I go down there sometimes. There's a nice little art gallery. That's where we met. We had coffee a couple of times, on the sea front. She told me she had bought the cottage on an impulse. It was almost derelict. I walked back there with her on one occasion. I could see from the lane that it was rather run down. I never went inside.'

'The thing is, I've no use for it myself. I'm not into all this rural idyll stuff. I've no time and it's too far away. Could you sell it on my behalf?'

'Well, yes, I could. But there's another idea you might want to consider. There's always a demand for holiday cottages round here. Your mother's cottage has superb sea views. It has real potential. I could have it done up for you and rent it out. It would be something to keep me occupied. I'm retired now, you see. You wouldn't need to bother about it at all. You can leave everything to me.'

She had already left everything about the funeral to him. Was she imposing too much on him? But he seemed willing, almost anxious, to receive this further commission from her. So why was she hesitating? He had been sympathetic. He was not to know that she did not need sympathy. He had not tried to pry into the reasons why she and her mother had not seen each other for so long. His conduct had been impeccable. It was just that there was something about his manner. She had felt uneasy when she had first met him, after the inquest. She had not been able to pinpoint the cause of her feelings, deciding in the end that it was her anxiety about the situation in which she found herself. Now she realised what it was. His eyes only occasionally met hers. The rest of the time they were looking around, as if he suspected somebody was following him. But that was no reason to reject his help. He was offering to take responsibility for the cottage off her hands. She would be foolish to refuse.

'Well, if you really don't mind. All right. It's agreed.' She fumbled in her handbag. 'Here's the key. And my card with my address on it in London. You can clear out all her personal stuff, if you wouldn't mind. Clothes and books and that sort of stuff. You won't find anything of value there, I'm afraid. Then you can do what you like with the place. Just keep the rent cheques yourself until you've covered your costs. Talking of costs . . .'

'The funeral? Leave that to me as well.'

'No, I couldn't do that. But take the cost out of the rent as well. Or send me the bill. Well, thank you for all you've done, Michael. I really was at a loss, and you've seen me through it. Thank Megan for coming, as well. I did appreciate it. I really have to be off now. I have to be back for work in the morning.'

They shook hands.

'Well, it was very nice to meet you, despite the circumstances. Do keep in touch. You must come and inspect your property. I'll let you know how I get on with the renovations. Goodbye for now.'

As she slipped into the seat of her car she was conscious of his eyes focusing intently on her. Why only now, when she was leaving? She looked up at him and waved. Megan had returned and stood behind him, waving and smiling. As she drove away she thought about the parting expression on his face. Was it really one of relief? Or was she reflecting her own feelings onto him?

5

Megan opened the door and peered through her horn-rimmed spectacles at her visitor, her familiar feather duster in her hand. Then she dropped it, put her hand to her mouth and squealed.

'Lord bless us, it really is you, Miss Madeleine.'

'Hello, Megan. Yes, it really is me. And it really is good to see you. Come here.' She had never hugged Megan before, but neither woman was embarrassed by the moment. Perhaps Megan had prepared herself for it as she had.

'You haven't changed a bit. And don't tell me I haven't because I would know you were lying. And please call me Madeleine. "Miss Madeleine" is a bit young for me now, and makes me feel like a character in an eighteenth-century novel.'

'And no harm in that, either. They had proper respect in them far-off days. But Madeleine it is from now on if that's what you want. Well, come on in and let's get you a cup of tea. You're really out for good? Not just on probation? They're not going to take you back? You didn't walk along the coastal path, did you? You've no car with you and I didn't hear a taxi.'

'I came by minicab. Asked the driver to leave me at the top of the driveway. I wanted to walk down. I'm trying to get used to walking again, a bit at a time. I'm certainly not fit enough for the coastal path yet. And yes, Megan, I'm out for good.'

'Have you no luggage with you, Miss . . . er, Madeleine? You will be staying, won't you? It is your house after all and it's been so empty and lonely without you.'

They had sat down in Megan's cosy parlour near the front door, where she did her knitting and from where she could look out for visitors. Megan made tea on a tiny Belling stove.

'To tell you the truth, Megan, I don't think I could ever live here again. I'm staying at the inn in Porthhella.'

'I do understand.' Megan served the tea, in large, steaming mugs.

'You don't mind me being here, do you, Megan? After what I did?'

'Of course not. Don't be so silly. And I'll tell you again what I told the police the day they came for you. You never did it. Nothing will ever make me believe you did. Not to my dying day. Either she died naturally or it were someone else. That's what I think and what I'll always think. I know you wasn't yourself at the time. But that doesn't mean you could ever kill someone.

'And you're not the first person to be driven out of their minds in this awful old house. There were young Master David before you. That time he were away for a week and we didn't know where. When he came back he didn't know Mr Wallace from Adam or me from Eve. Then he wandered off the top of the cliffs that night. Dreadful. Mr Wallace were like a shadow of himself after that. When you came and looked after him, it were like the sun rising again in this house. Then he died and you . . . well, you started acting very strange. You went away without a word. I knew you had something on your mind you couldn't tell anybody about. And when you came back and wouldn't say anything, I were so afraid the same thing might happen to you. Only thank God they took you away and they looked after you.

'We should have done that with him. Not let him live here and go out on his own like that. But Mr Wallace wouldn't hear of it, his being sent away, I mean. And in your case the loneliness of living here after Mr Wallace's death would have been enough to

47

drive anyone over the edge, if you ask me. This great big pile, out on its own, looking out into the Atlantic. Fine, if you're used to it, like me. But not for someone like you, used to all that fast living up in London. If you want to know what I think, I think you should sell it. Get somewhere nice and warm and modern and light. No need to worry about me. Mr Wallace were very generous to me in his will. Best housekeeper in the world, he used to say, just to tease me. I'll be all right. I can find a nice cottage somewhere near here. I've lived in Cornwall all my life and I've never been outside it. But you've travelled. You can choose to go anywhere you like.'

'Megan, that other thing you wrote to me about. You remember? In your last letter.'

'What was that, now? My memory's getting worse all the time.'

'You mentioned a notebook.'

'Oh yes. I remember now. Well, it were like this. You know those locked rooms upstairs in the attic? Well, when Mr Wallace were in hospital and I were paying him a visit, it were just the two of us there, and I were doing some knitting because I thought he were dozing, he called me to lean closer to him so he could whisper in my ear. He told me where I could find the keys to the upstairs rooms. The rooms where Master David used to have his studio, and Mr Wallace before him. As you know, after Master David died he kept the whereabouts of those keys a secret and he wouldn't even let me go up there to dust and tidy round. Did all that himself, until he were too feeble to get up the stairs. Now he were telling me that it were his dying wish that I should take everything out of those rooms and destroy it. Made me promise. Said he would have done it himself except he realised too late that he would never have the strength.'

Megan leaned forward and whispered in a conspiratorial tone of voice, though the nearest living soul had to be miles away. Her eyes shone.

'Luckily there were no Bible near at hand so I didn't have to swear on the Holy Book because that would have made things a bit difficult for me as it turned out. Anyway, I did promise but then I went and forgot all about it. The thing that puzzled me were, why didn't he ask you to do it, because you was far more likely than I were to remember. But he didn't. He asked me. And what's more he made me swear not to say anything about any of this to you. Well, I didn't, did I? Because I went and forgot all about it. He died the next day and that put it right out of my mind. Then there were the funeral and you being preoccupied and then all that business with you being taken away. I never thought about it until it came back to me one day, about a year on, when I went to change the flowers on his grave. It were as if he were whispering to me from the grave to remember what I'd promised.'

'This visitation is but to whet thy almost blunted purpose', muttered Madeleine.

'Eh?'

'Sorry, Megan. Just a bit of Shakespeare from my schooldays coming back to me. Go on.'

'Luckily I remembered where he had told me the keys was. So I went up there to have a look around. I found there were things I couldn't destroy. A lot of drawings and paintings by Master David, done when he were a boy. I don't suppose they were great art, but I couldn't bring myself to burn them. And there were other drawings, by Mr Wallace himself, wonderful things, I thought, though I'm no expert. It would have been vandalism to have destroyed those. There were some papers I got rid of. Old bills, estimates for building work and the like. Though I can't imagine it were those he were bothered about. The funny thing is that I didn't find what he'd told me I would find. It came back to me that he'd talked about a blue folder, sealed, with very personal papers. I weren't to look at anything inside, I were to burn it right away. Well, I searched high and low and never found that blue folder. But there were something I did find, lying on the floor. An old notebook. I had a quick look at the first few pages and decided I couldn't destroy that either. It were nothing to do with Mr Wallace, and for the life of me I can't imagine what it were doing up in that room. I brought it down here and left it in the bureau.'

'And the other stuff that you didn't want to throw out?'

'It's all still up there. The police had a quick look round there after you'd been arrested, but obviously they didn't find anything of interest.'

'And the notebook?'

'I forgot about that as well. Then, I suppose it were a year ago, I were tidying up in that bureau when I found it again. I wondered why I had kept it. Then it came back to me. I had seen your name in it.'

'On the cover?'

'No. Your name were there among the words written inside. On the first page. I never read beyond that. The impression I got were that it were your mother had written it. So if it belonged to anybody it belonged to you. It were not for me or Mr Wallace to decide to throw it out. So I wrote and told you about it and asked if you wanted me to send it to you. You said, you hoped to be out soon and would come and see me and pick it up then. I've got it here for you. Nicely wrapped up.'

'Thank you, Megan.' Madeleine fingered the small parcel Megan had handed to her. 'If it was my mother's, what on earth was it doing in this house, and locked away upstairs at that?'

'Well, that's the real mystery about it. I never met your mum. Mr Wallace knew her a bit. Enough to want to go to the funeral. You remember we met there for the first time. He were very insistent on me coming with him. Said he would feel very strange there on his own. And there would be so few people there, so he said, that just one extra person would make a big difference. So I went, though I weren't very keen on the idea. Some people enjoy them but I'm not really a funeral person. They remind me of my poor Fred's. He were so young when he died. Not yet thirty. I'm glad I did go as it turned out, because it became my first memory of you. I felt we were friends right away, even though it were another thirteen years before we met again. Anyway, Mr Wallace said as you and she were like peas in a pod. Those weren't his words exactly. So, after it's been all round the houses, here it is in your possession at last. You can decide what you want to do with it.'

'I'll take it back with me to the inn and have a look at it before going to bed. Thanks for taking such good care of it, Megan. And thanks for the tea and the welcome. You don't know how good it is to see your smiling face again.'

'It's been so good to see you again. Sorry I couldn't come and visit. But when you've never been out of Cornwall in your life, it's too late at my age to start gallivanting around foreign parts of the country on my own.'

'I understand, Megan. I know you were always with me in spirit. I was going to say that that thought kept me sane.'

She started to giggle. Megan joined in. By the time they parted on the doorstep, they were both laughing like schoolgirls.

6

There could be no doubt about it. It was her mother's handwriting. The pages were yellow and the ink had faded but not yet enough to render it illegible.

June 1961

So it's come to this. I'm having to write to you. Even though we still see each other every day. I cannot talk to you any more, Madeleine. I was getting desperate. Then I had a brainwave. It's a long time since I had one of those. I went out to buy this nice new notebook, specially. I'm not going to write anything else in it. Only the words intended for you. When I've written enough, I'll give it to you. Maybe weeks, months or years ahead. Then you'll understand.

What's happened between us? You ignore me. I start to talk to you and you turn away. You go off to do your homework, so you say, even though I know you've already done it. Or you go off to be with him. In his study. The two of you are so close now. You're shutting me out. I don't blame you. I've been so distant from both of you, so wrapped up in myself. When I go away I try not to be away for too long. But sometimes I can't bear the thought of coming back to a house where I'm a stranger. So I'm away for days at a time. And I know neither of you needs me any more. You have each other. Don't be too hard on me. It hasn't exactly been easy, paying for the mistakes I made when I was so young. I'm still young, for God's sake, only thirty-two. I wasn't in love with him, though I thought I was. I married him because I thought I needed someone to keep me calm and steady. I thought I could use him to make myself complete, to give myself the qualities I lacked. It didn't work of course. I felt my soul drying up. I ended up hating him for his calm and self-control, for the very qualities I thought I had needed for myself. I married him because I was wild and he was steady. Then I wanted him to be like me. Not wild and out of control. Just enough like me so he would understand me. Enough so we could share a love of life and beauty. I knew he had his loves, of books and poems and ideas and history. I should have been able to share some of those with him. There was a time when he tried to teach me about them, when I was his student. But I didn't pay enough attention. I've forgotten it all now. I was so obsessed with imagining I was in love with him that I never really tried to understand what he was trying to tell me. Now he is teaching you. The two of you are so self-sufficient. The way you look at each other, and whisper so I cannot hear. So now I am on my own. Perhaps it could never have worked, even if I had agreed to try to learn patiently from him. I just don't have the gift for it. At least I can do the things I do have a gift for. The things you're now just old enough to be disgusted by. Yes, Madeleine, I can see it in your face. Maybe one day you will make a mistake in your life which will haunt you for the rest of your days. Then perhaps you will judge me less harshly.

Her heart was thumping. What is this, Mother? You're saying you hated him? You're saying I was cold-shouldering you? Well, maybe it looked like that when he was still alive. How old was I then? Thirteen. I suppose you and he had grown a bit distant from each other. But I don't remember taking sides with him against you. And what do you mean, 'the things I'm old enough to be disgusted by'? I don't remember you having affairs.

The ink in which the next entry was written was less faded.

May 1964

I really don't know what's happening to you. I don't understand you. You're 16 now, nearly 17, looking more and more like me every day. At your age I was an outrageous flirt. Everybody told me how attractive I was. When I try to tell you how attractive you are now I feel a little ashamed because I know I'm talking about myself as well. Or myself as I was. So why haven't you any friends? Why are you so controlled and distant, obsessed with your studies? I did try to talk to you about sex, just that once. You remember? All you said was that you would be careful. I wanted to say that there was a bit more to it than that but you just turned away. I wanted to give you the benefit of my experience. That's the problem, isn't it? My experience. You're still disgusted with me, even though I no longer have affairs. It's like our hearts are dying. But at my age, after a failed marriage, that's perhaps to be expected. But you have barely begun to grow up. Why have you closed yourself off in this way from everything life has to offer? I want you to be like me, but better, happier, more successful. If you can't talk to me, I hope and pray you meet someone you can talk to.

Come on, Mother. You're making this up. Is this your idea of the truth or the draft of a novel? We were very close in those days after father's death. Like sisters. I told you about everything. Remember those shopping trips we did together? And of course we talked about sex. And I had lots of friends. No special boyfriends, but plenty of girlfriends. All right, if you can write all this rubbish I can write down the truth.

She went over to the table and took out a notepad from the

drawer. It had the name and address of the inn on each sheet. She had decided to make a list. Of the names of her friends, of the places she and her mother had visited together.

After half an hour the sheet was still blank. Those damn drugs they gave me, she thought. They said they were to calm me down. But they stopped me remembering. They're still stopping me. And all that time that stupid therapist was supposed to be helping me get my memories back. I don't suppose he ever asked what drugs they were giving me.

That was before they found out, of course. Then everything changed. At first, she had been with other female patients on a large, Victorian ward. Not that anybody took any notice of her. Each was locked into her own private world, some buried in silence, others sitting on the edge of their beds, rocking from side to side and moaning, others telling their story out loud, at length and repeatedly, to the unheeding space around them.

Then, without warning, she was moved to a high-security wing. She had a room of her own, furnished only with a hard, narrow bed, a chair and a table. She was locked in, day and night. When she wanted the toilet, she called out through an aperture in the door for the duty nurse to escort her.

On the main ward they had only given her tranquillisers. Now there was a new regime of frequent drug injections. At first she had resisted when they came to administer them. A burly male nurse entered the room first and stood by the door. Then a female nurse, almost as large as the male, entered, carrying a small white box. The male nurse took hold of Madeleine's arm. When she tried to pull it away he jerked it behind her back and pressed upwards towards her shoulders. Slowly, casually, ignoring Madeleine's screams, the female nurse took out a syringe, filled and tested it and injected the contents into the still imprisoned arm. Only when the injection began to take effect and she went limp and silent did the male nurse release his hold. Taking an arm each the two nurses half-carried and half-dragged her towards her bed.

That night, before lights out, the female nurse returned to watch her as she undressed, and to search through her clothes and her bed for sharp objects which she may have somehow found and hidden away during the day. She had been assessed as at serious risk of self-harm, the nurse explained. When the nurse had very slowly and carefully checked every inch of her body for any recent marks she was allowed to put on her night-clothes and get into bed.

Not that there was much chance of her hiding anything dangerous. Her meals were served with plastic cutlery, and even then she was watched closely as she ate. She was not allowed a pen or pencil. Her letters to Megan were dictated to a member of the hospital administrative staff, who came to her room once a week for the purpose. She was allowed to see the letter and check it but not to sign it.

The routine was the same every day, except that after the first day she decided she would no longer resist the administration of the injections. The agony in her arm and shoulder persisted for a week. She was allowed out into a courtyard for exercise for an hour a day, heavily escorted and at a time when no other patients were there.

Though nobody told her, she knew the reason for the move and the new routine. It was all because of that examination, a couple of weeks after her admission. What was that doctor's name, the one who specialised in genito-urinary medicine? Dr Simms, that was it. She had liked Dr Simms, at first. She was not like the nurses. She was young and pretty and smiled reas-suringly. She told Madeleine to undress and lie down on the bed. We just need to check you over, she told her, just a quick check. It was not at all like that. The examination was long, thorough, intimate and often painful.

A few weeks later she was taken back to the same room to see Dr Simms again. Dr Simms asked her whether she had ever used contraception. Not since she was 17, she had replied. She had had an abortion then, and there were complications. It meant she could never have children. Dr Simms, barely attempting to conceal the disapproval in her voice, read out a list of the various venereal conditions she had found in the examination. Most were not serious. They would treat them with drugs. But there was something else. Something which was very serious indeed. I know, Madeleine had said.

That had enraged Dr Simms. She had thumped the table in front of her, demanded to know why Madeleine had not informed her of the diagnosis. Because there was no diagnosis, Madeleine had replied. She had just known. It was a stranger. A one-night stand in a little place near Marseilles. Dr Simms then demanded a list of everybody Madeleine had had sex with since that night. The answer was simple. Nobody. Dr Simms stared at her, then decided to believe her. She gave Madeleine the piece of paper she had kept with her ever since. Then Dr Simms told her she would recommend her for early discharge, on compassionate grounds. The following day she was removed to the high-security wing.

She had learned her lesson from the time she had resisted the nurses' efforts to give her the injections. After that she was a model patient, always quiet and docile. She asked patiently and repeatedly to be allowed to send for some books from home. Eventually her request was granted, subject to the consultant in charge of her case approving of her choice. She sent Megan a list with directions on where to find them in Michael's library. They arrived within a week. She chose three favourites which she read and reread constantly, refusing to discuss them with the nurses whenever they asked about them. They were a volume of plays by Aeschylus, Sophocles and Euripides and some books by her father on the Greek myths.

One day, months after her interview with Dr Simms, after she had gone to bed and heard the familiar clunk of the heavy key in the lock, it came to her, like a voice from another world. The woman she had killed was David's mother. She did not know how she knew, but she had never been so sure of anything in her life. She was elated, though she hid the change in her mood, not wishing to draw any further attention to herself. Despite the withdrawal of the therapy her memories were returning. She waited. Now others would follow. Eventually she would remember why she had gone to see Laura, why she had killed her. Maybe there was a reason of sorts. It could never have been a rational action. But maybe there was a sort of twisted logic to it, a logic which might make sense to her, which might prove to her that at least on her own terms she was not crazy after all, that she had not committed a totally random act of violence. She continued to wait. No other memories returned.

After a few months, she began to suffer from increasingly serious bronchial conditions, with outbreaks of sores in and around her mouth. The infections spread to her kidneys. She spent more and more time under treatment in the infirmary, the last time for a total of six months. When she began to recover from her symptoms, they told her she would be discharged within a week, though under supervision. She knew it was not on grounds of compassion. Her recovery was temporary. They knew she did not have much time left. It would be an embarrassment for them if she died in their care. There would be difficult questions to answer, suggestions that she had caught her condition there, criticisms of the circumstances which had allowed that to happen. Far better for them to be rid of her, to let her take her chances on the outside. There would be no public criticism of her early discharge. She was no longer violent, no longer a danger to anybody else. There were no surviving relatives or friends of the woman she had killed. Nobody would make a fuss. Nobody would remember her case at all.

She turned her attention back to the notebook. Three years between the first two entries. What happened during those years? He died. And it doesn't even get a mention.

I remember he died of cancer, she said to herself, out loud.

Did my mother tell me that was what he had? What type of cancer was it? I know he smoked a lot. Lung cancer, probably. I don't remember visiting him in hospital. I don't remember the funeral. Perhaps I didn't go. They thought it would be too traumatic for me.

A year later I was in hospital myself. That doesn't get a mention either. You had a problem with sickness, didn't you, Mother? You couldn't write about it. So your notebook is a blank for three years.

Hesitantly, she started to write. She looked at what she had written. It was a name. John Carey. Of course. He was her English teacher. She had mentioned him to Dr Simms. Not by name, of course. She had forgotten his name. In fact she had not mentioned him at all. She had only mentioned the abortion and the consequences. Now more of the detail was coming back to her. That was good. It showed that her memory was improving at last. The talks with Brenda and Megan, the visit to the cottage, the notebook, her thoughts about her time in hospital, painful though they were, were all helping.

She had been 17 at the time. He was nearly 50. She had planned it meticulously. A week before, she had gone to see their family doctor. She had heard about this new pill that stopped you having babies. She had persuaded him to prescribe it for her without telling her mother. That was what she had meant when she had told her mother she would be careful. Her mother hadn't asked her what she meant. She must have assumed she meant she would avoid having sex. Another of her sad illusions, that her 17-year-old daughter could still be a virgin! Madeleine had asked Mr Carey if she could talk to him privately after school, about what subjects she should apply to study at university. They did talk, briefly. He told her English would be a very good subject for her. She would probably get a grade A in her A level if she continued to work as hard as she had been doing. But you knew that already, didn't you, he had said. She shrugged her shoulders. She followed him as he left the classroom. Outside the school gates she asked him if he could give her a lift home. She lived only five minutes' walk away, whereas his house was five miles in the opposite direction. He knew that and knew that she knew it. But he nodded and opened the car door for her. He took a route which led to neither of their homes, turned up a side-road into some woods and parked in a clearing. It was over in less than a minute.

That wasn't the first time. He had asked her that, immediately afterwards. Of course not, she had said. But why should she remember the first time with Mr Carey, when she could not remember the much more important occasion when she had done it for the first time with anybody? Had it been with another of her teachers? She was sure it was not with a boy of her own age. She had always treated them with the contempt they deserved.

Mr Carey drove her back and dropped her off just outside the school. Neither of them said a word during the journey. They met at the same time every week outside the school gates and went to the same place, for four weeks. Once she had tried to start a conversation. She had asked him if she was special to him. He had laughed. It was the end of their affair. She did not mind. He was certainly not special to her.

A few weeks later she discovered she was pregnant. That wouldn't have been in the notebook of course. Her mother had known nothing about it. She had told her mother she would be careful but she wasn't careful enough. Several times she had forgotten to take her pill. She had enough money from her father's will to pay for an abortion. She told her mother she was staying with a friend in London. The abortion had gone successfully, she was told. Except for certain complications. Irreversible ones. She had not minded. She had never been the maternal type.

She lay down on the bed, still fully dressed, and closed her eyes. After a few minutes she sensed that she was about to doze off. There was a low, whispering sound in her ear. She could not make out any words. Then she heard a different voice. Her own.

Insistent, desperate. David's mother. It was David's mother I killed. I know that. I don't know why I did it. But I know it was her. Now the other voice was laughing, a harsh, mocking sound. Then it whispered a word, very close to her ear. Special.

She woke up with a shout, rushed to the bathroom and was violently sick.

7

She sat at her dressing-table, staring into the mirror. Behind her the grey shadows floated, shifted and pointed. She ignored them. She was used to them now. She had had years to get used to them. She wondered what had made her sick. She would not use the restaurant in the inn any more. There was a cafe on the seafront. She would go there in future.

Her face stared back at her. It was sallow, thin and deeply lined. Her limp hair was a mixture of grey and white. Thank God you never lived to see me like this, Mother. Anyone seeing us together now would assume I was your mother.

She shuddered, stood up, undressed slowly and put on her pyjamas. They were the first things she had bought after her discharge. They were grey, made of a thick woollen material which eased the discomfort of her pressure sores.

She awoke again in the early hours and could not get back to sleep. She put on the light, picked up the notebook and resumed her reading at the third entry.

April 1965

After what happened yesterday you will understand that I have no choice. I have decided to leave Oxford. I've always hated it here. I only stayed here up to now because of you. At least you used to try to conceal your disgust with me. Now you scream it into my face. In front of everybody. You don't need me any more. On the contrary, I seem to be making matters worse for you. The doctor told me you should be out soon and that you intend to go to London to find work. He expects you to make a full recovery. So long as I don't try to visit you again. He didn't actually say that, but I could tell it was what he meant.

You don't even need me for money. You have your allowance from his estate. I'll probably sell the house and buy something smaller, somewhere a long way away, in the country. Cornwall, maybe. I don't want to go back to Wales. I want to forget everything about my past. I'll be comfortable enough. The house should fetch a lot of money. I'll pay your share directly into your bank. I will have the royalties from his books to live on. They still sell well, even better than they did when he was alive. To make things easier for you, I will not give you my new address, so you will not feel under any obligation to get in touch. Nor will I expect you to tell me where you are. You will need to tell Mr Wilson each time you move. You remember him, don't you, our family solicitor? I'll give you his card. In case anything happens to me. You'll inherit everything of course. But he'll need to know where you are. We can communicate through him if we have to. I will ask him to contact you from time to time to see how you are getting on. He will let me know. And if you need anything, tell him and he will pass it on. I will send you this notebook through him, when I have finished it.

I wish you every success and happiness. I know you will be successful. You have that determination about you. As for happiness, I think you may find it a bit harder to come by. And it will not come unless you make some difficult decisions. What I mean is that you must try to get over your father's death. And when you get this notebook and have read here what I have been unable to say to you, if you cannot understand me at least try to forget about your hard feelings towards me. I do love you,

Madeleine, and despite our coldness to each other I know I will
miss you terribly.

At last, a mention of Father's death! But what was all that
about me screaming at you? I don't remember that.

I remember the clinic, though. That nice big house out in the
country. It must have cost quite a chunk out of Father's estate to
send me there, even if only for a few weeks. I had developed a
little problem with drugs. It started at school, quite soon after I
had gone back after that time in hospital. There were drug dealers
outside the school gates every day. We all knew they were there.
They mingled with the pupils and parents in the mornings and
evenings. Some were only children themselves. They approached
me. They seemed to realise I needed their services. They could
tell just by looking at me. It was only soft stuff, of course. But
they put me onto other dealers near the council estate. In case I
needed anything harder. Which I did. The police caught one of
them in the act of selling to me. He got two years. I got probation, on condition I attended a clinic. I went willingly. I was
determined to kick the habit. The doctors were pleased with me.
I don't remember yelling at you when you visited me. I don't
remember you visiting me at all. Are you sure you're not making
this up?

I was expelled from school of course, just before I was supposed
to take my A levels. Not that I was in any state to take them.
Whenever I managed to stagger into school it was straight into
the toilets to inject.

So we had a serious quarrel, did we, according to this? I told
you I was disgusted with you and never wanted to see you again.
And you took me at my word. If it's true I can't say I blame you.
But if I was disgusted with you, what gave me that right? Maybe
you were having affairs. But I was hardly in a position to judge
you for that, a 17-year-old drug addict schoolgirl seducing her
teachers.

He and I were close, I'm sure of that. I was so proud of him, watching him becoming so famous as his books sold more and more, appearing on radio and television. He was working on a new book when he died. About the Myth of Narcissus. I remember helping him with it, reading the proofs, looking up references for him. He never finished it. 'Beauty in the young is a curse. It awakens evil.' I remember that bit, from the opening chapter. I never knew what it meant. I wanted to ask him but I was afraid he would think I was being stupid. He thought I understood everything he said and wrote. It's all I remember of it. Nobody could find the manuscript afterwards. He must have destroyed it.

So, Mother, how did you get on in Cornwall?

July 1965

I started very early in the morning. It was late June, the longest day. I wanted to get there before dark. I hate driving in the dark. I hated the entire journey. It was hot and dusty. There were long queues of traffic. Petrol fumes choked me when I opened the window. At last it was evening and I had the road to myself. It was nine o'clock and the road had only a few miles to go.

I don't know why I took that left-hand turn. I suppose it was the red sky. I wanted to see the sun going down, the dying sun marking the end of my life. In the car park near the beach, a few tourists were taking photographs of the sunset. I wanted to avoid them, though they were too preoccupied to notice me. At the end of the car park I found a path which led across the side of the hill above the beach. I could see the whole bay. I walked along for about half a mile.

It was on the way back along the path that I saw the dolphins. It was ten o'clock but still light. The tide was low. The water was calm and silvery. There were three of them, only a few dozen yards offshore. They were circling playfully around each other. Sometimes they jumped clean out of the water. They call that 'breaching', or so I have heard. When I was a child I had often seen dolphins in Cardigan Bay. Perhaps they were the same ones. After all those years when I hardly ever saw the sea they had come to find me again. Or I had come to find them. I was crying with happiness.

It was nearly dark now. I did not want to drive on. I did not want to go anywhere. I had heard voices from the sea telling me to stay. Just over the road I saw the inn. They had one little single room left. I brought in my bag, much too heavy for its size. Wouldn't they have been surprised to know it contained only some of my books? I could have left them in the car but I wanted to give at least the appearance of having luggage. I would have to buy some clean clothes and a toothbrush the next day.

In the morning I looked around the village. I found the lane behind these cottages. There was a 'For Sale' sign in the lane but I did not know to what it referred. I could see no houses. I was about to move on when a young lady arrived from the estate agents. She asked if I had come to view the property. Something made me say 'Yes', though I nearly asked 'Which property?' I followed her through a broken-down gate, which was nearly hidden by the dense foliage, and along the overgrown path. I gasped with shock and delight when I saw the cottage. She admitted it was in a bad state of repair and needed a lot of work. Nobody had lived in it for years. I did not care. I had already decided to buy it. It could not be expensive. It was not. After a quick look round I made an offer at just below the price she had named. I would have gone higher. She accepted immediately. I sometimes wonder what happened to the people whose appointment I had usurped. I am sure they would not have liked the cottage. It was meant for me.

It really was a case of love at first sight. I was drawn to its dishevelled appearance, its melancholy air of neglect and its defiant inaccessibility to modern forms of transport. Did I see it as a reflection of myself? It is so oddly put together. There are two floors, but the upper one seems to have been added at a later time, with no internal connection to the ground floor. To get downstairs I have to go outside, down by the side wall and in again by the back door. I would like to make my bedroom downstairs, but first I will need to get an indoor staircase installed. There's damp downstairs and draughts everywhere. There's no electricity connected yet. I'm using candles. But I love it. It's all mine. The views are heavenly. I love to sit and watch the sea, especially when it's raging against those rocks out in the bay.

April 1966

I've just had a letter from Mr Wilson. He says he spoke to you last week. You've got a good job in a merchant bank now. On the bottom rung of the ladder, of course. But you couldn't really expect any more, could you, not without any qualifications, not even A levels? You type, you take messages, you do odd jobs for the brokers and the analysts. But I know you do more than that, don't you? You watch, observe, listen and learn. You take any opportunity to show you can do more than they expect you to. You take any chance to surprise them, to make them remember you. One day an opening will come. Just a tiny one, a little crack, a chance to really shine. And you will be through that crack like lightning. And then you will be up and away. Nothing will stop you. Somehow I know it will be like that for you.

You were right about that, Mother. That's exactly how it was. You knew me better than I thought.

This week, spring has finally arrived, thank God. What a long, lonely winter it has been. I had the chimney cleaned so I could keep warm with wood fires, like the ones we used to have at home in Wales. There is a store on the sea front which sells firewood. I get my groceries there as well. I walk down there every day in all weathers, and struggle back up the path with the burden of what I have bought. The man in the store told me that he could deliver my purchases, for a small extra charge. I told him I was not on my last legs yet. I hope I didn't sound rude. I didn't mean to. He still smiles at me when I go in, but I can't get him to chat to me. Other customers, the ones who have been there for years, get all the gossip. I wonder how long you have to live here before they accept you? Not that I want to hear the gossip exactly. I just want to feel I belong.

My usual pastime, now the weather is better, is walking along the cliff-top path. My favourite spot is between the two headlands. Once I am up there, away from the village, I really feel that I do belong. I love all wild places. The other day I met a hiker there who was walking the coastal path all the way along to Porthcurno. He warned me that the cliffs between the headlands are particularly dangerous. People have been killed in falls there, he said. I am not afraid to go close to the edge. I love to look down at the water boiling and hissing below. Offshore there are huge rocky formations which were once part of the cliffs. The sea has cut underneath them and behind them. Their shapes are fantastic, like prehistoric monsters who have looked upon the Gorgon.

Many of the cottages round here are only occupied in summer. There are some nice old folk who retired here. I say good morning to them. I don't invite them to come round and they don't invite me. Why is that? Am I afraid of growing old? Do I think it might be infectious? There is a woman in the art gallery who is about 30, I would say. I look younger than my age, so I thought we could be friends. We might have some things in common. We've said hello already. I don't know her name yet. I have to say that she doesn't look at me in a very friendly way when I go in. She's very reserved. I ask her questions about the paintings. I'm not really that interested in them. She tells me what she thinks I want to know. But I really want to know about her. I can't draw her out. She goes back into her shell. It's as if she's a little frightened of me. I think she's rather sad and lonely underneath.

So that was how you first met Brenda. Obviously your efforts to make friends didn't exactly work out. What in God's name did you do to upset her? By the time I met her she still hated you even though you had been dead for 13 years. She had so much hatred in her that she was only too delighted to redirect it towards me.

That's it. No more entries. All the later pages blank. So why did you stop writing? And why did you never send me what you had written? And why, oh why, did this notebook end up on the floor in a locked room, two miles along the coast, in the house of a man you barely knew?

8

June 1995

All right, Mother. I've decided to return the compliment. You wrote to me in these pages so I'll write to you. You didn't really expect me to read what you wrote and I know you won't see what I'm going to write. You did it for yourself. So I'm going to do it for myself. To help me remember. Reading and thinking are fine as far as they go. But writing will be even better. And it does seem a shame, to waste all the blank pages in this lovely book.

After your funeral it was another 13 years before I went to Cornwall again, before I finally saw your cottage. What made me go there? The inquest and the funeral were enough to put me off Cornwall for life. I had vowed never to return. I kept telling myself I should write to Michael and tell him to sell the cottage. I never got round to it. Finally I forgot all about it.

Then everything changed. I got the sack. Can't blame them really. They found me slumped in the Ladies'. Combination of alcohol and an overdose of coke. They found supplies of both in my desk. I had kicked the hard drugs habit years before, but coke was different. It was part of the culture. Everybody there was at it. Only I couldn't handle it. Not with my history of addiction.

The writing had been on the wall for months. Unauthorised absences, increasing signs of poor judgement, slurred speech at meetings, even at seven in the morning. Luckily they gave me a generous pay-off and didn't involve the police. Didn't want the publicity, I suppose. I went into voluntary rehab (again!) for the drugs and joined AA for the other little problem. I stayed off all drugs after that. I carried on drinking but managed to keep it under control. Most of the time.

Of course getting the sack could have been a wonderful opportunity, once I'd recovered. I could have taken a year or two off, travelled the world. I had enough money. Then I could have set up a consultancy of my own. I could have stayed in London. I had all my professional contacts there. Instead, I ran away to the end of the country, just the way you had done. Why, in God's name, did I do that?

Was I, despite what the police and the coroner had said, still curious about your death, so sudden, so mysterious, so dramatic? Did I wonder about Michael and the part he had really played in your life? Or was I wondering even then about the question which has been going through my mind since I started to read what you wrote here. What exactly was it that had happened between us, and would I find clues somewhere in the traces you had left in and around the cottage and on the edge of those cliffs?

March 1986

Madeleine detested the village and the cottage from the outset, and decided to leave as early as possible the next morning. She walked down to the general store on the sea front to buy some groceries for her evening meal, a packet of cigarettes, a bottle of red wine and a bottle of single malt whisky. She was used to a lifestyle in which coffee at the desk was a permanent feature. She was already suffering severe caffeine withdrawal symptoms. She also regretted the weight of her purchases and did not relish the prospect of dragging them back up the lane to the cottage. She struggled with them into a small cafe next to the store and ordered a cup of black coffee. She sat down and lit a cigarette.

After a few sips she noticed that a stout, severely-dressed white-haired woman at a nearby table was staring rudely at her. Madeleine looked away. After a few seconds she looked back. The woman was still staring. Out of habit she found herself sizing her up. Late forties or early fifties. Unmarried, living on her own. Owns a dog or a cat. Probably goes to church. Methodist or Presbyterian. The woman stood up and walked over. Madeleine stubbed out her cigarette quickly. Perhaps the woman objected to her smoking. If that was the case she only had to ask. There was no need to stare, no need to approach her so aggressively. She stopped, a few feet away. A look of embarrassed relief swept across the woman's face.

'My God,' she said. 'You're just like her. I thought you were somebody I knew. Then I realised it couldn't be. Unless you were a ghost. I'm sorry I disturbed you.' She turned round and walked away.

'It's all right,' Madeleine called after her. A thought occurred to her. 'Maybe I am a ghost. Did you know my mother, perhaps?'

The woman seemed to freeze. She turned round, very slowly. Madeleine's smile faded under her gaze. A sort of smile seemed to form on the woman's face, but it could well have been a sneer.

'Ceridwen Williams?' She pronounced the syllables slowly, one by one, as if sipping a bitter-tasting medicine.

'Yes. She was my mother. My name's Madeleine Reed. Williams was her maiden name. Would you like to sit down?'

The woman took a chair from the next table, and half-turned it towards Madeleine. She sat down. She had gone pale.

'Well, well, well. I never knew she had a daughter. Fancy that. She kept that a secret. But then nobody around here knew much about her. She kept herself to herself. My name's Brenda Rogers. How long are you here for?'

'Oh, I'm not sure yet.'

She had already thought better of her plan to go back to

London the next day. What did she have to go back to? She was acutely aware that Brenda seemed to feel some antipathy towards her. But then Madeleine was an outsider. She could not expect to be welcomed right away. Perhaps the atmosphere between them would improve with conversation. It was worth a try.

'Actually, the truth is that I lost my job in London, so I've come here for a break. To take stock. Decide what to do. What do you do here?'

'I own the little art gallery over there near the harbour.' She nodded vaguely in the direction of the sea wall.

'Oh, that's interesting.' She tried to sound enthusiastic but Brenda's expression was not encouraging. 'How did you come to buy it?'

'It used to belong to Michael. Michael Wallace.'

'Yes, I met him at my mother's funeral. And he's been managing the cottage for me.'

'I ran the gallery for him. Got some of his former students' work on show there at the moment. Feeble imitators, all of them. They couldn't hold a candle to him.'

'Oh, so Michael's an artist? I didn't know. He never told me. I had him down as a sort of local businessman or an architect.' Her surprise was genuine. Artists don't have such a distinguished and businesslike manner, she thought. Artists are raffish.

'He's very eminent, a member of the Royal Academy. I'm surprised you didn't know.'

'He did tell me he'd retired. But he didn't say from what.'

'It's true. He hasn't done anything new for ages and probably never will now. His wife died, you know. A year or so after your mother. She'd been ill for years.'

'I suppose that's why he stopped. He never told me in his letters that his wife had died. Did you know my mother well?'

'No. She wasn't here for long. She used to come into the gallery sometimes. I met her there.'

'I suppose it depends on what you mean by long. I would have thought seven years was quite a long time.'

'She was never here all that time. She sort of came and went.' Brenda seemed to want to change the subject. 'I suppose this place must seem very dull and provincial after London.'

'I think that's what I need, for a while, anyway.'

'Not much high life here. No glamour and glitter. It's really very quiet.'

'I never really had time for high living. Just work and sleep, mostly. I assumed it was the only way to live. I'd like to see if there's another way.'

'But you said you weren't staying for long. Why should you, when there's so little here for you?'

Madeleine sighed. They were clearly not going to be friends. She stood up.

'Well, it was nice to meet you.' She tried to sound as if she meant it. 'I've got to be off now. Lots to do back at the cottage. Goodbye for now. Perhaps I'll see you over at the gallery. I might want to buy something for the cottage.'

Brenda made no response. She did not even look up. Madeleine picked up her shopping bags and went out, her face reddening. She made a mental note to avoid the art gallery. When she returned to the cottage, she was out of breath and her arms and shoulders were aching.

Michael came round to see her the next morning at eleven o'clock. She was just emerging from the shower when she heard the knock on the door. She slipped on her dressing gown and pulled back the heavy door. He smiled at her.

'Sorry, not too early am I?'

'No, of course not. Come on in.'

He wore a dark-grey suit, white shirt and red bow tie. He looked scarcely different from the time she had first seen him. Only his hair, a little whiter and thinner, betrayed the passage of 13 years. He had the same upright bearing. He gave the same impression of pent-up energy, though this time she found it less threatening. She invited him straight into the kitchen and made them coffee. They sat down at the table. He had brought with him a small flat parcel in brown paper. He pushed it to one side while he picked up his coffee cup.

'So you found the place all right?' he asked, after a pause during which each seemed uncertain how to begin.

'Yes, thank you. That map you sent me was exactly what I needed. It was so neat and precise. It must have taken you ages. I'd like to thank you for looking after the place so well. You've spent so much time and money on it.'

'Pleasure. I enjoyed it. It kept me occupied. And it was your money I was spending. The conversion of the roof space was the biggest item. But it paid its way. It means we can accommodate quite large family groups. I'm glad you approve. Visitors really do seem to like the place. We've had several people come back more than once. What about you? How do you find it?'

'I don't think it's my style really. I find downstairs a bit creepy. The old bit. I'm not sure about the village either. Not really my sort of place.'

He looked her in the eye constantly as she spoke. She found it a little disconcerting, but she preferred it to the evasiveness of his eyes when they had first met.

He seemed suddenly to become aware of her discomfort. 'Forgive me. I noticed the resemblance last time we met. But, now, well you've grown just like she was when she first came here.'

'Funny, I heard that yesterday. But it wasn't meant in a friendly way. From Brenda Rogers.'

'Oh, don't mind her. She's a bit odd these days. I don't see much of her now. Her gallery used to belong to me but I have nothing to do with it now.'

'I didn't know until yesterday that you were an artist. Brenda said you're famous.'

'I used to be quite well known in some circles, but that was a long time ago.'

'So you sold Brenda the gallery?'

'Sort of. An arrangement. Payment for services rendered, I

suppose you could say. How long were you planning to stay? I mean I'm assuming you'll be here a while but you may have other commitments. In your letter you said a few days.'

'Actually, that was a bit misleading. I have no commitments. I lost my job. I got a good pay-off and I'm taking some time here to think about things. I may be here a while.'

'I'm so sorry. What a shock it must have been. I can well understand you not wanting to mention that in your letter.'

'Oh, it's probably for the best. Things were getting very uncomfortable for me. I was getting too old for that way of life. I was tired of making money and never having the chance to do anything with it. Oh, by the way, I was sorry to hear about your wife. Brenda told me.'

'Yes, it was a tragic illness. Multiple sclerosis. A particularly severe form, with no periods of remission. But that was many years ago now. I've got over it. Look, you must come over to the house some time. You could drive up there. I've brought a map. This is how you get there by road.' She looked at the piece of paper he handed to her and smiled.

'You and your maps! Is that all you draw these days?'

'Yes, I'm afraid so. No more high art for me. Just useful stuff like this now.' She studied the map for a minute, disappointed with his response, then folded it and put it down on the table.

'Or you could come by the coastal cliff-top path,' he continued. 'It's much shorter as the crow flies, but it can be a bit strenuous if you're not used to that sort of thing. And don't stray from the path. Those cliffs are very dangerous. As you know, of course. Your poor mother.'

'About my mother. Where exactly did it happen?'

'It was very near here. Just the other side of the headland you can see from your front window. She must have been walking up there at night. Even in daylight it can be dangerous. It had been raining, so the edge would have been slippery.'

'Did she ever say why she came down here to live?'

'She never told you?'

'No. As I said when we met at the inquest, we had sort of drifted apart.'

'Perhaps it was because it's as far as you can go. She was desperate to leave her old life far behind her. For her it meant an end to that life, and the beginning of a new one. What a tragic shame that the new one was so short-lived.'

'Did she tell you all that? About making a new start?'

'Oh, no. I didn't know her that well.'

With a sudden movement that made her jump he slapped the table. 'Well, it's good to have you here, Madeleine. Please stay as long as you want.' He laughed. 'Sorry, of course you will. Silly thing to say. The cottage is yours. What I'm trying to say is, as far as I'm concerned, I'm delighted you're here, and you're always welcome up at the house.'

They stood up. At the door he turned back to her. 'Oh, I brought something with me. I left it on the kitchen table. It's a picture that used to hang above the stove in the living-room. Nothing special. A little one of mine. I put it in there when I was doing the place up. I took it down to repair the frame. If you like it, you can put it back up. I'll leave it to you. Goodbye for now.'

She returned to the kitchen and made herself another coffee. She lit her first cigarette of the day. She had not liked to do it while he was there. She was sure he did not smoke and did not approve of the habit. She liked him much better than when they had first met. Something has mellowed him, she thought. Or somebody. Perhaps he's remarried, and he's keeping it as a surprise for me. She picked up the parcel and, without opening it, put it in a cupboard next to the cooker. She had no interest in pictures and preferred her walls to be uncluttered.

9

June 1995

When the inn was not open and the weather was clement, Charley, George and Samuel liked to sit on a bench on the seafront by the lifeboat station. Unlike other benches along the front, this one faced towards the village. The three had no wish to look at the sea from which through the years they had wrought their precarious livelihood. But they did want to look at the passers-by and occasionally to make an appropriate comment.

Of the three, only George was still married. The others were widowers. Susan usually threw George out of their cottage by ten o'clock in the morning, claiming that she did not want him under her feet while she was trying to hoover. He would then repair to the bench and wait for his colleagues to join him. In bad weather they would meet at the pensioners' day centre, a tiny annexe to an almost equally tiny Methodist chapel tucked behind a large Victorian house.

'She's still here,' said George, continuing their conversation of the previous evenings. 'He's done nothing about it. Even though he promised.'

'How do you know?' asked Charley. 'She could have left this morning.'

'Are you blind? I can see her now, that's how I knows. She's coming this way. She'll bring nothing but trouble here. Some folks just don't seem to know as when they're not welcome. Folks as can kill others in cold blood.'

His voice rose as Madeleine crossed over and passed on the other side of the street. She looked straight ahead, pretending she had not heard.

'There's some sorts as we don't want here,' he continued, in an even louder tone. 'And that includes murderers.' His voice spat out the final word as she turned the corner towards the gallery.

'Murderesses,' muttered Charley.

'What?'

'Murderesses. She's a she. So she's a murderess. A murderer is masculine.'

George shook his head slowly. 'Well that's as may be. But I don't suppose there's any chance of her mistaking that I were speaking about her, not about some masculine murderer who just happens to be here as well.'

'Who's that?' asked Samuel. 'Is there another one? What in God's name is this place coming to?'

'No, of course not,' said George, irritably. 'We were talking about her. Only her.'

'Well, I still says it were that Michael Wallace as started it all,' said Samuel.

'Well, I would just go a bit easy, that's all,' said Charley. 'She might put a spell on you. And the rest of us. Close our mouths. Stop up our eyes. Make us lame.'

'You're lame already. Your eyes are hardly any use either. And I wish someone would close your mouth.'

'Remember that old woman who lived in the cottage up by the turning with the main road? She were a witch. Had a black cat, she did.'

'That were one hundred and fifty years ago. I course I don't remember.'

'I didn't mean remember personally. The stories about her.'

'Anyway, this one's a murderer . . . all right, murderess. Not a witch.'

'Maybe. But I'll swear that Brenda Rogers is a witch. And it looks to me as if those two are forming an alliance. Look where she's headed.'

They nodded, slowly, secure and contented in the shared knowledge of unnamed catastrophes to come.

Apart from Brenda, the gallery was deserted. Brenda looked up as Madeleine entered.

'Oh, it's you again. To what do we owe this privilege? You've never been in here before, have you?'

'No. I was never an art gallery person.'

She glanced round. Dozens of paintings and drawings had been crammed into the tiny space. Because the few windows were small and high the room was naturally gloomy, but Brenda had skilfully deployed artificial lighting to highlight details of the pictures. Six different artists were represented, mostly from St Ives, Newlyn and Penzance.

'Nothing here of Michael's?' she asked.

'I keep a few small ones of his at the cottage. I hang some of them here every now and then, to help to keep his memory alive. But he never intended this place as an outlet for his own work. He wanted to use it to give young artists a chance to display their stuff and get noticed. I try to stick to that. Michael did quite a lot of large canvases. They need space. You have to be able to stand back from them. Get the overall impression and then move in to study the detail.'

'I know. After his death a number of galleries rang me and asked me to take back their stock of his works. They said they didn't have room for them any more. They must still be up there at the house. I suppose they had decided he was too old-fashioned for them.'

Brenda snorted. 'Usually a painter's work goes up in price after his death, when people realise there isn't going to be any more of it. That didn't happen in Michael's case. He had stopped painting years before he died. There had been a short-term hike in the prices of his work when word got round that he had retired. Then his reputation began to decline. It's a cycle that happens to quite a few artists. Unfortunately Michael was still alive to witness the decline. He was always very painstaking. Would take months, sometimes years, over one canvas. Did he talk to you about his early career, when you lived with him?'

'He only told me about the time after he moved to Cornwall.'

'He was a late developer, not a young, spontaneous talent like David. He never even went to art school until his early thirties. He was in the army before that. Rose quickly through the ranks. Served in Greece and Cyprus. He was a major by the time he left.'

'I knew he was in the army. He never told me he was so senior.'

'He had done a lot of drawing and painting in the army. A lot of map work as well. That's why his draughtsmanship was so refined. He went to art school to consolidate and broaden his techniques. He hated it. Found himself fundamentally out of sympathy with almost everything he found there. Michael had never believed that to create a vital new form of art it was enough to challenge traditional ideas and media. He had always considered that an artist should find his inspiration in the beauties of nature and the human face and form. Nobody could produce vital or lasting work if their sole purpose was to imitate others or to react against them. New original work could not be created from feelings alone, he often said to me. There would always be scope for new techniques, but these needed to be founded on established ones, which had to be thoroughly mastered first. For many, that was enough for him to be labelled old-fashioned. So, how are you settling in?'

'Oh, wonderful. The locals are friendlier than ever. The landlord keeps asking me how long I intend to stay. I'm the only resident at the moment so I thought he'd be pleased to have me. He was welcoming enough at first. Now he's positively hostile.

Last night I tried to get something to eat in the cafe, but the lady refused to serve me. I can't blame them, I suppose.'

'That would be Susan Croft. She's the wife of one of the chorus of three ex-fishermen you see hanging about the place. They're not exactly rays of sunshine.'

'I've come across them. They know who I am. One of them called me a murderer as I walked past just now. I'll have to move out soon and go back up to the house. And I don't want to cause you trouble, just by speaking to you.'

'Don't worry about me. I can look after myself.'

'Brenda, can I ask you something? Do you think Michael and my mother had an affair?'

Brenda stiffened. 'What makes you ask that?'

'I don't know.' She was not going to tell Brenda about the notebook and where it had been found. 'Michael always said he knew her only slightly. I wondered, what with being at the inquest, and helping me arrange the funeral, and looking after the cottage . . .'

'That hardly amounts to evidence of an affair. Michael had time on his hands. He wanted to be helpful. And you lived with him up at the house all that time, before his death. Presumably he never mentioned it then. So why would he keep it a secret from you of all people? Anyway, the answer to your question is that I don't know and I don't care.'

'It was just a thought. I wonder, could I borrow the cottage key again?'

'Another trip down memory lane? All right. Here's my front door key. The cottage key is on a hook on the back. You can drop the cottage key through the box and return the door key to me here.'

Madeleine stepped out into the street, relieved that the three old men were not waiting for her.

As she was turning through the gate leading to the path down to the cottage, she stopped to watch the figure a hundred yards ahead of her on the lane. He had been there when she had first turned into the lane, stooping, shuffling along, staring at the ground. Even at that distance she could see he was very shabbily dressed. An old tramp, she decided. She had expected to catch up with him but to her surprise he had maintained the distance between them. She shrugged her shoulders and stepped down the path.

Once inside she stared at the drawing again. One of Michael's many models, she had thought when she had first seen it. But even then she had felt strangely drawn to it. Now she could see that it was much more than an exercise in line and perspective. There was a story here. These limbs were warm, relaxed, flushed. This was a woman who had just made love. Even though her face was hidden, the aura of satisfaction, of pleasure in her own body and her lover's, was unmistakable. Her lover was off-picture, just to the right. She was pushing herself into a seating position, so she could reach a nearby glass of champagne, so she and her lover could toast each other. Michael had caught all of this in a few strokes of the pen. No wonder he was pleased with it. No barely remembered model could have inspired this, she was sure of that now.

That did not mean it was her mother. But if it were, it would account for David's mistake. What was that phrase Megan had used? Like two peas in a pod. It would not of course explain how her mother's notebook had come to be up at the house. But at least it would mean there was some sort of connection between the cottage and the house. And it might help to explain why she had stopped writing in it and had then forgotten about it. Teenage girls keep diaries, she had read somewhere, until they start making love, because at that point their capacity to put into words what is happening to them fails. Why should not the same apply to a lonely woman in her late thirties?

She walked down to the bedroom. Michael had been a married man. It was here they would have met. But Brenda's question troubled her. Why had Michael always kept it a secret from her?

Why had he always claimed that he had only known her mother slightly? By the time Madeleine had moved in with him, Celia had long since died and her grief-stricken parents had soon followed her. There was nobody left alive who could be hurt by the knowledge. Not Madeleine. She would not have resented the thought that her mother had found at least distraction, and possibly some happiness, before the end of her life. Not Michael himself. Her mother would not have been the only one. There was Laura. He had given her a child, one he did not publicly acknowledge as his son. Maybe there had been others. But why had he continued to keep them all secret right to the end of his life? No elderly artist's reputation was ever damaged by the disclosure that he had had affairs.

She walked slowly through the hallway towards the front door. Then she spotted the envelope. It had not been there when she had arrived. She was sure of that. She picked it up. The single word 'Madeleine' was scrawled on it. She opened it. There was a single sheet of paper, heavily stained with dirt. The words, printed on it in the same red felt-tip ink as the name on the envelope, screamed at her.

I can tell you about their deaths. St Olave's Church, tomorrow at noon. Front pew. Left-hand side. Don't look round. Or you will find out nothing.

10

April 1986

Madeleine sat by the bay window with a cup of coffee and her third cigarette of the day. She would probably not bother with breakfast. Wait until lunch. The weather needed her undivided attention. In London she had scarcely noticed the passing of the seasons. Now, dark or light, foul or fair, sunny or stormy, windy or rainy, weather streamed into her consciousness from the moment she woke up. The cottage seemed to be saturated with it from all sides. Out to sea there could there be one sort of weather, and to the land on the right in the direction of the sunrise, yet another. She found herself attempting to predict changes by looking at distant cloud patterns and estimating where the wind might take them. One morning, when the air was still despite the huge waves that were bringing the surfers crashing into the shallows in a swirl of foam, she predicted gales by the evening. She was delighted to find herself proved right. The main advantage of her new pastime was that she did not need to leave the cottage. She could do it all by observation from the windows in the front room or from the lawn.

It wouldn't do, though. She would have to take some exercise. She was sleeping very badly. Her system was continuing to produce the addictive adrenaline which over the years had seen her through the highs and lows of her 18-hour days, the dizzying risks, the euphoria, the despair, the ecstasy of sudden, huge profits and the sickening lurches into nerve-wracking losses. She wondered how long it would take for her system to realise it was no longer required. Perhaps it would help if she cut back on the coffee.

At last a day came when she felt a perceptible increase in the temperature. Heavy winds over the preceding few days had given way to mild breezes, and dark leaden clouds to ones of the whitest cotton wool. She put on her trainers, a light, close-fitting jumper and jeans. She soon found the start of the coastal path but was dismayed to see that the initial slope was very steep. She would have to build up her stamina slowly. It would be some time before she could manage the walk to Michael's house. At last she struggled up to a small fort-like building where she stopped to catch her breath. It was still intact but the windows and doors were missing and a dank smell exuded from the interior.

'Dates from the war,' shouted a bearded man in a green anorak, striding past her, a huge pair of binoculars dangling from his neck. 'Observation point for enemy ships.' He had come up the path behind her and was not even slightly out of breath.

'Thanks,' she managed to gasp. 'Very interesting.'

From the observation point the path was reasonably flat and she felt sufficiently recovered to walk on. There was another headland beyond. The path followed the top of the cliffs between the two headlands. This must have been where she fell, she thought. In places along the sides of the inlet, grassy slopes dropped away from the path leading to a low cliff for a final plunge into the water. The most dangerous section was where the inlet reached the point furthest away from the open sea. Here the cliff started very close to the path and fell vertically away for several hundred feet.

She left the path and headed inland. She soon came to an area of grassland where the soil, though thin, was still able to support some bluebells and wild pink pansies. A girl with her back to her was sketching in a large pad on her knees. She had dark hair falling almost to her shoulders. As Madeleine came past she saw that she was wearing a large loose brown pullover and jeans. The face turned to look at her. Madeleine stopped and caught her breath. It was not a girl. She guessed he was about 19 or 20. He stared at her. She had to say something.

'I'm sorry. I thought you were someone I knew,' she stammered.

He frowned. His eyes were deep and black, glowering at her. They were telling her she had intruded, that she did not belong there. But she could not pull her own gaze away. The seconds ticked by. At last, he looked down and carried on working. She walked around him and looked over his shoulder.

'Gosh, that's brilliant,' she said with genuine warmth and surprise. With nothing more than pencil strokes of differing angles and thicknesses he had captured the sweep of the land in front of them as it tilted down towards the sea, the outcrops of rock near the edge, and the shimmer of the horizon where sea and sky met.

'It's a sketch for a watercolour,' he muttered.

'How long did it take you to do it?'

'I've been doing this one for about twenty minutes. But it's my third or fourth attempt at this view. I think I'll paint this one and see how it looks. I can do that back at the house. Look at the paper. Feel it. It's a special granular surface. You get an alternation of light and half-light. I could show you how it works when I've added the colours.'

A slight local tang beneath a public school drawl. She felt the paper between her fingers. The surface created a tingling sensation. Her hand was nearly touching his. She shivered, unexpectedly. The breeze up here must be colder than she thought.

'I'll leave you to it. Sorry to interrupt.'

He continued to work as she moved away, her presence already forgotten. She glanced back at him several times. His head remained motionless, his eyes fixed on the sheet in front of him, the pencil working furiously.

The next day she decided to take a walk in the other direction, along the seafront, past the inn and along the beach. Just before she reached the inn she changed her mind. Day-trippers, surfers showing off, screaming kids, sand in her eyes and her shoes. Definitely not her scene. Much better to go the other way. Only a few hikers and bird-watchers ever got up to that headland. And the occasional artist of course.

Not that he had been exactly sociable. Positively surly in fact. She was sure she did not want to see him again. But they did have a sort of arrangement, didn't they? Even though they had not put a day or time to it. He had promised to show her how watercolour worked. When he had added the colours to the sketch he had been working on. It would be rude not to go back to see him and talk to him. Even though he would probably have forgotten what he had promised her. He would probably not even remember he had met her.

If she hurried she would get there at about the same time as she had the day before.

It was as if he had not moved. She stood a few yards from him, taking care not to obstruct his view. He seemed to notice her without seeing her. He put the pencil down.

'I'm sorry. I didn't mean to disturb you.'

'That's all right. I'm getting a bit tired of this one.'

'Are you an art student?'

'Yes.'

'You're very talented.'

He shrugged his shoulders. 'My uncle's a painter too. That's where I live. With him. Along the coast.' He waved vaguely in the direction away from Porthhella.

'Your uncle?' In a moment she understood. She wondered when Michael was planning to tell her.

'May I join you? I'm a bit tired from my walk. I'm not very fit, I'm afraid. What's your name?'

'David.'

'Mine's Madeleine. I'm staying in Porthella. In one of the cottages there.'

'A holiday let?'

'No, the cottage is mine. I can stay as long as I want.'

'Are you here with your family?' he asked.

'My family? No, I don't have a family. My parents are both dead.'

'No husband?'

She laughed. 'No, no husband. Not even a boyfriend. I'm on my own.'

He stared at her. She felt naked in his presence. She had already admitted far more than she had intended to. She was a 38-year-old woman on her own, with nothing to do with her time. Already she sensed his disdain.

'I like to be on my own. I can't concentrate on my work otherwise.'

'I can take a hint. I have to go anyway. Shopping to do back in the village. Before they close.'

The good weather did not last. The next day, heavy grey clouds scudded across the bay. Rain rattled against the windows. Confined to the cottage, she watched from the window as the waves crashed against the black rocks at the base of the headland. The sort of weather in which her mother had been out walking when she fell, she thought. But who in their right minds would go walking up there in conditions like this?

Several days later, the sun reappeared. She put on a short-sleeved top, khaki shorts and her trainers, which now had a used, dusty appearance which their designers had never intended, and made for the headland. A few white clouds hung motionless in the light blue sky as if painted on it. From the sea came only the gentlest of breezes. David was there, sketching as before.

She sat down opposite him, waiting for him to notice her. After ten minutes he stopped and flicked back several pages in the pad. He looked up.

'Do you want to see this?'

She walked over to him. The pad was open at the landscape

he had been sketching when she had met him. He handed it to her. She caught her breath. It was transformed. Little of the pencil outline remained. From foreground to background hues shaded into each other from emerald to dark green to purple to azure to an ever-lightening blue with patches of dazzling white. It was difficult to tell where land, sea and sky met.

'I think it's fantastic, David. I know nothing about art. Until today I thought I didn't like pictures. But I really do like this. It's all so different now.'

He shrugged his shoulders and tore the watercolour out of the pad. Before she could stop him he had ripped it into tiny pieces. Some fluttered to the ground while others were borne away on the breeze.

She gaped at him. 'What did you do that for?'

'Best way of making sure my uncle doesn't see it. Not his style. He doesn't think it should be mine. Anyway, it was trivial. All landscapes are trivial. No resonance, no symbolic meaning. I have much more significant work to do.'

He turned to a fresh sheet and started to sketch, ignoring her presence. After ten minutes she turned away. It was some time before she realised he was following her.

'David, I have a small confession to make.'

He was sitting on her sofa, drinking coffee, occasionally glancing out towards the bay. She sat opposite him. He had not said a word since he had followed her into the village, up the lane and into the cottage and into her living room. She was sure she had not invited him. She had not spoken to him since he had told her why he had torn up the picture. She wondered if she had unwittingly given him a gesture which he had misinterpreted. Well, it could do no harm to offer him a coffee. And there was something she had to say to him.

'I have met your uncle already. We met for the first time thirteen years ago. He knew my mother. This was her cottage. Since then he's been managing it for me. I met him again very recently.

But he didn't mention you. I think he's keeping you back from me as a surprise. He said he was going to invite me over.'

'I knew he was looking after some property for somebody. I didn't know it was this one.' He sounded supremely uninterested.

'How long have you lived with him?'

'Since I was about six or seven. My parents were killed in a car crash when I was a baby. My father was his younger brother, George. My mother was French. That's what my uncle tells me, anyway.'

'You don't look French.'

'I don't feel it either. Look, we'd better not tell him we've met. He likes to control who I meet and where and when I meet them. He's very protective.'

'That's because he knows how gifted you are. I wouldn't blame him too much. Okay. We'll keep it a secret. When he introduces us, we'll pretend we've never met before.'

He stood up and wandered aimlessly around the room. He stopped in front of the wall above the stove.

'Looks as if there was a picture there,' he said. 'You can still see the outline where the frame was. And the hook's still there.'

'Somebody renting the place must have disliked it and taken it down and hidden it.'

'Or maybe somebody really liked it and took it with them.'

'Yes, that's a possibility.'

'So, David,' she said at last, sitting down and forcing a tone of normality into her voice. 'Who are your favourite painters?'

'Not the ones my uncle thinks I should like. His favourites are the old masters of the Italian Renaissance. He wants me to model my techniques on them. Titian, Bellini, Tintoretto. They were the Venetians. Then Raphael and Michelangelo. I suppose you've seen the Sistine Chapel.'

'Actually, I haven't. I did go to Rome once. It was for a conference. Some ugly modern building miles outside. That was all I saw.'

'Uncle sent me to Italy last year with a group of students from different countries, to study art on location as it were. Venice was the first stop. He told me to spend time in the Church of the Frari. Make a copy of a famous painting there by Titian. It's called *The Assumption*. Just sketch it and then work on it when I got home. I have been working on it, but not exactly in a way of which he would approve. I'm keeping it hidden. I take it out and work on it when he's away from the house. My own favourites are the ones he most hates. Munch. The German Expressionists. I must get back now.'

He stood up, walked straight through to the front door and shut it noisily behind him. She stared after him, shaking her head.

She drove much too fast down the driveway, the house looming up at her suddenly as she rounded a bend. With a flourish of squealing brakes and gravel-crunching tyres she pulled up before the main door. She stood back to register her first impressions. The windows were narrow, with cramped Gothic arches. All of them were shuttered. Five wide stone steps led up to a broad porch beneath a flat granite slab roof, supported on four pillars in a Doric style which clashed harshly with the windows. Set into the wall beside a massive, iron-studded oak door with a ponderous round iron latch was a small window of opaque, leaded, dark-red stained glass.

The door opened and Megan stood there, smiling.

'Hello, Megan,' she said brightly. 'I remember you from my mother's funeral. You haven't changed a bit.'

'Neither have you, Miss Madeleine. Not a day older. Come in. Mr Wallace is expecting you in the front room. Go on through. I'll bring in the tea in a few minutes.'

The hallway was dark and cavernous, with a lingering trace in the air of lemon-scented furniture polish. Against one wall stood a small, manual wheelchair, in grey metal except for a dark brown leather back. As she passed it she smelt oil and metal polish. From an ornate grandfather clock against the opposite wall came a slow, muffled click. Megan pointed to a door at the far end of the hall. She opened it gently. Late afternoon sunlight flooded through the French windows. Her eyes blinked as they adjusted to the change. The room was spotlessly clean and furnished like the lounge of a seaside hotel. It was as if she had moved from one film set to another.

Michael had rung the previous evening to invite her to the house the following afternoon for tea. She had thought of attempting the walk via the coastal path but had thought better of it. It was another warm day and she wanted to arrive looking fresh and smart, not exhausted and covered with dust and sand. She had put on a low-cut floral cotton summer dress incorporating a belt of the same pattern. A small white leather handbag and a pair of light brown high-heeled shoes, and the effect was complete. Well, it would be once she had got into her Porsche, lowered the roof and fastened a chiffon scarf loosely about her neck.

Michael rose nimbly out of a deep armchair, walked up to her and kissed her on the cheek.

'Madeleine, good to see you again. You look lovely. The air here must be doing you good. Can I introduce you to my nephew, David? He's lived here with me since my wife died. He's an artist too, but much more gifted than I ever was.'

David sat slouched in another armchair, his legs dangling over the side. He made no attempt to move, and barely glanced in her direction.

'Hello, David,' she said. 'Pleased to meet you.'

He was smartly dressed this time, in grey trousers and open-necked black shirt.

'Sit down, Madeleine,' said Michael. 'Make yourself at home.'

There was a third armchair opposite the other two. She sat down. Michael smiled at her, then beamed at David, apparently oblivious to David's rudeness.

'So what do you think of the house? Quite a setting, eh? You get fantastic sunsets from this room. Worth it for those alone. A local landowner bought the land in the last century. He had it levelled and built a house on rather flimsy foundations. It soon fell into disrepair and they knocked it down. The family had run out of money by then. This house was built just before the war. An industrialist from Bradford, would you believe? He sank really solid foundations, thank goodness. Then an American bought it on impulse. He read about it in a magazine and learnt it was for sale. He hated it from the start. I don't he think he took the weather into account, especially the winters. It fell into neglect. I got it fairly cheaply.'

Michael spoke mainly to her, occasionally taking in David with a glance. David continued to ignore both of them. Madeleine decided she had to make some attempt to draw him into the conversation.

'David, Michael says you're an artist as well. Have you been to art school?'

'Not yet,' Michael replied for him. 'He's going to my academy in September. I set it up in Portsmouth to teach traditional methods and techniques. I don't want him going to one of these places where all they do is mess around.'

David glared sullenly at him. She wondered what the chances really were that he would go to his uncle's academy.

'So, what sort of things will he do there?'

'Landscapes, still life. We have life classes as well.'

'You mean nude models?'

'Some.'

'Something to look forward to, David,' she said, turning towards him in a desperate effort to lighten the tone and elicit even one word from him.

David caught her eyes and held them for a few moments. Then, slowly, deliberately, his eyes travelled down her body and back up again to her face, his features distorted into an unmistakable sneer. Her cheeks burned. She pulled her eyes away and turned to Michael, wondering whether he would say anything to his nephew about his behaviour. Michael seemed to have noticed nothing amiss. He was smiling.

'I'm afraid I'll have to disappoint you there, young man. Most of the models in the life classes are old men like me.'

They all laughed, Michael heartily, David coldly, Madeleine with relief. At that point, Megan, with perfect timing, brought in the tea. David suddenly sprang into action, unwinding his leg from the side of the chair, and standing up awkwardly. He muttered something inaudible and left the room.

'He doesn't like tea,' said Michael, in a tone of confiding awe, as if this were another of David's special qualities which only a select few were entitled to know about.

'I'm sorry I didn't tell you about him,' he continued. 'I wanted it to be a surprise. I wanted to see how the two of you got on.'

'I don't think he likes me,' she said. And I certainly can't stand the obnoxious little shit, she almost added.

'Oh, I think he does. He's always very withdrawn at first with new people. I know he was a bit quiet today. But it's only an act. He discovered the sulky teenage thing a bit late. He only has a few months left until his twentieth birthday. So he's trying to get as much out of the role before it's too late and he has to grow up. He was always a very polite, well-behaved child. His parents died in a car crash in France when he was only a baby. After Celia died he came to live with me. He's been such a joy and consolation to me. He has a wonderful natural talent. He'll be up in his room working now. Sometimes a bit modern for my taste. I was always on the old-fashioned side, so my numerous critics said.'

'You sound very proud of him.'

'Yes, I am. And I know his father would have been too. I paid for his education at boarding school. The trouble is . . . well, I never remarried, so there was no feminine influence on him at home. Perhaps I should have. Remarried, that is.'

'I'm rather surprised you didn't. I'm sure many women would have been interested.'

'I suppose after Celia, nobody else could mean so much to me. Well, maybe the three of us can get together some time again.

Now that the ice has been broken, we can all start to get to know each other gradually. I'm sure you and David will begin to appreciate each other in the fullness of time.'

'Yes, I'm sure we will.' And pigs will fly. 'I'd better be off, now, Michael. Thank Megan for the tea.'

'Thank you for coming, Madeleine. I have enjoyed having you here.'

Not half as much as I'm enjoying leaving, she thought as she walked through the hall.

She drove back at an even faster pace than the one which had brought her there, often barely seeing in time the sharp bends as they loomed suddenly out of the shadows of the roadside walls and trees. She was furious with herself for not complaining straight away to Michael about David's behaviour. She was furious with Michael for being so besotted with David that he could not or would not recognise his rudeness to their guest. And above all she was furious with David. It wasn't that they had formed a friendship exactly. But she had thought that they at least had an understanding. She had admired his work, accepting the individuality which Michael had apparently been so far unwilling to accept. And had he shown any gratitude? On the contrary. The work she had praised he had torn up before her eyes. Despite that impulsive churlishness, she had hoped he would see her as an ally if he needed one to assert himself against his uncle's will. Well, whatever it was she thought they might have had was in the past now. He had ruined everything. The next morning she would go up to the headland to see him. She would demand an apology. And she would tell him that whatever troubles he had with Michael that she might have been able to help him with, he was now well and truly on his own.

11

June 1995

She called at the house the next morning at ten o'clock. There was no reply. Megan was probably out shopping. She had asked the taxi to wait. She returned to it, paid the driver and told him she would not need him any more. She would take the coastal path to St Olave's. There was plenty of time. Her appointment there was not until noon. She felt better than she had for many weeks. She was sure she would be strong enough, for that day at least. When she had lived with Michael it had been one of her favourite walks.

The path wound across the tops of cliffs which were mostly much lower and of gentler gradient than those between the house and Porthhella, leading gradually away from the Atlantic and into the English Channel, where the coast was sheltered from the harsh winds and high seas. The sun beat warmly onto her back as it ascended the sky. As the path sank towards sea level, the air grew stiller and hotter and the vegetation increasingly lush. The sea was now out of sight, though she could hear its muffled crash and swish on the other side of giant sand dunes covered in coarse grasses.

She took a side-path which led inland through dense woods. Midges and mosquitoes whirred around her eyes and ears. Deep-blue hoverflies darted along the path in front of her. A miniature

97

wooden bridge crossed a narrow stream splashing playfully over mossy stones. Huge Brazilian rhubarb plants closed to form a canopy overhead. The sun filtered through the translucent leaves. Beyond the woods the path led between fallow fields. She saw the squat Norman tower of a small church rise slowly from the sloping green earth. Near the church, at the side of the path, a Saxon cross, the carved inscription weathered almost to invisibility, marked the route of an ancient pilgrims' way. She crossed a stone stile to enter the churchyard, where derelict gravestones pointed up from the ground at every angle like the crooked teeth of giants.

She went up to the stones with which she was most familiar. She read her mother's: 'Here lies Ceridwen Williams, 1929–1973, who sought peace by the vastness of the sea and sky. May she rest in the arms of the Almighty.' She had left Michael to choose the wording. Nearby was a white smooth marble stone large enough for three more inscriptions. 'Here lies Celia Wallace, 1930–1974, beloved wife of Michael, remembered for a life devoted to others in spite of pain and sickness.' Beneath that was the one she had read most often: 'In loving memory of David Wallace, 1967–1986, beloved child of George and Sandrine, beloved nephew of Michael to whom he was as a son.' Very appropriate wording, that last bit. Finally, Michael's: 'Here lies Michael Wallace, 1926–1988, lovingly remembered as a devoted husband to Celia, loving uncle to David and artist to all who treasure beauty.' Her own choice of words. No more space beneath Michael's. Nobody to follow him. The end of the line.

She had walked slowly, still unused to exertion. Her legs ached. It was ten minutes to 12. She looked around the churchyard. It was deserted. She entered the church, blessing the cool and dark which greeted her. Front pew. Left-hand side. She sat down. Don't look round. Whatever happens.

She smelled a presence before she heard anything. It was a not unpleasant fusion of damp hedgerow and coarse fabrics thickened by sweat and dirt. Then she heard laboured breathing, very close to her ear. The kneeler immediately behind her creaked.

'I've seen you, haven't I?' she said. 'Yesterday. You're that tramp. You were walking along the lane leading to the cottage. You came back and left the message. Okay, so you know who I am. Who are you? How do I know I can trust you?'

She was aware of whispered sounds in the air around her head but could not form them into words. She let her body slump down to bring her ear closer to his mouth. His breath smelled of damp, hand-rolled tobacco.

'You don't. Yet.' A harsh laboured whisper. 'We have to go back. Start at the beginning.'

'Beginning of what?'

'Your mother. And Michael.'

'You knew them?'

'Not your mother. I knew Michael.'

'Have we met before? I took care of Michael for over a year, before he died. Did you ever come to see him then?'

'Oh, I saw him all right. But he never saw me. Neither did you.'

'Wait a minute. How old are you? When I glimpsed you yesterday I thought you were an old man. But there's something about your voice. Even though you're whispering.'

'I'm old, Madeleine. Very old. Older than death. About your mother and Michael. They had an affair.'

She laughed. The sound echoed around the church.

'Sorry, old man. You're too late there. I've already worked that out. And frankly I couldn't care less. Good luck to both of them, I say.'

'Oh, there's something else. Something you will care about. Remember, you mustn't look round. When I've stopped, I will leave the church. You must wait for at least five minutes. If you don't do as I say, there will be no more contact. If you do, we'll meet here tomorrow at the same time. Can you hear me? Do you understand?'

'Yes.'

'They had an affair. Then he killed her.'

The kneeler behind her creaked again. The door at the back of the church swung open. How could an old man have got there so quickly? She waited no more than a minute. She ran frantically around the churchyard, then into the hamlet, then back along the path she had taken from the coast. Nobody.

12

May 1986

The day after her visit to the house for tea with Michael and David, she was stepping out of the shower when she heard a loud knock on the door. She dried herself quickly, put on her dressing-gown and went to the door. She glanced in at the kitchen clock as she did so. Eleven o'clock. Not an unreasonable hour for a visitor, she supposed. But who could it be?

David stood there, in jeans and a red sweater, carrying a large, flat portfolio case. She folded her arms and stood in the doorway.

'What do you want?'

David did not reply but stepped forward suddenly, pushing past her into the hallway. He put the case on the floor, leaning against the wall.

She turned to him. 'I don't recall saying you could come in.'

He pushed past her again, this time returning to the door, which she had left open. He pulled it shut and stood facing her. Then he stepped up to her. She recognised the expression on his face. It was the same as the one he had worn at the house the day before, when he had looked up and down her. He put his hands on her shoulders. He was several inches taller than she was. She felt him pressing her down until her knees gave way. She fell backwards. He knelt above her and began to undo the top button on his jeans. He pulled the zip down. Then his weight was on her, crushing her as he thrust into her.

She was aware of him easing himself off her, picking up the case and walking through to the sitting-room. She pushed herself up into a sitting position and looked down at her body. Her dressing-gown, made of thin silk, was scrunched around her middle. Her breasts were exposed, her legs splayed out like those of a discarded rag doll. She pulled and smoothed the fabric back over as much of her flesh as it could cover in its severely creased state, then stumbled through to the sitting-room after him.

He was sitting in the armchair facing out to sea. She stood by the sofa opposite him. Then she walked over to the table, opened her handbag, and pulled out a packet of cigarettes and a lighter. Her hands were shaking as she fumbled with them. At last she managed to light a cigarette, sucking the smoke deep into her lungs. She returned to the sofa and sat down. He turned his head towards her.

'I won't, thanks. I don't smoke. You shouldn't. Bad for you.'

He turned his face away again. She stared at him for a full minute. He showed no sign that he was even aware of her presence. She coughed, wondering how her voice would sound when she spoke. As she would have to sooner or later, as it was obvious he had nothing further to say. She took several slow deep breaths.

'So . . .' The shake was too much for her to continue. She took another slow breath and coughed again. 'If you've got what you came for, why are you still here?'

He laughed. 'You really think I came all the way over here for that? Just to have sex with a fat, ugly old cow like you?'

'So why did you do it? If it wasn't what you came for?'

'I was just checking, that's all.'

'Checking what?'

'I'll explain in a minute. When I'm ready. I think I will have a cigarette.'

'I don't recall offering you one.'

He stared at her. She threw over the lighter and the packet. 'Help yourself.'

He turned his face to the window again, puffing inexpertly on the cigarette, coughing from time to time. Then he turned to her again.

'Why don't you make us some coffee?'

'Just tell me why you're here.'

'All right. It's very simple. I need somewhere to work. Away from the house. Away from him.'

'Work on what?'

'My version of *The Assumption*. I told you about it.'

'Is it in there?' She pointed towards the case.

'Yes. Don't worry. I'm not going to move in. Uncle will think I'm sketching out of doors. I'll just come during the day.'

She shook her head in disbelief. 'And what gives you the right to come round here and tell me what you're going to do in my cottage?'

'I told you. I need peace and quiet. I need to know there's no danger of him interrupting what I'm doing and interfering with it. I need solitude.'

'So what do I do? Walk around the village?'

'Whatever you want. Except when I want you here.'

'And what would you want me here for?'

'That's the other thing. I will need a model, some of the time. When I need to be on my own, I'll tell you.'

She laughed, a note of near hysteria in her voice. 'You must be the most arrogant, presumptuous young prick . . . What if I told you to get out, now, and never come back?'

'I would go. You have that right. But you haven't yet, have you?'

'What does "Assumption" mean?'

'It's when the Mother of God was raised into Heaven. Only I'm not doing it that way exactly. I'm making a few modifications.'

'And apart from her, are there any other figures in the picture?'

'No other women.'

'Let's get this straight. You want me to be the model for the Virgin Mary? David, if you knew how funny that was . . .'

'But I do know. That's the point. You're the opposite of every-thing she stood for. As I said, I'm making some modifications. Reinterpreting it, if you like.'

'No, I don't think I do like. You chose me because . . .'

'You're an ugly old cow and a whore. I could tell the former just by looking at you, of course. I was pretty sure about the whore bit but I wanted to check it. Now I know.'

She stood up, walked over to him and slapped him hard across the face. He grinned, stroking his reddening skin. Then he got up and pushed her back on to the sofa. He stood over her.

'Look, let's stop pretending, shall we? I know who you are and what you are. My uncle has no idea. Do you know why he's such a crap artist? He has no idea about people. He can't see through anybody. But nobody needs to see through you. You're all there on the surface. The way you were yesterday up at the house, smiling and flirting, wearing that dress showing your tits. You were turning it on for both of us. An old man and an obnoxious teenager. You don't care. Men are all the same to you, aren't they? You just turn it on automatically. Look at you now. You come to the door in that skimpy gown. You don't say, come back later when I've changed into something decent. Even now you've still got it on, though it hardly covers anything. I know you can't stand me. But you let me come in, let me fuck you without even asking permission. Has my uncle had you yet? Or are you expecting him later?

'I can see what sort of woman you are. You've never been married, have you? Never had children, never been in a proper relationship. I'm right, aren't I? Don't you dare criticise me for being the way I am. You may be older than I am but you're not superior. All right, maybe I am an arrogant young sod, but you are a whore. You can slap me again if you like but that won't change the facts. Oh, you may not take money for it. Money isn't what you need. But you need something. And you use your body to buy it. Tell me I'm wrong and tell me to get out. But inside you know I'm right.'

He turned away, lit another cigarette and sat down again in the same position, looking out to sea. She stared at him again, then started to laugh.

'My God, what a speech. And yesterday you couldn't put one word in front of another. All right. You're right. Everything you say about me. Shall I tell you about the bits you missed out? It hasn't just been sex. I've tried the lot. Alcohol, fags, drugs. Serious stuff, I mean, cocaine, heroin. Not just that pot rubbish I'm sure you tried at your highly respectable public school. I bet you thought you were so grown up, didn't you? Work was another drug for me. Right now, it's a drink I need. And I don't mean coffee.'

She got up, went into the kitchen and poured out two glasses of whisky. She returned to the sitting room and handed one of them to him.

'You know, David, it's almost a relief to meet somebody who understands me. Somebody who is totally and completely judgemental. Someone with a complete absence of sensitivity to anybody's feelings. Who holds nothing back. Who goes right for the jugular.'

He drained his glass, picked up the case and walked towards the hallway.

'Where are you going?'

'Home, of course. I can't expect you to model for me after everything I said, can I? It was a stupid idea, anyway. Forget it.'

'David, put the case back. I'll see you here tomorrow morning, ten o'clock.'

13

'How do you know who I am?'

'I've seen you before. I read about your case. Your picture was in the papers.'

'That was years ago. I've changed a lot.'

'I recognised you. I knew right away who you were.'

'You don't seem the sort who reads papers. Just uses them to keep out the cold. You haven't had a wash since yesterday, have you?'

'I sleep under the stars these days, while it's warm. In winter I might sometimes go to a hostel for a bath and change of clothes.'

Traces of a local burr, but underneath there was something else she could not pick up. Impossible to tell the accent of a man who only whispers.

'Let me know when you're next due for a bath and we can meet immediately afterwards.'

'Didn't think you'd be too particular, after the places you've been in the last few years.'

'Explain what you said about Michael. You said he killed my mother. That's impossible. I know how she died.'

'You know the official verdict. We all know that. It was an accident. She fell off the cliffs. Walked too close to the edge, in the dark and the rain.'

'He couldn't have killed her. If you want to kill someone you don't drag them up to the top of a cliff and throw them over. If he had killed her somewhere else and wanted to disguise it as an accident, he couldn't have hauled a dead body up there. Even if he could have managed it physically, there would have been tracks in the mud. In any case, the pathologist was definite that it was the fall which killed her. And say he had got her up there while she was still alive, there would have been the marks of a struggle at the top. The police found no evidence of that. So, what proof have you got, and what was his motive?'

'No proof exactly. But enough to convince me. This.'

A hand in a ragged glove pushed a dirty piece of paper onto the bench beside her. She picked it up and read it. She immediately recognised her mother's handwriting. There was no date or address at the top.

Dear Michael
It's been several years now. Things can't go on as they are. I only have a few days. I'm at the cottage, on my own. Where and when can we meet? Write to me here.
Ceridwen

She pushed the paper back. He made no move to take it.
'Keep it.'
She scrunched it up and put it in her handbag.
'Where did you get it?'
'I stole it. Let's leave it at that for the moment.'
'I suppose the police never saw it.'
'No.'
'This is hardly proof of blackmail.'
'Not blackmail as such. But she was putting him under pressure.'
'To divorce Celia and marry her? But Celia was ill and dying. Why didn't she wait?'
'Maybe she didn't know about Celia's condition.'

107

'Then why didn't Michael explain it to her? Tell her to be patient and wait a little longer? Sorry. I don't buy it. You haven't established either motive or opportunity.'

'I agree it's circumstantial. But, what if she wasn't prepared to wait? What if she threatened to tell Celia? What if Michael no longer cared for her, if he ever had? What if all that mattered to him was to get her out of the way?'

'So he arranged to meet her at the top of the cliffs. Then took the opportunity to push her over. But it still doesn't make sense. You don't meet someone who might see you as a threat in such a dangerous place, and then stand so close to the edge that you're positively inviting him to push you.'

'I haven't been able to work it out in my head yet. All I know is that it's too much of a coincidence. She puts pressure on him, then she oh so conveniently dies.'

'And he helps arrange her funeral, looks after the inscription, does up her cottage. Not something you do when you've killed someone you were desperate to get rid of.'

'Why not? Maybe he really did want her dead, but was stricken by guilt afterwards. That's why he did those things.'

'And why did he keep this letter? In his position, if I had done what you say, I would have destroyed everything that connected me to her.'

'That I can't explain. All I can say is that it wasn't the only thing of hers he kept.'

The notebook, she thought. She would have left it in the cottage. After her death he had gone and collected everything which might connect him to her. He might have glanced at the opening pages of the notebook and taken that as well, in case there were references to him in the later pages. He was not to know then that the notebook did not mention him. But he had not destroyed any of it. He had kept it all hidden in the house, even at the risk of the police searching the attics and finding it. The notebook had been left discarded on the attic floor. The rest had been put into a blue folder which he had asked Megan to destroy. Megan had been unable to find it, because somehow it had come into the possession of this old tramp. Could it possibly be true? Had she spent all that time looking after the man who had murdered her mother?

'Why are you so interested in all these things that happened so long ago?'

'I told you. I knew Michael.'

'You were a friend of his? What's your name?'

'No harm in telling you my first name. My name is Alan.'

'Is that your real name? Where do you come from? Do you have an accent? I can't tell when you're whispering. Why don't you speak up?'

'I can't. Operation. Throat cancer. Too much smoking. Yes, it's my real name.'

'Michael never mentioned anybody called Alan. Were you an artist?'

'I dabbled a bit once. Wouldn't have a clue now.'

'How would someone like Michael know a tramp like you?'

'I wasn't always a tramp.'

'What were you?'

'No more for now, Madeleine. I'm going now.'

'Will we meet tomorrow?'

'Yes. Same time. Remember the rules. You broke them yesterday. Five minutes after I've gone. Close your eyes. Stay there.'

Again she heard the church door creak open and clunk shut. This time she obeyed the rules.

14

May 1986

'How does this work?'

'You sit where I show you. Keep as still as possible. I'll make pencil sketches in the pad. Then I'll work them up into ink drawings. The drawings can stand alone. When I have one that's close to what I need for the larger picture I'll use that as a model. I won't work from life directly onto the main picture.'

'Where do you want me?'

'By the window. To catch the light.' He moved the armchair so it was facing the sunlight streaming through the window. 'Take your clothes off first.'

'Wait a minute. You're drawing the Mother of God and you want her naked? I may not know much about art but I'm sure it's not normally done like that.'

'That's right. I told you. This is not the normal version.'

'Are you sure you can face the sight of me this early in the morning, in this light?'

'I'm an artist, remember. I draw what I see. Beauty. Ugliness. All the same.'

She turned her back to him, took off her shoes, sweater, jeans, bra and pants, left them strewn untidily on the floor and walked over to the chair. David had opened his sketchpad on his knees. He picked up a pencil from a set of half a dozen he had spread on the floor beside him. He started to move it rapidly across the page.

'Look to the side, not straight at me. Keep still.'

He flicked the pages backwards and forwards, the pencil continuing to dash and dart. He was clearly working on several sheets at once. He did not erase anything. If something seemed to dissatisfy him, he shook his head and moved on to another page to start again.

'Spread your legs. Wider. Wider still.'

She forced them apart, her skin cringing before the merciless sunlight.

'Can I move my head? I've got cramp in my neck and shoulders.'

'Don't tense your upper body. Let yourself slump in the chair. Like a dead weight. Close your eyes if you want.'

After an hour he stopped and threw the pad on the floor. 'You can stand up now.'

She rose and stretched, feeling the blood flow back through her neck, legs and arms.

'Did you get anything?'

'Just outlines. All I was expecting to get at this stage.'

'Do you want to do any more today?'

'Later, maybe.'

'I'll go and lie down then.'

She walked stiffly past him and down the stairs to the bedroom. She lay on her stomach, stretching out her arms and legs towards the four corners of the bed. After a minute she heard the steps creak. Out of the corner of her eye she watched him undress. She remained motionless.

'So this was your mother's place, was it?'

They were lying in bed, smoking.

'That's right.'

'Uncle says her name was Ceridwen. Welsh. He says you're very like her.'

'I wanted to be like my father. He was a brilliant academic.'

'But you didn't end up like him, did you?'

'No. I was never anything like as clever. I was sure I could make money, though. I went into the City.'

'What did your father think of your choice of career?'

'He never had the chance to think anything of it. He died of cancer when I was fourteen. What do you remember of your parents?'

'Nothing. I came over to England while I was still a baby.'

'I suppose Michael told you about them?'

'He told me my father was an engineer.'

'Weren't you curious to know more?'

'Not really. Uncle always said to me that one day he would tell me the full truth about my parents, but not until I was older. On my eighteenth birthday he asked me if I wanted to know the whole story. I said I didn't. I've heard enough lies from him already.'

'Why lies?'

'I know when he's lying. I believe his brother and his wife died in a car crash. But if they were my parents why didn't he and Aunt Celia adopt me after the crash? I knew she wasn't well but I wouldn't have bothered her. I had a nanny when I first arrived and then I went to boarding school. I have some very vague memories of the time before I was brought here. There were different women looking after me. I thought one of them was my mother. But then this other woman, the one who took over from the one I thought was my mother and handed me over to my uncle, told me my mother died when I was a baby. I never really believed her either. I can see through people, you see. Tell when they're lying. I just have this impression that everybody's been lying to me all my life. So why should they stop now?'

'Do you have a girlfriend?'

'No.'

'But you weren't a virgin, were you, before you met me?'

'I worked on a farm last year, to get some money of my own.

There were two girls there helping out with the horses. Early twenties. Students. They had a bet as to which of them would deflower me first. In the end they decided to do it together. It was in the stables. All those grunting noises around. Like we were just three more farm animals.'

'You hate and despise women, don't you? You don't believe your mother died when you were a baby. You believe she couldn't be bothered to look after you. So she passed you on to another woman who passed you onto your uncle. You think your mother was a whore, don't you? And now you've found another whore. And you want to show the world what you think of women, and mothers in particular, by painting her as the Mother of God. Don't you think that's just a bit obscene, blasphemous, some might say?'

'Maybe. So why are you here? Why am I here? Why are you going along with it if you disapprove so much?'

'I don't know.'

With a sudden movement that startled her he had thrown the covers off the bed and rolled on top of her. He pinned her down by the shoulders, his face directly in front of hers. She closed her eyes.

'Open them. Open your eyes. Look at me.'

She opened her eyelids a fraction. 'More.'

She groaned. This was far worse than the previous times. The day before, on the hall floor, he had barely given her a glance. An hour ago he had been behind her, nothing for him to see but an anonymous arrangement of hair, shoulder blades, vertebrae, buttocks. Now his staring eyes could see everything at a few inches' distance, all the lines of age and pain that were etched on her face. She felt as if she were being flayed alive.

Afterwards, he dressed quickly and walked upstairs. Within a minute she could hear the scratch of his pencil. She knew he was drawing a face, filling in an outline. He did not need her any more that day.

*

'So how many's that you've done?'

It was three weeks after she had first modelled for him. He had come every day except Sundays, when Michael expected him to be home all day. The routine was always the same. He arrived at ten o'clock. By then she would have showered and put on her dressing-gown. After coffee she would slip off her gown and take up whatever position he directed. He would work for an hour. Exhausted, she would go downstairs and lie on the bed. He would follow her down, undress and enter her. Then they would sleep for an hour. After that he would either go home or order her upstairs for another session. From the time of his arrival to his always abrupt departure they barely spoke a word to each other.

This time Madeleine had ventured to ask him a question, hoping perhaps for a sign that his grim, relentless search for she did not know what would soon be coming to an end. The routine had been the same that morning. Except that after he had dressed and come upstairs he had neither left the cottage nor woken her for another session. That had never happened before. When she awoke and went upstairs she found him sitting at the table, leafing through his sketchpad. He was taking stock of progress, she thought. Now might be a good time to ask him. He gave no sign that he had heard her or even noticed her presence. Slowly and awkwardly, as usual, she picked up her gown and put it on. This was always a much harder task than slipping it off. By then her limbs were weak and aching, her actions as uncoordinated as a child's. She shrugged her shoulders and sat down on the sofa. She had decided not to repeat her question. Then to her surprise he pushed back his chair, yawned and spoke.

'Eleven complete ink drawings. About a hundred pencil sketches.'

'Can't I see them yet?'

'No.'

'Have you got what you need for the picture?'

'Not yet. Something's always missing. Maybe the next one.'

'Does your uncle suspect anything at all?'

'No. He's very trusting. Believes in me implicitly. Or in some image he has of me. I think I'll tell him. Everything we do. Every detail. I'd love to see his face.'

'No.' Madeleine almost screamed the word. 'You mustn't tell him a thing. God knows what he'll do.'

'To me or to you?'

'What do you mean?'

'Why do you think he'd bother about us unless . . .'

'Unless what?'

'Unless you're fucking him as well. I suppose that's it. He's fallen in love with you. Sort of stupid thing he would do. He's a real romantic. Sentimental old fool. He'd be jealous.'

'David, I'm not fucking him. That's the truth.'

'You can if you want. I couldn't care less.'

'Just promise me you won't tell him. You want to finish your picture, don't you?'

'And I can't do that if he kills either or both of us. All right, I promise. I'll go now. I'll be back in the morning.'

When he had gone she waited for a few minutes, then carefully opened the case which he had left on the table. The sketchpad was inside. Underneath were the ink drawings, on separate sheets of a harder, yellower paper. She leafed through them, shuddering. She took the pad and the drawings out and laid them on the table. Below them, taking up most of the dimensions of the case, was what she presumed was his sketch of *The Assumption*, a bizarre medley of pencil, ink, watercolour and crayon on a sheet of grey, granulated paper. She took it out carefully and placed it on the other side of the table. The case was not yet empty. There were two colour photographs inside. They looked as if they had been torn out of a book. The first showed an altar in a gloomy, ornate church. The photograph seemed to have been taken from halfway down the nave. Above the altar, partly obscured at the bottom by candles, was a painting. At first she saw only three horizontal lines, the top enclosed within a curved arch, with two fluted columns on either side. As her eyes became accustomed to the shadows she could make out a figure in red in the middle of the three lines. Small white figures gathered around the feet as if bearing it up. The other photograph was a close-up reproduction of the same painting. She could now see the details of the three horizontal lines. In the centre, haloed in a blinding white light, robed in red, was Mary, the Mother of God, gazing upwards, eyes blinded by an ecstatic vision. Along the bottom were the apostles, clamouring and pleading to her as she was lifted from out of their midst. At the top was God the Father, borne aloft by two cherubs, meeting her gaze, drawing her up to receive her into Heaven.

She placed the more detailed reproduction next to David's sketch. She was puzzled. At first she could find no possible connection. What was it he had said? A reinterpretation. What exactly did he mean by that? He had written the title in small pencil letters at the top of his sheet. The three horizontal lines were there all right. But they seemed to be upside down and in the wrong place. They were at the top of the sheet. And there was no sign of any central figure being lifted up, no God the Father at the top. But there were some ink scribbles at the bottom. She turned the picture round so that the title was at the bottom. She put her hand to her mouth to stifle a cry.

He did not come round the next morning. It was three o'clock when he knocked at the door. When she opened it he lurched unsteadily in.

'Where have you been? You're drunk.'

'Thought I'd call in at the inn on the way.'

'The inn isn't on the way. I want to talk to you.'

'About what?'

'About that.'

They were in the sitting-room. She was pointing at the large sketch, still on the table where she had examined it.

'You took it out. I told you not to do that yet. You nosy cow. Might have known you'd have to have a peep.'

'I've looked at everything you've done here. I'm not bothered about your drawings of me. But I am bothered about this. I've compared it with the reproduction. I can see what you're doing. It's not just a blasphemy. It's a perversion. You're sick, David. You need help.'

'Maybe,' he said, sinking into an armchair. 'They said that about Munch. And plenty of others.'

'She's not going to be lifted into Heaven, is she? You've turned God the Father into Satan. And he's dragging her down to Hell.'

'That's right. The title's ironic, you see.'

'Yes, I see now. And what I see is that I want no more to do with this . . . this obscene nightmare.'

'Oh, you don't, do you? Well, I've got news for you. It's too late. You're in this with me, up to your neck. Yes, we are in a nightmare. And the only way to get out of it is to finish it.'

'And how are you going to do that? You've been trying for three weeks now. You still haven't got the image you want. How long can this go on?'

'Today, Madeleine. Today is when we finish it. I know what's needed. You haven't given me the image I need because I haven't yet taken you where you need to go. Go downstairs.'

He followed her down, holding the railing unsteadily. In a corner of the room stood a full-length mirror on castors. He pulled it away from the wall towards the centre of the room, next to the bed. Madeleine was naked, already climbing onto the bed, about to take up her usual facedown position.

'Not there. Here. On the floor. In front of the mirror. Kneel down.'

15

June 1995

'Before you tell me anything else, tell me how you knew Michael.'

'I was related to him. Very closely. I never knew how closely until I found those papers he had been hiding.'

'What did you find?'

'My birth certificate.'

Madeleine shivered uncontrollably.

'How old are you really, Alan?'

'Really? It's funny how when you live rough you get to look old, almost overnight. When you have a beard, and the sun and wind crease your skin and the dirt gets into the creases and can't ever be washed out, and you walk with a stoop because you daren't look people in the eye because you don't want to see their contempt, or worse, their pity, then you look old. I wasn't really lying. I am old. Age and chronology aren't the same thing.'

'So how old are you, in terms of chronology?'

'I'm younger than you.'

'I was beginning to suspect that. And Michael?'

'He was my father.'

'I don't believe you. I would have known.'

'He never acknowledged me. But he was aware of my existence.'

'How did you find out?'

'It wasn't difficult. I came here to watch him. He didn't even see me.'

'Your mother?'

'No idea what happened to her. I was adopted. My adoptive parents are dead.'

'Did they tell you Michael was your father?'

'I said it wasn't difficult to find out.'

'When you came here, did you see his nephew?'

'You mean David? Oh yes. I saw him. I talked to him. Only he wasn't his nephew. He knew that. He told me. He was his son as well. My half-brother.'

'How did you feel about him?'

'How do you think I felt?'

'I can imagine. He took in one son, brought him up, loved him as a son. But his other son he disowned and ignored.'

'That's right. Maybe I wasn't the only one out in the cold. Maybe he had lots of little bastards all over the place. But David was the only one he was remotely interested in. The only one who seemed to have inherited his artistic bent. The only one he thought he could make into an image of himself.'

'But, why did you talk to David? You didn't tell him . . .'

'Oh no. I never told him who I was. He would have been frightened. I couldn't do that to him. He had been ill. Gone a bit funny in the head. I didn't want to scare him.'

'What . . . what did you want to do to him?'

'Why don't you guess?'

She felt as if the weight of the church roof were pressing down on her.

'You . . . would have wanted him out of the way. You were insanely jealous of him. But you had won his trust. He thought you were a friend.'

'And friends can go for walks together. On the coastal path. And we were both very young.'

'Young men aren't afraid to go near the edge. Or if they are they might dare each other. See who dares to go closest. Near

119

enough to look over. No young man wants to look like a coward.
Oh no . . .'

'Oh yes, Madeleine. Another accident. Same spot as your
mother.'

'They said he had been standing on unsupported earth. It had
given way. So after you killed him . . .'

'I went back there at night to dislodge the earth. Easy.'

'You stole a torch from the house and left it to guide the
searchers. They saw where the earth had fallen. They found the
body at the foot of the cliffs. And in killing David you got your
revenge on Michael as well. On the father who had pretended
you never existed. You destroyed him. Please go, Alan. We must
never meet again.'

'I'll go. But there's no need to be afraid of me. And you're
certainly in no position to judge me. You, Michael and me. We
have a lot in common. We're all killers.'

16

June 1986

'I've finished them. Both of them. The final ink drawing and the main picture.'

Madeleine was in bed, where she had stayed all day after taking a long, hot bath. She blinked open her eyes and gazed at him listlessly as he stood at the foot of the stairs. Her whole body felt numb. Her throat was raw.

'So what happens now?' Her voice croaked.

'I don't know. I'll leave what I've done here. You can destroy it all if you want. I need to get away. I don't want to go his bloody academy. It'll squeeze the life out of me. I'll take off tomorrow. Go hitchhiking around Europe. He'll cut off my allowance. So when I get back I'll have to get a job. Move up to London, I suppose. In the meantime I'm going down to the inn for a drink.'

He stamped up the stairs. A few seconds later she heard the door slam. Her eyes closed again.

After what seemed only a few seconds there was a loud knocking on the door. She struggled out of bed, put on her dressing-gown and stumbled upstairs. She opened the door, half-expecting David to be standing there, having changed his mind about going to the inn.

'Christ, it's you.'

'Aren't you going to invite me in?'

'Of course. Come in. God, Michael, what's the matter with you? You look terrible. Are you ill?'

'I could ask the same about you. Did I get you out of bed?'

'Yes. I am a bit under the weather. Spot of flu, I think. I'd rather you didn't go through there . . . Michael, please, come into the kitchen. I've got private stuff in here.'

'So I see. Interesting work. Very rough but I think I recognise the style.'

'What do you want, Michael?'

'David. I want my nephew back.'

'What makes you think I've got him? You'd better sit down. Catch your breath. You look as if you're about to collapse. You didn't walk the coastal path, did you?'

'No. I drove. Left the car at the bottom of the lane.'

So the short steep walk up the lane, which a few weeks ago would have been nothing to him, had exhausted him. God, he had changed. He almost fell onto the sofa.

'And the answer to your question is that I have information from a reliable source. He's been coming here during the day. Drawing. Now I know what. Or whom. While I thought he was out on the headlands. And he hasn't just been drawing you, has he?'

'For Christ's sake, Michael, stop behaving like a Victorian father. The boy's nearly twenty now. What he does, who he sees, who he fucks, is none of your business. Anyway, he's not here. So at this moment I can't give him back to you, as you put it. And don't you think it is about time you stopped treating him like a personal possession?'

'I know he's not here now. I saw him going into the inn. He never drank before. He never smoked. He never did pornographic rubbish like that. Have you any idea, you stupid, deluded woman, of the damage you've done? David was the most naturally talented artist I have ever come across, and I've met many in my time. In three short weeks you've destroyed his talent, destroyed his character, destroyed his future. And you've destroyed me as well. I trusted you. And you betrayed me.'

She stood up. 'No, Michael, I'm not buying that. You can say anything you like about me. But you can't build him up and then just knock him down because you feel like it. I know what game you've been playing all these years. You've been trying to live through him. Trying to make him into the artist you never could be. Well, now he's his own artist and his own man. You may not like either of them. But that's just too fucking bad. The game's up now. And you just lost. David will come back to you if he chooses to do so. I certainly won't keep him here. But two things are certain. He will never be the sort of artist you want him to be. And he never was the person you thought he was.'

He stared at her, hollow-eyed, shaking his head.

'Madeleine,' he gasped. 'You have no idea, no idea at all what you have done. You and he together . . .'

'You're disgusted because I'm twice his age? Michael, for God's sake, do you think that has never happened before? Don't be so naive. Maybe if you hadn't kept him locked up in that prison of yours he would have grown up to be a normal boy and have a girlfriend of his own age. But what chance did you ever give him of being normal?'

Michael staggered towards the door. She slammed it behind him. She waited until she heard the gate close and footsteps recede down the lane. She buried her face in her hands.

Half an hour later, she put on her coat and slipped quietly out. She walked quickly down the lane. On the seafront she turned right, in the direction of the inn. The yellow lights from the windows and the noises of laughter and shouting poured onto the road and the pavement. She ran past, looking straight ahead, seeking the darkness and the solitude of the beach lit only by a few early stars and a pale half moon. She found the path above the beach and ran along it. After a hundred yards, she turned and ran down onto the beach.

She stepped up to the edge and began to wade out, until she felt the still incoming tide pull and tug about her thighs. In front of her she saw grey shadows, hovering above the waves, floating silently towards her. She covered her eyes and screamed.

David was sitting in the armchair, staring at the play of bright moonlight on the water. There was a very strong smell of whisky. A bottle stood on the floor and he had a half-empty glass in his hand. On the floor beside him lay a flat, half-opened parcel. He shot her a glance, then looked away again.

'You're wet.'

'I went for a walk on the beach. I was by the water's edge. The tide was coming in. I didn't notice it until it was nearly up to my knees.'

'I didn't go down to the inn straight away. I waited for a few minutes. Saw him go in.'

'That's right. He knows what time you usually leave. Waits for you to go. Then comes in for a quick fuck. Drives back so he's home before you. For God's sake, David, stop being so bloody stupid!'

'I found this. I was looking in the cupboard for another bottle.' He picked up the parcel and tore the remaining paper off it. He stood up and handed it to her.

'Oh, I remember now. This is one of his.'

'Of course it is. It's got his signature on it.'

'He told me he put it in here when he was refurbishing the place. He brought it round just after I arrived, after repairing the frame or something. I didn't want to hang it back up. I never even looked at it. That's all. When you mentioned the space on the wall, the first time you came round here, I had forgotten about it. Hey, it's not bad, is it?'

'When did he do this?'

'I have no idea. It could have been years ago.'

'But you weren't here years ago.'

'Of course I wasn't.'

'So it could only have been a few weeks ago. Before we met, I suppose. You must have had it on the wall. You fucked him and he drew you. He gave you the picture. He even framed it for you. Then when I came round for the first time you had taken it down. You didn't want me to see it.'

She stared at him, then at the picture then back at him, her mouth open. Then she laughed.

'Christ, David, you think this is me! Is that it? Oh you bloody fool! I have no idea who this woman is.'

'Stop lying to me. Did you think I wouldn't recognise you? Of course it's you. I know your body. Better than you do.'

Slowly she placed the picture face down on the table. 'But not better than he does, is that it? That's the problem for you, isn't it? You always said I was a whore. You wouldn't have minded if there was a queue of men outside the door, so long as he wasn't one of them. Because he wouldn't see me the way the others would. Or the way you would. Anybody could fuck me. But only you could draw me. I was your possession. You thought you had bought me by putting me into your hideous drawings. You thought I was part of your sick, distorted vision of the world. You can't bear to think that I could also be part of his. That he could draw me like that.

'You were always operating in different worlds, weren't you? He with his traditions, you with your dreams and nightmares. And now you find you're in competition over the same model. The way he drew me undermines everything you've done with me over the past few weeks. That's what you can't stand. Because suddenly you've seen what a real man and a real artist can do, when he sees someone as a woman and not just as a piece of flesh, to be pulled around and abused. All right. I admit. This is a picture of me. And he fucked me before, during and after. Are you satisfied now?'

He stepped up to her and slapped her hard across the face. She gasped and jerked her head to the side. Then he rushed out of the door and slammed it behind him.

*

For a few minutes she stroked her stinging skin, smiling. Then she went over to the table and picked up a notepad and envelope. She wrote on the notepad.

June 1986

Dear Michael

This is just to let you know that I am leaving Porthhella and do not plan to return. You will find the key outside in the usual place. I would be grateful if you would put the cottage on the market. I no longer wish to be the owner. What you do with the proceeds is up to you. I will leave with my solicitor an authority for you to act on my behalf in the sale. His address is on the back of this letter.

David is not with me now and I know he will not come back here. Whatever it was we had together is finished. I am sure he will come back to you soon, probably this evening, certainly by the time you get this letter. I know he does not wish to attend your academy and I think you should respect his wishes. He needs to take a break from his work and was talking of going to Europe for a holiday. I suggest you let him have some breathing space and find his own way in his own time. Do not destroy your own health and peace of mind over what has happened. It was an unfortunate episode but I am sure he will look back on it as part of growing up. I am not proud of my role in it. I did not wish you or him any harm. I am sorry for having kept the secret from you. I wanted to save you unnecessary anxiety, but it seems that in the event I unwittingly caused you a great deal. I hope you will forgive me in time.

Madeleine

She put the note in the envelope. She then picked up another letter which she had received a few days before. It was from her estate agents in London, telling her they had found a suitable buyer for her flat. He had made an offer which they believed was a highly favourable one in the present state of the market. They asked for instructions to proceed with the sale. She left the letter on the kitchen table.

She packed a small suitcase and placed it in the hall. Was there anything else? Oh yes, the drawings. She gathered them together and leafed through them. When she came to *The Assumption* she paused, turning it round and observing the newly added image of the woman from different angles. Then she picked up Michael's drawing and placed it next to it.

So you think these are both me, do you, David? Which do you think is the truth? Yours or his? I know what you think. You're right. You resent his drawing but only because you thought I was your exclusive property. Not because you think it is better or more truthful. You despise him as an artist. He doesn't even try to capture the face. But you, you put it right in the centre of your work. And that face, that screaming, distorted image of evil being dragged down to Hell, is the mirror of my soul. How well you understood me.

She placed the drawings carefully in a folder, wrapped it in brown paper and sealed it with parcel tape. She walked down to the sea front and placed the letter to Michael in the tiny red postbox. She returned to the cottage and looked round for the last time. She lifted up Michael's drawing and hung it on the hook above the stove. She stepped back a few paces.

It's not bad, Michael. Really not bad at all. She could have been anybody, of course. Any one of the thousands of women with a figure like that. To you, she was just a model, an assembly of lines and curves. You probably don't even remember her. But there is definitely something about it.

She collected her luggage and took it down to the car.

She slept on the sofa, fully dressed, and made a very early start the next morning. She arrived in Dover in the late afternoon.

She found a small hotel and booked in for the night. The next day she made arrangements with a branch of her bank for the secure deposit of the parcel containing the drawings. She sent a letter to her solicitor nominating Michael to act on her behalf in the sale of the cottage. She rang the estate agents in London and gave them instructions for the completion of the sale of her flat. She found a second-hand car dealer who was only too pleased to take her car from her at the price she asked. She bought a rucksack and packed some of her clothes and accessories in it.

That evening she took a ferry for Calais.

17

July 1995

When I look back I suppose that was the moment when I really turned crazy. When I saw those shadows floating on the water. To me they were as real as my own flesh. Not substantial. I knew I couldn't touch them. But real.

I knew who they were. He had told me about them. I imagine he told you but I doubt if you were interested. They were the Furies. The Eumenides. Older than Christ, older than Zeus. It was Mother Earth who bore them, from drops of the blood of Uranus, the First Father. They avenge crimes against nature. Crimes like the murder of a parent. But why had they come for me? I hadn't killed him. I hadn't killed you. I knew I had done some wrong things in my life. I had become estranged from you. I had let David break Michael's heart and done nothing to prevent it. But surely they were not the only reasons why the Furies pursued me. Whatever the reason, of one thing I was sure. They would pursue me to the ends of the earth and for the rest of my days.

I travelled aimlessly through Europe for several months. In late summer I found myself in Paris. I rented a tiny room near the Jardins du Luxembourg. Every day I walked through the gardens, watching the little old ladies who hurried past, dressed in overcoats despite the summer heat, dragging their proportionately tiny dogs behind them on tight leads. In the evenings I drifted along the Boulevards St Michel and St Germain, stopping from time to time at the cafes and bars. Usually I went back to my room alone. Sometimes I let a man I had met in one of the bars come back with me. I never asked his name or gave him mine. I just drifted, in body, mind and soul, waiting for something, I had no idea what.

In the oppressive heat of late August, I at last found Paris intolerable. I hired a car and drove down to Marseilles. The roads were clear. Paris had been almost abandoned by its inhabitants for the holiday season and the *rentrées* had not yet begun. Marseilles was too noisy and crowded. I drove on along the coast, looking for somewhere quieter. I stopped at a dingy little hotel in a tiny port town and checked in for the night. I can't even remember its name. In the evening I went out, looking for a bar. I found one, down by the harbour.

I can't tell you what happened next. Not yet. It's not because I don't remember. I do. Every moment. But I can't write about it yet.

The Furies were with me all the time of course. But when I got back to Paris I sensed that their presence was less oppressive. I knew that in some way I had pacified them. They would not go away. But now they only watched, silently, from a distance.

With late autumn giving way to winter, I began to have a recurring nightmare. I was falling, endlessly, through swirling darkness and rain, to Tartarus, a place Father had told me about, a gloomy corner of the underworld. From the earth it would take an anvil nine days to reach it. At first I was alone. Then you were with me. The smooth, shiny rocks of the cliff-face rushed past us. Then there was a third person, falling with us. I awoke, calling out David's name.

The nightmare persisted. I wrote a letter to Michael, asking him how he and David were. I received his reply after two weeks. For three days I sat in my room, frozen with shock. Then I went down to the telephone in the hall and rang the airport.

18

July 1995

'So you've taken to coming round to see me at night have you? Do you know what time it is?'

'You weren't in bed, Brenda.'

'No. I hardly ever sleep. What time is it, anyway?'

'Eleven o'clock. I don't come out during the day now. I stay in my room. Keep out of sight. I'm moving out at the end of the week.'

'Come in. Sit down. So what do you do in your room?'

'Think. Try to work things out.'

'And what have you worked out?'

'That Michael and my mother had an affair. And you knew about it. You lied to me.'

Brenda sat down opposite her.

'All right. I lied. I admit it. I lied because it's humiliating and painful for me. So what do you want from me now?'

'I want to know why you hated my mother so much, and why you hated me. Take your time. Start at the beginning.'

'The beginning? All right. If you really want to know. I come from Newcastle originally. I went to art school there. It's not the most inspiring part of the world for an artist. So I came down here. I had heard about the artists' colonies. I never thought I would be good enough to be part of them, but I wanted to be in the same surroundings. I wanted to see if the light and the scenery would stimulate my rather feeble creative faculties. I got a job in a gallery in St Ives. That was where I first saw Michael's works, and where I first met him. He lived in Penzance then. He was in the gallery supervising the hanging of one of his exhibitions. I showed him some of my work from art school and asked him if he would take me on as a private pupil. He did. He was a good teacher, patient and kind. I fell in love with him. He never noticed. We both realised early on that my talents were very limited and there was little he could do for me. I stopped going to him for lessons. But I was still working in the St Ives gallery and saw him from time to time.

'When he moved to the house on the bay, he visited Porthhella and saw the capstan house. It was in a very poor condition. He told me he was thinking of buying it and converting it into a gallery. I went to look at it. I pleaded with him for the opportunity to work with him on it. I got in the best local designers and contractors. When it was ready he asked me to run it for him. I was delighted. I enjoyed the extra responsibility. I enjoyed seeing more of him than I had in St Ives. He let me run it more or less as I saw fit, but he came down regularly to visit. I travelled around, looking for new talent. He was always pleased when I discovered a promising young artist whose career we could promote by mounting an exhibition. It was the happiest time of my life. I still loved him but I knew nothing would ever come of it. He had married by then. Even if I could have interested him in an affair I don't believe in chasing after married men.

'Then she arrived. She had no such compunctions. Ceridwen. Your mother. They met there. She was admiring the paintings in the gallery. He was admiring her. All I could do was watch. I had never met Celia but I wasn't jealous of her. I knew he had married her to improve his social standing. Her family were well-connected county people. It wasn't a love match. This was different. They devoured each other with their eyes. I was sick with jealousy. I started following them. They met up on the headlands, then at the cottage. I spied on them. I know it made matters worse for me but I couldn't help it.'

'I'm sorry if it made you unhappy. But it wasn't her fault. And it certainly wasn't mine.'

'You still don't get it, do you? Of course it wasn't her fault. That's the whole point. She was just doing what came naturally to her. Can you imagine what life is like for someone like me? Someone whose face and manner are somehow soured from birth, who could never have friends, who could fall in love but never attract either love or hatred in return? The worst thing was that Michael didn't hate me, or despise me. He had very good reasons to be grateful to me. He admired me. He always said how efficient I was. But as for my other feelings . . . He never even knew! They lived somewhere inside me. They never reached my eyes or my lips. I didn't know how. I had never learned. God knows, I tried many times to tell him. The words just died in my throat. I wouldn't have minded if he had laughed at me. I'm sure he would have done. Laughed at me and despised me. I could have accepted that. Anything would have been better than just being regarded as an efficient assistant.

'Of course I hated your mother. She was everything I wasn't. She had never had to learn. She didn't have to try. She could just look at a man and that was that. Her eyes, her voice, her figure, her manner of walking and standing and just looking, just being – I mean, you would think God would have withheld one little gift from her. Just one which he could have spared for me. But no. He gave her everything. More than she could ever need. She just looked at him and she had his love, his whole being, from that second onwards. All I wanted was his contempt and I couldn't even win that. I hated her just for existing.'

'So, when she died . . .'

'I felt at last that there was some justice in the world. She had had far more than she deserved but at least it was all over. I had something on her. I was still alive.'

'Then I came along.'

'Yes. Ceridwen rising from the grave. The nightmare was starting all over again. You were the image of her. I always thought it would be you and Michael from the start. If I were God that was how I would have arranged it. As the most exquisite punishment possible for having wished her dead. When you took up with David, I was sick with relief. You were not like her at all.

'When it comes to the art of being a woman, Ceridwen was supreme. She was at her peak. She accepted everything about herself, accepted graciously and gratefully every one of the years she had lived and grown and learned. Above all, she had taste. She knew the sort of man who was worthy of her. She chose Michael. A philanderer, maybe, but a gentleman. A man who never deserted his sick wife. A great artist, but one who was humble enough to know the limits of his gifts and generous enough to give the world the best of himself. But you . . . you could have had that man, when he was still in his prime. You could have had Michael.'

No, Brenda. Never. Precisely because he was a gentleman.

'But instead you chose David. I could hate Ceridwen but I could never despise her. But I could despise you. You had never grown up. You had never accepted the passing years. You were trying to regain your youth by seducing a child. Thinking that opening your legs for a teenager would make you one again.'

'It wasn't like that, Brenda.'

'Then how was it? Don't tell me you loved him.'

'No. I've never loved in the way . . . you loved Michael. I had a lot of affairs. None of those men meant anything to me. But David was different. He was special to me. I don't know why.'

'He was special. He was a genius, so Michael said.'

'Yes. A genius. An abusive and totally self-centred genius.'

'As they often are.'

'Indeed. But I let him. I put up with it. I was thirty-eight. He was nineteen and I let him use me like one of the rags he used to clean the paints off his brush. And yet he was violently jealous. He became dependent on me. He was convinced I was having an affair with Michael. I knew by then it was all over between us. I let him think I was having sex with Michael so it would be easier for him to walk away and forget about me. I miscalculated. I didn't know he was so vulnerable.'

'So when you moved in with Michael, it wasn't because you loved him?'

'No. When I heard about David and went back I was sorry for him. And guilty. I had destroyed both of them. But Michael was still alive. Just about. I could make things a bit easier for him, maybe. I owed him that. That was all.'

'I would have looked after him. But he would never have wanted me that close to him. Perhaps it was just as well it was you. You could give him what he needed. I didn't despise you any more. You had grown up. You weren't just thinking of yourself. I hated you, of course. Because you were in my place.'

'Brenda, I know this is an awful thought but . . . do you think Michael could have killed my mother? Because she was making things too uncomfortable for him?'

Brenda shook her head. 'I know he loved your mother, but he couldn't leave Celia for her. Ceridwen was not the sort of woman who would just accept that and move on. She may have tried to pressure him. But I knew Michael. He wasn't a murderer. He could be a man of sudden passions. He might have killed in the heat of the moment, but we know that wasn't what happened. He couldn't have planned and carried through a murder in cold blood, working out exactly how to make it look like an accident, then carried his secret with him to the grave. That wasn't him. I know that. What gave you the idea?'

'I've been talking to somebody. There's this tramp who's been haunting the village. He's been following me.'

'I've seen him, but only from a distance.'

'Only he's not just a tramp. He knows things. He showed me evidence that my mother was putting Michael under pressure.'

'Really? And does this well-informed tramp have a name?'

'He told me his name is Alan but I don't know if it's real or not. He won't let me see his face. He says he's Michael's son. Michael never acknowledged him. He discovered his identity. Drifted aimlessly through life. Then at last he found a purpose. He met David and planned his revenge on him. Brenda, what is it?'

Brenda was not looking at her. Her eyes stared into the empty fireplace, her face contorting.

'No, it's impossible . . . It was all arranged. How could it . . .?' She looked up and seemed to remember Madeleine's presence. 'Did he give you any proof Michael was his father?'

'No.'

'He told you Michael killed your mother. Then he invented a son of Michael's who plotted to kill David. Well, I must admit it's a good story. One of the best I've heard. But forget it. He may have got hold of a piece of paper somewhere. But the rest is pure fantasy. Michael could never have treated a son of his like that.'

Madeleine stood up. 'All right, Brenda, maybe you're right. But hasn't it ever occurred to you that your image of Michael is rather biased? Isn't it at least possible that your views about what he could and could not have done might be coloured by your feelings for him? He may have had all the qualities you attribute to him. But he could have had other, less attractive ones as well. He could have killed my mother and he could have neglected and disowned one son in favour of another. He could pass one off as his nephew, but not two. And it's perfectly possible that he never knew about Alan's existence, though Alan says he did. The fact is that neither of us really knows. All right, it could be made up. But he was so convincing. I really believed him.'

'Maybe he believes it himself. That's why he's so convincing. He suffers from delusions. He read about Michael's life. Became obsessed with it. He knows he's an orphan, but he has no idea who his parents were. He became convinced he was Michael's illegitimate son. He probably never met David but he dreamt of revenge. When David died, he convinced himself he'd done it. You've got to admit it's a possibility.'

'I suppose so.'

'What are you going to do? When you move out of the inn, I mean.'

'Am I going away? You'd like that, wouldn't you? No, I'm not leaving. I'm going back to the house. It's a hideous, lonely place and it's full of ghosts. But it's where I belong.'

After Madeleine had gone, Brenda poured herself a glass of brandy and sat down. She realised she was shaking. She wondered if Madeleine had noticed.

'Is it possible . . .?' She asked out loud. Then, to herself, is it really possible that you were playing me along all the time? That right from the start you intended to betray me? You deserved to die even more than I thought. Of course, this poor lunatic girl could be right. Michael spread his seed far and wide. Everywhere but here. I can hardly blame the women, can I? I would gladly have borne him a bastard and hidden it away somewhere. This Alan could be who he says he is. Or he could be a liar or delusional. Maybe there really is nothing to worry about. But I need to find out. I'll close the gallery for a couple of days. Nobody's been over the doorstep for a week. The change of scene will do me good.

19

September 1995

I've moved back into the house now. Been back a few weeks, with only Megan for company. Such a relief to get away from the village, and the inn and those horrible old fishermen. I'm in my bedroom now. Plain and simple. A single bed, dresser and wardrobe. No pictures on the wall. Megan hasn't altered a thing. It's just as I left it. Only the face which stares back at me from the dressing-table mirror has changed. And the clothes in the wardrobe are loose and baggy.

I have to leave this notebook for now. The rest of the story, up to the time I left for Portsmouth to see Laura, took place here in this house. I need to go through it all again, in my mind. But first of all I need to be alone. And that means I have to devise a plot to get Megan away from here, for a few days at least.

20

September 1995

'The doctor were with you for ages this morning,' said Megan, glancing suspiciously up at Madeleine after a long silence.

They were sitting in Megan's parlour in the late afternoon, drinking tea, Megan getting on with her knitting. It had become a fixed part of their routine, from the day Madeleine had moved back into the house. They had the whole house to themselves, but preferred the cramped intimacy of the parlour. Neither of them ever went into the lounge facing the sea, except when Megan needed to go there to dust and polish the silverware. When Madeleine wanted to be on her own she confined herself to her bedroom or the library.

'That's country doctors for you. They have so few patients. They like nothing better than to gossip. I told him I was fine. He listened to my chest and prescribed some pills. That took five minutes. The rest was just chatter, passing the time.'

She had spent the previous two days in bed with a chest infection. The doctor had come at Megan's insistence, despite Madeleine assuring her there was no need.

'Changing the subject,' she continued, 'I've decided I will sell the house, you'll be pleased to hear.'

Megan put down her knitting and beamed. 'There you are. I knew you'd make the right decision in the end. I'm really delighted.

139

But it's not for my sake, is it? You're doing it because you want to. I told you you don't need to worry about me.'

'It's for both our sakes, Megan. But I'm not going to do it right away. There are things I have to think about first.'

'That's fine by me, my dear. You take your time. I hope you don't mind me asking, but . . . I've been wondering, what with you being so poorly lately. Were it really very awful for you in that place? I mean, I were consoling myself with the thought that it were a hospital so they would be looking after you. But when you came back, well, it didn't look as if they had taken much care of you. You lost a lot of weight there. And you're always frowning, when I catch you on your own, as if you're trying to remember things. They didn't help you remember, did they?'

'No. They had other priorities with me. I was a difficult patient at first. They needed to give me some injections. I had a panic attack when they first came to do it. I thought they were going to kill me. The nurse nearly broke my arm. They were better when I decided to behave. After a few months they were almost friendly. When they realised I wasn't a threat to them or anybody else. That was all they were bothered about. I can't blame them.'

Megan shook her head. 'Poor girl. What a dreadful business. And you still can't remember anything?'

'Yes, something. I must have known who Laura was. Because I know now and it came to me out of my own head. She was David's mother. Which of course means that Mr Wallace was his father.'

Megan stared at her. 'Are you sure? How did you find out?'

'I don't know. Mr Wallace didn't tell me, that's for sure. But he might have told me to go and see her after his death for some reason. She did come to visit him once, here, late at night. I do remember that.'

'I don't. I suppose I had gone to bed.'

'So had I. But then I got up again. Perhaps I heard the bell. I saw her from the landing. If I heard anything of their conversation I don't remember. Did you ever wonder about who David really was? I mean, it must have been a surprise to you, him just coming to live here like that.'

'No. I don't wonder and I don't pry. People choose to tell me things or not. It's up to them. Sometimes I believe them and sometimes I don't. He told me Master David were his nephew. It weren't my place to argue about that.'

'I can see you had your doubts. Do you believe me, about Laura being his mother?'

'I believe you believe it. But if you could remember how you found out, maybe the rest would follow. Did she tell you herself, when you went to see her?'

'Possibly. Though why that should lead me to do what I did, I don't know.'

Megan shook her head. 'Couldn't it have been an accident? Or maybe nothing happened at all. She just died. I mean, I'm old now and my skin is frail and thin. Sometimes I see bruise marks on myself and I'm sure they just appeared.'

'But if nothing happened, why would I forget the conversation we had? No, I know you'll never believe me but I did it all right. I accepted that a long time ago. Megan, do you remember that first time Mr Wallace introduced me to David? It was in the lounge. You served us tea. It was the first time we had met since my mother's funeral.'

'Of course I remember.'

'Did you ever hear anything afterwards, about David and me?'

'No. Village gossip never reaches here, and if it did, I wouldn't listen.'

'David and I took an instant dislike to each other. But we were drawn to each other at the same time. It was as if the only way we could dispel our feelings of animosity to each other was . . . Well, what I'm saying is that we met in secret. We had an affair. Mr Wallace found out. He came round to see me. We had a terrible row. The relationship had finished. I went away. After a few months I wrote to Mr Wallace to ask him how David was. I just had this bad feeling. He told me about David's breakdown and how he had died. All those terrible things that happened were my fault. I could have stopped it before it started. I was older. I should have been in control. But I wasn't.'

'Of course it weren't your fault, Madeleine. Master David . . . well, I'm not going to criticise the way Mr Wallace brought him up. That's not my place. But he were like a boiling pot with the lid on, ready to explode. I remember that time very well. One morning, there were a woman in the house. I had been in the garden and I hadn't seen her come in. But they was having some dreadful words. I heard them from the hall. I went upstairs so they wouldn't come out and think I had been eavesdropping. I didn't recognise her voice. I heard the front door slam.

'Mr Wallace went out later that day. He looked as if he had seen a thousand devils. He ignored me when I asked him if he were feeling all right. Stupid thing to ask, really. It were obvious he weren't all right. Master David had already been out since the morning. Mr Wallace told you the rest, I suppose. When you saw him again, you must have noticed how he had aged. His hair had gone white, he stooped, his back were bad, he had terrible angina. What you didn't know were that all that happened in the space of a few weeks. I never saw anyone fall off so quickly, from being a picture of health and energy. It were only you coming back that saved him.'

'Not for long. Megan, when David came back here, and he wasn't himself any more . . .'

'That's right. It were as if we was total strangers to him, and him to us.'

'Did he meet up with anybody else, any friends from his past, anybody he might have met while he was walking outside?'

Megan thought and shook her head. 'No. I don't think so. What sort of person are you thinking of?'

'Someone, a boy, of about his own age.'

'No. Nobody like that. He had no friends like that around here. He had kept in touch with some school friends, writing to them and making the occasional telephone call, but they never came here and he never went to see them. Mr Wallace didn't encourage him to socialise. I'm sure he never met anybody after he came back. He were in a world of his own by then.'

'You never saw anyone like that hanging around the house, before or after he came back?'

'Oh no. Nobody that I noticed anyway. Why do you ask?'

'Oh, nothing. I just wondered. Going back to what I was saying, about selling the house. There's something I need to do first. I need to spend some time here on my own.'

Megan gasped. 'But why, for God's sake? You, alone, in this dreadful old place, haunted by all that's happened here? After all you've been through?'

'That's the point, Megan. It's haunted. And I need those echoes of the past to help me get my memories back. I've been thinking that you need to get away for a while. I'm sure your niece in Truro would love to have you over for a few days. She's always inviting you, so you keep saying.'

Megan's eyes sparkled. 'And I suppose that's the deal?'

'The deal?'

'You don't do anything about selling the house and getting away yourself until I go away and leave you alone for a while.'

Madeleine sighed. 'You've got it in one, Megan. I should have known I couldn't slip anything past you.'

'I'll need to think about it. And I can't do that without another cup of tea and a nice piece of my home-made cake.'

Megan left the parlour and went through to the kitchen. As she rummaged in the cake tin she shook her head slowly. Then with a sudden movement she slammed the cake tin shut.

Come on, Megan, she said to herself. It'll be best for her to do it the way she wants. You can't do it for her. I will go and see Linda. Now, what about that tea. And there's jobs to be done afterwards. All this wondering and dithering won't get the baby a new bonnet.

She put two slices of cake on a plate and walked slowly back to the parlour.

143

*

'Megan, your taxi's here.'

Madeleine was waiting by the front door. After a minute, Megan shuffled through the door and down the porch steps.

'Here, let me take that for you.' Madeleine picked up her tiny suitcase and walked beside her. 'Are you sure you have enough things?'

'I don't have anything else to take. And if I need anything, Linda can get it for me. Are you really sure you'll be all right here on your own? I'm used to it, but for someone who's been through what you have, I'm still not at all sure it's the right thing.'

'I'll be fine, honestly. We've been through this many times. It's what I need to do. And you've been cooped up here for too long. It'll do you good to spend a couple of weeks away. I'll ring you at Linda's.'

'Every night?'

'Every night.'

'And if you want me back sooner you just let me know and I'll be here in two shakes of a lamb's tail.'

'I know. I'll let you know, I promise. Now off you go. The meter's running.'

Megan shook her head, sighed, hugged Madeleine and lowered herself gingerly into the back seat of the taxi. Madeleine waved as the taxi disappeared round the bend of the driveway. She smiled with relief.

She walked into the room which had served Michael as a library and writing-room. Old books, mostly on art, philosophy and history, lined the walls from floor to ceiling, with spaces only for the Gothic windows and a huge open fireplace. If the books had been catalogued according to a system, only Michael had ever understood it. He always knew instantly where a book on any particular topic could be found. A rosewood cabinet contained his favourite brandies. She served herself a large glass and looked around the room. It was still exactly as he had left it, just like the rest of the house. Megan had preserved it like a museum.

Was it already a museum when David first came there, Celia's wheelchair installed in the hall as a permanent reminder of illness and death? Whatever Michael had expected of him, it could not have been the joy and laughter of a normal, happy child. She tried to imagine David newly arrived in that huge empty house, alone and frightened, trying to come to terms with his new life, a life without his mother, a life with a strange man whose voice and manner must have seemed so severe and distant. She tried to imagine his terror and grief. Did Alan understand nothing of that? Did he not understand that he had no reason whatsoever to resent David, to envy him, to hatch plots against his life?

Two sons, one part of Michael's life, however reluctantly, the other a secret. One loved, however clumsily, the other scorned or unknown. But had Alan made Michael aware of his presence? Had Michael spent the time she had lived with him there in dread of the knock on the door, in fear of the spurned son's revenge? If so he need not have worried. The revenge had already been taken. Had Alan hidden near the house, after David's death, looked through the windows into the study, watched Michael's head bend low with grief, his hair turn white, his body stiffen and waste away? If so, he would have known his revenge had been absolute.

21

October 1995

I've managed it! I got Megan away and now I'm alone here. I won't deny that I miss her and that I'm scared. There isn't another inhabited house round here for miles. Just me, the sea, the wind and the sky. And the sunsets. The weather's remarkably clear and calm for the time of year. Sometimes, in the evening, I sit outside the house, facing the sea, watching the sun go down. From time to time a walker might come by, along the path below, sometimes a whole group of them. I wave to them and they wave back. None of them stops for a chat. But at least there's some human contact.

Of course I'm not completely alone. The memories are here, plenty of them. Just not the ones I want, not yet. So I've taken up the notebook again, to see if it helps.

When I got back to England, after receiving Michael's letter, I wondered if I was doing the right thing. I wanted to go and see him. There were things I had to tell him which I couldn't put in a letter. But what effect would it have on him, seeing his old adversary again, after all he'd been through? I booked into a hotel in London and stayed there over Christmas and the New Year. Then in January I made up my mind. I took the train to Penzance, then a taxi. It was late at night when I arrived. I knew Megan would have gone to bed. Perhaps he would have done

146

as well. Even if he heard me he probably wouldn't open the door. I would go back to Penzance and call again the next day. I would telephone first and talk to Megan, sound her out, find out whether he would be willing to see me. But the taxi had gone. The nearest phone box was miles away. It was too late to try to walk to Porthhella and get a room at the inn there.

I decided to try the door. If there were no reply I would return to the main road and walk towards Land's End. I might be able to flag down a passing car and ask for a lift to the nearest phone box, or to a hotel that might still be open. If necessary I would walk to Land's End and back. It would be morning by then. My heart thumping, I walked up to the front door. There was a faint light through the stained glass of the library window. I pushed the bell. The noise seemed to echo through the whole building. I had decided to push it only once. I would wait five minutes. I was turning away when I heard slow footsteps, shuffling through the hall, the inner door creaking open, sounds of panting and sighing, then the groaning of the bolts being pulled back, one by one.

January 1987

He looked up at her, trying to catch his breath. His mouth hung open, a drop of saliva crawling from his lower lip down to his chin. She almost shook her head as if to say that she had come to the wrong house. Then in an instant she was aware how ridiculous that idea was. It had to be that house. So that shrunken, stooping figure with thin, white hair had to be Michael, though all her memories of him told her it could not be he.

'Madeleine,' he whispered. 'It's really you? You'd better come in. You'll catch your death out there. Push the bolts back, will you? Come into the library. There's still a fire there. Sorry I took so long to come to the door. My back's so bad these days it takes me forever just to get up out of my chair. I'm always short of breath. Megan's in bed. She never hears the front door at night. I couldn't imagine who it might be.'

She followed him through the hall, very slowly, keeping her distance from him, letting him have the space and time he needed as he leaned on his walking-stick and inched forward. Once in the library he sat down near the fire, wincing with pain, placed the walking-stick across his knees and signalled for her to sit down opposite him. There was a half-full balloon glass of brandy on a small table next to his chair. He picked it up and sipped from it, his hand shaking. Despite everything he still kept up appearances, she thought. His shirt and trousers were clean and pressed, and he wore his favourite bow tie. She sat down, still unable to find any words to start their conversation. To her relief he spoke first, after a minute's aching silence.

'Thank you for writing to me from Paris. You hadn't heard a thing? It was in the papers here. Not over there, I suppose.'

'Nothing. It was a dreadful shock. I just wanted to know how you were. How both of you were. Then I got your letter back. Was it really the same place?'

'Yes. Exactly where your mother fell. It is truly an accursed spot. So, Madeleine, how long has it been?'

'About six months. I left last June.'

'Only six months? In that time I've aged twenty years. As you can see. You haven't aged. Not at all. I'm pleased about that.'

'Do you mind me coming? I didn't want to write again. I could never have found the words. I'll go away if you want. Right now. Just say the word.'

'No, no, of course not. You must stay. We should talk. It will be good to talk, after all this time. Good of you to come all this way to see a sick old man. You must have a brandy. Help yourself. I've still got this one. My brandy's all I have these days.'

'Thanks, I will.' She walked over to the cabinet and served herself in a much smaller glass than Michael's. She shook her head. She realised she had made a mistake. Brandy should be drunk from a large glass, one like his, to appreciate the aroma, a man had told her once. She had not paid any attention. Brandy had never been one of her drinks. In the days when she had only drunk to achieve quick oblivion it had seemed a waste to drink something valued by connoisseurs. Now she had been afraid of giving herself too much of something so important to him, afraid of taking from a man she had hurt so deeply, a man who because of her was only a shadow of what he had been. But it was too late now. And she desperately needed a drink. Maybe he wouldn't notice the size of the glass, or if he did he would make allowances. She returned to her chair. She coughed as she took a small sip of the brandy, then relaxed as she felt the warmth spread through her limbs.

'So where have you been? I sold your cottage. I never heard from you so I had no idea where to send the money. I've still got a cheque made out to you in the bureau. Signed but not dated.'

'I've been travelling around aimlessly. Genoa, Venice, Verona, Paris, Marseilles, back to Paris. Michael, I am so sorry. What happened to David was my fault. As is what's happened to you.'

He shook his head. 'No, no. My fault. All mine. You did what I asked. You gave him up. I destroyed him. Over all the years before you ever met him. I put so much pressure on him. Tried to make him into the sort of artist he was never intended to be. Sent him to a school that was never right for him. At the time I told myself, an artist's life is tough. He needs to be able to cope. But he couldn't. I should have seen that.'

'That night after you came to see me in the cottage, I decided you were right. I had to get out of his life. I decided to leave. I was going to leave him a note. He returned and we quarrelled. Violently. He stormed out. I wrote you the note after that. I assumed he would come straight back here to you.'

'He did come back to me. After a week.'

'A week! Oh my God.'

'I reported it to the police. They told me to wait for a couple of days. I told them about you. I wondered if he had gone away with you. Thought your letter might just have been a trick to put me off the scent. They tried to contact you but couldn't find you. You weren't at the cottage. Your London flat had been sold. Your solicitor didn't have an address abroad for you. The police said they would keep a lookout around here, but they were sure he had run away with you. There was nothing I could do. I had forgotten to tell them that his passport was still here in the bureau. I'd forgotten that myself.

'When he came back he couldn't tell us where he had been. He had had a dreadful breakdown. He had lost his memory. He didn't know who I was. He could only have found his way back through some sort of homing instinct. He couldn't draw or paint any more. He had forgotten that he ever had. He didn't recognise his own works when I showed them to him. The doctor told me he was suffering from amnesia, probably induced by a severe shock. But he seemed very content, almost serene. He was far more affectionate than he had been, to me and to Megan. He didn't say much, but he would follow us around. He helped Megan to prepare and serve the meals, though he ate very little himself. He sat with us at mealtimes and smiled at us. He helped me go for walks outside. He wasn't the same person. He was easier to love, God forgive me. But it was impossible to know what was going on in his mind. He was a stranger.'

'How did the accident happen?'

'He started to go on long walks on his own. I watched him at first from the house, and Megan would follow him a little. But it seemed safe. He never went near the dangerous parts of the path. Sometimes I would follow him from a distance and find him sitting and looking out to sea. It was always the same spot. He was looking at a view he had often drawn. I thought it would help him to remember. He seemed strangely happy. I didn't want to disturb him by taking him away. I didn't want him among strangers, in one of those awful hospitals, drugged like a zombie. Now I wish I had taken him away. To somewhere where he would have been safe. Away from the sea and away from the cliffs.

'One day he went out in the morning and came back as usual. Then the next morning he was missing. He must have left in the night. He had never gone out in the dark before, so I hadn't thought to lock his room. He never knew whether it was morning or afternoon, or even day or night. We called the police immediately. They checked the coastal path. Just by where your mother fell they noticed part of the earth had fallen away very recently. There was a torch there. One of ours. I think he must have been standing there and the earth gave way underneath him.'

He fell silent, staring into the fire. His head was bowed. His shoulders shook.

'I'll go now, Michael. I wanted to come in person to say how sorry I was but I only seem to have made matters worse. I'd like to take some flowers, pay my last respects. Where should I . . .?'

'Take them to St Olave's. The family plot next to your mother's grave. His inscription is on the same stone as Celia's. You can leave them there. There'll be another inscription there soon, the last one.'

'I'll go there tomorrow. Stay there, Michael. I know it hurts you to stand. Where do you sleep?'

'Next door. It's my bedroom now.'

'Do you get any visitors?'

'I've no family left now. The last was an aunt of mine. She died a few years ago. Sometimes an art lover with a long memory comes to pay his respects. I'm still something of a curio in these parts.'

'Do you want to go to bed now? Can I help you?'

'No, thank you. I don't sleep much. I go to bed about three in the morning. When the brandy starts to have some effect. Did you come by car?'

'No. Taxi.'

'Still there?'

'No. I sent it away. I didn't think about what I would do if nobody answered the door.'

'You can't walk out into the cold and dark like that. Stay here.

151

I'll get Megan up to fix something up for you in one of the spare bedrooms.'

'No. Don't disturb her. I'll doze here by the fire, if that's all right. Leave in the morning. Go back to Paris, I suppose.'

'Is there anything in Paris for you? Or anybody?'

She smiled. 'No, Michael. Nobody. It's just . . . where I ended up. So I might as well go back there as anywhere.'

'Of course. Why not? But stay here for tonight. Here by the fire, if that's what you want. Close your eyes now. You look exhausted.'

She was awoken by the morning light through the window, fragmented by the stained glass into a rainbow of colours which streamed across the carpet. She was alone. Somebody had put a blanket across her knees. Had he wakened Megan and told her about their unexpected guest? Very quietly she rose and stepped into the hall. Not a sound. She tiptoed to the door, eased back the bolts and closed the door behind her. She trudged up the driveway. A thin layer of snow which had fallen during the night crackled under her feet.

There was a bus stop near the top of the driveway. She looked at the timetable. There were only two buses a day, but by luck one was due in an hour. There was no bus direct to St Olave's but this one would take her to a village within an hour's walk. The bus was punctual to the minute. She was the only passenger. After the bus had dropped her in the main street of the village she walked round but could find nowhere to buy flowers. A few more weeks and early spring flowers would arrive from the Scillies. But not yet. She would have to go empty-handed. Perhaps she might find some snowdrops to pick in the nearby woodland.

An hour later she stood by her mother's grave. It was first time she had visited it since the funeral. The grave had been carefully tended. A bouquet of tiny white snowdrops in a vase had been placed there recently. She had intended after the funeral to ask

Michael if he would arrange for the grave to be maintained at her expense. She had forgotten but obviously he had done it anyway. Perhaps at first he had tended the grave himself, while looking after Celia's at the same time. But who had been coming there now Michael was ill? Who had placed the snowdrops there? Was it now part of Megan's regular duties? Or had they made arrangements with someone who lived locally?

She moved on to the white marble stone by the neighbouring grave and read the new inscription. She looked up and around the graveyard. The thin layer of snow sparkled in the pale winter sun. Her constant companions, the grey shadows and the black hooded figure standing behind them, were a few yards away, clustered under an oak-tree whose lower branches seemed to gather them together in its grotesque arms. Apart from the shadows she was alone.

Is this why you are always with me? Because I came between them? Or is it something else? Something from deep in the past, something I've forgotten? Something you want me to remember? Will you go away if I do? No, I know you'll never leave me. Do you torment Michael as well? No. His memories are all too vivid. He doesn't need you. He can see his guilt all too clearly. We belong together in that house. We're two of a kind. Two guilty creatures, waiting for death. I won't go back to Paris. I belong up there, with him.

She caught her breath and whirled round, sure she had heard the crunch of a footstep on the snow. There was nobody there.

22

October 1995

Yes, even then, before Laura, I knew I had a guilty secret. The therapist told me I had two locked doors in my mind. Laura was one. Behind her lay a second door, much older. The key to Laura's door also opens the other.

When I came back to these parts, after my release, I thought I could detach myself from my memories as they returned. I thought it would be like watching another person. As if the memories which led to the killing were no longer part of me. Now I know I was wrong. The truth is that I am terrified. I know that what happened in that room with Laura unlocked the second door, just for a moment, before I slammed both of them shut. If I bring back the memories of Laura I will release those ancient, buried demons once again. Will I then forget again? No. The defences cannot withstand a second attack. I might be sane for a moment, fully conscious of my guilt, seeing all the horrors I will have unleashed. But that sort of sanity leads inevitably to madness. Or I will plunge straight away into insanity, never having the chance to look myself in the eye and say, this is what you are and this is what you did.

I wake many times in the night, sweating, crying out that I cannot bear to face what is coming, that I must run away. But I know it is too late. I have chained myself in here, and the memories I cannot yet see prowl and growl around me. I can hear them, in the walls, in the gables, in the chimney pots. They are huddling together, grouping, gathering strength. Soon the walls in my mind will crumble and they will come for me.

In the meantime, back to my story. I came here to live with Michael, to see if I could restore to him some of the life I had taken away. We were two of a kind, both under sentence of death. But we deceived each other. I told him nothing about my condition. He appeared to recover, at least in part, but I think he was only making an effort for my sake. We knew it could not last. Time crawled along. It was as if we were locked into a perpetual winter. Finally the spring and then the summer arrived, seasons he had never expected to see again. We could even go out for short walks. And sometimes, when we stopped to rest, he was in a mood to talk.

July 1987

She helped Michael towards the bench set against the rock. Michael sat down gratefully, panting, placing his walking-stick across his knees. Though it had been a very warm, still day, he wore his waistcoat, jacket and bow tie. They watched the sun until it settled on the water, scattering blood reds among the blues, greens and turquoises of the water in the bay beneath them.

'You know, Madeleine, I used to think nothing of walking along the coastal path all the way to Porthhella and back, sometimes twice a day. Now I can barely make it this far. It's not practical for someone in my condition to live around here. And then there are the memories. But I couldn't move away from here, not now. I'm bound to the place. Part of the landscape. And there are times when I feel as ancient as these granite rocks.'

'How did you first come to live out here?'

'I came to Cornwall after the army and art school. Other artists had discovered it long before me. There is a very special quality to the light here. I rented studio space in Penzance. I knew the town slightly. Two of my aunts had settled there and I had visited them occasionally. I soon began to be noticed. I gave my first solo exhibition in the town hall. Celia and her parents attended. Her parents expressed an interest in buying some of my works. All the ones on display which were for sale had already gone. I told them I had more and promised to take them round to show them. That was how Celia and I got to know each other.

'We lived in Penzance when we first married. The marriage set the seal on my success. For generations her family were substantial landowners here. Her parents were widely respected for their work in the community. They were good people. They didn't remain aloof from the social and industrial changes around them. They set up charities for former tin-miners and fishermen and their families. They worked tirelessly to bring new industries into the area. They helped widows and orphans. Her father was mayor for a time. He disapproved of me at first, as a partner for Celia I mean. Later he decided that he could make something respectable out of me if he could keep me away from my painting for long enough. He helped me to secure a seat on the council. I became involved with charitable work. I was appointed to various committees. My motives were not at all altruistic. My artistic reputation grew with my standing as a pillar of the community. Celia was a perfect social wife and hostess. She organised my exhibitions. She arranged press conferences and previews. To the outside world we were a couple who radiated success and prosperity.

'On the inside, things were rather different. Celia provided me with a social cachet which was very important to me. The life of a painter can be a lonely and difficult one. Even when there is critical acclaim, there is often social scorn. It is not considered an entirely respectable way of life. I yearned for respect as a member of society. When I became Celia's husband, it was awarded to me overnight. I enjoyed my new status. I used it to spread my reputation. I needed it and welcomed it. At the same time, I resented it. The price was high. I had to develop a social persona with which I was often uncomfortable and which interfered with my work. I bought this house to give myself the space and solitude I required to paint. We kept our house in Penzance as a base for our community activities. Soon we began to spend more and more time apart. She stayed in Penzance, maintaining the social fabric of our marriage. I stayed here.'

'You never had any children?'

'Her parents were anxious that we should have children soon, but it soon became clear that we never would. Our doctor carried out tests. The fault, in medical terms, was Celia's. She became deeply depressed. Soon after that, he diagnosed in her the early symptoms of multiple sclerosis. Strangely, it was only then that I think I began to love her. She had done everything for me. I had felt resentful. Soon she would be dependent on me. We lived here quietly. Celia was still able to act as an efficient and charming hostess, though sometimes she would be exhausted for hours afterwards. Soon she would need to withdraw altogether from our social rounds. That prospect did not trouble me. I looked forward to it. I looked forward to the time when we could be alone together in this house and I would look after her. I had tired of the shallow society to which I had once yearned to belong.'

'How did you come to meet my mother?'

'It was like I told you at the funeral. I used to love to walk over to Porthhella from here and just wander around, soaking up the atmosphere. It was so relaxing after Penzance. I never knew who I would run into there. In Porthhella nobody knew me. I was fascinated by the old capstan house. When it came up for sale I bought it and converted it into a gallery. Brenda Rogers helped me, then she took it over. I met your mother there. I had gone over to see the work of some new artist Brenda had discovered. We met for coffee sometimes, in the cafe on the seafront. I think she was a bit lonely and enjoyed having someone to chat to. That was all.'

'Could you tell me about David's parents? If it won't upset you too much to talk about it?'

'I don't mind talking about it now. George was an engineer. He was a painter as well. A gifted amateur, you could say. He liked to experiment and try out new things. He had a very good feel for colour. He wasn't strong in the technical department. Couldn't draw to save his life. When I came to live here on the bay, George moved in with us for a while. He had been working in India. He was looking for somewhere to live. He had met a French girl in India, Sandrine. They had a relationship there, but she had broken it off. He came home. Sandrine returned to France and got in touch with him again. He went over to see her and they got engaged. They were married in France. David was born in Lyons. I hardly ever saw them. I was too busy with my life here. Celia was already sick.

'Two years after the wedding they died. They had been out to celebrate their anniversary, at one of those famous country restaurants. On the way back they collided with a lorry on a narrow road. They were killed instantly. David was with a babysitter. I went over to France to arrange their funeral and settle their affairs. That took months. Bloody French bureaucracy. Had to arrange for a nurse to take care of Celia. She wasn't too bad then. I brought David back to England, but with Celia getting worse all the time I couldn't move him in with us. He stayed with various relatives. When Celia died I brought him to live here.'

'I wanted to thank you for looking after her grave, by the way. My mother's, I mean. I had meant to mention it at the funeral but it slipped my mind.'

'It was hardly any trouble. Hers and Celia's being next door to each other. It was as easy to do both as to do one. And I couldn't have done Celia's and neglected hers, not with it right under my nose. Of course I couldn't do it any more when I fell ill. Megan carried on with the arrangements, bless her, using the same taxi service every month. It's such a relief that I'm well enough now to go back there myself, with your help.'

'But you did my mother's before Celia died.'

'Why not? I wanted to help you. I also felt it was my responsibility. It was my idea that she should be buried there. And to
tell you the honest truth, it was a relief to have an excuse to get
out of the house. That's another reason why I looked after her
cottage as well.'

'Didn't Celia mind?'

'No. I didn't tell her the whole story. I told her someone I knew
in London had bought a cottage here and had asked me if I
could find a managing agent. I said I had offered to do the job
myself, to take up some of my spare time. I was with her day
and night for most of the time. She couldn't object. Not when
we had a live-in nurse to look after her clinical needs.'

'Well, thank you anyway.'

'Now I want to raise something with you. That's why I asked
you to come out here with me. You can't deflect me from my
purpose by getting me to talk all the time.'

'Go on.'

'When you came back here that night and went away again I
presumed I'd never see you again. You came back the next day,
after you'd been to the churchyard. You said you'd been worried
about me. You asked Megan to make you up a bed for a couple
of nights. That was more than six months ago.'

'And I'm still here. Are you sorry I stayed?'

'Hardly. Look at me, for God's sake. Megan keeps saying that
you pulled me back out of the grave. She's right. I thought I was
dying. That night you came, I expected to live only a few weeks
if that.'

'You're still very ill, Michael. Your heart, your back. You have
to be very careful.'

'It wasn't me I wanted to talk about. You mustn't stay any
longer. You're still young and beautiful.'

'And you're still a flatterer, Michael. A gentleman, but a flatterer.'

She knew the truth. Every day the mirror told her what Michael

159

would not. She too was ageing rapidly. She knew when it had begun. That night in the dirty little hotel near Marseilles. And with each day spent in that house with Michael the process continued relentlessly.

'Sometimes you have to be one to be the other. But I'm not trying to flatter you. I was an artist, remember. I know beauty when I see it. You have your life ahead of you. Why don't you go off and live it? Away from here. Don't worry about me. My time will come when God wills. Don't waste yourself. You're so like your mother to look at. But there's something of hers you've lost. There was a wildness in her eyes, a vitality in her gestures, her walk, her laugh. Something flowed in her veins which is not there in yours. A moment in her company and you felt more intensely alive. That quality must be there in you. And I'm stopping you from finding it again.'

'But was she always like that, when you knew her?'

'Why do you ask?'

'Because it doesn't fit in with what the police showed me when I went to identify the body. Her clothes . . . it was awful. All worn and shabby, much too big for me, and I was supposed to be just like her. And her face . . . so worn and thin. I suppose that happens to all corpses. But she really must have aged, let herself go. She couldn't have been the way you describe. Not then. Not towards the end. Did you know her all the time she was here, right up to the time of her death?'

'Not really. Now I think of it, it had been some years since I had last met up with her. Of course I had to spend more and more time with Celia, as her illness got worse. So I can't really say what was happening to your mother then. But when I knew her, she certainly had that quality of life. It was so powerful I can't imagine anything which could have destroyed it. You must have it too. Go away from here and try to rediscover it. Be selfish. You have money. Go and enjoy it. Get back to the Mediterranean. I always loved it there. The sun, the laughter, the people living for today. That's what you need. Forget what happened here. You weren't to blame for anything. You and David . . . that was outside your control. Leave me here to grieve for him. I can grieve for both of us. If you were trying to make it up to us you've done that. If you ever owed us anything you've repaid it a hundred-fold. You will think about it? Do you promise me?'

'All right. I'll promise to think about it. Now let's get back for tea. Megan's waving from the window. Give me your arm.'

The months passed, the routine unchanged, except that Michael's trips out of doors became ever shorter and rarer. Autumn and winter came again, though they were by then barely aware of the passage of time. The anniversary of her return to the house came and went, unnoticed and unremarked.

One night in early spring she was sitting with him until after midnight as usual. The fire was nearly dead. Her eyes were closing, the words of the book she was reading no more than a blur. Michael's glass slipped from his hand. He slumped forward as if struck from behind. Suddenly she was wide awake. She rushed over to him, eased his head back and felt his pulse. There was saliva in the corner of his mouth. His eyes rolled, unfocused.

'It's all right, Michael, I'll get help.'

She ran out into the hall and picked up the telephone. Then she went up to Megan's room and knocked on the door.

'Megan, are you awake?' There was a murmur from within. 'It's Mr Wallace. I've sent for an ambulance. I think he's had a stroke.'

'Who's that?' asked Megan, as they followed the coffin into St Olave's Church. Madeleine looked behind her. Brenda was standing outside the church a few yards behind them, her face pale and drawn, her eyes red and swollen. Madeleine waved to her to join them in the church. Brenda shook her head and stood her ground.

'It's Brenda Rogers. Michael's former assistant. I wish she'd come in. It's so empty, just you and me the only mourners.'

'I recognise her now. She came to the house a few times, many years ago. She's really changed. Looks much older. Suppose we all do. Except you.'

'Especially me, Megan.'

'Why won't she come in?'

'It's me. We've only met once. But I think she really hates me for some reason. Let's go in.'

They were glad to get inside. A numbing wind was sweeping through the little valley from the east, sending brown leaves swirling about their feet and rattling the weathercock on the church roof. Apart from Brenda they had seen only a local reporter and a small group of hikers who had taken a diversion from the coastal path in the hope of securing some respite from the gale. No former students or fellow artists had come to pay their respects. The Royal Academy had sent a printed card of condolence. There was a short obituary in one of the broadsheets. In the history of the art of his time he had long since been no more than a footnote.

For the second time in her life Madeleine was forced to listen to a fulsome tribute from the Reverend Colm O'Brien, who had visited Michael only twice since she had returned.

'Michael Wallace was an adopted child of the West Country. He will be remembered as a skilful artist who drew inspiration from the wild landscapes which surround us, who was a model to his pupils and fellow artists of hard work and devotion to self-improvement. He was rewarded by a success which many would envy, though he remained clear-headed and conscious of his limitations. The other aspects of his life were less well known, but give a far better indication of the real man. He sought no refuge in aesthetic ivory towers. With the help of his wife, Celia, he strove tirelessly to improve the lot of his fellow country dwellers, and to use the material wealth with which God had endowed him to protect them from the worst consequences of the decline in the well-being of their communities. When Celia became ill in the full bloom of her life, he nursed her devotedly until her tragic, premature death.

162

'Then, at a time when other men in that situation would have withdrawn into isolation and self-pity, he found a new outlet for his need to care for others. He took into his home his orphaned nephew, David, also a gifted artist. He shouldered the solitary burden of bringing him up, providing him with a good education, showing him by example how to lead a good and upright life, and using his own knowledge and experience to nurture his artistic talents. In his final days, the shadows of three tragedies lay across his life. He and Celia had not been blessed with children. Her illness and death had affected him to the extent that he gave up the creative work which had been the core of his life and which had given, and continues to give, so much pleasure to others. Then came the final, cruellest blow of all. The nephew he had come to love as his own son had also fallen prey to illness and had met with a tragic accident, aged only twenty and barely at the threshold of his own artistic career.

'In the face of adversities which would have overwhelmed most people, Michael Wallace remained stoical and courageous to the last. He accepted without complaint his long, debilitating last illness, at the end of which death came with merciful speed. God had given him many blessings and, for reasons which only He can understand, had chosen to take some of them from him. Michael Wallace did not question those actions of God. He accepted His will. As we today must accept it as we remember Michael and give thanks to God for his life.'

As the coffin was lowered, Brenda stood some distance away. When the final prayers had been said, Madeleine turned towards her but she had already left.

23

October 1995

I've missed something out, of course. Laura. She came to visit Michael, a few months before he died. I never spoke to her. She never saw me. But some eighteen months later I went to see her and I killed her. I'm sure now that Michael never mentioned her to me, never asked me to visit her, never left any papers in the house about her. Why should he? So how did I find out who she was and where to find her?

Last night it came back to me. I made up the fire in the library and sat there in my usual chair, opposite Michael's, as I had each evening during his long and slow decline. I fetched myself a brandy as I had always fetched his and mine. During the evening he would drink three or four glasses, while I sipped just a few drops, enough to be sociable. We rarely talked. We sat there, with each successive evening wrapping the shades of the house ever more closely around us, becoming part of its rotting fabric. I would choose a book for him and one for myself. I would pretend to read and glance up at him from time to time. I had long since lost the ability to concentrate on a book.

Last night, after half an hour, I moved over to his chair. I took his place. I went back in time to the evening he had sat there, waiting for a knock on the door, even though it was late, long past the time when Megan and I would usually be in bed. Finally it came. Three sharp knocks on the front door. Not the bell. She had been told not to ring the bell. The hall and library doors had been left open to allow the sound of the knocks to carry to him but no further. But for some reason I was unusually restless that night. I couldn't sleep. I decided to go down to the kitchen and make myself a hot chocolate. I was crossing the landing when I heard the knocks.

December 1987

She caught her breath and stopped. Nobody could possibly be expected at that hour and the very few casual visitors only came during daylight hours. After a few minutes, to her intense surprise, she heard the sound of the bolts being drawn back. Surely Michael would not be so foolish as to open the door to a stranger? She moved quickly to the top of the stairs and was about to shout down to him when she saw the visitor. She had followed Michael into the hallway. She wore a thick, light-brown overcoat and a felt hat of the same colour. She was tall and upright. Her face was pale and strained. Her cheeks were sunken and her eyes bright. Madeleine judged her to be in her sixties, but illness could have aged her prematurely. He took her hat and coat and hung them on one of the hooks just inside the hallway. They looked at each other. Madeleine stayed at the top of the stairs, her hand on the banister. Neither Michael nor the visitor had noticed her presence.

'Well, Laura,' said Michael, after a pause which seemed to stretch to infinity. He was not smiling. 'It really is you. You still call yourself Laura, do you? You didn't change your name when you started your new life down under? Somehow I imagined you would.'

'I've nothing to hide. Unlike you. Laura James is my name.'

'You were Laura Peters when we knew each other.'

'You've obviously forgotten that James is my maiden name. I changed back to it when I went to Australia. I have no particular wish to remember my husband.'

'How long have you been back?'

'Four weeks. I'm staying with Naomi, my sister-in-law, in Portsmouth. She's on her own and doesn't mind company, even when the company's a sick old woman like me. We always got on very well. She never married, wise woman. Well, Michael? Are you going to ask me in or do I have to stand here in the hallway all night? Don't look so scared. You've nothing to fear from me. I'm not here to destroy you. It looks as if someone or something has already done that.'

'I'm sorry, Laura. I mustn't forget my manners. Please come on in.'

Laura walked slowly past Michael into the library. He followed her and closed the door behind them. Madeleine thought for a few moments. Michael had obviously been expecting Laura and had arranged the visit for a time when he could keep it a secret. That was his business. There was nothing in Laura's manner to suggest that she intended him any harm. So she would leave them alone. But she was still intent on the hot chocolate she had promised herself. She trod softly down the stairs. As she passed the door she heard a snatch of conversation. She paused, rooted to the spot. It was Michael who was speaking.

'You shouldn't have come back, Laura. We had an agreement, remember? You accepted the terms at the time. You agreed it was for the best. You went away. Nobody forced you. You should have stayed away.'

'So that's what you would call it. An agreement. I would call it undue pressure and influence for improper reasons. You lied to me, manipulated me, then bribed me, turning me into a shadow, then into somebody who had never existed. I wasn't strong enough to stand up to you. I wish to God I had. I wish I had never gone away, and I wish I had never taken your money. I wish I had done what was right. But you weren't bothered about what was right, were you? You were worried about your precious reputation. You wanted to avoid a scandal.'

'You know there was more to it than that. All right, maybe that was my main concern at first. But later, things changed. I wanted to do the right thing by the child.'

'The right thing? We're talking about my child, Michael, mine. Not just yours. Don't you think I was the one who was in the best position to say what was right?'

'You can't do anything about all this now. It's too late for all of us. So why did you come back?'

'I intended to come a few years ago. Even though you had told me not to. I was never sure I could trust you. I wanted to see for myself. Then you wrote to me with the news. How he had lost his mind, fallen off the cliffs. There was no point in me coming. I fell ill soon after that. Then my sister died. I had no reason to stay there. I wrote to Naomi and told her about my circumstances. I was sick and alone, in a country I had never liked, where I would never have chosen to be. She invited me to come and stay with her. After I had been there a few days I began to think about you, now you were only a few miles away instead of on the other side of the world. So I thought I would drop by. Just out of curiosity. I wanted to see you before the end, see what had become of you.'

'Curiosity? Or revenge? Are you sure you didn't come to gloat?'

'No, not revenge. I'm sorry to see you like this. My God, how you've changed. I've aged as well, I know. That's the illness. I've fought it for years and now I've no fight left. I've brought you this as well.' There was a rustle of paper. 'It's what's left over from the money you paid me. Most of it's still there. I lived very frugally.'

'Keep it. I've no use for it.'

'No. It's no use to me now. It never was any use. It poisoned me, contaminated me. I could never look at it or think of it without thinking of what I gave up for it. Now I'm paying the price for what I did.'

'What are you going to do?'

'Nothing. What I know is of no interest or use to anybody now. You won't see me again or hear from me. I'll go back to Portsmouth. It won't be long now. I know I don't look too bad. But the doctors in Australia said it would be only a few months. Perhaps a year.'

Madeleine heard her rising laboriously to her feet. She padded carefully away from the door and up the stairs.

October 1995

Yes, I listened to them at the door. That was how I found out that Laura was David's mother. That was how I learned that Michael had lied to me about David's parentage and early life.

My God, that poor woman! Sent to the other side of the world because Michael wanted her out of the way. She had only come back to die in peace. And I even took that away from her. How did I locate her? Through her sister-in-law. Naomi. Laura had said she had never married. She was Naomi Peters. As Laura's married name had been Peters. I looked up Naomi Peters in the Portsmouth directory. A year after the funeral, I went to Portsmouth to see her. And there the trail of my memories still goes cold.

24

She put down her pen and shut the notebook. She stood up and opened the cupboard. It was still there. The folder of 12 ink drawings David had made of her, together with *The Assumption*. After she had moved in with Michael she had asked her bank to forward them to her. She had put them away unopened. She had sent for them because she knew she needed to feel their presence. But she was very anxious that Michael should not even suspect they were in the house. If Michael had asked she would have told him she had destroyed them. To her relief he never did ask and she assumed he had forgotten about them. As the months went by she forgot about them herself.

She pulled out *The Assumption*, forcing herself to look at it. With a sudden cry she let it fall to the floor and sank to her knees. She gasped for breath. She could feel hands on her body, burning into her flesh, pulling her down. Her fingers clutched at her throat as if trying to loosen the grip of an unseen attacker.

After a minute she found her breath and struggled to her feet. She picked up the drawings and put them back into the folder. What had happened? It had felt like a nightmare from which she was trying to force herself to awaken. But she was sure she had been awake. Was it another returning memory? If so, was it the memory of a dream or of something which had really happened? Or was it simply a physical reaction to the drawing, a moment of terrifying identification with the scene for which she had served as a model?

As she put the folder down, she noticed there was another object on the cupboard floor. A spool of tape from an old-fashioned tape recorder. Only a museum now would have a machine on which it could be played. She had always kept the tape, but could never remember who had given it to her or what was on it. She had only known that it was important and that she had promised to keep it. She had brought it with her when she first moved to Cornwall. It had accompanied her on her travels through France and Italy, resting at the bottom of whatever bag she was using as her luggage.

Suddenly she felt overwhelmed by fatigue. She lay down on the bed and closed her eyes.

When she woke up the glimmerings of a grey dawn already hung around the room. She had forgotten to draw the curtains. She must have fallen asleep on the top of the bed, fully dressed. But she remembered having been in bed, between the sheets, in her new pink cotton nightdress. A different bed, a different room. A single bed, in a tiny, reassuringly bright and cosy room. Pink wallpaper with images of flowers. A room with no space for monsters to hide and frighten her in the night. Of course now she was 13 she was no longer afraid of monsters. She had heard the footsteps outside. They didn't matter. She knew that in her room she was safe. She snuggled further down the bed until the top sheet almost covered her, hugging her pillow, breathing into it, feeling the fresh crispness against her cheek.

She stopped breathing when she heard the voice. 'Are you awake, Madeleine?' Heard but did not see the handle turn, because she had screwed her eyes so tightly shut that it hurt.

25

For early October it had been unusually hot and still for several days. By the next evening it had turned sultry. Charley, George and Samuel stood by the lifeboat station looking out to sea. Over the horizon, just to the north of the Scillies, a black landscape of cloud massed in bizarre towers like a demon kingdom rising from the sea. After half an hour, during which time none of them had moved a muscle, another black cloud, flat like the underside of a huge alien spaceship, settled directly overhead, moving imperceptibly from the land behind the village. The two cloud masses, one turreted, the other flat, faced each other like opposing armies across the intervening miles of water and stood their ground. The water was like glass.

'Storm's brewing,' said Samuel at last.

'I would never put out when it were like this,' said George. 'Reckon it'll be like that one where your Tommy got lost.'

'Aye,' said Charley. 'Next day the boat was cast up between those headlands, all in splinters. No sign of him or the rest of the crew.'

'Always a bad sign, when the water's as still as that,' said Samuel.

'Some sort of trouble's stirring,' said George.

'At least that murderess has gone.'

'Not really. I hear she's back up at the big house. God knows what she's doing there but she's up to no good, I'll swear. And whatever it is, that witch is in it with her. They were talking together once late at night in the witch's cottage, so I hear. Definitely trouble ahead.'

They nodded in unison and walked slowly along to the inn.

Brenda watched them out of the corner of her eye as she opened the door to her cottage. Once inside, she walked over to the sideboard and took out the bracelet. She sat down on the sofa, turning the bracelet over in her hand, running her fingers around the edge.

So, Madeleine, how are you getting on up there, all on your own in that dreadful place? I hear you sent Megan away. So the deliveryman from the grocery tells me. He also told me you're still in one piece, or you were when you answered the door to him the other day. Have you remembered anything? Are you any closer to knowing what I did? When can I expect your next knock on the door? Whatever you decide to do to me, I'll deserve it.

What did I get in the end for all my efforts? This trinket I stole as a trophy. Trophy of what? She won in the end. Even the way she died was a triumph. It guaranteed she would always be remembered, even by people who never knew her. Who will ever remember me at all? Oh yes, she was that bitter old woman who ran the gallery and looked down her nose at everybody and died alone one night in her little cottage. She was always a bitter old woman. Even when she was young. What else did I get? Enough money to stay on here, not enough to let me get away and start a new life somewhere else. That pathetic little gallery. The contempt of my neighbours. Well, the feeling is mutual. What did I get from him? His grudging gratitude. And his final rejection. And the knowledge that what I did set in motion a chain of tragedies that I was powerless to stop.

She put the bracelet away and walked upstairs to her bedroom. She stared at herself in the mirror.

I got this as well, of course. A face which with every passing year is more lined with bitterness and hate. If her death had

172

really set me free I wouldn't have had to look at a face like this in the mirror every day. Yes, I would like to be set free. But there's only one way that can happen now. I have to confess. To her! To the woman I hated almost as much as the one who came before her. Christ, I need to get out of here. I really would like to find that tramp and talk to him. I have an idea where he might be staying.

It was still early evening as she threaded her way through the maze of cottages which led to the coastal path. She was surprised to find it stiflingly warm. She wished she had left her coat indoors. By the time she reached the observation point she was panting hard. A few days before, she had seen the tramp in the distance moving towards it, his step rapid and sure, too rapid for her to catch up. She would only get a chance to talk to him if she could catch him at home.

She stooped beneath the low doorway and stood inside what was left of the building. Cigarette ends, used matchsticks, sweet wrappers and empty lemonade bottles littered the floor. There was also a newspaper. Greasy and dirty but quite recent. A headline caught her attention. She picked it up gingerly. It was open at an article about Madeleine's release. There was a blurred photograph of her face, barely recognisable, probably taken at the time of her arrest. There were other photographs, one of the house and one of the cliff where Ceridwen and David had fallen. She read through the article.

Over decades this wild beauty spot in the extreme West of Cornwall has lived under the shadow of a terrible curse. Nobody knows the original cause. Twenty-two years ago a woman called Ceridwen Williams fell from these cliffs to her death hundreds of feet below. Thirteen years later, the nephew of famous local artist, Michael Wallace, went mad and fell from exactly the same spot. Mr Wallace died soon afterwards of grief. But even then the curse had not run its course. The daughter of Ceridwen

Williams, Madeleine Reed, had lived with Michael during the final months of his life. After living on her own for months in that house of sickness, madness and death she too fell prey to madness, committing the senseless killing of a dying woman. Miss Reed has spent years in a secure hospital. This paper interviewed her on her release last month. She still cannot remember the killing or what drove her to it. She told us she was intending to return to the same part of the country, though she doubted if she could ever bring herself to live in the house again. Is some strange malign Fate drawing her back? Does the curse still have further to run, or has the evil finally spent itself? Only time will tell.

Brenda snorted. So, I was right, she said to herself. It's you, isn't it? You're the man who's been talking to her, spinning her stories. Nothing but an old tramp. This is where you've set up home. You found the newspaper, read the article and that started your imagination going. You came here. You recognised her and started to follow her. Or . . . maybe you really are who you say you are. There's something not quite right about you. I never knew an old man walk as quickly as you do.

She stepped outside, looked out to sea, saw the leaden clouds gathering over the Scillies. Looks as if there's a storm coming up. Better get back.

Madeleine too had noticed the change in the weather. She had put out a chair on the patch of sand and coarse grass on the seaward side of the house, hoping to watch the sunset. There would be none that evening. Time to go indoors. She made herself a cold snack, ate it in the kitchen and walked through to the library.

After half an hour she heard a distant boom of thunder. Then another, much closer. There was a pitter-patter of rain against the panes. She got up, stepped into the hall and stood there in the dark. Her hand searched for the light switch. She found it and flicked it. Nothing. She swore. Always happens round here during storms. Bloody power cut. Then the knock on the door.

This time it was an insistent hammering. Not Laura's almost apologetic knock. She ran to the door, pulled back the bolts and swung it open. Nobody. Her bones froze. She was sure that what she had heard was nothing to do with her lost memories. It came from a time before she had ever seen the house. Why not? The ghosts from her own time were not the only ones to haunt that house. But why now? And why had it responded to her presence, whatever it was?

Outside, on the path leading by the side of the house, she heard running footsteps. Running past the house, onto the coastal path, in the dark and the rain. From here. Suddenly she knew.

'It was you, Mother, wasn't it?' she shouted. 'That's why I heard your knock just now. It was you. You came here. And you ran from here. Not from the cottage. From here. On a night just like this.'

She rushed outside, still in her pullover and jeans. She turned left and ran up the path, the rain and wind lashing against her face. She thought she could see movement ahead of her on the path, but in the darkness it took no discernible shape. Then the wind brought a sharp cry to her ears. She ran on, here slipping off the path onto the grassy seaward slope, there grazing her knee against the rock on the other side. Now she was on level ground. She could hear the crashing of waves against the rocks. Then another cry. Possibly a seagull.

She turned around again to face the sound of the waves. She stepped forward, rainwater streaming down the inside of her blouse, her shoes squelching in the mud. Ahead, a jagged line, black against dark-grey. The cliff edge. She could just make out two silhouettes. One was standing right on the edge, its back to the void. Another stood in front of the first, gesturing. It seemed to be trying to coax the other forward, away from danger. The figure at the edge turned and held out a hand. Then Madeleine found herself facing the outstretched hand, holding up her own to meet it. Her back was to the sea. She was standing exactly where the first figure had been. Her heels were slipping in the mud. There was nothing underneath to support them. But it didn't matter. She was safe. The hand of the figure in front of her was reaching out to save her. All she had to do was let it take her hand and pull her back. Her hand tried to grasp the arm in front of her but found only air. It was too late. She was already falling, backwards, into the black emptiness. She let out a piercing scream.

26

She was still breathing. Her hands could feel grass and slime. Rainwater poured into her open mouth. There were no sharp rocks, black and glistening with salt spray. The sea was still hundreds of feet below her. But she had felt everything. She even remembered the sensation of falling, the lurch of her stomach, her hands flailing helplessly, the cliff-top rushing up to the sky. The endless wait for final oblivion. She pushed herself upwards and into a kneeling position, feeling the mud yield beneath her. She was still some 20 yards from the edge, in the position where she had seen the two silhouettes.

She clambered to her feet and stumbled on down the path in the direction of Porthhella. The skies were gradually clearing, the rain abating. She kept her bearings from the distant glimmer of the lighthouse. The shadowy shapes of the sleeping village emerged at last, huddled beneath the cliffs as if taking shelter from the storm. She staggered to Brenda's door and knocked loudly.

'I've got to talk to you, Brenda.'

Brenda stood at the door, pulling on her dressing-gown.

'Hello, Madeleine. I've been expecting you. Though not at this hour in this weather. You must be soaked to the skin. You'd better come in and get dry.'

'I came by the coastal path.'

'What? You really are crazy. What are you trying to do? Follow your mother down the cliffs?'

'That's what I have been doing. Following her. Then, for a few moments, I was her.'

Brenda pushed Madeleine into her tiny bathroom and turned on the taps.

'Here, get those wet things off, and have a good hot soak. I'll get you a brandy and some dry clothes for you. Mine will probably fit you. Your figure isn't as full as it once was.'

She cast a critical eye down Madeleine's body as she undressed. Madeleine was too exhausted to mind the scrutiny.

'What are those marks?'

'What? Oh, those. I was in the hospital infirmary for weeks at a time. Some chest and lung infection I couldn't shake off. The nursing was a bit primitive. I got pressure sores. They're not as bad as they were. Most of the time I'm not aware of them.'

She stepped gingerly into the bath. Brenda picked the wet clothes up from the floor and carried them into the living room where she lit the log fire. Then she went into her bedroom, took off her dressing-gown and night dress and put on a bottle-green suit. It was her smartest outfit. She combed her hair and put on a touch of rouge. She checked the effect in the mirror.

A criminal facing a judge and jury should always look her best, so they say. I can never look much. But the least I can do is make an effort, out of respect for her, and Madeleine. A bit late to show respect, I know that. Well, here goes.

She returned to the living room, put Madeleine's clothes on a clothes horse in front of the fire, went over to her drinks cabinet and poured out two brandies. Carrying her dressing-gown over her arm she took one of the brandies into Madeleine, who was by then covered in warm water and foam, her eyes beginning to close.

'Here you are,' said Brenda. 'I think you need it. We both do.'

'Thanks,' Madeleine murmured. She took the brandy off Brenda, her hand still shaking.

'Take as long as you like. Wash your hair under the shower and come and dry it in front of the fire. Use my dressing-gown here until I can look out some proper clothes for you.'

Brenda hung the gown on a hook on the door, and returned to the living room. She swallowed her brandy in one gulp and refilled her glass. She sat, waiting.

An hour later, both women were seated in front of the fire, Madeleine wearing a loose matching tweed jumper and skirt which Brenda had given her. Her wet hair was gathered in a towel. She unwrapped the towel and let her hair hang loose before the fire. Steam began to rise. She rubbed her hair fiercely with the towel then wrapped it around her head and sat back in her chair.

Brenda stared at her for a full minute. Finally, their eyes met.

'You know, don't you?' she said.

Madeleine nodded.

'Thank God. You have no idea what a relief that is to me.'

'I came here tonight to get it out of you one way or the other. So go on. Tell me everything. I want to know what you and he did to her. First of all, I want to know how and when you knew that she was pregnant.'

27

'One evening Michael came to see me, just as I was closing the gallery. He was extremely agitated. Your mother was going to have a baby. There would be a scandal. He was a big cheese on the council in those days. And he was on all sorts of important committees to do with the arts. And then there was Celia. She was of a nervous disposition and her health was delicate. She would be devastated. Her family would make sure his name was mud in all the high circles he was now moving in. There might be a messy and expensive divorce. His career could be ruined. He had to fix an abortion. He did not know how to go about it. He did not want word to get around that he was doing it, or that would be even worse. I told him to calm down. I would sort everything out for him.

'When I first went to live in St Ives I shared a flat with a girl who had been to college in Portsmouth. She had become pregnant after a one-night stand and had decided to have an abortion there. I was still in touch with her. I rang her and asked her for the name and address of the doctor who had arranged it. She laughed and said she was surprised at me. She thought I was much too straight-laced to get into trouble the way she had. I didn't disabuse her. She told me the name and gave me the number. Smith, or Brown or something like that. Almost certainly not his real name. I didn't care. My friend told me he was the sort who didn't ask too many questions. That was enough for me. I rang

180

him and explained the circumstances. He said he would be very pleased to help. He gave me details of the clinic where it would take place.

'I went to see her. I had been looking forward to it so much. I introduced myself. She had been to the gallery so we had already met and exchanged a few words. I had been polite to her but no more. She smiled and invited me in. We went into the living room. That wretched picture of her was on the wall, where it still is.'

'It's definitely her? I was beginning to wonder, the last time I was in there. I never really noticed it before. Not being interested in pictures.'

'Oh yes, it was her all right. Drawn from life. Drawn in a way he had never drawn anybody before. She sat there, half-turned towards me, looking out to sea, ignoring me, feeling her belly from time to time, though it was still early days and there was nothing to show, looking all smug and serene. I was calm and business-like. There was no point in showing her how much I hated her. I was about to get my revenge. I was savouring every moment. I told her I was there on Michael's behalf. He had asked me to organise some things in connection with her pregnancy. It was a rather delicate matter so he could not come himself. In fact, he could not come at all. He could never see her again.

'I told her I was sure she did not want to ruin both their lives by staying there and letting the pregnancy continue. So he had authorised me to offer her an arrangement which would be greatly to her advantage. He would pay for her to have the preg-nancy terminated, at a clinic in Portsmouth. He would buy a house for her there, where she could go to live while she was waiting for the operation. Afterwards she could stay on there. Or she could ask him to sell the house and let her have the money so she could move somewhere else, so long as it was at least as far away. The only condition was that she must leave immedi-ately and never return to Porthhella. I would give her one more day, so she could pack her things. I would fetch her the next day.

181

She said nothing. The expression on her face never changed. I asked her if she had understood. She nodded. She was still sitting there when I left.

'When I went back the next day I thought I would have to explain it all again. But to my great surprise she was packed and ready to go. She smiled and got into the car. It was as if we were going somewhere for a day out. I had expected hysterics. I had at least expected a fight. This was almost too easy. I drove to Portsmouth, where I had booked single rooms for us in a small hotel. The next day, I took her to see my friend's doctor. There was another doctor there with him. I think he was Smith or Brown as well. They examined her and completed the paperwork. They asked her if she had ever been depressed. She said she had often been on antidepressants when she lived in Oxford. Was that true?'

'I don't know. It's possible. She was unhappy. I realise that now. She was suffocating, married to an older man wrapped up in his researches, stifled by the petty social niceties of the life of a don's wife.'

'She gave them the name of her doctor so they could contact him to confirm it. They seemed very pleased about her having been depressed. They wrote down exactly what she said about it. They told us the clinic was comfortable and very discreet. Hygiene and clinical care, before and after the event, would be of the highest standard. I went there with her for her next examination. It was very nice. Not at all seedy. She seemed pleased with it.

'I spent the next few days looking for a house for her. She did not want to come with me. She stayed in her hotel. I found one I thought would be ideal. It was small and comfortable, in a quiet suburb. Nobody would pay any attention to her there. I took her the photograph and description the estate agents had given me. She agreed, without even seeing the house. I completed the purchase quickly on Michael's behalf. I did not want to draw attention back in Porthhella to what was happening by sending for the furniture from the cottage. I bought some for her locally. She showed no interest in coming with me to choose it. She said she had confidence in my taste. I was with her when she moved in.

'The next day I went round to ensure she had settled in. She seemed comfortable and relaxed. I told her not to worry about the operation. It would be quick and painless. Then the whole sorry episode would be over. She could get on with her life. She said she was looking forward to that. I asked her if she would like me to sell the cottage for her. She said she would send me written instructions. In the meantime could I look after it for her, for a regular small payment? I told her I would do it for nothing. When we parted we kissed each other on the cheek. Inside, I was crowing.

'I drove back to Porthhella. I told Michael everything was arranged. He was almost ill with relief. My reward, and the price for my continuing silence, would be a cash sum and ownership of the gallery. He was paying me off. I knew he didn't want to see me again. He did not want to be reminded of what I had done for him.

'The years went by. I ran the gallery. The authority to sell the cottage never arrived. She had given me a spare key so I could look after it, as I had promised. I was meticulous about that. I did not want her to have even the slightest pretext to come back.

'But she did. After seven years she returned. Without any warning.'

'How did she look?'

'Look? I didn't really notice. I remember thinking she had put on weight. That's all. I never looked closely. I didn't want her to see me. I had gone round there one Saturday to clean, as usual. I saw her through the window. Thought it was a burglar at first. When I had got over the shock I wondered if I should warn Michael. But he had made it clear he no longer wanted anything to do with me. And what was there to warn him about? She might have simply decided that after all those years there could be no harm in visiting what was still her property. I decided to tell Michael nothing. If she wanted to get in touch with him that was between the two of them. If I ran into her in the village I would ignore her. I never did run into her. She died soon after.

'Celia lived on for a few months. When she died I wrote to him to offer him my condolences. He wrote back and told me it would be nice if we could get in touch again, after all those years. I went round to the house, and we drank some brandy together, to drown his sorrows. He was very lonely. With your mother and Celia both dead, I could be no danger to him now. I could come in out of the cold. I didn't mind. I understood why he had kept me away all that time. I was pleased to be back, on the fringes of his life. I knew I could never come any closer than that.'

'When did you find out she never went ahead with the abortion?'

Brenda took a deep breath. 'Only recently. After the last time you came to see me. Even then I never found out for certain. But that was when I became sure in my own mind. When you told me about this Alan chap, who claims to be Michael's son, I dismissed the idea at first. Then a thought occurred to me. Perhaps your mother had decided not to go through with it. Perhaps this Alan was her son by Michael.

'I went back to the clinic. It was a long time before I could persuade them to talk to me at all. I told them your mother had died recently and I was acting on behalf of a beneficiary of her will. She had also left money to a child who could not be traced and whose very existence was in doubt. There were several beneficiaries and potential beneficiaries who were disputing the will. There was doubt about her mental state. She had always acknowledged that she had once had an abortion at their clinic. Then remorse had put her into a state of denial. She had started to claim that she had the child and put it up for adoption. If I could just see proof that the abortion had taken place the matter would be settled. I was not seeking to see any confidential clinical records. I let them know that my client was a well-known journalist and dropped hints that if they weren't cooperative articles might appear in the press making dark hints about the clinic's rather shady past. They have a squeaky clean image these days.

'In the end they gave in. They told me she had had five appointments arranged, two preliminaries, one for the procedure itself, two for follow-up. They showed me their records. The trouble is, this was before the 1967 Abortion Act. The clinic took their share of the money but were careful not to accept any of the responsibility. That was entirely a matter for the doctors. They were just hiring the clinic's facilities. The case notes were never at the clinic. There was no way to confirm the appointments had been kept. And there was no way of tracing who the doctors really were. It's hardly surprising. The law in those days was very uncertain. Any doctor carrying out an abortion which was not an immediate response to a life-threatening situation risked prosecution. They found ways to protect themselves, to muddy the waters, to stop the trail leading back to them.'

'It all sounds rather familiar. I had an abortion in those days. A couple of years before my mother did, or was supposed to. She never knew of course. The place I had it wasn't as nice as the one you describe. Poor hygiene, inadequate back-up. They might have killed me. As it was they just made me sterile. So she changed her mind at the last minute?'

'Or she never intended to go through with it and was playing me along.'

'And now you think Alan is her son. My half-brother. It all fits, I suppose. My mother couldn't face bringing him up on her own. So she had him adopted. Somehow he found out about his father. I wonder if he knows who his mother was, and who I am. That might explain why he made contact with me.'

Brenda shook her head. 'I don't think he knows who you are. He has his reasons for following you. You're Michael's heir. And that's what he thinks he should be. He wants what's his. Real tramps never stay in one place. But he does. He's camping out in that disused observation point on the headland. I had a feeling he might be there. So I looked in earlier this evening. He wasn't at home. But there was stuff of his lying about. Not just normal tramp's stuff. There was a newspaper article about you.'

Brenda stood up and walked over to the sideboard. She took out the bracelet and handed it to Madeleine. Madeleine turned it over in her hands and looked questioningly at Brenda.

'A present from Michael to your mother. When I came back to the cottage, I found it on the bedroom floor. Perhaps she had dropped it there by accident. Perhaps she had thrown it there in anger, after hearing from me that Michael had rejected her. I should have returned it to him. But I didn't. He never mentioned it. Either he forgot it or he assumed it was still with her. I kept it. God knows what use I thought it would be. At the time it represented my victory over her. But the victory was always hers. Look at me. Look at the life I've led. Look at the person I was, the person I am now. None of this would have happened if I hadn't behaved the way I did.

'When your mother first came here, she was lonely. I could tell that. She tried to . . . well, not to make friends with me exactly, but to make contact. I rebuffed her. She was never hostile to me, but I chose to hate her. I know it was Michael who wanted her to have the abortion. But I didn't need to help him. I could have told him to look elsewhere for the assistance he wanted. It was nothing to do with me. But I didn't just help him out of loyalty for him and concern for his position and his peace of mind. I did it with such relish. I was so pleased at the chance to get back at her. To make her suffer for her pleasure. And look what happened.

'I had my revenge all right. She lived in exile all those years, her boy lost to her, not daring to contact the man she loved for fear he would reject her again. When eventually she plucked up the courage to return it was to meet her own death. I could have stood by her, against Michael's scheming. We could have defied him. She could have stayed here and had her baby. God knows she needed a friend then. All she found in me was an implacable enemy. And she had done nothing to hurt me.'

Brenda sat down, her face in her hands. Madeleine turned round and peered into the blackness outside the window. After a few minutes she looked away again, her eyes travelling around the room, then to the door, then again to the window, everywhere except where Brenda sat. Then she spoke, very quietly, almost to herself.

'You weren't the only one who could have helped her but didn't. She had a daughter. I could have helped her. I was old enough for that. But I couldn't. Because I knew nothing about it. I keep asking myself why she didn't tell me. Now I think I know why. I found a notebook my mother had written in. It was up at the house. Michael must have found it in the cottage and taken it back there. She started writing it when I was still a teenager. As I read it I found it hard to believe what I was reading. I didn't recognise myself. I had persuaded myself that we had had a good relationship then, and only drifted apart after she came down here. But the truth was that I had withdrawn from all contact with her, from the age of thirteen. My mother obviously thought I was disgusted with her because she was unhappy and having affairs. A year later my father died of cancer. But that seemed to drive a further wedge between us. She thought I felt she had got over it too quickly. So when she came here and had an affair with Michael and had a child, she decided to keep all that from me. She thought that if I knew I would judge her and despise her.'

Brenda looked up. Madeleine was staring out of the window again.

'I realise you must hate me very deeply.' Brenda's voice was shaking. 'It's funny, isn't it? I was always the one who hated. I never thought what it must be like to be at the receiving end. Now I know. I'm not so stupid as to ask you to forgive me. Maybe one day you might forgive me for the way I behaved towards you. Though why on earth should you? But you can't speak for her. She's the one I most need to ask for forgiveness. But it's too late. She's gone. And I have to live with my share of the responsibility for that. Anyway, the choice is yours. We can decide never to see each other again. Or you can let me help you. If I can. Not to make me feel better or to make you feel better about me. I won't expect that. It's just that I'm beginning to sense how awful this must be for you. Trying to find the truth among your lost memories on the one hand and all the secrecy on the other. And you're probably wondering whether the truth is something you will be able to bear when you do know it.'

Madeleine stared at her, then shook her head. 'I don't hate you, Brenda. I'm too tired to hate. And I'm too tired to carry on searching. You can't help me.'

'All right, the choice is yours. You can leave now and we'll never see each other again. But maybe you want to think about it first. I think you do need help. You can't do it on your own, as you've just admitted. And believe it or not, I'm on your side now. I want to know the truth. I want to know about Michael and your mother. I want to know who this Alan is and what he's up to. I want an end to the tragedies that have been going on around here for too long. I don't want anything more to happen to you, not after what you've already been through.

'And my story will have told you something about me. Not just that I'm a malevolent old bitch. I'm certainly that. But I'm also resourceful, clever and cunning. Maybe you could use a bit of that. So before you decide to cut me out of your life, how about giving me a try? Stay a bit longer. Tell me everything you've seen and heard tonight. Tell me everything you're thinking about what happened here and what's happening now. Let's see what we can make of it between us. You're a highly intelligent and resourceful woman as well, I know that. But at the moment it's very hard for you to make sense of anything. You are tired and I can tell you're not well. So why not let me help?'

Madeleine smiled, weakly. 'All right. I haven't the strength to move, even if I wanted to. We can talk. Just while I'm here. First things first. How about a cup of tea?'

28

When Brenda returned with the tea, Madeleine's eyes had closed. They flickered open when Brenda touched her hand and held the cup in front of her. They sat in silence for a few minutes.

'Do you want to go and lie down?' asked Brenda. 'You can have my bed. I'll rest on the sofa.'

'No, thanks. Let's carry on talking. I'm exhausted but I couldn't sleep. Did you tell Michael about David and me?'

'As this is confession time . . . yes, that was me.'

'You watched us? The way you watched Michael and my mother?'

Brenda nodded. 'It was easy. I slipped through the front garden and down the stone stairs by the side of the cottage to the lawn by the front. I could see straight into your bedroom. You never drew the curtains. He was usually there during the day. I could see everything. There was no danger of either of you seeing me. Not with your face in the pillow and him behind you like that.'

'Like animals, you mean. So, did you enjoy the show?'

'No. You didn't enjoy it either, did you? It wasn't the way it was for your mother, was it?'

'Only you can say, Brenda. You're the only one who's seen both of us in action.'

'Me? I can't say. What do I know? I was never that interested in sex. There was only one man I would have wanted to teach me. When it was obvious that wasn't going to happen I never thought about how it might be with anybody else. I sometimes wonder what sort of pupil I would have made. Probably no better than I was as his art pupil. Your mother, she didn't need lessons, by God. I couldn't see them. Usually it was dark. If it was during the day they drew the curtains. I heard them, though. Mostly her. Sometimes it was as if she was singing. No words, just voiced sounds. They seemed to be coming from deep inside her throat. It was almost a man's voice, though I knew it wasn't Michael's. Later there were words but I couldn't understand them. I'm sure they were Welsh. Very soft and low, soothing, caressing. He wouldn't have understood them but he must have loved the sound of them. It was never like that for you, was it? I might not know much about sex but I can tell the difference between sounds of pleasure and pain. He hurt you. Why did you let him?'

'If I knew that I might be able to explain a lot of things. So why did you watch us, if it wasn't for your enjoyment?'

'I felt I owed it to Michael. David was his life. I couldn't stand by and watch both of them being destroyed. I needed to be absolutely sure, to see with my own eyes. He refused to believe me at first. Said I was a gossiping bitch who was just jealous of people being friends. He told me he had introduced you and David to each other and you had only met in his presence. I had never seen him so angry. He became violent. He shook me by the shoulders and almost threw me out of the house. A few days later he rang to apologise. He said he would sort out the situation himself. When you left, I assumed he had paid you off.'

'You said you sometimes wondered if David was his son. Why did he go to such lengths to hide that fact, even after Celia had died?'

'Michael's world was built on flimsier foundations than most people realised. His family weren't wealthy. He never made much as an artist. At one time his larger works fetched high prices but there were few of them. He married money and social status. Everything he bought, the house, the gallery, the place for his academy in Portsmouth, was paid for by Celia's father and put into her name. None of it would come to Michael until after both Celia and her father were dead. I had to wait until then before I could be paid for what I did. Your mother's house in Portsmouth was bought with a legacy from his aunt, paid from a separate account so neither Celia nor her father would know anything about it. When Michael decided he wanted David to move in with him he was playing a game with very high risks. If Celia's father as much as suspected that David was his son, that Michael had betrayed his daughter, he would have changed his will. And he would have done everything in his power to destroy Michael while he still had strength to do it. Once Michael had started the deception he had to continue with it. He could not tell David the truth until he had reached an age when he could handle it.'

'And by then David wasn't interested.'

'Earlier on, you said you had been following your mother tonight. What did you mean?'

'I haven't just been remembering things. I've been seeing them, feeling them. I think I know what happened on the cliffs, when she died. Michael didn't plan to kill her, and he didn't lure her up there. She came back because she desperately wanted to see him, to speak to him. She went up to the house. Perhaps he had refused to come to the cottage or meet her anywhere else.'

'And that was the one place where he didn't want her to come.'

'Because of Celia.'

'Precisely. Your mother would not have known how sick she was. How could she? By then she was confined to a wheelchair. I told you it was never a love match. But the more dependent she became on him, the more he loved her.'

'He loved both of them?'

'Why not? Different types of love. One intense and passionate, the other caring and devoted. In long marriages one type may give way to the other. With him it was both at the same time, for two different women. At that time, Celia had to have priority. He could never have left her.'

'And where did Laura fit in?'

'No more than a distraction.'

'From both of them?'

'No, just from Celia. God knows, he must have needed distraction from time to time. He must have met Laura before he met your mother. Maybe she was an old flame from his early days in Portsmouth. Before Celia became too ill for him to be away from these parts he used to spend a lot of time in Portsmouth, setting up that academy of his. He would have looked up old friends while he was there, revisited old haunts.'

'I wonder why my mother was so insistent on speaking to him. Maybe she thought she could get Alan back if she and Michael were to marry. Perhaps Alan hadn't been formally adopted. Perhaps he was only in care. Maybe she thought the courts might order him to be returned to her but only if she and his father were a couple. It's just the sort of crazy fantasy my mother would have pursued. But if she had known Celia was in a wheelchair she would never have gone there. Can you imagine the scene? Michael opens the door. My mother forces her way past him. Tells him that they have to talk. If necessary she will confront his wife. Michael is terrified. If Celia hears about the child, the one thing she had never been able to give Michael, it could kill her. So he takes my mother into the library, tries to calm her down. But inevitably voices are raised. Celia is in the next room. She hears everything.

'When my mother comes out she sees Celia, in the hallway. She is horrified. You never told me she was like this, she tells Michael. If I had known . . . She is overwhelmed with shock and remorse. She rushes out and onto the coastal path. By then it's very dark and raining hard. But she knows the path well. Or she thinks she does. Michael follows her, telling her it's not her fault, they can talk things over, sort something out. She is younger and stronger. He can't keep up with her. By the cliff-tops she loses her way, runs off the path and on towards the cliffs. Just in time she stops. Right by the edge. Michael runs up to her. She can't move. She's frozen with terror. Michael tells her to turn round slowly.'

192

'You saw all this, tonight?'

'Yes. At first I was following them. Then I was in her place. Not just in her place. I was her. I was a woman who had loved Michael, who had carried and borne his child. Those memories of pregnancy and childbirth were inside my body, the memories of holding the baby were in my hands and arms. They were her memories, not mine. My own child was aborted when I was seventeen, before I even began to sense its presence. But tonight I sensed Alan growing inside me, pushing out of me, clinging onto me. All those memories compressed into a few seconds. And I was standing in front of his father. He was holding out his hand to help me. I held out my hand. I started to fall back. My hand was searching for his but it wasn't there.'

'Maybe he was just too late to reach her.'

'Or maybe he held back. He had seen something come between them, an image before his eyes. An image of Celia back at the house, the look of betrayal on her face which he knew would now never leave her. My mother was no longer the woman he had loved, she was the woman who had destroyed his peace of mind forever. So his hand did not meet hers. He dropped it. She fell.'

Brenda rose and started to pace about the room. 'Yes, of course. That's it. Now I understand it. Why he never drew or painted again. A moment's cold rage stopped him from saving her. Imagine the expression on her face as she fell backwards. Where was the hand that was supposed to save her? That image must have haunted his every waking moment thereafter, and stalked though his dreams at night. It all fits. That was the time he stopped drawing and painting. People said it was when Celia died. But I knew it was before that. It was when your mother died. How could he have carried on? Every time he tried to lift a brush or a pencil her final image would have been there. What a terrible burden he had to carry. Until later, when even greater ones came.

'Of course, it's only supposition. What you saw and felt tonight could just be your imagination. It might not have happened that way at all. She could have been alone up there. Fell over accidentally. Or decided she would never convince Michael to go back to her, and jumped off in despair. Or she could have gone to the house as you said. Only Michael didn't follow her. Or if he did he was nowhere near her when she fell.'

'I know all those explanations are possible. But I don't believe them. I believe she communicated with me tonight. Told me what really happened. It explains why he seemed to be trying to make it up to her, arranging the funeral, taking over her cottage.'

Brenda slumped down again in her chair. In less than a second an expression of intense fatigue had come over her face. After a minute she spoke, wearily. 'So, Madeleine, what are you going to do now?'

'Go back to the house.'

'Why, for God's sake?'

'I said before that I was too tired to go on searching. I am. But I know I have to carry on.'

'You mustn't be there alone. I'll come with you. If you want to stay alone in your room I'll leave you to yourself. But you must have someone in the house.'

'I'm not alone. Megan's there.'

'And you're lying. I know you sent her away. I have my groceries delivered as well, you know. By the same man. He keeps me informed.'

'I won't deny that I'm scared. But I don't think the memories will return unless I'm on my own.'

'There's something else I'm worried about. I think you may be in danger.'

'Me? Why? From whom?'

'From Alan. Because you're in his place. You inherited Michael's house and most of his money.'

'As far as I'm concerned, if he can prove who he is, he can have it all. I have enough money of my own. And I can't stand the house. And if he really is my brother, I need to help him to get back to some sort of normal life. If he'll let me.'

194

'He may not understand any of that. He's obviously paranoid. Thinks everybody has been plotting against him. If you
tell him you're his sister he won't believe you. But he will believe
it's a plot to take back a share of what he wants to take from
you. He may decide that if he killed David he might as well
get rid of you. He got away with it once, he might get away
with it again.'

'He's no danger to me. I'm sure of that. I could sense it.'

'Look, I'm not trying to scare you. Just let me come to the
house with you. Spend the rest of the night and tomorrow here.
You need the rest. Then tomorrow evening I'll drive you back
there and stay with you.'

'You can drive me back. I'd be grateful for that. But you must
leave me there.'

'You can be stubborn when you want to be. All right. I agree.'

Madeleine's eyes had already closed.

'What are you smiling about?' asked Brenda as she turned off
the engine. They had parked in front of the house after a journey
in complete silence.

'I don't know. Perhaps it's the thought of Alan being my brother.
He's a dirty tramp. At best he's a fantasist and a paranoid. At
worst he's a killer. Then I thought, I can't exactly be anybody's
dream of a sister. Actually, we're ideally suited to each other. A
tramp, a paranoid schizophrenic, and a killer – does that remind
you of anybody?'

'Come off it, Madeleine. There's no comparison. You had a
bath last night.'

Madeleine stared at Brenda for a few seconds. For a moment
she could have sworn she saw the trace of a smile flicker across
the older woman's face. She shook her head. She must have imagined it. She had never seen Brenda smile and was sure it was too
late now. Her features had been set too hard for too long.

'If that's all you've got to say in my defence I'd better get
inside. Thanks for the lift.'

'Are you really sure about this? You don't want me to stay with you? I could at least wait outside in the car until you give me the all clear.'

'No thanks. It's best this way, honestly. I'm sure I'll be all right.'

'Have it your way.'

Madeleine waited until she heard the engine start. Then she opened the door and stepped into the hallway. She flicked the light switch up and down several times. Still nothing. She groped her way up the stairs and into her bedroom. She heard a muffled sound behind her. Before she could cry out she felt a hand clamped against her mouth as the door slammed shut behind her.

29

There was a loud knocking at the front door. In an instant the hand pulled away from her mouth and pushed her towards the bed. She heard the bedroom door open and heavy footsteps clump down the stairs. As she fumbled her way out of the bedroom towards the top of the stairs she heard a sharp cry followed by the crash of the front door slamming.

'Madeleine, are you all right?' Brenda's voice from just inside the hall.

'I'm up here. I'm all right.'

'Is there any light?'

'There was a power cut during the storm. I think it may still be off. I know where the fuse box is. You stay there.'

She crept carefully downstairs, her fingers tracing the top of the banister. She saw Brenda's shadow near the front door.

'What happened?'

'There was someone waiting for me in my bedroom, in the dark. When he heard your knock he decided to leave.'

'I know. He nearly knocked me over as he ran out. Did you see who it was?'

'No. But it was Alan. I know his smell.'

'How did he get in?'

'He must have a key. Here we are. There's a torch somewhere . . . There it is. Could you shine it here, please? Inside this cupboard.'

Madeleine flicked a switch in the cupboard just inside the front door. The hall light flooded back on, dazzling the eyes of both women.

'The bastard! The power must have come back on and he switched it off deliberately. So he could lay in wait for me. Why did you come back?'

'As I was turning out of the driveway I looked into my mirror and realised that I hadn't seen any lights come on. So I came back to check. Are you all right? He didn't hurt you? Don't say I didn't warn you.'

'I know, Brenda. You did warn me. And I didn't listen. Thanks for coming back.'

'And I'm staying. No arguments.'

'All right, Brenda, no arguments. But you must leave me alone. I'm going upstairs now. You can get yourself a drink in the library. You know where it is. And you know where the kitchen is if you need anything to eat.'

'Yes, I know. Off you go. If you need anything just shout. In the meantime I'm going to bolt the front door and check all the windows.'

Madeleine lay down on the bed. After a few minutes she sensed there was another person in the room. She forced herself to lie still, not to scream. He sat down on the side of the bed and started to speak, softly, with a Welsh lilt.

30

'You weren't asleep, were you, Madeleine? I could tell. I wanted to have a little chat with you. I hope you don't mind. I'm feeling a bit lonely, I suppose. Your mother's away again. Left us on our own. I don't mind. That's what she wants and that's what we want, don't we?'

He took a cigarette from a crumpled packet and lit it, slowly and deliberately. Her heart was pounding. Underneath the bedclothes her hands were shaking. But she did not want him to go. She wanted him to continue talking to her, just to her, the two of them alone in that room. She loved his voice, but it had been so long since she had heard it just for her. She loved the sound of his words, like a Welsh harp, very soft, with a slight rise and fall, a cutting off of the breath just before the end of each syllable.

'We were close once. Your mother and I. Or so it seemed. Two wild Celtic souls. That's what she called us. But that was her. It wasn't me. She saw a reflection of herself in me, God knows why. She was so young when I met her. Eighteen. I was thirty-two. She was one of my students, did she tell you that? Brilliant prospects. Then she got pregnant. Had you at nineteen. So we married. She never finished her degree. Then we found out how little we had in common. She hates it here in Oxford. Always has. Me, I couldn't survive anywhere else. I wondered whether our marriage had served any purpose at all. Whether it had not all been a dreadful mistake. But now, when I see what you are becoming, I know it wasn't. It had a purpose. The purpose was you.

'You know it as well, don't you? I've seen it, in the look in your eyes. You have them all. Your mother's eyes, your mother's face. Even your body is beginning to swell like hers. But you have my understanding. I can see it all now. Your mother was the conduit to you. That's all she was ever meant for. I don't care if she's throwing herself at other men. She doesn't matter now. Only you and I matter. She was made of the common clay of life. In you, the clay has been touched with a divine spark. I never noticed it before. The transformation is so gradual, you see. You are like a flower in bud, delicate, subtle and suggestive, not yet ripened and coarsened by the sun. We are two special souls. We are destined to be special together. There are certain rules in life, of course. There have to be. Every society in history has had them. But they don't apply to us. How does that make you feel, Madeleine? I know how it makes me feel. It makes me feel like a bird on the wing, in full song. It's something I've never felt before. Sorry, I know I'm not making sense. Don't say anything. Go to sleep now.'

Such a way with words. Almost a poet. But what did he mean? She was not aware that she had looked at him in a way which could have provoked him to say what he had said to her. And what was that about her mother's body? Already, at the age of only 13? Of course she had been aware of the changes in her shape. They had disgusted her. She could hardly bring herself to look at herself naked in the mirror. Not that her mother was disgusting. She had heard people speak of her mother as a beauty, her figure full and ripe, her eyes wide and seductive, her personality warm and open. Her mother was a real woman. She had longed for her mother to notice her, to teach her how to be like her. To teach her how to accept the changes in her and the future which beckoned because of them. Now she realised that would never happen. It was too late. Despite her youth, her inexperience, her fear, her ignorance, she was to take her mother's place, to fulfil the role in which her mother had failed, to be her father's soul mate. They were to be 'special together'. Whatever she learned would come from him and him alone. He would discuss his researches with her. Tell her about his new insights into classical mythology and history. They would pore together over his dusty old books. She would love that. But the bit she did not yet understand was where her body came into it.

She would not understand that until the following night.

'I want to make it easy for you, Madeleine. It will be best if you don't see it. You're very young and it might frighten you. Take off your nightdress. That's a good girl. Now turn over. On your stomach. That's good. It might hurt at first. Try not to scream. Just relax. There'll be less pain that way. Please, Madeleine, don't scream. That's right. My Madeleine. So special. So very, very special.'

31

Brenda poured herself a large brandy and sank into an armchair in the library. She nodded approvingly. Michael always had a good taste in brandies. Pity there were only a few bottles left.

After a few minutes, she rose and went over to the bookshelves. Might as well find something to read to pass the time. She had seen the inside of the library before but had never had a chance to look in detail at what was there. A very impressive collection, she thought. It must have taken him a lifetime to put together. Just like his brandies. But unlike the brandies most of these look as if they've never been touched since they were placed here. Except for those few there. No dust on the top. And not neatly flush with the edge of the shelves. These have been taken out and read recently, perhaps many times.

She took out two of the books and returned to her chair. She placed one on the table and opened the other. For a few moments she stared at the flyleaf. Slowly, her hand shaking, she closed the book and placed it on the table next to the other one. She stood up and opened the door into the hall. At the foot of the stairs she heard sounds from the bathroom on the floor above. She returned to the library, sat down and waited.

After a few minutes Madeleine pushed open the door and sat down opposite her. She was carrying a folder under her arm. She placed the folder on the table next to the books. Her face was a ghostly white.

'I heard you being sick. Are you all right?'

Madeleine nodded. 'I see you found some books to read.'

'Yes. I picked out a couple, from that shelf over there. Well, you know precisely where they were. This one looks interesting.' She picked up the book she had opened. '*The Myth of the Kindly Ones*. By Dr Andrew Reed. What does it say about him on the back? "Andrew Reed is Tutor in Classical History at St Stephen's College, Oxford. This is the fourth book in his highly acclaimed series aiming to interpret the Greek myths for a modern audience. Dr Reed lives in Oxford with his wife and daughter."'

'Yes.'

'Your father?'

'That's right.' Madeleine's voice was barely a whisper.

'What does the title mean?'

'It's a euphemism. The Kindly Ones were the Furies of Ancient Greece. They pursued people for unnatural crimes.'

'Unnatural?'

'Like Oedipus. Sleeping with his mother. That sort of thing.'

'That sort of thing.' Brenda repeated the words slowly and deliberately. 'This inscription on the flyleaf. It surprises me. "To the one who is special, part of me, body and soul." That's very moving. A wonderful thing for a man to write to his wife or lover. For someone like me who's never attracted any sort of love it's almost unimaginable. I thought your parents weren't happy together. That was why your mother had affairs. That's what you told me. But to be loved like this . . . I don't understand it. But if this were dedicated to her you would think he would have addressed her by name. But there's no name. Unless . . .'

'Unless he was addressing someone else.'

'Exactly. Someone else. Was this in Michael's collection when you came here? Or did you bring it yourself?' Madeleine covered her face with her hands. 'All right. I know you find it difficult to talk about this. So let me help. Let's see, when was this published? I have trouble with these Roman numerals. Can you help me here?'

203

'It was published in 1961.'

'Thank you. How old were you at the time?'

'Thirteen.'

'This is a first edition, isn't it? And he gave this one to you, with the dedication inside. When you were thirteen. You brought this book here, didn't you?'

'No. I'd forgotten all about it. My mother had a small collection of books, really awful ones, trashy rubbish. This must have got mixed in with them. I suppose she brought it with her when she came to live in the cottage. I never found it there.'

'Yes, I remember now. After your mother moved to Portsmouth I found them and wrote to her to ask her if she wanted me to send them to her. I didn't want her to have any sort of excuse to come back, such as wanting to fetch her favourite books. She told me to leave them or get rid of them. She said they were trash too. I left them there. I never looked at them. I don't go in for reading much. And I knew her tastes would not be mine.'

'Michael must have found it when he sold the cottage for me. He would have known it was one of my father's. He already had some in his collection. He never mentioned it. He put it on the shelves with the others.'

'Did you look at it since?'

'No. I took them off the shelves from time to time to browse through them. And I asked Megan to send them to me in the hospital. That one was part of the package she sent. But somehow I never wanted to open it.'

'Because it would have reminded you how you and he were special, part of each other, body and soul. But now you have remembered, haven't you? That's why you were sick just now.'

'Yes.'

'Did you tell anybody what was happening?'

'No, of course not. It was our secret. Our special secret.'

'Did it go on for long?'

'No. A few months. Then he became very ill.'

'Yes. Cancer. You told me.'

'No. Not cancer.'

'Why would you lie to me about that?'

'I wasn't lying. It was something I had made up to keep my memories buried.'

'But you remember the truth now.'

'Yes. Would you like to hear about it?'

'All right. If it will help you. What did he die of?'

'They came for him.'

'They?'

'The Furies. He had been writing about them while he and I were . . . It was as if he were defying them, provoking them. In the end they came.'

'Madeleine, do you see them? There, looking at me, pointing at me.'

'Don't be silly. There's nobody there. We're all alone. You must have fallen asleep. You were having a bad dream.'

They were in his room in college. As usual she had come straight from school to help him read the proofs of his latest book. For over a week now they had made little progress. He could not concentrate. He smoked continuously. His eyes were red with lack of sleep. He talked wildly, incoherently. He hardly ever came home, preferring to catch what moments of sleep he could in the armchair from which he conducted his tutorials. She always brought in some cakes and sandwiches, nearly always took them away again untouched. Sometimes he did not recognise her, mistaking her for one of his students. Once he had thrown her out of the room, calling her by her mother's name, calling her a slut and a whore. She urged him to see a doctor. He told her it was too late. She was becoming increasingly anxious. Her mother was away and she did not know where she could contact her.

'No, I see them,' he whispered urgently. 'Over there.'

'Who are you talking about?'

'The accusers. The Eumenides.'

'For God's sake, that was only a book! Your book. You brought them alive but only on paper and in your imagination. They're not real. They're mythical. You've been overworking, that's all.'

'No. Not mythical. Real. You should see them, too. Look, look. Over there.'

'I can't see anything.'

He shook his head. 'I don't understand. You should see them. We both committed a crime, you see. Against the Gods. We defied them. Mocked them. Now they're taking revenge.' He grasped her hand, so hard that she winced with pain.

'If you can't see them now, that means they will come for you in the future. That would be too horrible. What we did was very wrong, you see. We were special, not like other people. We set ourselves up against their laws. I kept expecting you to tell me that you were seeing them too. But they will come, unless we stop it. The guilt was yours as well as mine. It started with the changes in you. I didn't realise until I saw it in your eyes. I didn't realise what you were, what I was, what we had to be to each other, how we had to rise above the rest of common humanity. It was wonderful, wasn't it, to be up there together on the clouds? But it couldn't last. Our punishment had to come. You will understand it when we're together again. I dictated something, when I was trying to understand it myself.' He rummaged among the papers on the top of his desk. 'Here's the tape. Should destroy it really but there's no time.'

'I'll destroy it if you want.'

'No, no. No time.' He was almost screaming. 'It's discreet. It doesn't say what we did. If it fell into the wrong hands, nobody would understand. It'll be all right. Just lock it away. In the cabinet over there. Here's the key. Do it now. There's no more time.'

'There's plenty of time. But if it helps I'll do it now.' She obeyed him. 'That's it. Safely locked away. Rest now. It was just a dream, as I said.'

'No, not a dream. It's real. Madeleine, do something for me. It's too dark in here. Go over to the window. Draw the curtain. That's my girl.'

She released his hand and walked over to the massive case-ment overlooking the quadrangle. Outside she heard the chatter and laughter of undergraduates, looked out and saw them running across the uneven paving stones, their gowns flapping, clutching armfuls of books and papers. Behind her she heard a drawer open, a sound like a clicking of metal.

'What was that, Father? I didn't hear you. What did you say?'

She was sure he had said something. Just a couple of words. But the noises from the quadrangle, and the sound of the opening drawer had obscured them. She turned round. Then she was deaf. She smelt the smoke, saw the gun on the floor, saw the door open, people rushing in, mouthing at her, dashing over to the body slumped in the chair. She heard nothing.

'Two months after his death, I was in a child psychiatric unit. My mother had discovered that I was mutilating myself. Nothing too drastic. Stubbed cigarettes out on my skin. Scored marks across my arms with a knife. It wasn't because I enjoyed the pain. It was just that I felt this enormous sense of relief when the blood began to flow. I tried to be careful but one day she saw the marks on my arms. She was furious. Told me it was about time I got over my grief. If she had managed it, why couldn't I? She was sorry but she had no choice but to have me detained. When I was discharged after a few weeks I was cured, supposedly. All that meant was that I was out of immediate danger of suicide or serious self-harm.

'But I was hardly cured. I had affairs with my teachers. I became pregnant and had an abortion. A year later I was a heroin addict. I still needed the drugs, you see. The ones they had given me in hospital had suppressed my memories and my feelings. Once I was out I needed other drugs to keep them suppressed. I had to keep the lid on, to stop the memories breaking through again. In the end only the hard drugs would do it. Our doctor arranged for me to attend this very expensive private clinic.'

'Your mother must have been out of her mind with worry.'

'I didn't notice. All I felt was how disgusting, how repulsive I must have been to her.'

'Did the treatment work?'

'Oh yes. I kicked the habit. But by then I had the lid down really tight. Nothing could get through. I could function, but only as an automaton, not a human being. I had been expelled from school, of course. I had planned to go to university but there was no chance of that now. I went to London and got a job in a bank. Started at the bottom and worked my way up.'

'What I don't understand is why you and your mother didn't become close again as a result of what you were going through. Once you had got through the rehab successfully, why wasn't she there for you?'

'Because I had made sure she couldn't be. In the notebook she wrote about me screaming my disgust with her into her face. I remember what happened now. It was in the clinic. I had been there a few weeks. She used to visit but I wouldn't talk to her, wouldn't even acknowledge her. One day I turned on her. The doctor in charge of my case was in the room with us. I screamed at her, telling her to get out and never come back. I used the word "disgusting". She thought I meant her, because of her affairs. But I didn't. I meant me. I couldn't bear her to look at me, even to be in the same room with me, because I was sure she had to be totally and unbearably disgusted with me.

'By then I couldn't remember exactly why I thought she should feel that way. But inside I knew I had done something monstrous, something repulsive. And I sensed that even if she didn't know what had happened she would see it in my eyes, hear it in my voice. So I had to shield her from me. That was why I had been so distant from her, ever since she had returned to the house after it had happened for the first time. So she went and I never saw her again until the day I identified her body. When she had gone the doctor asked me why I felt she was disgusting. He had misunderstood as well. He seemed to think she had abused me, which was why I was in such a state as to need the services of his clinic.

He said he would make sure she would not visit again because it was obvious her visits were obstructing my recovery. By the time I got out she had moved down here and we only communicated through our solicitor.'

'And you had really forgotten everything?'

'Yes. What he had done to me. What he had said before he died. I had even forgotten how he died, forgotten that I was there when it happened. I had no sense or image of myself. Not until David provided me with one. Here. Look at those.'

Brenda picked up the folder and leafed quickly through the contents. She shut it and handed it back to Madeleine.

'I've never seen any of his work before. Thank God.'

'Michael said he was a genius. Far more naturally gifted than Michael ever was. I'm no expert. But when I first met him he was sketching something on the headland. He took it back home and made it into a watercolour. He showed it to me. I thought it was beautiful. He tore it up as soon as I praised it. Told me landscapes are trivial. He said he had more significant work to do.'

'Like this?'

'That's right. *The Assumption* was meant to be his first major work. Weeks of intensive effort. A hundred sketches.'

'And you as his model? Poor you. Maybe Michael was right about his natural gifts. But gifts need to be protected and nurtured, not abused. If this is genius, it's in meltdown. His talent was destroying itself just as he was destroying himself. To me this isn't art. But then what do I know about art? Only what Michael taught me. And he was a traditionalist and much maligned for it. If you want to know what I think, I think they're monstrous. You should destroy them. Burn them.'

'What? Destroy the only proof I have that I exist at all? David was the only one, since him, who understood me, who saw into my soul.'

'These aren't about you, Madeleine. They're about him. I'll destroy them for you if you find it difficult.'

'No, I can't let you do that. I have to keep them.'

'All right. Have it your way. Have you remembered everything?'

'No. I still can't remember about killing Laura. But the other night I remembered how I found out she was David's mother. I overheard her talking with Michael, that time she came here to see him. He had paid her off, as I thought. She gave David up to him and went to Australia. She came back after she heard he had died. She was already ill by then.'

'And Michael never mentioned her afterwards?'

'No. I'm sure of that.'

'He never gave you a message for her?'

'No.'

'So it was your own decision to go and see her. You have to go back there. In your mind. Back to that room in the hospice. The same way you went back to that room where your father shot himself.'

'I can't.'

'You must. You can't stop now.'

'All right. But I can't go to that room. Not yet.'

'You went to see her sister-in-law first. That's what you told me. What was her name?'

'"Naomi.'

'That's right. How did you know where to find her?'

'Simple. I looked up her address in the phone book.'

32

'Miss Reed? I'm Naomi. Come on in.'

Naomi was a plump, bustling woman in her sixties. Her smile was broad but did not disguise the lines of worry about her eyes and forehead. She wore an apron covered with flour which she was trying vainly to brush off her hands. Madeleine followed her into the living room of the tiny terraced house. The furniture was old and shabby but the room was spotlessly clean and tidy. Naomi had been keeping herself busy, cooking and cleaning, distracting herself from thoughts about her dying sister-in-law.

'Sit down, please. Cup of tea? And a scone? I've just baked some fresh.'

'That's very kind, but no thanks.'

'Well, Miss Reed, it's as I explained on the phone. She's been in the hospice for a few weeks now. It's only a mile from here. They call it a home for palliative care. They used to call it St Agnes' Hospice. But everybody still knows what it's for. They're very kind there. They look after her better than I could here. And the hospital can't do any more for her. It's a very peaceful place. If you still want to see her, it's best if I go with you. They know me there. What did you want with her, anyway?'

'I knew an acquaintance of hers, Michael Wallace. You may have heard of him. He's a well-known artist. Well, he was. He died recently. I think she would want to know. Could I ask you something? Michael never really told me anything about her. Did she have any children?'

'No. None that I'm aware of. She and my brother certainly didn't have children. She was only thirty when he died. As far as I know she never remarried. But she could have met someone else and had a child. If so, I don't know anything about it. Nobody's come forward, since she's been ill. Not that she has any money or property to leave, even if they did. She's never mentioned anybody. She hasn't bothered with a will or anything like that. She's literally penniless, so what's the point?'

'Does she have any other living relatives?'

'No. Her parents died when she was in her twenties. She had a sister. That was the one who went to Australia, the one Laura went to stay with when she went out there. She died, so Laura came back here. She was already very ill. The doctors had only given her a year or two to live. They've been proved right. She's sinking fast. It really could be any day now. I was terribly shocked when I saw her. She just appeared on my doorstep. Said she had come back to die. I could see she wasn't joking. She was old far beyond her years.'

'Will she be able to talk?'

'I think so. I was there this morning. Her memory is still quite sharp. She might enjoy meeting someone new. She must be sick of the sight of me by now. I only hope they haven't given her too many drugs. Let's go now. I'll take you in there and introduce you but I won't stay. She's had enough of me for today. I'll come back here. Do you want to stay the night here, or will you go straight home?'

'I'll probably go straight home. Thanks anyway.'

'Fine. Let's go.'

Laura was in a private room. Naomi went in first. She came out after a minute.

'She's awake. The nurse is with her. I've told her what you said about why you want to see her. Laura's keen to meet you. I think it'll do her good. I'll go now.'

She went in. Laura was sitting up in bed. The curtains were drawn. Madeleine blinked until her eyes adjusted to the dim light. Perhaps sunlight disturbs her eyes, she thought.

Madeleine barely recognised Laura. Her cheeks were now deep hollows. Only the bright, staring eyes were familiar. Her gnarled hands lay on the blanket in front of her. An intravenous drip was attached to her arm. She looked blankly through Madeleine, who sat down and held Laura's hand. The nurse nodded to Madeleine and told her she would wait outside. If she was needed there was a red emergency button near the bed. When the nurse had gone, Madeleine pulled a chair close to the bed and sat down.

'Laura. My name is Madeleine Reed. I was living with Michael when you came to the house. I saw you when he let you in. You talked with him about the past.'

'Yes.' Laura shifted and tried to sit up. Madeleine helped her to adjust the pillow.

'I remember. How is he?'

'He's dead, Laura.'

She coughed. Madeleine had the impression she was trying to laugh.

'Dead? The old bugger beat me to it. Sorry. I picked up some bad habits down under.'

'You were talking to him about your child. Do you remember?'

'That was a private conversation. I don't remember anybody else being there.'

'I didn't mean to be nosy. I was just passing the room. I overheard you. After Michael died, I remembered you, and what you said about a child. I wondered if you were all right. If you needed help. Michael hadn't mentioned you to me. But I traced you here, through your sister-in-law. Laura, would you like to talk? Would you like to tell me about you and Michael? I'd like to hear about it, if it wouldn't upset you or tire you too much. How did you first meet?'

'Here in Portsmouth. That's where we met. I come from here,

born and bred. I met Harry, my husband, here and we married here. He ran a small garage. Always told me how well it was doing. Very impressive he was. Sharp suits, flashy motor. Lots of charm. I fell for the lot. We bought a little house in a nice quiet area. He looked after all that. The house was in his name. I trusted him completely. Everything was looking rosy. It was only when he died I discovered there were several mortgages on the house. He had debts. Business debts, gambling debts. You name it. I inherited the lot. I sold the house to a landlord and rented it back. But I got behind with the rent almost immediately.

'If only . . . if only Michael hadn't seen the boy. It would all have been different. We would have struggled but at least we would have stayed together. He would have let us alone. But he saw him. While Michael and I were talking he came running into the room, to show me something he'd just drawn. I told him to go back and finish it off and not to disturb us because me and the gentleman were talking. Michael, well, he looked as if he had been struck by lightning. He asked him to show him what he'd been drawing. He told him not be afraid of him, because he could see he was. Michael, well, he wasn't used to children, was he? He didn't have the right manner or voice. I could tell he was trying to be kind.

'Well, he looked at the drawing and said it was very good indeed. He looked at it for ages, holding it up to the light, turning it round at different angles. Then he asked me how much money I owed. He had seen the unpaid bills I had left on the table. All I ever did with them was shuffle them around to make space for new ones when they arrived. I told him. It wasn't much really, but it was far more than I could cope with. He wrote me out a cheque on the spot. Told me there would be much more where that came from. He sent me more cheques from time to time. Small amounts but enough to keep me afloat. He insisted that I never got in touch with him and never told anybody about him or what he was doing for us. Later on, it was much worse. The things he made me do. But I was helpless.'

Laura was crying. Madeleine leaned forward and held her head in her arms. Then she poured some water into a glass from a jug by the bedside and held the glass to Laura's mouth while she sipped. After a minute Laura continued.

'He wanted the boy to live with him under a new identity. So he could make a completely fresh start. That's what he said. I had to tell him his parents had been killed in a car crash when he was a baby.'

'What! You had to tell David he wasn't yours?'

'That's right. Technically the law was on my side. I knew that. Michael was the biological father but that didn't give him automatic custody rights. Until then he had never publicly acknowledged him, not for the whole of the first six years of his life. Now he had seen him and decided he wanted him, just like that. So at first I told him he could get lost. He wasn't going to bribe him away from me by paying a few of my debts. Then he told me he could get custody. He could prove I had been in debt, that I was not a fit person to be his mother. He would employ the best lawyers. I had no money at all. Only what he chose to give me. I couldn't fight him. He was just too strong. Too powerful. I knew the court case would ruin me completely and I would lose anyway. In the end I gave in. I accepted a promise of money from him to go away to Australia. He bought my ticket for me. I delivered David into his hands. I surrendered my heart and soul at the same time. I never recovered them.

'After I had been out there a couple of years he sent me the payment he had promised. I had long since given up expecting it. There was a letter saying this was the final communication between us. But it wasn't. I got another letter from him, many years later. He told me how David had died. My sister died soon after that and I realised it was the end for me. There I was, alone, in a country on the other side of the world, a country I had always detested. I had nothing here either. I knew I was sick. I decided I couldn't die there. I came back while I still had the strength to do it. To die in the town where I was born. I went to see Michael to pay him back what was left of the money he had given me. For the first time I felt free. Now I'm waiting for death. I didn't hate him any more. Not when I saw what had happened to him.' Her eyes began to close.

'Laura, I'm going now. I know it must have been awful for you. Losing your child like that. I'm sorry to have brought back such bad memories. But there must have been a time when you loved him. When you were together. When you were first pregnant with David. There must have been some happy times for you then. Try to think about those. Think about what Michael was to you then.'

'What? I'm sorry, I didn't catch that. I thought for a moment . . . Come closer, will you? I can't see you properly. Open the curtains. Let me see your face . . .'

'Don't stop, Madeleine. Not now. Why have you stopped? What happened next?'

'I can't . . .'

'What? You can't remember, or you can't bear to face the memory? So what did you come here for tonight? Go on. You have to. What happened?'

'Stop. You're hurting me.'

Brenda had stood up and moved behind Madeleine's chair. Her fingers were digging sharply into her shoulder blades.

'Yes, and I'll carry on hurting you until you continue. For God's sake, breathe!'

Madeleine's breath forced itself into her lungs with a harsh, whooping sound. She cried out as the fingers pressed harder and harder.

'She . . . she . . . For God's sake, Brenda . . . she . . . recognised me.'

33

'It's you! It really is. You've come back to me. You've come to say goodbye. Come here. Hold my hand.' Laura's face lit up.

'Laura, we've never met before. Who are you talking about?'

Laura stared at her, frowning. 'It is you, isn't it? But how can it be? She's dead. But you're the image of her.'

'Of whom?'

'Of my closest friend. Of Ceridwen. Yes, I remember now. She had a daughter. She told me. I had forgotten the name. Now I remember. Madeleine. I saw you outside the church. After the funeral. He wouldn't let us go inside until after the coffin arrived. And we had to leave before it came out. He didn't want us to see or be seen by anybody else there.'

'But I don't understand. You and my mother were friends? But how did you meet?'

'She moved in next door to me. Here in Portsmouth.'

'But that's impossible. She never lived here. She lived in Oxford, until I went to London. Then she moved to Cornwall. She stayed there until she died.'

'No, my dear. She left Cornwall, came here to make a fresh start.'

'But why here?'

'I have no idea. All I knew was that she was on her own and needed a friend. I was lonely too. The baby was a real bond between us. We looked after him together, always popping in and out of each other's houses. When he started school we'd take it in turns to take him and then fetch him. It was like he had two mothers.'

'Just a minute, Madeleine. This doesn't make sense. She recognised you. She and your mother were friends. Your mother went to Portsmouth to have an abortion, but decided in the end to have the child. So we think. Michael's child. Laura had Michael's child. So two women with his love-children end up next door to each other in a town hundreds of miles away from here and become friends. That's impossible.'

'Only one child, Brenda. Laura only mentioned one child. Not two.'

'Fine. Your mother did go ahead with the abortion. There was only one child. Alan is nothing to do with this after all. Just a tramp who's trying to pass himself off as Michael's heir, as I always thought. Or maybe he's a love-child of someone else entirely, someone we don't know about. But you're still saying that two of Michael's lovers from different parts of the world came by chance to live next door to each other. That's preposterous.'

'I agree. So none of this is working. I can't be sure if I'm remembering things or making them up.'

Brenda returned to her chair and thought for a minute. 'Wait a second. Your father's death. What was the date?'

'Let me think. 1962.'

'Yes, but the date. The day and the month.'

'I'm trying to think. I can't remember the day. It was summer. There were exams going on. Finals. June, probably.'

'Okay. June 1962. If your memories of your father's death are correct there'll be records. Newspaper reports. Reports of the inquest. Do you have a copy of his death certificate?'

'No. I never saw a copy. There wasn't one with my mother's effects. I suppose she had one but lost it or threw it away.'

'But there'll be the entry in the register. Did he leave a will?'

'Yes.'

'Who would have handled that?'

'Our family solicitor, I suppose. A Mr Wilson.'

'Do you have his address?'

'Yes. His card is in the bureau. What's this all about, Brenda?'

'What I'm getting at is that your account of your father's death is a memory we can verify, or otherwise. We'll know if you are recovering real memories or just fantasising. If you are remembering the truth we can take it from there. Find out what really happened in Portsmouth. Go to the house, talk to the people there now and the neighbours, things like that. See if anybody remembers.

'But first things first. Let's check what happened to your father. Go to the bureau. Write down everything you can remember about it. Every detail. I know it must be very unpleasant for you to go back over it again, but we need to have your own account in full before we can check other accounts against it. And get Mr Wilson's card.'

Madeleine went over to the bureau and started to write. Brenda left the room and returned 20 minutes later with two mugs of hot chocolate and some tiny white pills on a plate. Madeleine rose.

'I've written it down and put it in this envelope. Mr Wilson's card is in it as well.'

'Give it to me. Now, drink this and take these pills.'

'What are they?'

'Sleeping tablets. They have no effect on me but I take them anyway. Do you want to go up to your room to sleep, or would you prefer to stay down here?'

'I'll go upstairs.'

Brenda watched her as she swallowed the pills. 'Good girl. Off you go. You look totally exhausted. And that's how I feel. Get a good night's sleep if you can. Tomorrow we'll go to Oxford. Pack a bag in the morning, in case we need to be away a couple of days. We'll collect some of my stuff on the way. You'd better ring

Megan before we leave to say you may not be here when she returns.'

'Where are you going to sleep?'

'Down here. Just in case Alan comes creeping back. If he has a key and tries to get in by the front door the bolts will stop him. But I'll hear him. And old and frail as I am I'd love to have a go at chasing him and catching him. He'll wish he never came near the place.'

'I doubt if he'll come back tonight. Brenda, I've been thinking about what happened. I don't think he meant to harm me. I think he just wanted to talk to me. He turned the lights off so he could talk freely without worrying about the possibility of me seeing him. He grabbed me so I wouldn't rush out and fall down the stairs. If he had wanted to harm me he had plenty of time to do it.'

Brenda grunted. 'Well, maybe. But I'm not taking any chances. Goodnight, Madeleine. Turn off the light as you go out.'

'Goodnight, Brenda.'

Brenda settled herself comfortably in the armchair. There was a rug nearby on the floor. She picked it up and pulled it over her lap. She wondered if it had been Michael's.

She shuddered awake. She was sure she had heard a scream. Her first reaction was surprise to find she had fallen asleep at all. Sometimes she was awake all night. Sometimes she dozed for an hour or two before dawn. But this time she had been deeply asleep and the clock showed that only an hour had passed since she had picked up the rug. Her second reaction was fear. Had Alan got into the house and attacked Madeleine upstairs?

She threw off the rug, ran to the door and out into the hall. Swearing, bruising her legs against the unseen furniture, she searched for the light switch. When at last she found it she dashed upstairs, surprising herself with her agility. At the top she quickly found the landing light. There were several doors off the landing. Which was Madeleine's room? She called out her name. She tried the first door she found. There was a narrow staircase behind it, leading to the attics. The next door opened onto the bathroom. She opened the door next to it. She gasped with relief. The light fell on Madeleine's motionless form, under the covers, her hair spread on the pillow. She was silent, apart from the sound of light, regular breathing.

Brenda's eyes raced round the room, peering into the shadows. She stepped inside the room, feeling into the corners. She opened the wardrobe as quietly as she could. Nothing. Madeleine was alone and apparently undisturbed. Had she imagined the scream? She padded across to the bed and touched Madeleine's shoulder. Madeleine stirred slightly and murmured. Brenda stepped back slowly through the door and closed it behind her. Half an hour later she was fast asleep again in her armchair.

When she awoke the clock showed that it was already past nine. She had slept more that night than she had for the whole of the previous month. She rose stiffly, walked into the hall and through to the kitchen to put on the kettle. Then she returned to the foot of the stairs and called out Madeleine's name. There was no response.

We must both have been completely shattered last night. I'll leave her for a few minutes. Then take her a cup of tea. The rest will do her good.

Ten minutes later she stood by the open door to Madeleine's room. It was empty and the bed had been made. Had she got up early and gone through to the lounge to wait for Brenda to wake up? Leaving the tea she had poured for Madeleine by her bedside she searched slowly and methodically through every room on the first floor, then downstairs. Nobody in the library or the lounge, or in Megan's little parlour. Then a thought occurred to her. What about the attics? She returned upstairs and on up the narrow staircase. The door at the top was locked.

Back in the library, she swore, loudly. She had not even heard the bolts being pulled back. What in God's name was the girl playing at? Had she gone crazy again? She wondered if she should search the coastal path. Or even call the coastguard. Madeleine had gone up there the other night, imagining she was seeing her mother fall over the edge. God knows what ideas were going through her head after all that stuff she had remembered about her father. Perhaps she had decided she could not cope with the memories she had recovered. And who would blame her?

Then she noticed something on the small table near her armchair. It was the envelope which Madeleine had given her the previous night. The contents were still inside. On the back of it, she had scribbled a short note:

Sorry, Brenda. I have to do this on my own. M.

Although it was only just after ten, Brenda decided it was time for a large brandy.

34

The tall steeple, fashioned out of warm Cotswold stone, was far too imposing and elaborate for a parish church. Brenda felt intimidated as she stood in its shadow. In the distance she saw a female figure standing motionless by the side of one of the graves. As she approached she saw that the woman wore a long black coat with a black scarf over her head. As Brenda's footsteps crunched on the newly-fallen crisp brown leaves the woman looked round. Madeleine's eyes met Brenda's for a moment, then turned back towards the grave. They had registered no surprise or alarm, no visible signs of emotion at all.

'I never came to the funeral,' she said, quietly, almost to herself. 'I must have been in shock. I suppose I was staying with a relative. I had an aunt in Woodstock. She died before I went to London. I suppose I stayed with her. I've never been here before.'

'Is that why you dressed in black today? To make up for not being there at the time?' Madeleine nodded. 'May I look?'

'Of course.'

Brenda stepped up to Madeleine's side and looked at the gravestone. It was small, no more than waist-high. Brenda read the inscription out loud: '"In memory of Andrew Reed, beloved husband of Ceridwen and loving father of Madeleine."'

'I expected much more. Nothing about his fame or success. His contribution to learning. Could be anybody. I'm sorry about running away like that. How did you know where to find me?'

'I had Mr Wilson's card you gave me. I drove up yesterday afternoon. Found a little hotel. I went to see him this morning. It's young Mr Wilson who runs it now, of course, as you know. But his father was there as well. Retired now. The one who handled your father's will. He was there because you had just been with them. Young Mr Wilson had called him in so he could tell you about your father's death. They told me too, when I explained I was a friend who was anxious about you. Everything fits your account. They told me you had come on here, to pay your belated respects. They gave me directions. Well, have you?'

'Have I what?'

'Paid your respects. Or did you come here for another purpose?'

'I came here to ask for his forgiveness.'

'Forgiveness?' Brenda realised that she had shouted, and turned to apologise to anybody nearby for having disturbed the peace of the graveyard. But they were alone, as far as she could tell. 'Forgiveness? After what he did to you?'

'I remember something he wrote in one of his books. "Beauty in the young is a curse. It awakens evil." The words kept coming back to me, all down the years since he went. I never understood what he meant. I understand now.'

'So do I. You had her beauty, all right. The beauty I hated her for. You already had it, even at thirteen. And it awakened evil in him. And you asked for his forgiveness?'

'The evil was in me too. It started in me. That was what he meant. Yes, I asked for forgiveness. Why not? If he had never had me for a daughter, or if I had behaved differently, none of this would have happened. He would have lived on. Still been alive now, maybe. He was quite well known by the time he died. But he was never really recognised as a great scholar. He never had the time for that. Never had time to become a professor, to be revered all around the world. Never had time to become a great man, proud and happy in his achievements.'

'He destroyed himself. And you.'

'No. I started it. I was alone, you see. Mother never noticed what was happening to me. I was terrified. I turned to him instead. It must have been the way I looked at him. My eyes must have asked him, what's happening to me? What must I do? What am I? Who am I? Not just my eyes. I used my whole body to call out to him. And he responded. He told me who I was. He told me I was special. He told me I wasn't alone. And he didn't just say it. He made me special. Part of him.'

'You accepted what he did because he made you special? But surely it was far more terrifying than being alone.'

'Yes. The first time, I thought I was going to die. I didn't understand why he wanted . . . the most disgusting parts of me. Why I had to display those parts to him, naked, on my belly, as if crawling in the dirt. Why he was breaking me into pieces. And all the time he was calling me special. Later, I understood. He was breaking me so he could remake me in his own image. So we could be together, above the rest of mankind.'

'As God remakes the sinner. It's all right. I haven't suddenly turned religious. I went to church regularly when I was a girl. But the sinner is made whole and taken up into Heaven. He wanted you in Hell with him.'

'Yes. That's where I belong.'

'And was it worth it? Once he had remade you, as you put it. Was it worth it, being a stranger to your mother, to the people who might have been your friends, your lovers? Was it worth it, going through life as a shadow because you had given everything away, heart, body and soul, when you were a child of thirteen to an evil man, a coward who could not go on living with what he had done, who could not face the consequences of his actions? But he left you to face them, didn't he? So look me in the eye and tell me it was worth it. Can you do that? And if not, what in the name of all that is holy are you doing here, asking for his forgiveness, when he should be screaming up from the depths of Hell to ask for yours?'

Madeleine's eyes blazed. 'Worth it? Of course it was. How could you, how could anybody possibly understand? When we

225

were together, working on his books and articles. When he was trying to explain his thoughts to me even before he had formed them himself. When I felt that together he and I had the power to reinterpret the world, to make it afresh. After that, how could I be interested in anything anyone else might do or say to me, least of all the girls at school with their inane chat about boyfriends and make-up? So, what if they thought I was stuck-up and superior? What if they did hate me? What if I had no friends? What if I could do nothing but despise every man I met since because it could never be with them the way it was with him? What if I had to live my life alone because what I shared with him could never be shared with anybody else?'

'What if? I'll tell you what if. Because he took from you everything you could and should have been, that's what if. What would I have done with a fraction of the heart and the beauty and the intellect you were born with? You've wasted them all. You lost your mind, killed a woman who had done you no harm, spent all those years locked away, and now God knows what else is wrong with you and how much time is left. So what gave you the right to do that to your life? And what gave him the right to take all that from you?'

Madeleine shook her head. 'You're right about the life I've led. But it wasn't meant to be that way. The Furies came for him. And I betrayed him.'

'What are you talking about? They only came for him. Not for you. He was the guilty one. Not you.'

'You're wrong, Brenda. They did come for me. Later.'

'Because of you and him? Or something else? What was it you told me about the Furies? They pursue people for unnatural crimes. A mother and son. Or a father and daughter. Forbidden relationships. But there are others, aren't there?'

Madeleine stared at her. Then she smiled. 'Well done, Brenda. You are clever, aren't you? You worked it all out, didn't you? You've solved the puzzle. Of Laura and my mother and the child.'

226

'Yes. I worked it out. On the way up yesterday. And you remembered it, didn't you, during the night? When I heard you scream. What I saw you and David do together . . . You were doing what you did with him, weren't you? In exactly the same way. Displaying what you call your disgusting parts so he could break you and remake you. Maybe that was the way you always did it. With all the men you slept with. Only they didn't matter. With David it was different. With David it was the nearest to the way it had been with your father.'

'Yes,' whispered Madeleine. 'A family affair.'

'Had you any idea at all?'

'Not consciously. I needed David because somehow I knew he would give me a reflection of myself. That had only happened to me once before and I had buried it in my subconscious. I didn't understand at the time why I knew David could find it for me again. I just knew. So now we both know everything. Except why Laura had to die.'

'Why do you say you betrayed him?'

'Did they tell you there were two bullets in the gun?'

'No. How do you know that? It would be in the ballistics report, I suppose. But how did you hear about it? And what does it matter? He would have had more than one in case he missed with the first.'

'I didn't read about it. I just know. The second bullet was for him. The first should have been for me. But he couldn't bring himself to do it. So he told me to follow him. I didn't catch what he said at the time. I only remembered while I was standing here, before you came. I was supposed to pick up the gun and follow him. I didn't. Then I forgot. He wanted me to die with him so we would be together and I would be spared the horror of the Furies. You see, he would never have wanted me to be here on my own. Unable to be with him but imprinted with his image. Not fit for this world but not knowing how or when to leave it. He would never have done that to me. But I didn't understand. So they came.'

Brenda walked up to her and put her hand round her shoulder. 'Madeleine, when I couldn't find you in the house yesterday morning, I thought you had decided to kill yourself. I thought you had gone to the cliffs. I thought you couldn't live with the memories you had uncovered. When I found out you were still alive, and again when I saw you standing here, I felt sick. Sick with relief. Your mother's death is on my conscience. The thought of yours being as well . . . If that sounds selfish, too bloody bad. And there's something else, too. Just as selfish. With you gone, I have no idea what I'll do with myself. I resented you coming into my life, when you were discharged. Now the thing I'm going to resent more than anything else is you leaving. And I don't like the way you're talking, about guns and not being supposed to be here and going to be with him.'

'It's all right, Brenda. I don't have a gun. And I'm not going to jump off the cliffs. That's not my way. I'm too much of a coward. There's no need for anything like that, don't you see? I am following him. I've killed myself already.'

Brenda pulled her hand away and covered her mouth with it as she let out a little cry. Then she ran over to a nearby bench and sat down, sobbing.

An elderly couple strolled by, carrying flowers. Madeleine smiled at them. 'It's all right. She always gets upset like this when we visit her uncle. Even after all these years.'

The couple smiled back at her, then turned towards Brenda to smile at her reassuringly. Brenda did not notice them. Madeleine walked over to the bench.

'I'm sorry, Brenda. I shouldn't have put it like that. I shouldn't have been so brutal. It was years ago. While I was abroad. Before I came back to live with Michael. It's not because I remembered what he said. Not consciously. But his words must have registered somewhere. It's just taken a lot longer with me than it did with him, that's all. I know you realise that something is the matter. So I didn't think I would shock you. I'm sorry.'

Brenda took a large cotton handkerchief out of her handbag and blew her nose noisily.

'But what if you're wrong about all this? What if you're horribly wrong about the whole business? What if you don't have to follow him? What if he was just an evil, cowardly man who shot himself and all that's in the past? That means it's not too late. Whatever happened in that room with Laura it was your final confrontation with the past. It's all over now. You did a terrible thing when you had no control over your mind or body. But you served your time. There's still a life ahead of you, if you can just believe it. For God's sake, can't something be done? There must be some treatment somewhere, abroad perhaps? What about America? I haven't got money, but you have. What I do have is time and energy and plenty of cunning. I'll help you. I have nothing else to do with my stupid little life.'

'No, Brenda. I've seen plenty of experts already. It's too late. I'm on borrowed time as it is.'

'All right. I'm sorry. I won't mention it again. So long as you promise you won't do anything to cut short the time you do have, borrowed or not.'

'I promise. But there's something I want you to promise me.'

'What's that?'

'Don't tell anyone what he did.'

'That may be difficult. But I'll try.'

'You must promise. Not before I go, and not after. You're the only person alive who knows. And you must take the secret with you to your grave.'

'All right. But why?'

'For a start, nobody would believe you. They'll ask where you got the information from. You'll say you got it from me. But she was crazy, they'll say. She was crazy from the age of fourteen. Officially diagnosed. That's why I could never have told anybody when I was alive, even if I had remembered. They'll think you're crazy too. But some mud may stick. The college set up a memorial fund in his name. He left a lump sum to start it off, together with a legacy, a percentage of the posthumous earnings from his books. There's a new lecture theatre named after him. I went there to look at it this morning. I paid a large sum towards the initial costs, anonymously of course. More importantly, part of the fund goes towards scholarships for poor students. There are a lot of other sponsors, here and in the States. If there were rumours about his conduct, all that could be threatened.'

'All right. You have my word. None of that makes up for what he did, but it would be wrong not to let it continue. How are you feeling?'

'Tired.'

'Let's walk. I want you to tell me more.'

'About what?'

'About Laura. The bits you haven't yet told me. They could be very important. I want you to tell me everything you now remember, about why you went to see her. Come on, on your feet. The walk will do you good.'

Madeleine rose unsteadily. They linked arms and walked slowly along the path between the graves.

35

'After Michael's death I was desperate to settle his affairs and get away, anywhere. But I couldn't. He and the Furies kept me in the house.'

'When did they first come to you?'

'Before I went abroad. It was when David and I had finished whatever it was we had together. Everywhere I went on my travels they were with me. After Michael died, they were still there. But by then my father was with them. He had become one of them. He was the chief accuser. The only one who spoke. They were keeping me in the house until I confessed my crimes. My father was accusing me of something to do with David. But I didn't understand. My father died before David was born. What possible connection could there be? The Furies avenge crimes against nature, he said. Remember me telling you that? You are guilty of such crimes. First me, then David.

'What do you mean? I replied. I had never been unnatural towards you. I had always loved you. No daughter could have loved a father more. If anything we were too close. Yes, he said. That was it. We were too close. Unnaturally close. Your love for me wasn't right. It was not natural. I don't understand, I said. What do you mean? You know very well what I mean, he said. And your love for David was unnatural as well. When was it that the Furies manifested themselves to you? Only after you and David had joined your bodies together. They had held back the first time, decided that they would take me first. Now your time has come. You are just like me, corrupt and evil, through and through.

'Don't you know who he was? Don't you know who his mother was? No, I said. You're wrong. You've made a mistake. You can go back to Hades and take those odious creatures with you. I can prove you're wrong. I heard her. Laura. The way she had spoken about David. "My child," she had said. But not her natural child, he replied. She never said he was her natural child. All right, I said. I'll prove it to you. You can hear it from her own mouth. "David was my natural child." I'll get her to say those words.'

'So that was why you went to see her. Not to help her. To save yourself.'

'But she wouldn't say those words. I was doing everything I could to prompt her to say them. But she wouldn't.'

'But surely you didn't kill her for that?'

'No. Why would I do that? But that's still the bit I can't remember.'

'Come on. Let's get away from all these graves. It's getting dark and I'm feeling quite spooky. Where are you staying?'

'Hotel just up the road from here.'

'Let's fetch your things, then mine.'

'Are we going back to Cornwall?'

'No. Portsmouth.'

36

A pair of semi-detached thirties houses in a quiet suburban street. Brenda parked the car on the opposite side of the street. She pointed to the houses and nodded to Madeleine.

'Those two? Which was my mother's?'

'The one on the left. Number thirty-two. The one I bought for her with Michael's money.'

'It's very small.'

'Large enough for a woman on her own. And she didn't have to stay there. It was only meant to be a temporary arrangement. While she had the abortion and recovered. She could have moved away afterwards. I never thought she'd be here for more than a few weeks. She could have asked Michael to sell the house and give her the proceeds. She could have sold the cottage as well. I had promised to do that for her. She could have got somewhere a lot bigger, if she had wanted.'

'Yes. She could have moved anywhere, so long as it wasn't back to Cornwall. Or anywhere near.'

'That was the agreement.'

'But she stayed. Because she had a child. And a new friend next door. And hopes that one day she and Michael might be together again. She wanted to stay somewhere where Michael knew he could find her, if he changed his mind. I suppose Laura's was the other one in the pair.'

'I suppose so. There's a "For Sale" sign outside.'

The front door of the first house opened. Two girls, about four and six years old, rushed outside and began to play with a doll in a toy push-chair. Then one of them noticed the women in the car on the other side of the road, watching them. She ran to the open door and shouted through it. Their mother, a plump, red-faced young woman, came to the door and looked over at them, an expression of suspicion and hostility spreading over her face.

'Wait here a minute,' said Brenda. She opened the car and strode over the road with a brisk and business-like air. Madeleine watched for a few minutes as Brenda engaged the mother of the two girls in conversation. The girls forgot their game and watched, fascinated by this unexpected arrival of a stranger. The mother smiled and disappeared into the house. Brenda came back to the car and opened the door.

'Come on. We're going inside. I told her we were supposed to meet the estate agents here but they've obviously forgotten the appointment. That lady has a key. She's going to let us in to have a look round. We're prospective buyers, don't forget. The place is for me. You're my niece, come along to help and advise me. I'll be enthusiastic while you pretend to be much more doubtful. Well, are you coming?'

Madeleine shrugged her shoulders, climbed out of her side of the car and followed her over the road. The other woman was already opening the door to the house which had been Laura's. She smiled broadly at them, clearly pleased at the prospect of a single respectable lady for a new neighbour.

'I'll let you go in and have a look round on your own. Then you can make up your own minds. Better than having all that sales chatter in your ear. It's been empty a while so it's a bit bare and bleak. But I'm sure between you you'll be able to make it homely again.'

She glared at her children who were still watching, as if to warn them to be on their best behaviour and show what good neighbours they would be. 'When you've finished just knock next door and let me have the key back.'

They walked through into a lounge with a threadbare beige carpet and peeling wallpaper. In one corner of the wall all the paper had been removed, revealing mottled plaster beneath. The only furniture was a low cushion-less settee with protruding springs. There was an air of chilly damp in the room.

'I wonder if this is her stuff,' said Brenda. 'What's left of it. I can't imagine anybody's lived here for years. Looks as if she started to decorate. Maybe that was when Michael sent her away.'

'It wasn't her house by then. She was renting it. Or trying to.'

'So the landlord came back and started to peel off the wall-paper. Then he decided not to bother. He put it on the market to get whatever price he can. No wonder nobody wants the place. So this is where Michael first saw his son. Maybe in this very room. Let's sit down.'

'I don't want to stay here.'

'We won't. Just a few minutes. Just the time it takes you to tell me what happened when your mother left David here with Laura. In Laura's words. Go on. Start again at the point where she told you he had two mothers.'

'Two mothers? What a lucky child he was. But only a natural mother can love a child the way you loved him. He was yours, wasn't he? The way you spoke to Michael about him. You had to be his mother. You said so yourself. You said David was your child.'

'No, my dear. You misunderstood what I was saying because it wasn't meant for your ears. Michael and I knew what I meant. David was only mine because it was in her will and I had accepted responsibility for him.'

'Her will? But I know what was in her will. Everything came to me.'

'That must have been her previous one. Before any of this happened. After a few years she told me she had decided to go to Cornwall to see the father. Then she said that she had been having nightmares. She was afraid she might not return, might not see the boy again. I told her that in that case she shouldn't go. Why not just forget about the father and concentrate on bringing up the boy, if she was that concerned? She said she had to go. She wanted the father to meet his son, see what sort of boy he had become. Wanted him to leave his wife so they could become a family. But in case anything happened to her she had decided to make a new will. I told her she was just dreaming. But I couldn't put her off her plan. I wish to God I had managed to. I should have locked her up until the madness had passed. But I couldn't stop her.

'While she was away I tried to keep my mind off what she had said, about being afraid something might happen to her. I took him out to play in the park, kept him amused, reassured him she would be back soon. All the time there was this feeling of dread in my heart. I wrote to her at the cottage, telling her he was well but missing her terribly. I didn't hear from her. Then I saw it in the papers. I was in shock, wondering how to tell him. Wondering if I should go to the police down there because they were saying they didn't know who she was, this woman who had fallen from the cliffs. But I knew in my heart it had to be her.

'Then he came to see me. I assumed he had come from the landlord, about the rent. The posh suit and the fancy car, I supposed all that was to intimidate me. No point, I thought. You can't get blood out of a stone. I started to explain my situation, and he told me, no, he hadn't come about the rent. I still wonder about what he was going to say. Probably that he was a friend of hers who had lost contact and was trying to find her. That he had tracked down her address to next door, called there but got no reply. Did I know where she was, did I know who she had gone to visit? He must have seen the letter I had sent to the cottage. Got my address from that. Realised I was her next-door neighbour. He wanted to know if I knew about him. If she had left me his details. She hadn't. I didn't even know his name. If I had, I suppose his plan was to buy me off or find some other way to get me to stay out of the way. He didn't want the police finding out that she had gone to put pressure on him and then died in mysterious circumstances. This is what I thought later, when I began to suspect.'

'Suspect what?'

'That her death wasn't an accident, of course. But at the time I was completely in the dark. Anyway he never did carry out his plan, if it was what I thought. He saw the boy and that changed everything. After that, he decided to play a different game, a very dangerous game, for much higher stakes. Before, he had only wanted my silence. Now he wanted that and the boy. And that meant I had to disappear. I don't know if he worked all that out at the time. But he knew right away how to get to me. That was when he asked me how much I owed. Who the hell are you, I asked? He told me his name. I was none the wiser. Then he told me he was the boy's father, but the boy must never know. He said Ceridwen was dead. An accident. A fall from the cliffs. But how did he know it was her, I asked. According to the papers she hadn't been identified yet. He told me not to ask questions or he wouldn't give me the money. I agreed. He handed over the cheque and left.

'His car was still outside though, for another couple of hours after he had left me. I could hear him next door, in her house, rummaging around. Within a week he had the whole place cleared and up for sale. I had a key she had given me but I had to hand it over to him. All he gave me from the house was a box full of the boy's toys and the drawing and painting stuff she had left there. I felt it was a sacrilege, him tearing all the memories out of her house like that, the whole life she had had there, the two of them. But I couldn't do anything about it. The house was in his name.

'When David died, falling from the cliffs in the same place she fell, I decided Michael must have killed her. David's death was divine justice. A mercy to David because his mind had gone, so Michael had said in his letter. A terrible retribution for Michael. He had to live on with the knowledge of what he had done. If

237

you can call that a life. May all their souls rest in peace. He wasn't mine, my dear. Not in the way you thought. I never had children of my own. But I loved him as if he had been mine. When you heard me talk to Michael about my child, that was how it felt to me. My child.

'She was already pregnant with him when she arrived. There was nothing to see then. But when it started to become noticeable I asked her about the father. She didn't want to say much about him. She said he had bought the house for them and sent them money from time to time. She hinted that he was an important public figure. He was married and needed to avoid a scandal. At first she was happy to stay out of his life and keep his identity a secret, for his sake. Later she changed her mind about that. Decided she had protected him for long enough. When she first admitted to me that she was pregnant she said, you don't think I'm a bad person, do you? You're not ashamed to be in my company? I told her not to be silly. I was never the one to go around judging people. I was delighted in fact. As I said, it was a sort of bond between us.

'I was with her in the hospital when she had it. She always said she wanted a boy. She had her wish. I was so happy for her. She called him Hywel. After her father. David was the name Michael wanted him to be known by. Michael had a new identity ready for him for the time he would go to live with him. Still trying to avoid a scandal. Michael told me to tell him his real name was David and that his real parents had been killed in a car crash when he was a baby, like I told you. When I told him I don't think he really took it in. How could he at that age? But he took to his new name readily enough. I imagine he forgot his real name after a few years.

'Are you all right, my dear? You're very quiet. You're still there? I can't see very well. Is that you over by the window? Come over here again. Close to me. That's right. I want to tell you about the will. She told me she wanted me to be her executor and Hywel's legal guardian in case anything happened to her and his father still refused to acknowledge him. Then there was you. She told me she had a daughter. You had gone to work in London and had done very well for yourself. Said you were the image of her. She sounded so proud of you. But she was very sad as well. I had always been able to tell she was sad about something, not just about not being with Hywel's father. Now I knew what it was. She said you had fallen out when you were still in your teens. She didn't say what it was about. Only that there had been some awful misunderstanding. In your eyes she had done something dreadful to you but she was never quite sure what it was. She hoped you would be reconciled one day.

'I told her, never mind about Hywel's father. Write to your daughter, make contact again, try to sort out what had happened between you. Maybe the two of you could be friends now. Then think about the father. No, she said. Not yet. Later. When I've seen him. I couldn't persuade her. But you were in her will. Half of what she had was to go to you and half to Hywel.

'She had a solicitor but he lived in Oxford. I knew a local one. He'd looked after Harry's affairs, in a manner of speaking. He agreed to act for her. He drew up the will, she signed it and I witnessed it. Before she left, she gave me Hywel's birth certificate, and other papers, school reports and stuff like that. For safe keeping.

'After her death, Michael eventually agreed that we could go to her funeral. He refused point blank at first. I pleaded with him. In the end he relented. But only on condition that nobody else saw us. We had to wait in the churchyard until the coffin had gone into the church. Then we could go in but we had to stay at the back. Under no circumstances were we to talk to anybody. When he gave us the signal we had to leave. As the service was drawing to a close he turned towards us and nodded. That was the signal. But we didn't leave the churchyard and go home, which was what he wanted us to do. I couldn't just go. Not like that. I wanted to watch her being lowered into her grave and hear the final prayers. So I could go up to it afterwards, when they had all gone, and pay my final respects. So we hid, among the gravestones.

'Then you came out. I had seen you in the church. I knew right away who you were. I wanted to go up to you. To tell you she had always remembered you. That she had been sorry for what had happened between you. That she was sorry for any wrong she had done you. That she had intended one day to make it up with you. David ran towards you. Do you remember? I pulled him back. I lost my nerve. I thought, if Michael came out now and saw me approaching you, perhaps even speaking to you . . . God knows, the last thing I wanted was for him to take David away from me. But I knew he could provide him with a future. I persuaded myself I was going along with it for the boy's sake. But I was sure that if I didn't follow Michael's orders he would cast both of us off. I would lose David anyway, I thought. How could I be a mother to him with no home and a mountain of debt? He would be taken into care.

'I wish I had been stronger. Told Michael to do his worst and tried somehow to make a life for the two of us. But there and then, at that moment in the churchyard, I lost my nerve. I pulled David back and we left. I never spoke to you. I lost my nerve and I never recovered it. If we had only managed to exchange a few words, if I had only been able to tell you who we were, what was going on, get you on our side . . . It would all have been different, wouldn't it? So very, very different. I'm so sorry, my dear. For everything. I wish to God I had been stronger.

'When I got back I asked my solicitor to let me have her will. I told him I wanted your solicitor to put it into effect, because he was the only one who knew how to contact you. But of course I never did get in touch with your solicitor. Michael had asked me if there was a will. When I told him there was, he told me to get it and give it to him. When I surrendered David to him I handed over the will and his birth certificate and all the other papers she had given me. I suppose he burned the will. I had told him I had a sister in Australia. She was ill and I had not

240

had the chance to visit her there. In exchange for the boy, and my own heart and soul, I got a one-way air ticket to the other side of the world. And, later on, a few thousand pounds to make sure I stayed out there.

'When I came back to England my sister-in-law was shocked to see the condition I was in. I've come home to die, I said. She burst into tears. She's been good to me. Very good. I never told her what had happened. We had lost contact since Harry died. She keeps telling me, you don't deserve this, Laura. You're a good person. I know something happened after Harry's death to make you want to go away. But I'm not going to ask you what. All I know is that this is not what you deserve. But she's wrong. It's everything I deserve.

'That's all, my dear. There's nothing else to tell. I'd like you to go now. I'm very tired.'

'Is that all?'

'Yes. Everything she told me.'

'The last thing she said was that she wanted you to go because she was very tired. And you can't remember what happened next?'

'No. I'm sorry. I am trying, Brenda. I just can't.'

'Come on. There's somewhere else we have to go. Go and wait in the car. Here are the keys. I need to talk to the lady next door again.'

Twenty minutes later they were outside another building. They had driven away from the city centre and the inner suburbs to the fringe of the countryside. Detached, double-fronted houses were set well back behind tall hedges that bordered long, leafy avenues.

'Every city has this sort of area now,' said Brenda. 'Huge, expensive houses for the gentry, which get sold and converted into nursing-homes and the like. I know my way around here. We just passed the clinic where she was supposed to have the

241

abortion. I was there very recently, as I told you. Did you see that sign outside? Centre for Women's Health. There's a euphemism for you. And you know the area as well, don't you? That sign's another euphemism. St Agnes' Centre for Palliative Care. Why does everywhere have to be a centre these days? Why can't they just be hospitals, or hospices or nursing homes? This is the place isn't it? You told me Naomi had said it was once called St Agnes' Hospice. I asked the lady who gave us the key for directions.'

'Yes.' Madeleine's voice shook. She slumped low into her seat as if trying to become part of it. 'I can't do this, Brenda.'

'Oh yes you can. Because you have to and you know it. So tell me, is this place private?'

'Yes. It was when Naomi brought me here. She paid for Laura's room with what little money she had left. Laura had none. She had some left over from what Michael gave her but she had given that back to him. Brenda, we can't just go in.'

'Yes we can. Private places need customers, don't they? And that's what we are. You're my niece, remember. And we're looking for a bed for my elder sister who's dying of cancer. The NHS can't do any more for her. And we don't like the conditions in the ward they've got her in. We want somewhere quiet and pleasant where she can spend her last days, don't we? The standards of nursing care and medical cover need to be adequate but not intrusive. I'll do the talking, don't worry. I'll be very convincing. You don't have to say a word.'

'But what if someone recognises me?'

'They won't. I don't want to be cruel but you have changed. Wrap that shawl closely around your head. Anyway the chances are that nobody who worked here then is here today. All these places have a big turnover of staff.'

A minute later they were standing in the reception area. Madeleine stood back, covering her mouth with the shawl, while Brenda talked to a young lady in a crisp grey suit carrying a black folder. The young lady smiled, nodded and disappeared into an office. Brenda ran back towards Madeleine and grabbed her by the arm.

'Come on. She's gone to get someone to show us round. When she comes back she'll think we've changed our minds and gone away. Now, which floor?' Brenda shook her arm. 'Which floor, for God's sake?'

'First. Up those stairs.'

Brenda frogmarched Madeleine up the stairs. 'Which room?'

'On the right. Just round that corner. Brenda, there'll be somebody in it.'

'If there is, there is. We'll just have to see. It might be empty. This one?'

'Yes.'

'Are you sure?'

'Positive. I remember that nursing-station we passed just there. That was where the nurse was. I could reach her from the room by pressing a red button.'

'But there was nobody there. So maybe all the rooms along here are empty. It's very quiet here. No staff and no visitors.'

Brenda knocked gently on the door, then pushed it open. The bed was vacant, the bedding stripped off, the equipment idle against the wall. Brenda pulled Madeleine into the room.

'Don't worry. If anybody comes in we'll say we lost our guide so we thought we'd look into some of the rooms. Where were you standing, exactly?'

'There. Just by the bedside.'

'This side, nearest the door?'

'Yes.'

'How close? Near enough to touch her? Show me.'

Brenda lay down on the bed and stretched out. 'Was she like this? Where were you when she finished telling you about your mother and David and Michael? Show me.'

Madeleine moved towards the bed, stretching out her hands. When she was still a few feet away she pulled them back and clamped them over her mouth.

Brenda pushed herself off the bed and grabbed her by the shoulders.

'Madeleine, open your eyes. It's all right. You're safe. He's not here. It's only me. He was never here. You imagined it then and you did the same just now. But it was never real. Not then. Not now.'

Madeleine's eyes opened, wide, staring. Then with unexpected force she pushed Brenda away from her and ran towards the door. She was outside the main entrance and nearly into the street before Brenda caught up with her. She stared at Brenda as if she did not know who she was. Brenda shuddered. She pulled Madeleine into her arms.

'Madeleine, look at me. Don't do this. You mustn't forget again. Not after what you've just done. It's safe now. You can remember. Just tell me. Tell me you remember where we were just now. Tell me you remember what we just did. Look at me. Focus on my eyes. Madeleine, where were we? A few minutes ago? Come on.' She shook her violently.

Madeleine stared at her for a minute. At last her features relaxed and a faint smile crept over her face.

'Brenda?'

'Yes. It's me. Where were we just now?'

Madeleine pointed. 'In there. We went in so I could remember.'

'Thank God. And did you? Tell me you did, please, because I don't fancy going in and doing it all over again.'

'Yes. I remember. Everything. It's true. You were right. She wasn't there any more. It was him. He was there in her place, on the bed. The Furies were there too. All around me. Pulling me down to Hell. Then he was gone. She was there again, in his place. I didn't know why I was there, what we had talked about. But why? I mean, why did I resist him? Why did I try to get away? They were right to come for me. I had committed incest. Not once. Twice. I was guilty. I don't understand.'

'It doesn't matter what you understand. Not at the moment. There'll be time for that. All that matters now is that you never forget again. Keep trying to remember what happened. Keep going over it in your head. Each time it will be less painful. Come to the car. We'll go back to the hotel now. You'll be in shock for a while. I'll take us back tomorrow. You can stay with me and I'll keep an eye on you. You've done all you needed to. Just let me take care of you now. Come on. Don't be afraid.'

She felt Madeleine squirming in her arms, gasping, struggling to get away. She held her firmly.

'If you want to have hysterics I don't mind,' she continued, in a soothing voice. 'I'd quite understand if you did. I'm sure I would. But not here in public. You mustn't run away and you mustn't make a scene. I can't let you do that. You mustn't draw attention to yourself. Not here, of all places. Do you understand that? That's right. Come with me now. This is nobody's business but ours. You've been very brave. Far braver than I could have been. I really never thought I would get you to go in there and do what you did. You just need to be brave for a few more moments. Until we get into the car and get the hell out of here. Come on, this way.'

Madeleine resisted the tug of Brenda's hands. 'Brenda, I'm all right. I'm not going to get hysterical. But you're not listening to me. I said he took her place. But that was only for a moment. I remember seeing her there again. She was looking at me as if I were mad. I was mad. I'm trying to imagine the expression on my face. She must have been totally bewildered. But I never went near her. I went no closer to her than I did with you just now, when you were lying on the bed.'

'What are you saying?'

'Brenda, I'm not mad now and I'm not hysterical, though I don't expect you to believe me.'

'I do believe you. You imagined he was there for a moment. Then she came back. You thought it was still him. You pulled the pillow out and covered his face with it, to get away from him, to stop the Furies pulling you down.'

'Brenda, you're still not listening to me. The moment she told me who David was I stood up. I turned my back on her. When I turned round again, he was there instead of her, pointing at me and laughing. I could never have gone up to him or touched him. I was rooted to the spot. I wanted to run away but all my limbs were frozen. I tried to scream. Then she was there again, in his place. But I had no idea who she was or what I was doing there. I was still a few feet away from the bed. I was suffocating. All I knew was that I had to get out of there. I left. She was alive when I left the room, staring after me. I remember that now. Brenda, I didn't kill her.'

37

'Did you ring Megan?' Brenda called out from the kitchen, where she was making the sixth pot of tea of the day, although it was barely mid-afternoon.

'Yes. While you were out walking. Were those fishermen about?'

'Ex-fishermen. These days they wouldn't know one end of a boat from another, they're so sozzled all the time. I didn't see them. I expect they were in the inn.'

'Good. Megan says she wants to come home tomorrow. Linda and her family are going on holiday so she can't stay any longer.'

Brenda returned to the living-room, bearing a tray laden with biscuits and cakes, as well as the teapot, cups and sugar-bowl. For a fortnight, since their return from Portsmouth, she had devoted herself to feeding Madeleine up. She had had some limited success, though Madeleine always complained that she had no appetite and was only eating what Brenda put in front of her to please her. They sat down near the fire.

'Do you think she believed you when you rang her last week?'

'About her having to stay away a bit longer because a prowler has been seen in the neighbourhood, which is why I'm staying with you? Yes, I think she believed me. But I'll have to go back tomorrow. Be there for when she gets back. I still think Alan is no threat.'

'Probably not. Just as a precaution I went to have a look inside the observation point while I was out. Nearly froze to death on my way up the path. Not to mention nearly being blown over the cliff edge by the wind. There's no sign of any of the stuff of his I saw there before. No sign of life at all. I'm sure he's moved on. Hardly surprising. Nobody in their right minds would stay up there now winter's setting in. I reckon he's moved away. Whatever strange ideas he had he's forgotten them. Whoever he is. We had him down as your half-brother. We now know he's not that, but that's all we do know.'

'I still think he's Michael's son. By another woman. Not my mother, not Laura.'

'And I still think he's a fantasist, who's given up on that particular fantasy for now. How are you feeling?'

'Much better. I'll be all right up at the house. Megan will keep an eye on me. And it really is about time you opened up the gallery again.'

'I'll open it the day after tomorrow. Not that I'm expecting many customers.'

'Why not tomorrow?'

'I'll come round to the house with you. I want to check it out, just in case Alan has moved in permanently. And then get some of the rooms heated and aired. After that, I'll leave you alone, I promise. In the meantime we need to talk about something. I've been waiting for you to recover a bit from what happened in Portsmouth. I think you're ready now. Don't worry. I'm not going to ask you to prove anything. I do believe you.'

'About what?'

'When you said you didn't kill her. So how did it happen that you thought you had? And if they thought you were mad, why did they think you were telling the truth about that, when there was no evidence and no motive?'

'I never admitted it. I told them I couldn't remember. They didn't believe me. They interviewed me for hours. Repeating the same questions but in a different order. Trying to trap me. Putting to me statements they said I had made but which I thought I hadn't but couldn't be sure. In the end they sent for a doctor. A psychiatrist. He had looked up my records. Found I had been detained when I was fourteen and treated in a clinic for drug addicts a few years later. When the police heard about that they changed tack. Kept asking me if I was still on hard drugs. If I made a practice of passing myself off as a relative or friend of hospital patients so I could steal their cash to feed my habit. That line of enquiry didn't come up with anything. I mean, why would I spend half an hour with a patient who didn't have a penny to her name?

'They called in the psychiatrist again. He asked me about my parents. Whether I had a happy childhood. Yes of course, I said. My father had died young and I was sad about that. But my mother and I had been very close. I could tell he didn't believe me because he asked me why I had cut myself. I told him it was an accident. I was clumsy. My mother had overreacted. I believed what I was saying but he obviously didn't. So why had I then gone onto hard drugs? I had been young and stupid, that was all. I was experimenting. It just happened. I went to the clinic and sorted it out. He asked me about my relationships with men. I said I had lots of boyfriends and always enjoyed sex. I had just been too busy to settle down, that was all. I sensed all the time that he didn't believe me.

'Then he asked me why I was always looking across the room, away from him. I laughed. Of course, he couldn't see them. But I could. They were always there, watching me, pointing at me. Who, he asked. The Furies, I said. He had never heard of them. I told him about my father's book, about how they followed you for particularly vile crimes. Were they there because of Laura, he asked. No, I said. Not for anything like that. Other things. What, he asked. But I couldn't tell him. By then, he knew I was hallucinating. But he didn't know I could be violent. I didn't know until then. There was a particular word that set it off.'

'Set what off?'

'It was a trigger. For me to lose control completely. He found it by accident. He wanted to talk about relationships again. It was obvious he wasn't satisfied with what I had been saying. He asked me if there had never been anybody who was really special to me. That was the word. Special. It was my father's word for me. He used it constantly. Especially when he was . . .' She stopped and made a choking sound. Brenda stood up and put her arm round her shoulder.

'It's all right, Brenda,' she whispered. 'I'm all right. I just need to breathe for a few moments.'

'Take your time.' She felt the tremors running through Madeleine's body as she gasped for air. Gradually they ebbed away. Brenda returned to her chair.

'I went for him. There was a table between us. I was trying to climb across it to get to him. I was screaming at him. The door to the interview room was behind him. I suppose he knew from experience always to sit there, so he could get away. He got out of the door and closed it behind him. The doctor, the ordinary one, and a nurse came in. They pinned me to the floor and gave me an injection. When I calmed down they took me back to my cell. The next day I saw the psychiatrist again. He told me what I had said. I couldn't remember, of course. I had said something like, how did he dare to accuse me of not having had anybody special in my life? What could he possibly know about it? He asked me to tell him about it, about that special person. I said I was lying. There was nobody special. I suppose he'd unwittingly triggered a memory the day before, but it had gone again.'

'If only he had realised that,' said Brenda. 'If only he had worked patiently with you to bring it back again.'

Madeleine shook her head. 'He did realise, I'm sure of that. But it wasn't his job to cure me. It was to decide whether I was fit to stand trial. He had to make a report for the courts. He diagnosed paranoid schizophrenia with severe short-term and long-term amnesia. He said I was obsessed with punitive figures from Greek mythology and had hallucinations that they were pursuing me for crimes I could not remember committing. He said I had a propensity to violence and was a potential danger to myself and others. I should be detained in a secure unit while receiving treatment, including therapy to help me recover my lost memories. They appointed a lawyer to act on my behalf. A young woman, very bored, very anxious to get on with something more interesting and lucrative. She told me what was in the report. She said I should plead guilty to manslaughter on grounds of diminished responsibility. The court would accept that. I agreed. I thought I had killed her. Everybody was telling me I had. So I believed them.'

She was sobbing uncontrollably. Brenda leaned forward and held her. After ten minutes she released her hold and let Madeleine settle into her chair, her limbs heavy, her eyes closing. Then she went into the kitchen to make yet another pot of tea.

Madeleine rushed to the door when she heard Megan's knock. Megan stepped back in surprise.

'Why, Miss Madeleine, and I'm sorry to keep calling you that, but I'm so pleased to see you looking so much better. There's something like a touch of colour in your cheeks and I haven't seen that for a long time. Come here.'

Megan hugged her and the two women walked over to the taxi to fetch her luggage. When they returned Brenda was standing at the door, with Megan's feather duster in her hand. Megan stopped, open-mouthed.

Madeleine laughed. 'It's all right, Megan. Brenda isn't the new housekeeper, and she'll be delighted to let you have your duster back. She's been helping me get the house ready again. You remember I told you I've been staying with her, because of the prowler who's been seen around here? She's the only other person I know in this part of the world.'

Megan stepped up and shook hands with Brenda. 'Come to think of it, I do remember you. You knew Mr Wallace, didn't you? You came here a couple of times although I only saw you enter and depart. Mr Wallace told me you had very private things to discuss so I weren't to bring you tea or anything.'

251

'That's right, Megan. I run the little gallery in Porthhella that Michael bought and did up. It is good to meet you at last. Madeleine is always saying how well you take care of her.'

'In that case I think you've been doing another of my jobs for me, she's looking almost blooming. Thanks anyway. And there were really no need to get the house ready, though I do appreciate it.'

'I've just made some tea,' said Brenda. 'Shall we have it in the lounge or the library? There's fires in both rooms.'

'How about the library?' said Madeleine.

'Fine by me,' said Megan.

They let Brenda walk into the library ahead of them. Madeleine was about to follow when Megan caught her arm. She whispered into her ear.

'That woman. I also remember her from somewhere else. She were at Mr Wallace's funeral, weren't she? Only she stood apart from the rest of us. Never came into the church. You said it were because she hated you. So what's happened since?'

'It's all right, Megan,' she whispered back. 'We talked things over. We're quite good friends now. Nothing to worry about. I'm safe with her. Honestly.'

Megan frowned as if she were not entirely convinced. Then she looked down at the floor by the front door.

'Just a moment. What's this envelope? Looks as if it's been pushed under the door. Addressed to you, Madeleine. Marked personal.'

Madeleine's heart leapt into her mouth as she took it from her. 'Go through to the library and start on the tea. I'll join you in a minute.'

She ran upstairs into her bedroom and tore open the envelope. The writing was familiar, as was the message.

St Olave's, tomorrow, noon. Usual arrangements.

38

'You're smelling a bit cleaner, Alan.'

'Thanks. I've had a bath and a change of clothes.'

'I thought the bathroom had been used recently.'

'I found the key to the attic. There were some clothes there that fitted me.'

'David's? Your brother's? You kill him and then you wear his clothes. How could you do that?'

'He doesn't need them any more.'

'Did you steal a key from David, to get into the house?'

'Yes.'

'Why did you attack me?'

'I didn't. I was having a look round and I heard a car coming. I turned the lights off.'

'To stop me seeing you.'

'That's right. When you came upstairs you nearly bumped into me. I put my hand over your mouth to stop you screaming. As soon as I got a chance I got out of there. I hope your friend's all right. I didn't mean to knock her over.'

'She's fine. She found out where you were staying. Said you had newspaper articles about me. So why did you come here in the first place? Why did you tell me all that about Michael and my mother?'

'I'm not new to these parts. I've been coming and going for a long time. I saw you, here with Michael. Looking after him. I wanted you to know what he was really like. The sort of man he was. Would you have looked after him if you had known he had killed your mother?'

'We don't know anything of the sort. I knew him better than you did. I know what sort of man he was. Whatever his sins, he was overwhelmed by grief and sickness. I had helped to make him that way. Anyway, it's none of your business.'

'Actually it is.'

'Oh yes, you say you're his heir. Well, if you can prove it you can have the house and the money he left me. I never wanted them.'

'I will prove it.'

'So you keep saying. I used to think I believed you. Now I don't. I don't believe you're Michael's son. I don't believe you killed David. I don't believe you ever knew him. You couldn't have known him. He had lost his mind, forgotten who he was. He would never have talked to you.'

'Why would I pretend I killed him?'

'I don't know. Because it makes you feel important, pretending that for once you had the power of life or death over someone.'

'Yes, I do know what that feels like. More than you could possibly imagine. No more now. Remember the rules? Same time tomorrow.'

'Bugger your rules.' She turned round. But it was too late. The door had already closed. And she knew that if she ran outside as quickly as her legs would take her she would never find him.

When she arrived at the church the next day it was empty. She waited for ten minutes. She was about to leave when she noticed something. In the place where she had sat the day before was a blue folder, creased and dirty. On top of it was a piece of paper. A note had been scrawled across it in red felt-tip pen.

M. Go to the cottage. Take the picture out of the frame and look at the back. Then come back here. Look at the inscriptions.

Read them, don't just look at them. Read these papers. You will understand everything. A.

She tucked the folder under her arm and walked to the phone-box just outside the graveyard to ring for a taxi.

Brenda had given her a key to her own cottage the day after their return from Portsmouth. Asking the taxi to wait, she let herself in quietly, took the key to Cove Cottage off the hook and walked round to the lane, keeping a sharp lookout for the fishermen. To her relief there was no sign of them. She had thought about dropping into the gallery to let Brenda know what was happening. But what would she tell her? She decided to wait until she knew what was going on.

Had Alan been in Cove Cottage himself? He could have stolen Michael's key. Michael would have had his own while he was managing the cottage and might have kept it after he sold it. Alan might have discovered it in the blue folder or in the bureau in the library. But how would he have known what the key was for? Maybe there was a label with the address on it. Or had Alan only heard about the cottage and the picture from David?

She took the picture down, placed it on the table by the bay window and carefully eased it out of the frame. She turned the fragile paper over. Some words were written on the reverse, in faded pencil:

For Ceridwen. This is the best of me. Without you I would never have known.

Of course. She had realised eventually that it was her mother. If she had only known Michael was in the habit of writing on the back of his portraits she could have proved it to David at the time and prevented that absurd misunderstanding. But what did this have to do with Alan?

What else did she need to do? Oh yes, look at the inscriptions. What inscriptions? The ones in the graveyard, presumably. No, not 'look at', 'read'. She had to read them. All right, she would humour him. She would go back and read them. Maybe he would be there and she could ask him what this was all about. Carefully she restored the drawing to the frame and hung it back on the wall. She returned to Brenda's cottage and replaced the key. The taxi was still waiting.

She stood in the churchyard. She had read through them several times. What was it she hadn't spotted? Suddenly her breath caught in the back of her throat. When she was finally able to release it she swore, slowly and loudly. Then she heard the church door bang against the oak frame. Someone had just gone in and shut it behind them. Her feet felt like lead. Very slowly she dragged them towards the door, pushed against it and nearly collapsed inside. Her heart pounded agonisingly as she crept towards the figure in the front pew and knelt down immediately behind it. The figure did not move.

39

'You killed her.'

There was a long pause.

'Yes.'

'And let me take the blame.'

'I killed two birds with one stone. Well, one bird was killed. The other went to prison.'

'Hospital.'

'You were still locked up. I bet it felt like a prison.'

'Go on.'

'What?'

'Tell me why and how.'

'Why? She gave me away to him. She was supposed to look after me. But she gave me to him. I saw her come to the house. She came during the day, more than once, looking round, trying to summon up the courage to ring the bell. Then she came late one night. Went straight up to the door and knocked. So I knew it must have been arranged. He was expecting her. After she had gone and he had gone to bed I broke in. I had done it before. The little window to the pantry in the back. I broke the glass the first time and nobody noticed for months. In the bureau drawer in the library I found a letter from her, asking him if he would agree to see her. There was a reference to me in the letter, and to the circumstances under which she had given me to him. So I knew it was definitely her. I couldn't be absolutely sure, just from seeing her. She had changed a lot. But now I had the evidence. I felt Fate had brought us together again and put the evidence into my hands. Did you ever find it, the letter I mean?'

'No. He must have burned it.'

'There was an address in Portsmouth. I stole some money as well. He always kept cash in the bureau. I don't suppose he ever noticed any of it was gone. I took enough to get me a shave and a change of clothes, and to get me to Portsmouth and live cheaply for a while. I don't need much, as you know. I went to the address and made some enquiries around the neighbourhood. I found out she was in a hospice. Found out where and which room. It wasn't difficult. Then I became invisible. I'm good at that too. Who's the one person who never gets noticed in a place like that? That's right, the maintenance man, the odd-job gaffer. I borrowed some overalls from the maintenance room in the basement, and a clipboard and a box of tools. Drifted around the place trying to look busy. Nobody stopped me. Nobody gave me a second glance.

'I never intended to kill her. I just enjoyed popping my head round the door from time to time, watching her die. One day I would go in there, pretending to do a job, and take the opportunity to tell her who I was, tell her what I thought of her and what she had done. But it would need to be near the end. Just when she was trying to settle down to a peaceful death, come to terms with her past, make her peace with whatever god she believed in. I would take that away from her. I thought she had no right to that. So I waited.'

'Then I came to see her.'

'Yes. What a surprise that was. I couldn't imagine what you were doing there. If you're bringing some guilt money from him, you're too late, I thought. I saw the two of you coming along the corridor. I had seen her before. Some sort of relation, I presume. When I saw you I nipped into an empty room, leaving the door open. After a few minutes I saw the other woman come past again. I came out and walked along the corridor, past the nurse, past the room. The nurse never saw me. She was on the phone, chatting. I looked in through the window in the door and saw you in there with her. I went on to the end of the corridor. There's a door there, leading to a fire escape. I saw you come out. I slipped quietly into the room.

'She was wide awake. I told her who I was. I waited to see that she understood, that she believed me. I mean, she wouldn't exactly have recognised me if we had passed in the street, would she? I held her hand. I asked her if she believed me when I told her who I was. Then I told her things only the two of us could have known. When I saw it in her eyes, the terror, the realisation, then I killed her. It was very easy. She went out like a light. Another day or two and she would have been dead anyway.'

'You could easily have been caught. Anybody could have come in.'

'So what? If they'd caught me with the pillow in my hand I would have said I was doing a job in the room and she had asked me for help in making her more comfortable. If they'd caught me pressing it down on her it wouldn't have mattered. That's the thing about being dead. You can do anything and you're not bothered about being caught.'

'Michael forced her. It broke her heart. She had already paid. Did that never occur to you? No. You were like one of those avenging angels from the Old Testament. You said nothing afterwards, when they arrested me. You hated me as well.'

'I hated Michael. You had an affair with him. So I hated you.'

'I lied to you about that. To finish things between us.'

'Then why did you go and live with him?'

'He needed somebody. I owed him. That was all.'

'He killed my mother. Don't you hate him for that? She was your mother too.'

'We don't know he killed her.'

'I showed you that letter. How else do you explain what happened?'

'I think she may have come to see him at the house. To confront him about you. For some reason she rushed out onto the path. She lost her way and fell.'

'Possible. But you think there was more to it than that, don't you? I can tell by the tone of your voice. Maybe he followed her. That's what you think, don't you?'

'I don't believe he meant to kill her.'

'Maybe he didn't try too hard to save her. It amounts to the same thing.'

'It would do, in your book. The book of wrongs done to you. The book you think gives you the right to sweep through the world with a sword of vengeance in your hand. Was it only because of Michael that you hated me?'

'You never told me who I was. That was really sick, letting me fuck you. I was your brother, for God's sake. I suppose you had tried everything else.'

'I didn't know.'

'He must have told you.'

'No. He was going to tell us both later, when we were friends. Not that there was much chance of that.'

They sat in silence for several minutes. At last he spoke again, whispering so that she had to lean forward to catch his words.

'I never thought they would lock you up. I just wanted to cause you some grief. Kill two birds, as I said. I thought you would tell them she had been fine when you left. They might not have believed you. But with no motive, I didn't think they would charge you. I wasn't to know you'd forget and they'd lock you up for being crazy.'

'But you didn't come forward.'

'Who would have believed me? I don't officially exist, remember. You can kill me if you want. I've got a penknife here. Not exactly a sword of vengeance but it would do. I'd let you. I'd show you exactly where to put it. We couldn't do it in church, of course. We'd have to go outside.'

'Don't be so bloody ridiculous. Do you think I'm like you? Do you think everybody is like you? Obsessed with taking revenge on everybody who's hurt them in some way? Do you really think I care now? I'm dying, for God's sake.'

'I was already dead. But that didn't stop me. Okay, have it your way. Don't say I didn't give you the chance.'

'I know now what happened in the cottage, after I had left. Did you forget right away?'

'I don't know. I wandered around, on the headlands, through the fields and woods, just walking. I slept under hedges. I was having a slow breakdown I suppose. I forgot to eat. In the end I think I forgot everything. I found myself by the house but I didn't know why I had gone back there. Megan saw me from the window. She seemed to know who I was. I was vaguely aware that I had a connection to the place but I didn't know their names. I didn't even know my own. Gradually it all came back. But I kept it from them. I didn't want to give him the satisfaction of knowing I had returned. I didn't want to give him the chance to take me over again. Not after everything that had happened. I didn't want him to give me another bloody breakdown.'

'I can't believe I'm hearing this. You said he was a useless artist because he didn't understand human nature. Do you really think you do? Couldn't you see he was completely broken by what had happened? Did you really imagine he could behave in the same way again?'

'Maybe not. But I couldn't really be sure what would happen if he knew I had recovered. I couldn't take the chance. But what if I killed myself? He would have no power over me then. And that might really make him sorry. So I planned it, down to the last detail. Even the exact spot. I knew the earth was very thin there. You can see it overhanging from the path on the other side. And I knew it was close to where she died. I thought that would make it more poetic somehow. The only problem was that once I was dead I wouldn't be able to see how he would react.

'Then I had a brainwave. I could stage my death and disappear. Come back and see. Haunt him like a ghost. Not many people get that chance. To see how other people react to their deaths. So I dislodged the earth. It was very dangerous of course. I might have fallen. But that was my first plan, anyway, so I didn't care. When the earth fell but I was still there, I decided it was Fate again. I hung around and watched him. I enjoyed that. I saw you come back. I was so bloody angry with you for that. I wanted him to die alone.

'After I had disposed of Laura and they had taken you away I had no reason to hang around. I took to the road. Went up north. Did odd jobs here and there. Mostly I just walked and stole. Then I read about you being released. Thought I would come back and make contact. You know the rest.'

'So why did you decide to end your little game today?'

'I thought you would have guessed long before this. Then I realised you weren't going to, not unless I helped you. I also realised you were ill. I didn't want you to go while still believing you killed her. I hated you, but not that much. And I wanted to say sorry. Not for killing her but for letting you take the blame. Give you the chance to take revenge.'

'And have you finished now? I mean, they're all dead, aren't they? All the people who did you wrong. Including me. Or is there anybody else I don't know about?'

'No. I'm finished. Just one more thing. What was she like?'

'Our mother? I hardly knew her. She wasn't like me, I can say that for certain. Only to look at. She was wild, impulsive, passionate, trusting, naive. Things like that.'

'No. Definitely not like you. It was her fault as well, wasn't it?'

'What do you mean?'

'About us. She never told you about me. So when you came down here after her you didn't know she hadn't just left you a cottage. You didn't know she had left you a younger brother hanging around the place as well. So why didn't she?'

'We'd fallen out. We were leading completely separate lives. As I said, we were different. What will you do now?'

'I have a few plans. Nothing that need concern you. And no, nobody else is going to die or get hurt. You won't see me again.

No more notes. No more secret meetings. I'll disappear again. Close your eyes.'

She did so. She sensed him rise and glide past her. With a single motion she pushed herself off the bench and into the aisle. She rushed towards the back of the church but he was already closing the door behind him. She pushed her weight against it but it would not move. She swore loudly. She put her eye to the keyhole but could see nothing through it. He must be blocking it. She put her mouth to the hole and shouted through it.

'It's all right. I won't follow you. I won't look at you. I just want you to listen to me. For a few minutes. You won't have to say anything. Just stay there. I'll stay here. I won't try to open the door. I promise. Just knock on the door to show you understand.'

She heard him moving, his breath rasping. Then she heard a harsh grating sound. The key was in the lock. That was why she could not see through it. Now he was turning it, slowly, painfully, finally forcing it into place with a heavy clunk. She turned round, leaned against the inside of the door and sank to the floor, the cold of the stone spreading through her body. She spoke as if addressing someone directly in front of her.

'All right. Have it your way. I don't suppose you intend to leave me locked in here. So I'll wait here until you unlock it. The door's heavy. By the time I get it open you'll be away. In the meantime I'll say what I'm going to say. You can listen to me or not. That's up to you. But I can't just let you go without saying it. You see, we are bound together. We're brother and sister. You can run away but nothing can alter that. You'll take me with you and leave yourself behind with me. So why do you keep disappearing? I won't look at you. I don't want to. I don't want to see the face I made. Any more than I can bear to look at my own. Can you hear me?' She heard a slight scraping movement on the other side. Perhaps he was sitting down as well.

'You were right to hate me. But not for the reason you think. Not because of Michael. Because of us. You said you were sorry. Well so am I. Sorry we ever met. Sorry I wasn't the one you needed. Sorry I wasn't the one who could see you were drowning and pull you out. I wasn't the one who would set you on the road to your brilliant, arrogant future, the one who would somehow prise you away from him without destroying either of you. You might have met someone like that. Instead you found me, an unknown sister on a lifelong mission to destroy herself.

'We each of us knew from the start it was wrong. We knew the only way ahead was madness. But we could do nothing about it, not once it had started. I could have prevented it. I should have suspected. I should have asked Michael what was going on, refused to put up with his lies and evasions, insisted on the truth. I should have made him tell me what he and our mother really were to each other, and who this so-called nephew really was. I didn't because I needed you. I needed you to help me finish off the task I had set myself. So I was blind, deliberately blind. I know you won't understand. I'm only beginning to understand it myself. I was beyond saving. But you could have been saved. So what right did I have to drag you down with me? Are you listening?'

Again there was a sound of movement, heavy, shuffling, fidgeting.

'I can tell you're still there. So I'll carry on. I tried to set you free in the end. I thought it might still be all right for you. That horrible stuff you did with me as a model . . . maybe you saw that as your first rebellion. Yes, I was really thinking that. Or trying to convince myself of it, against all my instincts. Perhaps you would move on, break with him altogether, find your own way. It was crazy, wasn't it? Because you knew something was wrong, terribly wrong. Of course you did. You knew we had both done something dreadful. Something neither of us could live with and stay sane. And soon enough you found out exactly what it was. How could you move on from that? I was still blind, still under the illusion you could be saved.

'When I heard what happened to you, I was shocked but I wasn't really surprised. I kept having these strange dreams. I must have known something had happened. I wrote to Michael, asking him how you were. Why would I have done that if I hadn't known, deep inside? I had tried to get away from you, from us, from our past. But I had taken you and all of that with me. Of course I had. As I said, we are brother and sister. I came back because I had to talk to Michael about it. When I looked after him it was a sort of attempt to make it up to both of you. As if I ever could.'

She heard him rise to his feet, clumsily. The key made a groaning sound in the lock.

'Wait a minute. Not yet. Don't open the door. I haven't finished. What you did to me wasn't important. I couldn't remember any reason for killing Laura. I couldn't even remember what happened. So I didn't feel responsible. If I had no reason, then I was mad. And if I was mad, I wasn't responsible. And if I had a reason but I couldn't remember, then I was just as mad. And if I was mad anyway, they would have locked me up sooner or later. You didn't do that to me. I did it to myself. And I was already dying, starting to rot away. So I might as well rot there as anywhere else. Don't be sorry about me. Be sorry about the ones you hurt who didn't deserve it. I am. Because I helped to make you what you are now, and that means I'm also responsible for the things you have done. Promise me it's all over now. Is it? Will you find some sort of peace, now you've seen them suffer, now they're all dead? You can really be free, now, can't you?'

She thought she heard a sobbing sound, followed by a metallic grinding noise. The door yielded suddenly behind her and she fell backwards. When she had scrambled to her feet and turned round the porch was empty. As she knew the churchyard would be, and the hamlet, and the path to the sand-dunes and the pilgrims' way across the fields. She knew that wherever she looked he would be nowhere to be found.

40

Megan and Brenda were taking tea in the lounge, which had belatedly caught some of the weak late afternoon sun, when Madeleine walked in. She had the folder under her arm. She noticed that Megan had been crying. She was still dabbing her eyes when she looked up and smiled.

'I closed the gallery at midday,' said Brenda, in response to Madeleine's enquiring glance. 'Nobody over the doorstep all morning. Thought I'd come over and talk to Megan. Tell her everything, as we agreed. I've just finished. She tells me she always believed you never killed Laura.'

'Which is easy enough for me,' said Megan. 'But what makes me so happy now is that you believe it, Madeleine.'

'I didn't leave out what I told you about me and your mother,' said Brenda. 'Now she knows what a monster I am, and she still made tea for us.'

'I don't judge people, Brenda,' said Megan. 'That's never been my role in life. And I'm happy to be friends with anyone who's been such a friend to Madeleine these past couple of weeks.'

Brenda looked closely at Madeleine and frowned. 'What's the matter with you? You look as if you've seen a ghost.'

Madeleine sat down and took the cup which Megan handed to her. 'You never said a truer word, Brenda.'

'What's that you've got there?'

'Some interesting papers. I looked through them on the way back.'

'Back from where?'

'St Olave's.'

'You said you were going to visit your mother's grave. So where did you get that?'

Megan had said nothing but stared intently at the folder. Then she spoke. 'Just a minute, Brenda. Madeleine, I can see that it's a bit soiled and faded but would I be right in saying that that there folder is blue?'

'Yes, Megan. Just like the one Michael asked you to destroy. Only you couldn't find it. Why? Because someone had removed it. And that someone has just given it back to me.'

'You didn't go to see the grave, did you?' said Brenda, disapprovingly. 'You went to see Alan again. That was what that note under the door was all about. So what did he have to say for himself this time?'

'First of all, just one question, to both of you. Did you know that no body was ever found?'

Brenda stared at her. It was Megan who answered. 'You mean Master David? Of course. They searched everywhere. All along the coast from here to Porthcurno and to St Ives in the other direction. That were the worst thing about it for Mr Wallace, not being able to bury him. The coroner refused to declare him to be presumed drowned because he hadn't been at sea when he disappeared. He said it were possible he were killed by the fall and his body carried out to sea on the next tide. But until the body were found he couldn't be sure of the cause of death, or even that he were dead. So Mr Wallace knew that unless the body turned up he would have to wait seven years to have him declared legally dead. And he knew he would never live to see seven years.'

'It was in the local papers,' said Brenda. 'But you were abroad at the time.'

'It's not that unusual, round these shores,' said Megan. 'Why,

young Tom, the son of one of those fishermen, were lost in a
storm off those headlands and never found. There've been about
half a dozen such cases in my time here.'

'But didn't Michael tell you?' asked Brenda.

'When I first came back I think he was trying to, but I never
gave him the chance. I asked where I should go to pay my last
respects. He told me to go to St Olave's. That's all he said. I can
well understand why he wouldn't want to talk about it afterwards.'

'So what has this to do with those papers?'

'Look.' She handed over the folder. Brenda leafed through
them, her jaw slackening, her breathing becoming increasingly
laboured. Megan looked from one to other, a bewildered expression on her face. At last Brenda put the folder down on the table.

'Bloody hell,' she said. 'I need a brandy. Anyone else?'

'Yes please,' said Madeleine.

'Megan?'

'What? Oh, no thanks, Brenda. Bit early for me.'

Brenda returned within a minute with two glasses of brandy
and handed one to Madeleine. They looked at each other.

'Where is he now?' asked Brenda.

'He's gone. He won't bother us again.'

'Hang on a moment,' said Megan. 'You were talking about
Master David a minute ago . . .'

'No, Megan. I never mentioned that name.'

Megan sank back in her chair. 'That tramp you were just telling
me about, Brenda? The one who claims he's Mr Wallace's son,
and is convinced Mr Wallace killed Madeleine's mum?'

'That's right. He was christened Hywel. Michael renamed him
David. And he decided to call himself Alan.'

'Oh, my God. Could I change my mind about that brandy?'

'You certainly can.' Brenda left the room. Madeleine turned
to Megan.

'That folder Michael asked you to destroy. It contains some
very interesting things. There are two birth certificates. One in
French, an *acte de naissance* issued in Lyons in 1967 in the name

of David Wallace, the parents' names entered as George and Sandrine Wallace.'

'So Mr Wallace really did have a nephew.'

'Oh yes. He told me George and Sandrine died in a car crash. His story was that David was not with them. But according to the local newspaper article also in the folder, all three of them were killed instantly.'

'That's what I thought it meant,' said Brenda, returning at that moment with Megan's brandy. 'Only my French isn't as good as yours.'

'Michael was in France for some time, sorting out their affairs,' continued Madeleine. 'Presumably the deaths were not reported in the English press or the cuttings would have been in the folder as well. While he was there he must have had a lot of time to think. There was plenty to think about. He had a son who was David's age, one whose identity had to remain secret or it would cause a scandal. Not just that. If the news got out, it could cause Celia terrible psychological damage. She had never been able to have a child of her own. And Celia's parents would have withdrawn the financial support they had been giving to Michael. It would have been a disaster for him. But at that time he could not be sure he could keep it a secret.'

'You think he kept it from Celia and her parents that the real David was dead?' asked Brenda.

'Yes. He could have told them David had stayed in France, in the care of Sandrine's relatives. They would have had no reason to doubt the story. He brought his birth certificate back with him, having no doubt destroyed his death certificate. Already he was building a new identity for Hywel in case he needed it later. When he first saw Hywel, at Laura's house, he would have begun to plan the transfer of identity right away. In case Laura threatened to disclose who Hywel really was. It wouldn't just be his word against hers. He would have documentary "proof" he was his nephew called David. But there was no danger of Laura talking to Celia or her parents. She knew nothing about them. She had no idea what a powerful weapon she had in her hands. If only she had, and had dared to use it. And a new identity would be essential for his longer-term plan, to bring Hywel, or David as he was by then, to live with him.'

'But by the time that happened, Celia and her parents were dead. He didn't need a cover for him.'

'That's right. But he wasn't to know that when he started to hatch his plans. And Hywel had already been told he was really David, so Michael had to continue with the deceit.'

'What's the other birth certificate?' asked Megan.

Madeleine opened the folder and picked up a faded beige envelope. 'This contains Hywel's. The full name is given as Hywel Williams, mother Ceridwen Williams, no name entered for the father. Place of birth, Portsmouth.'

She took out another piece of paper from the folder. 'This is my mother's final will, appointing Laura Peters, née James, as her executor and legal guardian of Hywel Williams in the event of her death. There's also a letter from my mother to Michael, telling him she had decided not to go ahead with the abortion. Just imagine the shock of reading that your own father originally wanted you aborted. No wonder he hated him. What else? A letter from Laura to my mother, addressed to her at Cove Cottage, saying Hywel was well but missing his mother. Wanting to know when she was coming home.'

'Poor woman,' said Megan. 'She never did go home. Never saw her son again. And Laura, waiting for her all that time, wondering what had happened, wondering what to tell the boy.'

'I think Michael wanted you to destroy the folder for my sake,' said Madeleine. 'By the time he decided to do it he was too frail to get up to the attic on his own. And it was vital that I didn't suspect its existence. It wasn't until he was in hospital that he could talk to you on your own, without me being around, and swear you to secrecy. The secret he wanted to take with him to the grave was that the boy I had been sleeping with, the boy I thought was his nephew, was my own half-brother. He did intend to tell us one day. Then he found out we were lovers. That was the shock that destroyed Michael, even more than the fatal accident, as he supposed it.'

'I suppose he became Alan after that, when everybody thought he was dead,' said Brenda. 'A new beginning. Yet another new identity. You went up to the attics to look for the folder, Megan, but Alan found it first. But how do you think Michael managed to get hold of all those documents, especially the letter from Laura?'

'He got the will and Hywel's birth certificate from Laura. After my mother's death, he must have gone down to the cottage, looking for things he didn't want the police to find. I don't suppose he thought they'd suspect foul play. He just didn't want them to make the connection, in case it all came out, my mother being his lover, their having a son. He found that letter. That was how he knew Laura's address. He went to see her to find out what she knew about him, and also to check out my mother's house in case there was anything there to connect her with him. When he was talking to Laura he saw Hywel. That changed everything. He decided he wanted him with him. He already had David's identity documents from France. To complete the transfer he took from Laura all the documents which could prove who Hywel really was. Some he needed to keep against the day he might want to restore Hywel's identity to him. Others he kept because he could not bring himself to destroy anything connected to my mother. Not until the end, when he saw it had to be done.'

'But wasn't he taking a risk? What if the police searched the attics?'

'Not really. The stuff was much safer here than in the cottage. They'd have needed a warrant to search this house, which means they'd first need to have reasonable grounds for suspecting he was involved in her death. He did everything he could to satisfy himself that nobody would connect him with my mother any more closely than he was ever prepared to admit, namely that he had met her a few times and they were no more than acquaintances. He contacted Laura to find out if he might need to buy her silence. He attended the inquest, to confirm that the police did not suspect foul play.'

'He could have done that by reading the verdict in the papers. Wasn't he taking a risk just by being there?'

'He had another reason to attend. He wanted to check that there were no family members around who might cause trouble by asking awkward questions. He must have had a real shock when he saw me. Almost as bad a shock as you had, Brenda, that time in the cafe when we first met. But he kept his head. He befriended me, saw I was out of my depth, took over the arrangements for the funeral. With my agreement he buried her where he knew he would lie beside her in his turn. He brought you, Megan, with him to the funeral, knowing you would help to put me at my ease.

'He must have been so relieved by what he saw of me. He would have known from the moment he met me that I would not make any trouble for him. I obviously couldn't have cared less about my mother's death and I couldn't wait to get away. He knew it would be safe to rent out the cottage rather than sell it. I wouldn't interfere. I had my life to get on with, such as it was. Many years later, when that life had finished, I returned and became part of his plans.'

'You mean, to bring together two siblings who through an unfortunate chain of circumstances had up to then been unknown to each other,' said Brenda. 'A final link in the chain of restoration he had forged to make it up to your mother for what he did to her.'

'That's right. When he found out we had met and become lovers, the only thing that mattered then was to maintain the secrecy to the end of his life and beyond.'

'Tell us what happened at the church.'

'I saw Alan there yesterday. I asked him why he had followed me and spoken to me. He told me he had watched me return to the house and look after Michael. He wanted me to know Michael had killed my mother, so I would realise what sort of man he was.' Megan gasped. 'I think he really believed it. The only evidence he had was a note from my mother to him, asking him to meet her. This was just before she died. That note must have been in the folder as well. It only proved that she had come here to put pressure on him. But he took it as proof positive that he had killed her. He also claimed to have killed the boy we all knew as David, out of jealousy.'

'And you never guessed who he were?' asked Megan.

'No. Don't forget, I always thought that David's body was buried at St Olave's. And as Alan he never showed me his face. He disguised his voice as well. With the life he's been leading, I probably wouldn't have recognised him anyway, even if I had known he was still alive.'

'How did he say he killed David?' asked Brenda.

'You remember that the earth at the top of the headland was dislodged? Everybody thought he had been standing on it and it collapsed beneath him. His story to me was that he dared David to go near the edge, pushed him over, then dislodged the earth himself to make it look like an accident. Which was all true, except that nobody went over.

'That wasn't the only revenge he had. He told me he saw Laura come here to visit Michael. He thought he recognised her as the woman who had given him away to Michael. He broke in and found some papers which confirmed his suspicions. He found out where she was spending her final days. He planned his revenge on her. He didn't intend to kill her at first. Just watch her die, after reminding her what she had done. Then he saw me visit her.'

Brenda's jaw dropped again. 'My God,' she said at last. 'I never doubted you when you said you remembered leaving her alive in that room. But I couldn't get past the question, if you didn't kill her then who did? Who might have had a motive? The answer was always the same. Nobody.'

'Nobody living, certainly,' said Madeleine. 'But somebody we all thought dead had a motive all right.'

273

'And he admitted it?' asked Megan.

'Yes. He saw me visit her, and took the opportunity to kill her and let me take the blame, because of my involvement with Michael.'

Megan shook her head. 'Oh dear. I wanted you to be proved innocent. So your name could be cleared. But not to know it were him taking revenge on both of you.'

'And because he doesn't really exist, and nobody else but me heard him and nobody will ever find him again, we can't use his confession to clear my name publicly. But that doesn't matter to me now.'

'Well,' said Megan, 'I'll tell anybody who'll listen that there were someone who confessed, even though I won't be able to say exactly who. Brenda told me how you found out he were your brother. But did he know you was his sister?'

'I was coming to that bit. Today there was nobody in the church when I went there the first time. Only that folder left for me, with a note to go to the cottage. The note told me to take the picture out of its frame and look at the back. This was a picture Michael had done of my mother, only I hadn't recognised her. Before I left to go abroad David saw the picture, decided it was me and decided that I was also having an affair with Michael. Which I wasn't. I denied it at first. Then I admitted it, so we could finally put an end to a relationship that was destroying both of us. Today I looked at the back of the picture and there was my mother's name on it. I had realised it was her long ago. So what was Alan trying to do, leaving me a note telling me to look at the back? Then I realised he was telling me that that was what David did. Don't forget that at this stage I still thought they were two different people. David was there on his own. I had gone. He was looking at a picture he knew was of me. But now he knew it was of my mother.'

'Two peas in a pod,' said Megan.

'Exactly. He must have remembered that Michael used to put the names of his models on the back of his portraits. He took it out of the frame to prove it was me. He realised he had been wrong. Then he realised something else. This was the woman Michael had loved. Another woman he remembered as a child. Remembered her hair, her laugh. He stood here, looking at a picture of his mother. And his sister. Two images in one. He had abused me, made me the focus of all his hatred and suspicion of women. Now he had found out I was his sister. No wonder his mind broke.'

'He were a shadow of what he had been,' said Megan, shaking her head sadly. 'Didn't even know who we was.'

'So when did you realise who Alan was?' asked Brenda.

'Not in the cottage. I hadn't read the folder. I was just carrying it around. I still thought that he was telling me what David had told him. I couldn't understand why David would tell a stranger so much. The note he had left me in the church also told me to read the inscriptions in the churchyard. So I went back to do that. I realised when I read them properly for the first time. His is the only one on that stone that doesn't say "here lies" . . . How blind and stupid could I be? I went into the church. He was there. That was when he told me he killed her.'

Megan was looking out of the window and scratching her head. Then she turned round, a little smile playing across her features. 'This picture you were talking about. I haven't seen it myself. Could you describe it?'

'Of course,' said Madeleine. 'It's an ink drawing. Nude. The face isn't visible. It's beautiful. Mr Wallace thought so too. On the back he wrote that it was the best of him.'

'Really? How big is it?' Madeleine drew an outline in the air. 'That's really interesting. There's just the one like that, is there? No more?'

'No. Just the one.'

Megan stood up. Her smile was now broad. 'Feeling fit, ladies? I'm going into the library to fetch the key. Then we're all going up to the attic. I've got a surprise for you.'

41

The door at the top of the narrow staircase to the attics gave onto a small landing beyond which there were two further doors. Megan pushed open the first door and stepped inside. The others followed.

'Where did he hide the key, Megan?' asked Brenda.

'In a secret drawer in the bureau. There's a lever which opens it, hidden at the back of one of the pigeonholes. You have to feel for it. It took me ages to find it. I thought at first it didn't exist. I wondered if he'd imagined it. This is the room where he kept his secrets. Just take a look at these and you'll see what I mean.'

They followed her to a corner where a pile of framed drawings had been stacked. Between them they laid them out neatly on the floor. Brenda whistled.

'Eleven. All the same size as the one in the cottage. All framed in the same way. All ink drawings of a nude woman, her face invisible. Eleven, and the one in the cottage.'

'Did he frame them himself?' asked Madeleine.

'Oh yes,' said Brenda. 'He was very skilful. I imagine there's still wood and glue and framing equipment in one of these cupboards.'

'That's right,' said Megan. 'That one over there. I searched through here like with a fine-toothed comb, looking for that folder as had disappeared from the face of the earth.'

Like David's drawings of her, thought Madeleine. Only these were tender and intimate. As eloquent of Michael's love as David's had been of his hatred. This room had been a shrine to her mother.

'You were right, Megan,' she said. 'It would have been unthinkable to destroy these.'

'Nothing else he did compared with these,' said Brenda, almost to herself. 'To the world he gave admirable, meticulously crafted, lifeless artifices. But when love inspired him to real greatness at last, he hid the results away.'

'Except for the one in the cottage,' said Madeleine. 'He made a set of twelve. He chose one, his favourite, as a special present to the woman who had been his secret muse. One which he felt belonged in the cottage because out of the whole set it was closest to being a record of what they were to each other.'

'How come it's still there?' asked Megan. 'Why didn't he bring it back here, to go with the others?'

'He did,' said Madeleine. 'After her death. When I went to live in the cottage he decided it would be safe to put it back. It might even have been part of his plan to tell David and myself eventually about his affair with her. He brought it round the day after I arrived. I never looked at it. I left it unopened in a cupboard in the kitchen. David found it, when he was looking for a fresh bottle of whisky, after he had finished off all the others I had. I would never have recognised it of my own accord. He did, assuming it was me, but then he had an artist's eye. And as he said, he knew my body far better than I did myself.'

'But why didn't he take it back when he sold the cottage?'

'I can answer that,' said Brenda, standing up straight and shaking herself. Up to that point, she had been lost in contemplation of the drawings, barely listening to the conversation. 'Someone told the new owners I was in the market for cleaning jobs around the village. I went round to see them. I was surprised to see it still there, as you can imagine. I told them I knew Michael and I thought I had seen the picture in his house. Had he sold it to them? They told me he had offered it to them on long-term loan, on condition that it stayed in the cottage. He said it had a particular sentimental value, but only if it stayed there. If they sold the cottage they had to return it to him. They had agreed but I could tell they were puzzled. They weren't bothered about pictures in general or that one in particular.'

'We have to bring them back together, as a set,' said Madeleine. 'Put them in your gallery, or sell them on to another one. Surely they'll force the art world to reappraise his work.'

Brenda stroked her chin. 'He's almost forgotten now. These really could put him back on the map. The loan agreement would have expired with Michael's death. So the one in the cottage belongs to you now. As they all do.'

'They're yours now, Brenda. They may be of my mother, but you're the one who knows how to make best use of them.'

'I'll do my best. About the one in the cottage. I don't think we even need to bother the owners. I'll slip it out quietly, without telling anybody. I've got this gouache of his of about the same size, a sunset, somewhere in my cottage. I'll put it in its place. They won't even notice. I'll need to think about what to do with them. I could devote a wall to them in the gallery. But it's so cramped there. And it rather goes against the spirit of the gallery. It's always been about giving space to young artists at the beginning of their careers. While I'm thinking about it they can stay here. They're as safe here as anywhere.'

'What's in the other room, Megan?'

'Nothing much. Just rubbish, really. You can have a look if you like.'

They returned to the landing and Megan pushed open the other door. Within were two small rooms with a connecting door. One was a bedroom. It contained a single bed, two chairs, a wardrobe and a dressing table. All were covered with sheets. The other room was a studio. An easel had been placed beneath the skylight, a large sheet of white paper pinned to it. Faint charcoal lines swept across it. Madeleine stared at it. She could not discern any recognisable shapes. It was as if a child had picked up the charcoal to play with it.

'He was here too,' she said, after a minute. 'Maybe he came in here after he had picked up the blue folder from next door. He drew these lines, wondering if they might show any vestiges of his former gifts.'

'There's no trace of them, if he did,' said Brenda. 'He must have realised that. What did he feel, I wonder? Sorrow, relief, both at once?'

'I don't think he has any yearnings left for what he once was. He told me he had dabbled a bit in the past but didn't have a clue now. That was his disguise speaking but I honestly think that is how he really feels about it.'

There were several cupboards in the room. Madeleine opened them while the others looked on. In one she found dried-out paints, crayons, inks, pens, brushes and paper. Another contained randomly stacked drawings and paintings. No toys or child's books. Not here. Not anywhere in the house. Not now, not ever. She noticed that Megan was crying.

'Let's go downstairs.'

'He really loved her, didn't he?' said Megan. They were in the library. Megan had just returned the key to its hiding-place. 'I could tell as soon as I saw the drawings.'

Madeleine stared at her. 'But you didn't know about her and Michael when you first saw them?'

Megan smiled. 'Oh, I knew it were your mum he had drawn. That was why he wanted them destroyed. And why I knew I couldn't destroy them. I couldn't recognise her from the drawings, of course. Not directly. But I knew it had to be her.'

'You said you never met her. How did you know?'

'It's true I never met her. But she did come to the house.'

'Go on, Megan,' said Brenda, half-glancing at Madeleine.

'Well, as you know, my bedroom is at the back of the house nearest the sea. Once I've retired to bed there's no way as I'd

279

normally hear if anybody came to the door. But that night, there were a storm and I were a bit scared to tell the truth, with the wind rattling the windowpanes like blue murder. So I came down again and went into my parlour and made myself a cup of tea. I must have dozed off in my armchair. That side of the house were sheltered from the wind so it weren't so noisy. Then I were woken up by this sound of knocking and shouting. A woman's voice. I'm under instructions not to open the door at night, so I stayed put. But I did allow myself a little peep out of the window. I saw her there. She had only a thin coat on top, nothing on her head. She were dripping with the rain, shivering, her hair plastered down, a wild look in her eyes. I heard Mr Wallace pulling back the bolts. He said something on the lines of, God, it's you, what the hell are you doing here, I told you never to come here, and all sorts of stuff like that.'

'Did he call her by name?'

'Yes. Ceridwen. I heard it as clear as a bell. She said she had to come. He had given her no choice, and she had to have it out with him and with Mrs Wallace if need be. Then they was in here and I couldn't catch everything they said. Later on the voices was raised so I could hear something. She were saying something about a child, their son, how he had a right to know his father. Then I heard the door slam, a lot of crying and shouting, and she had rushed out of the front door. I heard her footsteps on the gravel outside, leading to the coastal path. I heard his footsteps following her. I thought as they must be both crazy going out onto the path in those conditions.

'About an hour later Mr Wallace came back. Normally I would have gone to see how he were, got some dry things for him, made sure he had a good strong brandy so he didn't catch pneumonia. But I didn't want him to know I were not in my bedroom. I didn't want him to know I had heard. So I stayed put. Mrs Wallace must have been in the hall. He said, "There's been an accident." That's all. I couldn't catch everything she said in reply. Something to the effect that whatever he had done his secret was safe. So long as he never mentioned . . . well, I'm afraid she used some rather bad language.'

'Go on, Megan,' said Brenda and Madeleine in unison.

'So long as he never breathed a word in this house or anywhere else about that whore or her bastard child. Then Mr Wallace said he had to go out again, urgently. Over to the village. And the next day he would need to go to Portsmouth. She said something like, fine, do what you have to. Just remove all traces of her from the face of the earth. I heard him go out and slam the door. When I knew she had gone to her room I crept back up to bed. I never heard him come in again. By the time I were up the next morning he had left.

'He were away for a few days. When he got back he looked totally exhausted, but relieved at the same time. A few days after that he had recovered all his former energy. There were a spring in his step again. I would catch him almost running about the house, making notes and little drawings. It were like he were making plans for the future. But if he were, she had no part in them. They barely spoke to each other, or even looked at each other. He had been so tender and loving with her for so many years. But now, it were as if he blamed her for what had happened. He left the nurse we had living with us to look after her, with me helping out as well as I could. She went downhill rapidly after that. She lasted less than a year.'

'And when David came to the house . . .'

'I knew it were him. Ceridwen's boy. Mr Wallace's son. He were proud of him as only a father can be. And hard on him as only a father can be.'

'Megan, did Michael ever say anything about what had happened that night, when he followed my mother onto the coastal path?'

'Only one thing and it never made sense to me. It were that time he asked me to find the blue folder and destroy it. Well I never did that, although I promised to. So I'll tell you this, though I promised I wouldn't. After he had asked me to destroy the folder he fell asleep and when he woke again he were muttering things. It were like he were rambling. Then he took my arm, and looked right into my eyes. "She fell," he said. "I never pushed her. But I didn't save her. I stood there and let her fall. Don't tell her. She mustn't know."'

'"She" meaning me, I suppose,' said Madeleine.

'But he could never have saved her, could he? I mean she had a head start on him and she would have been gaining on him all the way. What's the matter with you two? You're glaring at me as if I'd just told you I'd killed her myself. You believe me, don't you?'

'That's just it, Megan,' said Madeleine. 'We do believe you. Well, I certainly do. When I was here on my own, I saw it happen. Just what you described. From the moment she ran from the house. I told Brenda, but she thought it was just my imagination.'

'What you saw happen on the cliffs still could be,' said Brenda. 'We only know what Megan saw and heard in the house.'

'And what Michael confessed to her. And that was the confession of a dying man, remember. Megan, all this means that when I told you about the affair between David and me, you knew then that we were siblings.'

'Yes. But I couldn't tell you what I knew. I knew it were what you were trying to remember. I wondered if it were what had driven you mad when you thought you had killed Laura. Perhaps you had found it out then and after that it had all gone blank again. I didn't know what it might do to you if I just told you what I knew. I had to let you find out for yourself. I hope I were right about that.'

'Yes, Megan. You were right. Thank you.'

The three of them sat in silence for several minutes. Then Brenda stood up brusquely.

'Well, this has all been fascinating. But I must get back now. There are so many things I need to think about. So many things I never began to understand.' She frowned. 'I need to think about the people I've known, or thought I knew. You two, Michael, David, Ceridwen. I mean, I always thought I could size people up. Make the right judgements about them. You'd think knowing so few people in my time I would have got some things right. But I never did. I'm getting old now and I haven't even started to learn. So many of these things I've found out today and in the last few weeks . . . if only I'd been able to understand at the time. There's so much that's happened that needn't have done. And so much of it was my fault.'

'Don't be hard on yourself, Brenda,' said Megan. 'Some things are just meant to happen and we can't have the wisdom of hindsight before they do.'

'No, Megan. But sometimes a little foresight would come in handy. Anyway, we shall have to see what we can salvage from the mess. At least I am in a position to do something about that. I'll talk to you about those pictures soon, Madeleine.'

'Before you go, I have to tell you both something,' said Madeleine. 'I have to go up to London. Tomorrow afternoon. I have a series of appointments. Some tests I have to have. And depending on the results I may need others. So I'll be away for a couple of weeks.'

'You mean, medical tests?' asked Megan.

Madeleine nodded. At the same time she glanced up at Brenda who by then was standing behind Megan. Brenda shook her head. So she had not told Megan all she knew about her condition, thought Madeleine, with a surge of relief.

'I realised as soon as you came back from the hospital that you wasn't well,' said Megan. 'I thought, I hoped, it were just the effect of all those years locked away. I hoped the sea air would soon put you to rights again. But you're saying it's something as needs a bit more than sea air to put right?'

'That's right.'

'And you'll be back in a couple of weeks?'

'Yes. And I haven't forgotten what I promised. We had a deal, didn't we? You agreed to let me stay here on my own. And I promised to look into selling the house. I'll do that as soon as I get back.'

'I'll take you to the station tomorrow,' said Brenda. 'What time shall I pick you up?'

'About three o'clock will do.'

'I'll help you pack in the morning,' said Megan. 'And I'll come with you to the station, if Brenda doesn't mind bringing me back here afterwards.'

'Of course. I'll see you both tomorrow then.'

The following evening the tramp stood on the coastal path at the exact point where he had first seen the house come into view. This time he was not approaching the bay from Porthhella. He was returning from the direction of the house, pausing to look back at the red on the water. It was a different red now. Not the uniform blood red from the setting sun. That had been and gone an hour ago. This was a mixture of darting crimsons and flickering yellows. The breeze was off the land now, blowing acrid fumes into his eyes. Fragments of ash and cinder pinched and stung his cheek. He raised his hand. Several times he described a long, slow arch through the air.

42

The Reverend Colm O'Brien pushed open the door leading from the sacristy into the church. He was carrying a thermos flask of coffee and some sandwiches wrapped in foil. He laid them down on a pew near the back. From the organ loft above came thin, reedy sounds from the few pipes which were still working. The noise stopped suddenly. There was a sound of shuffling followed by the thud of steps coming down the narrow staircase leading to the nave. The tramp saw the coffee and the sandwiches and sat down. He started to unwrap the foil.

'Thank you, Father. These look very good. Did you make them yourself?'

'I told you, I'm not a Catholic. I'm an Anglican. Colm will do fine. No, I didn't make them myself. My housekeeper made them. I told her I was going for a long walk along the coastal path. I've never done that since I've been here so she's convinced I've gone mad. What was that you were playing?'

'A Bach prelude. Sort of. Half the notes on the organ are missing.'

'I know. I never knew you could play.'

'I had some piano and organ lessons at school. But he wouldn't hear of having any musical instruments in the house. He only cared about his bloody pictures. That was all he let me care about.'

'Did you have a comfortable night up there? Was the sleeping-bag okay?'

'It was all right. You should get that window repaired. The draught blows through the broken pipes. It sounds like some ghostly pibroch.'

'There's a lot of repairs I'd like to get done. Your uncle . . .'

'Not my uncle. I told you. My father.'

'So you did. Your father left the church some money but it all went on the new roof. I've started a new fund for the windows and the organ, not to mention the dry rot in the woodwork. But with an average attendance of three for Sunday services the outlook is not looking at all good. I have a feeling we'll get decommissioned at the next review. The police . . .'

'Are you going to ask them to donate?'

'No, of course not. I was saying that the police came round to the manse this morning. They had your description.'

'What did you tell them?'

'I told them I hadn't seen anybody who answered it.'

'You lied, Father.'

'That's right. And if I were a Catholic priest, and deserved to be called by the title you insist on giving me, I would have to go to confession. As would you.'

'That's obstruction, lying to the police. You could go to prison for that.'

'And you could go for a lot longer.'

'But you don't think I deserve to. Would you like some of this coffee?'

'No thanks.'

'Anyway, you couldn't betray me. I had claimed sanctuary.'

Colm laughed. 'Claimed sanctuary? Is that what you call being found fast asleep by me, next to the font, smelling of petrol as well as everything else you smell of? It's small wonder I didn't recognise you at first. Not until you told me who you were. Even then I wasn't sure. Not until I had insisted on you telling me everything which had led to your being here. You could never have made all that up if you hadn't been genuine. As for the right to claim sanctuary in a church, that was abolished a long time ago. The only sanctuary I could offer you was my own goodwill, freely offered.'

'And accepted. Don't think I'm not grateful.'

'Look, it's not for me to judge what you deserve. But you shouldn't have done it, David.'

The tramp banged his fist on the pew. 'I told you,' he snapped. 'David's dead. I killed him. He's really dead now. All traces of him. All the disgusting things he left behind him.'

'All right. Alan. You can't blame me. I always knew you as David, right from the time he brought you to the house to live with him. I still say you shouldn't have done it.'

'David was evil. You of all people should approve of what I did.'

'Not evil. I always felt sorry for you, I mean, for David. Such a lonely place for a boy to grow up in. But I wasn't talking about that. I was talking about burning down the house.'

'I checked it was empty. There was no danger of anybody getting hurt. He hated the house, towards the end. Because of everything that had happened. She hated it too. Megan can't have liked being there on her own. I was doing them a favour.'

'Where did you find the petrol?'

'There were some sealed cans in the garage. Must have been there for years. So, did you believe my story?'

'Yes, I believe you. It's a strange tale, and a sad one. This is where I would normally say that I've heard a lot stranger and sadder back in Ireland. But I'm not sure I have. But don't worry. I'll keep my promise. I won't breathe a word of it to anyone. Do you still hate him? If you had only seen him in his last few months . . .'

'I did see him. Yes, I hated him.'

'Even then?'

'Even then.'

'I can understand your feelings. One day there may be room in your heart for some compassion.'

287

'There is. But not for him.'

'So what now?'

'You mean, when am I going to get the hell out of here and leave you in peace?'

'Something like that.'

'It depends. Have you found out where she is?'

'Yes. I went round to see Brenda. Megan's staying with her but she was having a nap. She's still in shock. Brenda told me that when they got back from taking Madeleine to the station they saw the glow in the sky from miles away. It was only when they got near that they realised which house it was. Megan was convinced it was her fault. Thought she'd left something burning on the stove. She was so relieved when the police came round and told them it was arson.'

'The station? Why were they taking her to the station?'

'Oh, she's gone up to London to have some tests done.'

'Tests?'

'Yes. Medical tests. I suppose you realise she's very sick.'

'Do they have her address?'

'I didn't ask. She's staying in a hotel near the hospital where she has to go for the tests. Why do you want to know? Is it about the pictures?'

'Yes. They're hers. Have you got them safe?'

Colm nodded. 'I wrapped them up for you. Made a nice, neat parcel. It's safe in my study in the manse. Did you know there's another one?'

The tramp glared at him. Then he started to laugh, hoarsely and with an edge of hysteria.

'Quiet, Alan, for God's sake. Anybody passing will hear you.'

'Sorry,' he whispered, once he had brought himself under control. 'Yes, I do know there's another one. I have good reason to remember it. It's in the cottage she used to have. Cove Cottage.'

'Oh no it isn't. Brenda's got it. It's on her wall. I don't know anything about art but even I could tell it's part of the set. She knows it as well. She told me there were others but they were destroyed in the fire.'

'That bloody cow! She stole it from the cottage.'

'Calm down. She didn't steal it. It's Madeleine's, like the others. Brenda took it from the cottage with her agreement. It had been on loan to the current owners up to the time of your father's death. Brenda was going to collect the set together and put them up in her gallery. With Madeleine's agreement. So, this is what I think we should do. I'll take the others round to Brenda. I'll tell her they were left here in the church. She can draw her own conclusions about who left them. She'll be delighted. She was distraught about the loss. Said they were the best things he ever did.'

'They are. They're the only things he ever did. All right. I agree. Take them round. But let me get away first.'

'You'd better lie low here for a couple more weeks. I'll ask around. See if the police are still searching.'

'You're a wicked man, Father. Aiding and abetting a criminal.'

'I know I am. And for the last time I'm not your father.'

'Sorry, Colm.'

'That's better. I'll get you some books to read. You'd better get back up in the loft. The cleaner's due in a minute. And keep away from the organ. If she hears it playing and no sign of anyone around she'll be asking me to call in the Archbishop for an exorcism.'

43

November 1995

This is the final entry, Mother. Tomorrow they're admitting me. That's a very bad sign. It means I have a few more weeks at best. Maybe just a few days.

I still haven't told you about the man in the port near Marseilles. He was the Third Man in my life. Of course there were more than that, if you count all the ones who fucked me. Not that I ever did. Count them, that is. What would be the point? No, there were really only three.

There was the First One. You know who he was. Then David. He was the Second. Then the stranger, the Third. They were a Holy Trinity, three in one. The Father, the Son and the Holy Ghost. The First made me, the Second forged my image so I could see myself, and the Third was the envoy of the First, sent from Hades to bring me down to him.

The Trinity were not at all like the others. For the Trinity it was never just about sex, and certainly not about pleasure, for them or for me. Don't get me wrong. I don't want you to think there was never any pleasure for me. I was your daughter. I inherited from you all the necessary electrical wiring for that. For a long time it was a solitary business. I was the only one who knew how to switch on the current. But later others shared in the experience. The first was a woman, an older work colleague.

290

We were staying overnight at a conference in one of those soul-less business hotels. For some reason she decided to share my room and my bed. Then there were men, usually married, with a flat in town for those late nights at the office and a house in the country for weekends. At most there would be dinner, drinks and a midnight hour in their midweek bed, no more than that, and never more than once. Sometimes it was the floor of their office or mine, after an end-of-the-day gin and tonic. None of them ever came to my flat, in case one might want to stay. That was the way I wanted it.

One encounter was a bit different. It lasted a whole week. He was a young Italian student, in Verona. He thought he was in love with me. But mostly he was in love with himself, with his skill. He spent the whole time coaxing moans and cries and spasms out of me, looking for the person inside who wasn't there. When he realised I was only an empty shell, he left. I cannot remember his name, or the name of anybody else who gave me pleasure. That's the difference between you and me. I bet you know all their names. For you pleasure was everything. For me it was nothing.

I remember the Three, though. The ones who gave me pain. They were high priests of sodomy. For them it was a sacred ritual, a solemn sacrament. They were putting me into their equivalent of a state of grace. The First One did it that way when I told him I had started my periods. It was a necessary precaution, he said. We must not create a child who would be an abomination to the Gods, a child to whom I would be both mother and sister. As if what we were doing wasn't enough of an abomination already. The Second One did it to get the image he needed for his great masterpiece. Thank God it's gone up in flames now. The Third One knew from experience that it was the most effective way to pass on the seed of death. Each of them told me not to scream. Even the Third. I knew that was what he was saying, even though he spoke a language I could not understand. I did scream of course. They knew I would.

291

That was the moment when they knew I was transformed, when the sacrament was complete.

I had been searching for the Holy Ghost all my life, without knowing it, ever since the Father had gone, like those disciples in the Gospel story who waited in fear and secrecy after the Crucifixion for they did not know what. This Holy Ghost did not give me the gift of tongues. I could not understand his words. But I could understand the burning hatred in his eyes. He knew nothing about me. It was enough that I was a woman. A woman had condemned him to die. So he would condemn me and as many others like me as he could find in the time left to him. He hoped we would transmit it to others. Maybe he had worked out that the same seed which had sentenced him might sentence thousands of others in the time it would take him to die. Maybe that thought gave him some comfort. But if he was thinking that about me he would have been disappointed to know that I did not pass it on. What he gave me stopped with me.

One tiny glass of hideous, gut-wrenching local brandy and the deal was done. I left the cafe and he followed me. I never looked round. I walked back along the quay, through the pitch black of the cobbled streets stinking of urine and rotten fish to my hotel, collected my key and went up to my room. All the time he was there behind me and I never turned to look at him. The room was filthy, infested with cockroaches. Why had I chosen it? I could have afforded something much more luxurious. It just seemed appropriate for what I sensed was going to happen in that place. I walked in and he closed the door behind us. I undressed and lay down on the bed, face down, in the sacramental position. He had not yet touched me. The first time I felt his flesh was when his weight pressed down on me and the narrow flimsy bed groaned and creaked.

I could not be absolutely sure, of course, not until it was over. I might have got it wrong. He might not have been carrying anything. I might have misunderstood the nature of his hatred.

He might just have been an ordinary strangler or stabber. But when he left immediately afterwards, without another word, I knew I had been right. He was the One I had been waiting for, searching for.

So tomorrow's the big day. I've already seen the ward. They took me up there so I could prepare myself, so they could show me how nice it is, they said. The funny thing is that they're right. It is nice. It's not like a normal hospital ward at all. There's so much life and humour around. The patients are mostly young men, apparently in perfect health, apart from the drips they're attached to as they rush around, greeting their visitors, chatting to the doctors. I'm looking forward to it. With any luck I'll spend Christmas there.

So that's the whole story, Mother. I wanted to write it down so I could help myself to get my memories back. And to see if I could work out what really happened between us. But that's really quite simple. You went away to have your affairs. One day you came back and found I had become a stranger. It was all over between us. You had a second go at love and mother-hood. And look what happened. Your tragedy wasn't that you died young. It was that the two men you chose to father your children abused them in their different ways. And you could do nothing about it. Did you watch the child you had christened Hywel growing up, becoming David, turning into his own kind of abuser? And did you then watch helplessly as we found each other, the fruits of your womb coming together in one compound monstrosity? Now my body is rotting away, waiting to follow where my soul was taken all those years ago. And your son is a grotesque, despised creature on the margins of existence. That's hardly a great success story, is it, Mother?

But at least you tried, which is more than you can say for me. At least you lived. One can admire a stranger and so I admire you. I admire your courage in living your life by the light of your illusions, right up to the end. I admire your love for Michael, that whirlwind of destruction that swept through both your lives. I admire the foolish honesty and credulous fidelity with which you held onto that love through all the desolate years when he betrayed you. You never betrayed him for an instant. Even at the moment on the cliffs when he let you fall, you still loved him, still trusted him to save you. Your passion lived then and it lives on now. It still haunts those wild places, screaming its defiance to the winds and the waves.

She closed the notebook and put down her pen. She started to pack her bag. Not that she had brought much. A change of clothes, a hairbrush, already matted with the grey hair that was now coming out in clumps. No make-up. No point in that. Toothbrush and paste. Some ointment for her sores. She wouldn't need that. The nurses would take care of that once she was in the ward. Tomorrow she would take a taxi to the main entrance, go to the admissions reception, wait for the clerk to process the paperwork. Already a corpse, waiting to be buried.

What should she do with the notebook? It was private to her, and to her mother if she had been in a position to read it. It was nobody else's business. She would take it with her. Later on, she would ask Brenda to destroy it, unread.

The following morning, she checked out and hailed a taxi in Sloane Square.

'Where to, love?' asked the driver, cheerfully.

'The Chelsea and Westminster.'

They crawled through the heavy traffic along the King's Road. At last he pulled up outside the main entrance.

'Here you are, darling. Do you need any help to get to reception? Hey, are you all right? You look as if you're having a fit. Do you want me to go and get a nurse or a doctor to help you inside?'

Madeleine was clutching her throat, trying to breathe. At last she managed to force the air through her throat and shake her head.

'I'm sorry. I'm fine. I just lost my breath for a moment. Must have been the thought of going in there. Then I remembered. I've got the wrong date. Stupid of me. I'm supposed to be in Oxford today. Can you take me to Paddington Station, please?'

44

'So, he's gone as well.'

'As well as who?'

'As well as that murderess.'

'Who are you talking about?'

'That tramp. The one who burnt down the house on the bay,' said George.

'I'll tell you something,' said Samuel. 'That weren't no tramp. That were a ghost. A departed spirit.'

'Departed fiddlesticks,' snorted Charley.

'It were a ghost, I tell you. Have you ever seen an old tramp move so quickly? He just glided above the ground, he did. Anyway, I saw him close up I did. So I knows.'

'What, you managed to see his face with his head held under his arm?' said George.

George and Charley banged the table so hard that all three beer glasses jumped an inch off the surface. Samuel did not even smile. The expressions of glee on the other two faces faded.

'Ignorant,' said Samuel, with a sneer. 'That's what you two are. Just plain ignorant. Don't you know nothing about history? It were only those as had had their heads chopped off in proper executions for high treason and the like who carried their heads under their arms when they came back to haunt. Not every ghost, you idiots.'

'Not necessarily,' said George, anxious to regain some credit for knowledge and wisdom in the eyes of his companions. 'Maybe his head was knocked off when he died a violent death. Then he could . . . carry it under . . .' His voice trailed away under Samuel's contemptuous stare.

'Anyway, I knew who it were,' continued Samuel. 'Many years ago, I saw that young chap as went mad and disappeared over the cliffs and were washed out to sea. Young artist chap. When that murderess lived up Cove Cottage he used to visit her there. I saw him walk past me one day, right at the start of the coastal path. His face was inches away from mine. As near as yours is now. He turned his eyes on me. They were the eyes of the devil himself they were. Then a few weeks ago I saw those eyes again. I just turned the corner into our lane and there he were. Right in front of me. Then he were gone, in a flash. Gliding away. But I could never mistake those eyes.'

'And what about your own eyes? They're hardly any use to see you to your own home these days. Drink and the fancies it breeds. That's what that was all about.'

'Don't be so bloody daft. My eyes are fine, thank you very much. Look, it stands to reason. He came back to take his revenge.'

'Revenge on who?'

'On that Michael Wallace, his uncle. That Michael Wallace were in love with her as well. I reckon as she were playing one off against the other. The old one took his revenge. He were walking with the youngster up on the cliffs one day and they argued and had a fight and he threw his nephew over. The nephew came back and haunted the house, until in the end he frightened the old man to death.'

'Then why should the ghost come back now? All that were years ago.'

'Because there were unfinished business. The house. All the memories in it. He couldn't rest in peace while it were still there.'

'Tell me, how does a ghost burn a house down?'

'I dunno exactly. But he found a way.'

They sat in silence for a few minutes, unity restored.

'It's a shame, though,' said Charley at last.

'What is?'

'Well, having a ghost and a murderess about the place did make it quite interesting for a while. Things could be a bit dull now.'

'Maybe he left because he knows some real trouble is coming. I expect he heard it from that witch, Brenda Rogers.'

'That's right. And what's more, there's two of them now.'

'Two of what?'

'Two witches. Together in her house. That one who used to live in the big house. Mr Wallace's housekeeper. Megan's her name. Now if there were ever a name for a witch, that's it.'

'Two witches together is much more powerful than one. But they only really gets supernatural powers when there's three of them. That's what they call a cove of witches.'

'If that murderess comes back to join them, then there'll be a cove.'

'Just what I were thinking. And then troubles will rain down on this place like a plague of locuses. There'll be one disaster treading on the ankles of the next.'

'Heels.'

'"Eels"? What are you talking about?'

'He means a plague of eels.'

'No, I don't. Are the both of you deaf and stupid? I said, "heels", not "ankles".'

'Well, whatever.'

They nodded and sipped their beers in quiet contentment.

45

Yet another taxi. This time from Penzance Station.

'Where to?'

Porthhella. No, not there. Not where Brenda or Megan or the fishermen might see her. Better to go from the house.

'Tregarnon House.'

'That's the place that burned down, isn't it?'

'Yes, that's right. I hear the site's for sale. I want to take a look.'

'Fine. Will you want me to wait and bring you back?'

'No thanks. I'm staying nearby.'

'Right you are. Wherever it is it'll be quite a walk. But you're the boss.'

No expressions of concern from this one about how ill she looked. Thank God. She had her story ready, just in case. Food poisoning on the train. Can't trust railway caterers these days.

She sat back in her seat, watching the familiar scenery unfold. Though the sun had shone fiercely all day the hard frost from the previous night persisted in shaded parts of the meadows and under the trees. The sunset would be spectacular. She would be there just in time. If her strength held out.

'Miss Rogers? Brenda Rogers?'

'That's right. Who is this?'

There was a crackle on the line which made his voice hard to hear.

'James Wilson. Madeleine's solicitor. From Oxford. You remember we met, when you came up here to find her. You left your name and number in case we found her first.'

'Yes, of course. Mr Wilson. I remember. What can I do for you?'

'It's about Madeleine again, I'm afraid. She came up here yesterday to see me. She's very ill as I'm sure you know, and she came to sort out her will. The fact is, I hadn't expected to see her. She was in London, waiting to be admitted to hospital. We had an appointment for me to go there today. When she arrived here yesterday she told me her admission had been delayed by a week. So she thought she would come and see me first and get it all sorted. The fact is, I'm very worried about her. She barely had the strength to get through the meeting. I'm no doctor but in my opinion she needed to be in hospital right away. I have some contacts in the medical world here so I asked her if she wanted me to get her into the Radcliffe without risking the journey back to London. She was absolutely insistent that she would be all right. Frankly, I didn't believe her.'

'I did know she was ill, Mr Wilson. She told us she was having a few tests done and then coming back here. Obviously they decided they would have to admit her. But what surprises me is that she didn't ring and tell me. I don't even know where she's staying. Do you know?'

'I know where she was staying. I rang there after she left. She had checked out before she came up here. I then rang the Chelsea and Westminster. She was booked to be admitted yesterday, a serious priority. No delays on any account. She never turned up. They've been trying to locate her as well. They had the number of her local doctor down your way. They rang him in case he had referred her elsewhere and the message hadn't got through to them. But he had no idea where she was.'

'Oh Christ!'

'I wondered if she had arrived back there. I mean, she would stay with you, wouldn't she? I heard what happened to the house.'

'Yes, she would. If she were coming here. But what makes you think she would do that?'

'Well, my father was here as well, yesterday. You know he's supposed to be retired but he can't stay away. And he's an old family friend. So he drove her to the station. He hung around to make sure she got on a train all right. She didn't have a return ticket. And he swears he heard her buy a ticket through to Penzance.'

The sun hung blood-red on the surface of the water. She sat on a rock, writing in the notebook. There were still a few walkers about. But in an hour it would be nearly dark and much too dangerous to be so close to the cliffs. She would be alone. She was not sure of the exact spot. But she knew it was where the old path had been roped off. The edge was closer now than it had been then. Ever since he had dislodged the earth. She was only a hundred yards away. She could crawl there if necessary. She had half-crawled much of the way as it was, refusing several offers of help. She just needed to finish what she was writing.

A few more minutes and it was done. She looked up. Only traces of red on the water now. She clutched the notebook to her chest.

'What did the police say?' asked Megan.

'They traced the taxi driver who picked her up at Penzance. Definitely her. Fitted the description I gave them. Looked as if she was about to expire, so he said.'

'So where is she?'

'He didn't take her here. He took her to the house.'

'What house?'

'Her house, of course. Only there's no house there any more. As she bloody well knows.'

'Maybe she's gone and forgotten again.'

'No such luck. In that case he would have brought her here or back to the station or somewhere she could stay. No, she told him she wanted to see the site because she was thinking of buying it. And she didn't want him to wait. She went there deliberately. I have an idea where's she going. But it's nearly dark now and the coastguard won't come out until morning.'

'The coastguard? You don't think . . .?' Megan covered her face with her hands.

Brenda guided Megan to the sofa and eased her into a sitting position. She put her arms around her for a few moments. Then she stood up abruptly.

'It's no use, Megan. I've got to do something. I can't just hang around here waiting. I'll get round there in the car and look around. No, wait a minute. I'll go from here. It's shorter though the path's much steeper at the start. There's a torch in the cupboard. Here we are.'

'Where are you going?'

'Up to the headland, to where her mother fell. That's where she's going, I'll swear it.'

'Brenda, don't, please. It's much too dangerous.'

There was a loud knock on the door. Both women jumped.

'Who's that, for God's sake?'

'Maybe it's the police,' said Megan. 'Maybe they've found her. Oh please God they've found her.'

Brenda jerked open the door. Five men stood outside. She recognised Charley, George and Samuel, and John Foster, the landlord of the inn. The fifth man was young, probably still in his twenties, with a rucksack on his back. Brenda stepped back, startled.

'Hello, John. Gentlemen. What . . .'

'Brenda, I'm sorry to disturb you,' said John. 'I thought you should know. These gentlemen said you were friends with her.' The trio nodded. 'Madeleine, I mean. I had a call from the police in Penzance to say she might be missing and near the coastal path. They found an overnight bag near the site of the fire which they think might be hers. The sergeant said she was very ill and in no state to be up there. Then this gentleman came into the bar.'

302

The young man smiled, stepped forward and shook hands. 'Bill Johnson. I think I might have seen her.'

'Go on, young man.' It was Megan who spoke. She had come up behind Brenda as soon as she had opened the door.

'She was struggling up the path on the other side, towards the bay. That was well over an hour ago. I offered to help her but she refused. I came on here but I couldn't get her out of my mind. I decided I should go back. But it was getting dark by then and I thought it would be a good idea to get help. So I went to the inn. Mr Foster told me she had been reported missing. He offered to join me. Then these three gentlemen who were in the bar said they were locals who knew the coastline better than anybody and they offered too.'

'And I was about to go up there on my own,' said Brenda. 'And bloody terrified at the thought. I hate going up there even in daylight. So I'm pleased to see you all. Gentlemen,' she addressed the fishermen, 'I'm surprised you want to help. After what I've heard of your behaviour to her.'

George stepped forward. 'I wants to apologise for that, Miss Rogers. On behalf of us all. Miss Megan there saw us the other day when she were out shopping and explained it all. About how someone else confessed to the killing. And how she's so sick now. We're all three of us very sorry. And we're here to help. I can find my way up to that headland blindfold. And so can my friends.'

'Come on then,' said John. 'We're wasting time here.'

'Hang on a minute,' said Brenda. 'I'll get my coat and torch. I'm coming with you.'

She crawled forward, her hands numb, her legs without feeling. Every few feet, she checked to see that the notebook was safe. Already the frost was hardening the mud and the tufts of grass. The day had been calm. The waves below were no more than a distant swish in her ear, beneath the much closer sound of her rasping breath. She waited and listened. Then she smiled and rolled slowly onto her back. She forced herself into a half-sitting position, opened the notebook and scrawled three more words under the last entry. Three final words. She could not see to write them. But she was sure they were there on the page.

Now it was over. Nothing more to be done. The darkness pressed against her eyes. She closed them. Slowly, silently, she fell through the endless night.

46

They passed the spot several times before they saw her. She was lying on her back, close to the edge, as still as the surrounding rocks. Instinctively they laid their coats over her, although there was no sign of movement. It was Brenda who thought to shine her torch into her frozen eyelids to see if there was any response.

'She's dead, gentlemen. We shouldn't move her. But we can't just leave her like this. We'll take it in turns to watch her. Three on, three off.'

'You go back and sleep, Miss Rogers,' said Charley. 'The three of us will watch. We've spent many a night on the decks of our boats in much worse weather than this. We've got hides as tough as leather.'

'All right. You other two come back with me. We'll be back in an hour with flasks of hot coffee.'

'Then Bill and I will relieve you,' said John.

'I'll ring the police and the doctor,' said Brenda. 'They'll be here as soon as it's light. Just give me a moment alone with her.'

The men stood back. Brenda knelt down by the body and fumbled underneath the coats, looking up every now and then to check that none of them was watching her. Shivering with the chill which despite the covers seeped from the body into her fingers, she at last found the notebook. She prised it away and tucked it inside her jacket. She stood up and looked down.

You used up every last ounce of your strength to come up here to die. So why did you do that? What were you thinking of? You can't tell me now. But maybe this book will. I'll leave you here to watch over the place where she fell. Good night, Madeleine. God bless.

47

It was the sunset that drew you here. And the dolphins that told you to stay. And when you met Michael you understood why. Was he the reason you stopped writing to me? Was it because of him that you forgot you had ever written to me, that you left the notebook to gather dust? Or did you think that once you, Michael and Hywel were a family you might find me again, make me part of your new life? That could never have happened. You were too late, 20 years too late. I've reread what I wrote above about you being a stranger, one I could admire from a distance. But that was all nonsense, wasn't it? We were never strangers. You're never a stranger to someone you've betrayed as you betrayed me.

I remembered, just as I was about to go into the hospital. I thought I had remembered everything. But not that. Not the moment I knew I was lost. The moment you betrayed me. He had told me to be quiet. But I wasn't. I cried out, to you, for help. You weren't there. Of course you weren't. So I was quiet, all through the rest of the agony and the terror.

The next day I went down early but he was already up. I think he had been up all night. He looked at me. For a moment I think he was afraid, in case I would run away in fear or horror. He was wondering what he had done, not to me but to the two of us. I showed no fear, no repulsion. I was calm and self-possessed. Overnight I had grown beyond my years. I looked him in the eye and asked him if he loved me, if he would always be there for me. I was thinking of you when I spoke. He said, of course I love you. It's special, isn't it? Our special love. You don't need anybody else.

He never betrayed me. You did. That is why I have come here to the place you died. To accuse you of betrayal. If you had been a stranger you would never have returned to me that night, would you? So why did you show me what happened to you, here in this place? Were you telling me that you too had been betrayed? Was that supposed to make up for your betrayal of me? Why did you take possession of me, enter my mind, let me feel your last moments?

I need you to do that again, Mother, now, this minute. Before I die. I want to be you again. I want you to watch your daughter, doing those dreadful things with him. I want you to see her evil nature. I want you to tell her she's evil. Then I will know why you betrayed me. Because you knew before it happened that I was evil and always had been. Because you had to get away from me, from both of us. Then I can go to him. I will lie with my face pressed into the earth until his hands rise up and pull me down. I'll go to the edge, now. That's where I'll find you. That's where you'll tell me.

48

The office of Wilson & Partners, Solicitors, was a single, dusty, ill-lit room above an antiques shop in the High Street, accessible only by means of a steep, narrow staircase. About halfway up the stairs turned sharply to the right. On this cramped landing files and heaps of papers had been stacked, apparently at random. More were to be found at the top of the stairs, just outside the heavy oak door panelled with opaque glass. To the left a cubicle with a telephone and old-fashioned Olivetti typewriter accommodated Mrs Radley, the receptionist and secretary. She was 75, tall, fit and severe, her white hair tied in a bun. She was as indispensable to young Mr Wilson as she had been to his father. Only she understood the filing system. Only she could open the safe and work the telephone and only she knew where the tea and biscuits were kept. Fortunately she had no difficulty with the stairs.

Mr Wilson senior, on the other hand, though a year younger than Mrs Radley, was finding it increasingly hard to negotiate the stairs as his arthritis and shortness of breath made steady advances. But today he could still manage it, just about. He was pleased about that. He was determined to be there for the reading of Madeleine Reed's will. And Miss Rogers had specially asked for him to be there. A fine lady, that Miss Rogers, he thought. Somebody who respects age and experience.

Young Mr Wilson, as he was generally known though he was

by now well into his forties, and Brenda were already there, drinking tea which Mrs Radley had served from a silver tea set dating from the days of the senior Mr Wilson's own father. Brenda knew from her previous visit that she would enjoy the tea, which was nearly as strong as Megan's. They rose as Mr Wilson senior entered. He offered his hand to Brenda, nodded at his son, sat down in the corner chair which was reserved for him and waved for them to continue.

'So as I said, it's all pretty straightforward, Miss Rogers. She left the sums of money I mentioned to you and to Mrs Megan Jenkins, formerly of Tregarnon House. The balance will go into two trusts, one to run the residential home on the site of the former Tregarnon House and the other to administer what I believe you are going to call the Michael Wallace Memorial Gallery.'

'That's right,' said Brenda. 'It's not going to be anything very fancy. Not a new building or anything like that. But the gallery I inherited from Mr Wallace is very small and cramped. Fortunately the old harbourmaster's cottage next door has come up for sale and we've put in an offer. By "we" I mean Megan and myself. We're partners in this now. It's because of her we've still got some very precious drawings by Mr Wallace, which by a great stroke of luck were saved from the fire. We're going to convert the harbourmaster's cottage into an annexe and put the drawings in there. I do have a few contacts in the art world who are interested in becoming trustees. We'll get together what we can of the rest of Mr Wallace's stuff. A lot of it was destroyed in the fire, of course. But we'll advertise. See if any of the private owners are interested in selling. This way we'll have enough for a fitting tribute to Mr Wallace and still have space for work for new artists.'

Mr Wilson glanced at his father. 'Miss Rogers, I understand you asked for the opportunity to speak to my father again. Is it in connection with the will? My father did not actually deal with any of Miss Reed's affairs, so . . .'

'No, nothing to do with the will. It's really personal curiosity.

I hope you don't mind, sir.' She turned towards Mr Wilson senior. 'Miss Reed confided in me a great deal towards the end of her life. I suppose you could say we became friends. She told me about her father's death, as I mentioned last time we met. But there were some things she obviously didn't want to talk about, or couldn't remember. I just wanted to be sure about them, to complete the picture if I can. I've led a rather isolated life. I've never gone in for friendship. So her death is a great loss to me personally. It would just help me to come to terms with it.'

Mr Wilson senior smiled encouragingly. 'I'd be happy to offer any help I can, though my memory is not what it was.'

His son stood up. 'I'll leave you two alone then, if that's all right. I have another client to visit. I'll see you both back here at lunchtime.'

He shook hands with Brenda and left the room. Mr Wilson senior moved over to the desk and with an air of pride and satisfaction took the chair which he had finally ceded to his son 15 years ago. He waited for Brenda to speak.

"Mr Wilson, you remember my asking you last time if you could confirm that Miss Reed's father committed suicide. You did so. Do you remember anything more about the circumstances? What I mean is, did you see him in the weeks beforehand and what was his apparent state of mind? Did he leave a note? Did he seem the sort of person who might kill himself?'

Mr Wilson smiled again. 'I'll gladly answer your questions, Miss Rogers. I do remember it all very well. I attended the inquest. I was a witness in fact. The questions you have just asked me were put to me then by the coroner. Afterwards I remember speaking informally to the police officer in charge of the case. I'll also answer the question you haven't asked but which I think is uppermost in your mind.'

'What's that?'

'Was Madeleine suspected of killing him?'

'On my mind, yes. But not uppermost. Not that one. So was she?'

'For a while, yes. Of course she was. She was there alone in the room with him. She could have killed him and placed the gun in his hand afterwards. Whatever had happened, she had been the last person to see him alive. Whatever his last words had been, she was the only one to have heard them. So they interviewed her repeatedly, in her mother's presence of course. But she was in no state to answer questions. She either couldn't say anything about it, because of the shock, or she genuinely couldn't remember. Shock does cause amnesia, so I've heard. They took her fingerprints. The police report cleared her. Only his fingerprints were on the gun. There was nothing she was wearing or holding or had access to in the room which she could have used to hold the gun, or there would have been marks on it. And of course she would have had no conceivable motive. She adored him. And in any case, where would a 14-year-old girl get a gun from, in this city in those days? I'm surprised he managed to get hold of one.'

'Did he leave a note?'

'No. But there was a tape. The police found it when they searched the room. It was locked in a cabinet of private papers. The key was on her. She told them he had asked her to lock the tape away, just before he died. She was hysterical when they took it away for analysis. Kept saying he had entrusted it to her and nobody else must see it. They analysed it but couldn't make anything of it. The police psychologist gave evidence about it. He couldn't find anything in it which might have explained why he killed himself. It was all about some ancient Greek myths, apparently. But that was his life's work. In the end the police thought and the coroner agreed that the tape was entirely to do with his research and he had given it to her to lock away for safe keeping. Perhaps he had given her some instructions on where to file it when she had transcribed it, but she had forgotten. That was the sort of thing she used to do for him when he was working on a book.'

'What was the tape about? Anything to do with the Furies,

perhaps? The Eumenides, as they are sometimes called. Mythological agents of the vengeance of the Gods.'

'Yes, I think it was some nonsense like that. Nothing to do with his death at all. They gave her the tape back after the inquest. She kept it close to her all the time after that. As if it were some sort of charm to protect her from evil. She was in a dreadful state, getting worse all the time. Her mother had her committed. Later on there were problems with drugs. But I suppose you know all about that.'

'Would you say that he was in a deeply disturbed frame of mind?'

'Oh yes. No doubt about it. He made a will about three weeks before it happened. Nothing unusual about that or the content, only the timing. He was lucid and rational enough when he came to see me. But he seemed dreadfully agitated. He was very thin and I could tell he hadn't been sleeping. I suggested he should see a doctor. He said he had been overworking, that was all.'

'What sort of man was he? I mean, normally, before he became disturbed.'

'Very quiet, dry in manner, absorbed, a typical academic if there is such a thing. Not an easy man to know. Not one to form attachments readily.'

'Not one given to violent emotional outbursts?'

'I wouldn't say so. But perhaps only his doctor would have really known. If he had gone to see one, that is. But I rather doubt he did. I don't think he trusted doctors.'

'Not his wife?'

'I didn't see her much at that time. Only afterwards, when I was settling his affairs. But no, I don't think so. I don't think they were close to each other. I doubt if she really knew much about him. Or he about her. Now he and Madeleine on the other hand, they were close. She was his research assistant in the few months prior to his death, even though she was only 14. It was such a tragedy for her. I never knew any girl so affected by her father's death. I don't suppose she ever really got over it.'

'No, I don't think she did. Was the ballistics report read out at the inquest?'

'Ballistics? I'm not sure. Not read out, I think. I seem to remember the police witness saying there had been two bullets in the gun. Only one was used.'

'Two bullets? You're sure of that?'

'Yes, I am. Pretty sure. Is it important?'

'That depends.'

'On what?'

Brenda was surprised to find herself smiling. She could barely remember smiling at all for most of her life. Since meeting Megan, that had changed.

'On whether at some point we decide to be frank with each other.'

Mr Wilson returned the smile. 'Forgive me, Miss Rogers. I've been retired from the law for many years. But old habits die hard. This may not be a client-to-lawyer conversation, but I'm still not sure exactly what it is. So my instincts warn me to protect the interests of someone who was once my client. I know you have something on your mind and you feel I can be much more helpful than I have been so far. You may be right about that. Please be as frank with your questions as you wish. I will do my best to respond fully and honestly. If the nature of certain questions causes me to hold something back, I hope you will understand.'

'I found your choice of words interesting. When you said she adored him. Later you said, after some hesitation when you seemed to be searching for another form of words, that they were close. Much more the sort of words you would use in court. I felt that in the first case a shutter opened, and in the second that it closed again.'

He laughed. 'What's your background, Miss Rogers? Were you ever a barrister? If not, you would have made an extremely good one.'

'Nothing so grand. I tried teacher training but gave it up. At one stage I had ambitions to become an artist. I ended up running a tiny art gallery at the far end of the country. So now you've cast me as a barrister, let me pursue my line of questioning. Did you think their relationship was very intense? Do you think he felt the same way about her?'

'Yes, to both questions.'

'So if he loved her as much . . .'

'I think I can anticipate your next question. It puzzled me a great deal at the time. If he loved her so much, why did he put her through the agony of seeing him shoot himself in front of her? If he had decided he had to go, why didn't he choose a more discreet time and place?'

'But this question no longer puzzles you.'

'I meant I stopped thinking about it.'

'The shutter has come down again, I see. That's the first incomplete answer since you invited me to probe you further.'

'Touché, Miss Rogers.'

'Mr Wilson, I also am in a difficult position. Possibly more difficult than yours. We each know something. You have a duty to a former client. I am sworn to secrecy.'

'Suspect. You may know. She was your friend, she confided in you. I only suspect. And that is the truth.'

Brenda stood up and walked over to the grimy window. She looked down. A convoy of buses of different colours, shapes and sizes threaded its way slowly along the High Street, each fighting the other for space at the bus stop, each competing for the dwindling number of passengers as midday approached. Above them the sandstone buttresses and towers of the prestigious colleges, proud to have secured such a prime location, gazed impassively at the scene. She turned to look at him.

'Is St Stephen's one of these?'

'Dr Reed's college? No. But it's close.'

'Could we take a walk there? I need some fresh air.'

They soon found the new lecture theatre which bore his name.

'I'm sworn to secrecy because of this,' said Brenda, pointing to the plaque with its list of donors. 'Not just the building. The various funds and donations attracted in his name. If I told what I know, all that could be at risk. But the knowledge is a terrible burden to me. If I could only share it with one person, a person I could trust, someone discreet, someone used to safeguarding secrets . . . Tell me, do your obligations extend beyond the death of the person concerned?'

'I should say instantly that they do. Then our conversation would be at an end and we would go our separate ways, each with our burden. But I don't want that and I know you don't. I don't know how much longer I will be around. Not many years, I would think. I am no longer in the best of health. I do not know how many more chances I will have to be of some use. And at my age I think I am entitled to bend the rules a little. After all, what can anybody do to me? So I will answer your question by saying that it depends. And that answer is intended to open, not close the shutter. As for your oath, it was taken to safeguard certain interests. Maybe, at some time in the future, many years hence perhaps, when neither of us is around, the danger to those interests may have passed. The most important thing then will be the truth. That's all the scholars in this place ask of the past. That it yield up the truth to them.'

They turned and walked slowly through the first quad towards the porter's lodge.

'Do you know where it happened?' she asked.

'Up there.' He pointed towards a first-floor window. 'That was his room.'

She looked up, shuddered and turned away. Just before they reached the lodge he stopped and placed his hand on her arm.

'Miss Rogers, I know you are torn. You care passionately about what happened. Not just up in that room on that terrible June day. But what led up to it. Your secret is unbearable, I can see that. Tell me what you want me to do.'

'Not here. This place stifles me.'

'All right. Let's go to Christchurch Meadow.'

*

316

They sat on a bench by the river.

'I don't really know this place,' she said. 'What are the towers?'

'The one over there, to the north, is Tom Tower. Part of Christchurch. The one we came past to reach the meadow is Merton. The one over there is Magdalen. Listen. The Angelus bells. I love the way they always seem to be answering each other.'

'So beautiful, so peaceful. How could these things have happened here, of all places? That's what I'll never understand. You said that what the future expects of the present is for it to yield the truth. But for that there needs to be a reliable record. Buried if necessary until such time as it can be safely released.'

'I agree. An ideal repository for such a record might be, for example, a family firm of solicitors, handed down through the generations. From father to son to grandson.'

'You have a grandson?'

'Only ten. Very like his father. I'm sure he will carry on the tradition.'

She half-smiled. 'I think we have a deal. Shall we shake on it?'

'Gladly.' They shook hands. 'Do you have a full record of the history which she confided to you?'

'Not yet. I have this notebook.' She took it slowly and carefully out of her handbag and gave it to him. He whistled as he turned it over in his hands.

'God, this has been in the wars.'

'It's a long story. Her mother started it. She didn't know what was going on but she realised Madeleine had changed. She could not communicate with her any more. The notebook was her way of saying to her the things she had to say. Except that Madeleine never saw it until many years after her mother's death. Then she continued it, writing in it until just before her own death. On its own it isn't enough. There are too many gaps and oblique references. As soon as I get back home I intend to devote my time to writing the rest of her story, and that of the others involved. That includes me. There were other tragedies, and I played my part in bringing some of them about. But it was here it all started. In this town. In their home. When she was thirteen.'

'She really told you everything?'

'Yes, when her memories returned.'

'And it was she who swore you to secrecy, for the reasons you mentioned?'

'Yes. Tell me, did you really think the tape had no significance?'

'On the contrary. I had read his book on the Eumenides. He always sent me copies of his books on the day of publication. When the police inspector showed me a copy of the transcript of the tape I knew what it was about. He seemed to be saying that the Furies were real, that he had seen them. But that could only be the case if he had committed a crime against nature. Of course the police never understood what it meant. Towards the end of the tape he addressed her directly. Called her "special", "part of me, body and soul".'

'How did the police take that?'

'There was no mention of her name, of course. So they were puzzled. One of them was a bit more perceptive than the others. He wondered if he had dictated something he was reading, for future use as a reference. Something for his own book. It's plausible enough. There was nothing to indicate that the words he had spoken into the machine were his own. And in any case, what did all this mythological stuff have to do with him topping himself?'

'You knew that it had everything to do with it. And he had already finished and published his book on the Eumenides. But you didn't disabuse them. I saw those words as well. That bit about being "part of me, body and soul". In his handwriting. He had written her a dedication in the copy of the book he gave to her. No name again. The book was in Mr Wallace's library, but it was destroyed in the fire.'

'And the tape?'

'If she kept it in the house, it would have been destroyed as well.'

'Pity. Still, a copy of a copy of the transcript might suffice.'

She stared at him. 'You mean . . .'

He laughed at the expression on her face. 'You needn't look so astonished. You should know by now that lawyers are the most cautious of people, and I was more than most. I copied everything. I asked the inspector to lend me his copy of the transcript so I could study it. I took it back to the office, photocopied it and filed it. It's in a private cabinet. Not even Mrs Radley knows about it. Then I gave the inspector's copy back to him and told him I thought it meant nothing pertinent to the case. I'm not sure why I copied it. Something told me it might be useful one day. We have the notebook as original material, which your account, although second-hand, will clarify. All that should be sufficient.'

'Could I see your copy of the transcript?'

'Certainly. In fact, I'll make you a copy, back at the office. Why did you ask me about the bullets?'

'There was no note and from what you've told me the purpose of the tape was, to say the least, obscure. So I wondered if it had occurred to you that this might have been a case of a suicide pact that went wrong?'

'Yes, it occurred to me. One bullet for each of them. But he would have shot her first, not expected her to pick up the gun from his hand.'

'I think that was exactly what he did expect. He probably thought about killing her first but when the time came he couldn't bring himself to do it. So he did expect her to follow him. She couldn't because she lost her memory.'

'Was it a pact then?'

'Not as we would understand it. He had decided they were both guilty and they should both die. He thought he was protecting her from the Furies. It was never her decision. But she did follow him in the end. The notebook and what I'm going to write will explain it all.'

'Did she share his beliefs, do you think?'

'In the ancient gods and the Furies? She saw them and she knew who they were. But she sometimes wrote in Biblical terms as well. Her father taught her one belief system and I suppose her school taught her the other. But I don't think she had a chance to build a real one for herself. How could she? She lost her sense of self and her memories at too young an age. For her the Furies were simply external images of suppressed guilt and buried memories.'

'Look, this is what we'll do. Come back to the office. Leave the notebook with me and I'll put it in the safe with my copy of the transcript. I'll get another copy of that for you to take away with you and read at your leisure. Go back to Cornwall. Write up your account. When you have finished it, bring it to me in person. I'll draw up and witness an affidavit from you, swearing it is a true account of what she told you. I'll handle it all from then on. I'll leave written instructions for James and if necessary his successor. While you are alive nothing will be done with the material without your permission, I can assure you of that.' He looked at his watch. 'James should be back by now. You'd be welcome to join us for lunch.'

'Yes, I'd like that.'

'What are your plans after that?'

'Oh, I thought I'd visit someone I know. In North Oxford.'

49

It took her some time to find the grave again. By then the rain which had threatened all day had begun to fall heavily and she had forgotten her umbrella. However there was one advantage to the weather. She could be sure of being alone.

Hello, again. Dr Andrew Reed. Remember me? Brenda. Madeleine's friend. This time it's just the two of us. Nobody to ask for your forgiveness or any nonsense like that. Only me, your accuser, one of only two people left on earth who know what you did. But I'm going to be fair, Dr Reed. I'm not going to rant and rave. Not your style and certainly not mine. I'm going to try to imagine how it all happened.

First of all, your upbringing. A small remote village. Your parents distant and severe. The only joy you could find was in your studies. At school you were withdrawn, a loner. You went to church, or chapel more likely, but you never believed in it. Am I doing all right so far? Up to this point I could be talking about the two of us. But from now on there are important differences. I never needed faith. You did. As you read and studied the classics you decided you preferred the harsh, capricious gods of antiquity to a merciful Christian God. You could believe in them. You went to university, here in Oxford, got a first class degree, then a doctorate. You were elected a Fellow of an Oxford college at a relatively young age. Your reputation grew. You published books. Your entire world was your research and your teaching and your writing. You were in your early thirties by now. But you looked older. You were happy enough, so you thought. Safe and secure in your sheltered world.

You had never been particularly interested in the opposite sex. Then you met a young student, beautiful, vibrant, impulsive. You married. Maybe you sensed you lacked something she could provide. Maybe you felt that by that stage in your career you needed the security and status of marriage. Whatever the reason you never really loved her, never understood her. The two of you drifted apart. You buried yourself even more deeply in your work.

Then something happened. Something catastrophic. Something which shook your world to its foundations. Or rather someone. We need to give this new thing a name. That's something you could never have done, because it was totally outside your experience, your view of the world. Let's call it . . . passion. For want of a better word. I know a little bit about that. I know how it can take you over, just when you think you have your life completely under control. I know how it can give you a capacity for evil you never thought you had. It certainly did that with me. A young woman came into your life.

Of course she had been there before. But as a child. An inconvenience. A distraction. You had ignored her as much as you could. Now you were overwhelmed. There she was, the perfect embodiment of beauty in your eyes, innocent, lonely, fearful, trembling on the verge of womanhood with nobody to help her, her mother an absent stranger. She had had no time to build defences, to learn how to manipulate, to be cynical, to use others and avoid being used. She was a pure, perfect human being in your eyes. And beautiful. Beautiful in a way she could never have been before and never could be again. 'Beauty in the young is a curse. It awakens evil.' She told me you wrote that in one of your books. Her beauty was a curse indeed. On both of you.

The emotions which raged inside you were all the more violent for having been suppressed for so long. One thought tortured you above all others. She was not intended for you. Soon she would attract the attention of others. Boys, then men, fighting for her time, her attention, her smile, her words, her affections, her body. She would be corrupted by the world outside the two of you, that strange, messy, threatening, unknown world. You had to prevent that. So you took everything she had to give before she had a chance to give it, before she even knew what it was you had taken. You made her yours, forever, or so you thought. You had a new god now. Passion, ecstasy, the joy of possession of perfection, call it what you will.

You knew the old gods you had once revered had prescribed punishments for what you were doing. But you defied them. You told them you no longer believed in them. But it didn't work. The old gods were jealous and outraged. They sent their agents of punishment to torment you. The Furies. You had even written a book about them, recklessly daring to consign them to myth and superstition. They came and took their revenge. They drove you to kill yourself.

But that wasn't the end of it. You expected her to see them as well. You thought her as guilty as you were. You expected her to follow you. You assumed she would never be able to live on after you. In a way you were right about that. If she hadn't forgotten, she would have killed herself. But she did forget, and she survived, after a fashion. But if our lives are built on the memories of what made us who we are, then she had no life. All she knew was that she was different, special, not like other people. Unaware of what was driving her, she sought out men to take your place. I can hear you laughing about that. Of course nobody could take your place. But she had forgotten you. You had to find her again. You had to pursue her, even after death. Of course you did. She belonged to you, didn't she? So you and the Furies drove her to seek out that final encounter in a dirty hotel room, the one which would ensure that in time she would follow you.

The rain had started to ease. She moved to the nearest bench, wiped off the pools of water with her scarf and sat down.

Let's go back a little. I don't want to get ahead of myself. Let's

323

go back to the time she was drifting through life, searching for the man who might show her once again the image of herself you had given her. At last she met such a man. A brilliant young artist, someone whose genius justified any amount of bad behaviour. Or an intolerably selfish and abusive young man. Whichever way you care to look at it. He made her feel special all right. They were brother and sister. Nobody had told them. But I think they each suspected, deep down. He would not have had conscious memories of his mother. But subconsciously she must have reminded him of her. He focused his hatred of women on Madeleine because of those memories of the first woman who abandoned him, as he saw it.

He was sure Michael was his father. He must often have wondered who his mother was. Madeleine must have told him Michael had known her mother. Maybe that made him wonder even more. But what finally broke him was seeing that picture, that image of his mother and sister rolled into one, both of them the objects of his abuse. He looked at the picture and saw his own evil nature. He took refuge by forgetting, and later by killing off the person who had done those things, and becoming Alan.

She must have had her suspicions as well. The picture, Michael's actions following her mother's death, arranging the funeral, having her buried next to his own family plot, looking after her cottage. She must have felt there was something strange about the way he always denied he had known her mother more than slightly. Then David turning up out of nowhere, just the right age. I believe that deep down she knew this was another incestuous relationship, forbidden by the gods. So when the relationship ended, the Furies pursued her, as you had prophesied. Her moment of truth finally came when she spoke to Laura.

But in the meantime the Furies had driven her to do something terrible. I know her illness was not just bad luck. She sought it out. Although she did not realise it at the time it was her way to follow you, as you had told her to. After she spoke to Laura she did what David had done. She forgot. She buried the truth among her other lost memories. And in the hospital where she served her time for a crime she had not committed she protected herself by taking literally some words she had overheard Laura say, that she was David's mother. Conveniently, that was all she remembered about Laura. And that delusion was enough to protect her when she came back to Porthhella and started to find out all over again that her mother and Michael had had an affair. It even protected her when she realised her mother had been pregnant, and that somewhere she might have an unknown brother.

But the real truth was still there, trying to break through. And the one who embodied that truth was you. You were trying to reach her, trying to take possession again, your image, your words, your deeds, forming slowly through the fog of her lost memories. Although she wanted to remember, at the same time she was terrified because she knew that when her memories returned, so would you.

I never believed in ghosts, Dr Reed. How could I? A hardheaded northerner like me. But when you've lived down there by the Atlantic, looking out towards the Scillies over the drowned lands of legend that lie between, you maybe get less sceptical. You begin to sense that there are spirits around you. Madeleine sensed that too. She sensed you, trying to get through to her. A departed spirit with unfinished business, or simply that part of you which you had left in her psyche, who knows?

But she sensed someone else. She told me how her mother had tried to tell her about the way she had died. She was trying to tell her they were only strangers because of you. You had driven them apart. While her mother was away trying to find herself or lose herself through her affairs, you stepped in and took Madeleine, body and soul. She came home to find her daughter a complete stranger, a shadowy, manipulative, secretive person she couldn't begin to recognise. And she had no idea what had happened to make her like that so suddenly. When she came back to Madeleine that night at the house, she wasn't just telling her how she died. She was telling her she finally knew and understood.

325

God knows, there was a lot in her life for her to regret. So many wasted opportunities. But the biggest waste of all was Madeleine. She was telling her that what she regretted most was that she never saw her until it was too late. Never had the chance to take her by the hand and say, we're going to make up for lost time, you and I. There's nothing we can't be together, nothing we can't do together, we can take the earth and the heavens by storm with the love that is finally going to grow between us. But she never had the chance to say any of that, did she? And the reason for that was you, and what you did.

Now, shall I tell you something, Dr Reed? You may think you won in the end. But you didn't. You lost. That's what I came to tell you here today. You lost for two reasons. The first is this. In the end Madeleine knew and remembered enough to choose. And that was something she had never been able to do before. You had always thought you were in charge, that she could never choose. But now she could, and she did not choose you. How does that make you feel? She went up to the cliffs to die because she couldn't face dying in hospital, still not knowing what she had to know. She knew from the notebook that her mother did not know what you did. Maybe that was wrong of her mother. She should have realised something was amiss. There must have been warning signs, but she didn't notice them. She was absorbed with her own problems. Even if she hadn't suspected abuse she must have thought afterwards that it was at least in part because of her that her husband had killed himself and her daughter had gone off the rails.

But at the end Madeleine was prepared to forgive her and herself. But first she needed to know how her mother would react if she did know about the abuse, if she actually saw it happening. Would she agree with you that Madeleine was evil as you were? If so, you would have won. She would have accepted your right to take her down with you to Hell. At the end of the notebook Madeleine put that question to her mother. Then she walked, or more likely crawled, to the edge. To the last place on earth where her mother had drawn breath.

So how do I know how her mother answered? Because her mother had once before been inside her mind, that night when Madeleine saw how she had died. She told me she didn't just see it. She felt it. She stood on that spot, she fell to her death. I believe that happened again. I believe Madeleine was her mother once again. I believe she saw what happened to her daughter, when she was alone in her bedroom, when you went to her. And what mother, seeing that, wouldn't kill to protect her daughter if she could? And what mother, seeing her lying there afterwards, alone, terrified, in agony, would tell her she was evil, that she was to blame, that she belonged to you forever?

No, I believe that that cry for help from all those years ago was finally answered. If it hadn't been she would have destroyed the notebook, thrown it over the cliffs. She would have turned her face into the ground. The Furies would have dragged her down to you. But she died looking upwards, holding the book closely to her. And there on the last page is the final entry. Just three words. Barely legible. I believe she wrote them at the moment of death. 'No More Sea.' I remember those words from my Sunday school. From the Book of Revelation. And I think I know what she meant by them. She had her answer. The sea of destruction and estrangement which had torn and held them asunder was no more. Her face was peaceful. The Furies had finally left her. And so had you. And now I'll leave you to howl down there on your own for all eternity.

She had started to walk away when she remembered and turned back.

Oh, I nearly forgot to mention the other thing. I swore not to tell anybody what you did and I've kept that promise. But there is someone else who knows and who will guard the secret and hand it down. And one day the story will be told. And believed. I may never live to see that day, but I know it will happen. And that's the only thought that at this moment is stopping me from desecrating your grave and strewing your bones all over the shop. So put that in your pipe and smoke it.

Goodbye, Dr Reed. It's been an unexpected pleasure talking to you. And if you can rest in peace after all I've said, then by all means go ahead.

She walked slowly to her car, suddenly overwhelmed by a feeling of intense fatigue. Time to get back to Megan, she thought. I've been away long enough. There are things to sort out. I'll tell her about the inquest. Natural causes. The pathologist said she had gone into a coma and never came out of it. She died of heart failure. Her constitution had been severely weakened over recent months by HIV-related infections. I won't tell Megan she had AIDS. I'll tell her she had a chronic heart condition from childhood. If she thinks I'm lying, too bad. And in a sense it's the truth, isn't it? I'll tell her about the will as well. With her legacies from Madeleine and Michael there'll be plenty for her to buy a nice cottage near me. So I'll be able to keep an eye on her. I'm sure Madeleine would have wanted that.

She settled herself into the driving seat, preparing herself mentally for the long journey ahead. She would stop and phone Megan on the way.

Oh, there was one other thing. The copy of the transcript. It was short. She would read it first, before she started the engine. Think it over as she drove. She took it out of her handbag, unfolded it and began to read.

50

I have always found the Christian idea of Hell inherently ridiculous. An eternity of torment for an instant of sin. Only a madman could invent something like that. The Greek myths offer more potent and credible forms which we can recognise from our own lives. What worse hell can anybody imagine than to be hounded to death by loathsome tormentors who follow you everywhere you go? But for people like us, this is no myth. Mankind devises euphemisms for concepts which it finds painful or frightening. The Furies were real enough to the Ancient Greeks for them to find such a euphemism. They were so afraid of them they never referred to them by their real name. They called them the Eumenides, or the Kindly Ones.

Orestes and Oedipus were pursued by the Furies, each for crimes against their parents. Orestes killed Clytaemnestra, his mother, in revenge for her murder of his father, Agamemnon. Oedipus, unknowingly, killed his father and married his own mother. It seems that the Furies specialised in the pursuit of those who had broken the taboo forbidding any violent crime against a parent.

I believe the Furies of ancient times are still with us, though they may no longer have serpents for hair, or the heads of dogs, or the wings of bats. We fashion them according to whatever image suits our purposes. As for the crimes they pursue, they too have changed to suit the evolution of our modern taboos.

Maybe it is our consciences that call them forth, but they are real. I believe in them as many believe in God and the Devil. I can attest to the reality of the Furies as others have attested to apparitions from the Virgin Mary. Those who saw such apparitions were special, like Saint Bernadette, or the children of Fatima. Some say they were mad or were liars. They were not. They simply saw what others could not. I too am special, like them. And so are you, the one who is part of me, body and soul. We are special. But unlike those saints, our place is not in Heaven but in whatever dark corner of Hades has been set aside for us.

51

30 April 1996

Brenda stooped and laid the fresh shop flowers on the grave. That's funny, she thought. I'm sure I didn't put those others there last time. Look like weeds to me. Somebody's idea of a joke. She turned and walked back to where Megan was standing, looking at the three inscriptions on the neighbouring stone.

'I'm just reading her inscription, underneath her mum's,' said Megan. '"In memory of Madeleine Reed, beloved daughter of Ceridwen Williams." I'd have put on it that they was two peas in a pod but because of a careless cook they got separated into two different saucepans. Only that doesn't quite seem the right sort of language for a gravestone.'

Brenda laughed. 'It sums it up pretty well, though.'

'I were just thinking back to her funeral. I still find it funny to think of those fishermen carrying her coffin into the church. All dressed up in their Sunday best.'

'The night she died they watched over her all night, up there on the cliffs in the freezing cold. John and that hiker chap offered to relieve them but they wouldn't hear of it. So what possessed you to go and talk to them?'

'I were never planning to. But I were so angry about what you had told me about the way they'd behaved. And when I went down to the shop on the seafront that day there they was, large as life, sitting on that bench across the road. I knew it were them right away. So before I knew what I were doing I crossed over and introduced myself. Said I were Mr Wallace's housekeeper for over thirty years, and I were there all the time she were there to look after him. I said I knew her and they didn't. I knew she had a kind heart and a good soul which were more than could be said for them. I said someone else had admitted to the killing, though who it were were none of their business. And even if she had done it, what right did they have to judge her, especially now she were sick and dying. I turned my back on them and stormed away, wondering what had got into me.'

'Good for you. But you should have told me. You could have knocked me down with a feather when they turned up on the doorstep insisting on helping to find her. Megan, I wonder if you could do me a favour? Let me have a few minutes alone here.'

'Of course, dear. I'll go and sit in the church. It'll be cooler there.'

Brenda stared at the stone, seeing only Michael's inscription. She looked round to make sure she was alone.

Hello, Michael. I thought it was about time we had a frank talk. There are so many things I never said to you while you were alive. If I had . . . Well, maybe some things would have been different. Who am I kidding? It would all have been different. You had to carry a heavy burden in your final days. Well, that's mine. Knowing I could have stopped it all.

I loved you. Wherever you are, you should know that by now. You've dominated my life and my thoughts from the moment we first met. Not that you had the slightest idea, or would have given a damn if you had. You were far too busy elsewhere. But the awful truth is that it was an image of you I loved. I never really knew you. Even when I helped you send Ceridwen away I was too obsessed with my own revenge on her to judge your actions as I should have done. I hadn't hesitated to judge her, had I? Or her daughter. Or anybody else who presumed to cross my path.

But the one I should have judged, should have condemned, I excused, out of my own blindness.

That wasn't the end of your crimes, not by a long chalk. You sent Laura away, separating her from the boy she had come to love as her own son. You took her place and his mother's. You tried to be his father. And what sort of father were you? You loved him. I never doubted that. But you never knew how to show a father's love. You couldn't find the right words or the right gestures. He grew up in fear of you. I never admitted this before, even to myself, but you got everything wrong. You sent him to that awful school so he could learn to stand up for himself in the world. That wasn't right for a child like him. He learned only to sneer at the world and take what he thought was his.

Then Madeleine came along. His sister. You thought you could put everything right through her. Arrange for him to have the sort of love you had taken from him, the love you could never give him yourself. But you made one dreadful, catastrophic mistake, worse than all the others. You kept their identity a secret from them. Why in God's name did you do that? Did you think they wouldn't believe you? Did you want to see first if their natures were compatible? Did you want to spare them the shock of being told a stranger is a sibling? Or were you just addicted to secrecy, to the control you thought it gave you? Could you not bear to lose that control until the time came when you had to accept the inevitable? Was it you rather than them that you needed to prepare?

Whatever the reason, you had it all planned, didn't you? I have to admit, it was a beautiful scheme. They were going to become friends at first, under your supervision. Then one day you would reveal all. They were really brother and sister. Their friendship could flower into sibling love. Madeleine was older. She could give him the sort of maternal love and guidance you could not. You could withdraw, leave them to it, proud of what you had achieved at last, satisfied with the way you had so exquisitely, so triumphantly made amends. Maybe they would set up house together, until he left to pursue his career, in Paris, or Rome, or

Venice. He would get married and bring his bride home to show to his father and sister. Yes, Michael, it was a perfect plan, except for one thing.

For God's sake, did you know nothing about human nature? Had you never heard of what can happen between siblings who are not brought up together, who then meet in later life? They may have hated each other, but they were drawn together irresistibly. I saw the result with my own eyes. I told you and you never forgave me for that. I understand your reaction now. How could you ever have forgiven me? And you, who were tormented daily by the image of Ceridwen as she fell to her death, now had another horrible vision to contend with. Another nightmare which you had created. The physical union of a brother and sister you had brought together, each bound to the other until their minds and their hearts and their souls finally broke.

Some people, like me, never love enough, Michael. They are too afraid, only half alive. They bury themselves in places like this, sometimes allowing themselves a thought of how things might have been, if only . . . You were never like that. You loved too much and too widely, destroying here to nurture there. You dreamed of being surrounded by love and beauty. But you could only do that in art. And even there your art was flawed. I'm not talking about your technical deficiencies. You overcame most of those, through sheer hard work. I'm not even talking about your greatest fault as an artist, your inability time and again to realise the warmth and passion of your inner being on the canvas or the page. So often you hid yourself from the world when you desperately wanted to show yourself. Something stopped you from being the artist you should have been. Only in those drawings of her did you let your feelings emerge, and you never intended those for the world.

No, I'm not talking about your failures as an artist. I'm talking about the dishonesty of art, all art, even the greatest. You taught me about that. A trick of line here, of perspective there. Illusion everywhere. All the great artists did it, you told me. But in real life you have to pay for dishonesty. Beauty dishonestly formed gives way to ugliness and pain. Look at the pain you created in those whose lives you touched. Celia, Ceridwen, Laura, David, Madeleine. I was only spared because you cared nothing for me. You tried to create your idea of beauty directly in life rather than in art. But however terrible your mistakes, you paid for them. God made you pay by forcing you to see what you had done, to feel their pain as well as your own, to live long enough to see all the seeds of horror you had planted come to fruition.

I have to live with what I did and what I omitted to do, as you had to live with the knowledge of what you had done. I am content to be judged for my sins. But as the God who punished you is my witness I'm not going to judge you now. Rest in peace if you can, Michael Wallace.

Megan was waiting for her by the door of the church. Very slowly, they walked back along the path between the gravestones, arm in arm.

'He did some bad things, didn't he?' said Megan. 'There's no denying that. But I can't think ill of him. All I know is that he were always very good to me.' They sat down on a stone bench, near the stile.

'You know,' said Brenda, 'when I come here on my own I sometimes imagine how it might have been if I had acted differently.'

'Is that what you was thinking about by his gravestone just now?'

'That's right.'

'You didn't need to tell me what you did, Brenda. You know I don't judge people. These things are between ourselves and the Almighty. I know you've tried to make up for it since.'

'I wanted to tell you. I wanted to give you the chance to tell me to get lost. I wouldn't have blamed you if you had.'

'So what is it you imagine?'

'I imagine that when Michael asked me for help in procuring an abortion for Ceridwen, I told him I would have nothing more to do with him. Then I went to see her. Apologised for rejecting her earlier overtures of friendship. Told her what I knew about her condition and offered to help. Looked after her when she had her baby. In time she would have told me about Madeleine. I would have got them together, made them talk about the past. Maybe Madeleine's memories would have come back there and then. Or I would have got her professional help in getting them back. They would have sorted everything out between them. She would have met her younger brother. He would have grown up very differently from the way he did, would have been a different sort of person, someone who knew how to love and trust. They would have been a family.'

'With Aunt Brenda bringing presents at Christmas?'

'Why not?'

'But that didn't happen. So why torment yourself with what never were and were never going to be?'

'Because I need to be punished too. That's why I never let myself forget what I did or how things could, just could, have been different for them. For them, not for me. I was never going to have a real life of my own. But at least I could have prevented myself from destroying others.'

'Maybe you enjoy your dreams as well, just a bit. It's not completely a punishment, is it? Imagining how you might have done some good for others. Anyway, you're taking care of me now and keeping me company and don't think I'm not grateful. So let's get to the phone box and ring for that taxi. You've got an appointment at the chiropodist's, remember. Without me I think you'd forget your head.'

'Megan?'

'What?'

'How about a trip to the Scillies tomorrow? If the fine weather holds. We can get the boat from Penzance.'

'I don't know. I've never been there. Is it part of Cornwall?'

'It used to be, before the sea level rose.'

'I suppose that's all right then.'

Epilogue

April 2007

The Provost's room, panelled in oak with a huge desk stained with a dark red that she suspected had its origins in spilled port wine, seemed massive to Brenda. But over recent years the progressive deterioration in the condition of her spine had brought her eyes closer and closer to the ground so that everything looked massive. The only small thing in the room apart from her was the Provost himself. She had had difficulty in spotting him when she had first entered the room, buried as he was behind a newspaper in an armchair in the corner. When he had leapt to his feet to greet them she was surprised to see that though fully erect he was even smaller than she in her bowed stance. She had guessed he was in his early seventies, a good few years younger than she was. But if she had been told he was a 200-year-old pixie she would have had no difficulty in believing it.

Once he had seated his visitors in the chairs facing the desk he settled himself behind it, unlocked a drawer and took out a file of papers. Without a word or a glance down at the file he looked up at them over the rim of his spectacles and pushed the file over the desk towards them. He sighed and sat back in the chair, his eyes towards the ceiling. It was as if he were returning a particularly inept essay to a particularly exasperating student, one whose performance did not merit a single verbal comment. There was insufficient

337

power in the push to carry the file more than halfway across the desk. James Wilson stood up and retrieved it.

'Have you read it all, sir?' he asked.

'What? Good Lord, no. It's been decades since I read anything in full. I've read enough. Quite enough. I'm grateful to you for consulting me.'

'May we go ahead?'

'With my blessing? I won't go as far as that. But I don't suppose the press will bother us too much. I'll get the bursar to handle it. If it's important to you, then go ahead. I suppose your publishers have checked out the legal aspects.'

'They think we're safe enough.'

'Jolly good. I wasn't around at the time and I never knew him. I've no interest in protecting the bastard's reputation. I'll mention it to anybody here who did know him. But the real truth is that he's forgotten now. The sort of stuff he wrote has gone right out of fashion, replaced by more sophisticated scholarship. It's probably all out of print.'

'What about the state of the memorial fund?'

'The inflow of new money has all but dried up. But the funds we took in in the early days were well invested. It's all pretty safe now. And we have many other sources of income now to supplement it, especially from alumni. No, there's no problem there. Well, thank you for giving me the chance to see this. I appreciate the courtesy. And I wish you luck.'

He had disappeared. Then he seemed to reappear as if by magic around the corner of the desk, offering his hand with a gesture of aristocratic dismissal.

'Miss Rogers, I'm sorry we have no lift to take you downstairs. Can you manage? Perhaps Mr Wilson could take one arm and I could take the other. Or I can find a burly young undergraduate to carry you.'

She was not sure from his expression if he really was joking. 'Thank you for your time, sir, and the offer of help. I'll rely on Mr Wilson and my stick.'

And if you had been difficult you might have been surprised to find out what a crippled old lady can do with a stick like this, she thought.

A week later, the last day of April, Brenda hobbled to the bench which the thoughtful parish council had installed for her at the foot of the steep incline leading up to the headland. It had been three years since she had been able to visit the place where Madeleine and her mother had died. After Madeleine's death she had gone back to the exact spot where she had found her body and marked it with a small pile of stones. Hikers, perhaps imagining the stones had been placed there to mark their route and keep them well away from the cliffs, added to the pile as they passed until it finally grew into a large cairn. But these days her legs could carry her no further. On that particular day she very much wanted to speak to them and would have preferred to do so up there. But she would have to be content with looking up in the direction of the cairn and sitting on the bench.

She started to talk to herself, half out loud. She had spoken to them before from there, many times. So she did not bother to check first that she was alone. Nobody in the village would have minded. They knew her eccentricities well enough by now. As for any strangers passing through, they would dismiss her as a local madwoman who had wandered away from one of the new nursing homes which had been built above the village.

Forgive me, Madeleine. I know you swore me to secrecy. But that was before you found your mother again. And before I found you and took the notebook off you. You wanted me to find it, didn't you? It was your way of telling me it had all changed. Now you wanted your story to be told. Not right away. But when the time was right. When it was safe. That time is now. Megan's gone. I know it would have hurt her terribly to know. Why put her through that pain? I could never have done that. But there's no danger now. Any day now it will all be revealed. And I will be there to vouch for the truth of it. For as long as there is still some breath in this broken old body. So the two of you can rest in peace now, up there on the wild headland you both made your own. The place I can only look at from afar.

She rose and struggled slowly and painfully back to her cottage, past the gallery which was now a branch of a much larger one in St Ives. These days she never went inside. New managers came and went, learning their trade. The collection was unchanged, though. That had been a condition of the sale. It was just before opening time and already a queue was forming at the door. The book she had published the year before about Michael's career, with the help of a ghost writer and a well-known art photographer, including detailed reproductions of the drawings on display there, continued to draw the curious from far and wide. The book had given only a slight and highly sanitised account of his personal life. Soon the world would know the whole truth. Almost. The only detail she had omitted was his confession to Megan about what had happened on the cliff-top when Ceridwen had fallen. She was sure his reputation would not suffer from the revelation that he had been a ruthless philanderer. But a killer was a different matter.

Perhaps in the end nobody would read it, despite the interest promised by one respectable newspaper, and a number of more prurient ones. Maybe she had wasted her rapidly declining stock of time and energy. As she had wasted over two years in her efforts to secure a posthumous pardon for Madeleine. She had always known that would be a hopeless task. She had been treated with sympathy and kindness but in the end nobody believed her. And who could blame them, with only her word and her faltering memory to go on? Megan had always told her there was no point. They were the only two people left who had known and loved her, and they knew the truth. That was all that mattered. But still she felt she had to try. For the first time in her life, and only now that it was drawing to a close, she had felt the need to fight for what she knew was right. And now the fight was almost over, she knew her time would come soon.

So who would read Madeleine's story? Maybe nobody. Perhaps it would only live on in the folk memory of the village, as Charley, George and Samuel, now confined by old age and infirmity to their cottages, told it to their grandchildren, with particular emphasis on their heroic vigil on the headland on the night of her death. And God only knows how they would embroider and embellish the tale beyond recognition.

She had ordered a taxi to take her round to the church. A local shop had already delivered the flowers she would take with her. For years she and Megan had followed the ritual together, visiting the graves, changing the flowers. They did that frequently of course. But the last day of April was special. It was on that day that she had first noticed the flowers had been changed. She had noted the date in her mind. To her astonishment exactly the same thing had happened the following year. She took shop flowers with her, placed them on the grave and found them replaced after they had spent time inside the church or walking near it. Sometimes they watched and waited, but they never saw anybody else approach the grave. They never discussed who it might be, simply exchanging glances of understanding. But one thing neither of them could explain was why that particular date had been chosen.

For the last five years, Brenda had visited the graves on her own, Megan's now being one of them. It had all been very quick and easy. A sudden change in the weather, a cold, an attack of pneumonia, all at home, all within a few hours. Brenda, and her niece who had just managed to get there in time from Truro, and the doctor, had all been at her bedside.

Today Brenda thought again about the date. Not her death, that had been in the depths of winter. Not her birthday, he probably never knew that. Then what else, but the date they had met?

She placed her flowers on the grave and turned towards the church where she would say her usual prayers for them all, nearly always alone. As she did so the tramp crept noiselessly around

341

the corner of the building. He moved towards the graveyard, silently, almost gliding along the footpaths. A long, thin hand, wizened by sun and wind, moved the flowers to one side and replaced them with a crumpled, sweat-dampened bunch of wild meadow flowers.

Then in a moment he had gone, moving like a shadow, unseen, unheard, over the stile, past the Saxon cross, along the ancient pilgrims' way.